A Threat of Home

A Threat of Home

RITA MORRISON

Matador
9 Priory Business Park,
Wistow Road, Kibworth Beauchamp,
Leicestershire. LE8 0RX
Tel: 0116 279 2299
Email: books@troubador.co.uk
Web: www.troubador.co.uk/matador
Twitter: @matadorbooks

ISBN 978 1 8004 6473 5

British Library Cataloguing in Publication Data.
A catalogue record for this book is available from the British Library.

Printed and bound in Great Britain by 4edge Limited
Typeset in 11pt Jensen Pro by Troubador Publishing Ltd, Leicester, UK

Matador is an imprint of Troubador Publishing Ltd

for
Soren
Millie
and Freya

Katie's Tale

Duisburg 1939

Katie was careful where she sat on the train to Cologne. There were a couple of women with large bags on their laps at one end of the carriage and she decided to sit opposite them although there were a few roomier spots in the middle. It was always safer to be nearer other people on the trains and trams, especially on quieter weekdays. She exchanged a "Good morning" with the women who smiled and shuffled their legs and bags a little to accommodate her before continuing their conversation. The train trundled and clattered its way slowly out of Duisburg Station and Katie, elbow on the little window ledge, settled her chin into her hand and began to think about Eric.

The kiss at the station before he had caught the train to take him back to England a few weeks before had been quick and polite but the kiss in the kitchen that same morning had been altogether different. They had been alone, and he had taken her very firmly in his arms. The kiss was urgent, had left her breathless. "Come to England, Katie, come really soon – promise me!" She thought of his face, his eyes bright behind their horn-rimmed glasses. She liked the glasses; they made him look clever, as indeed he was, she reminded herself. He knew more about German literature and history than she did. She thought again about the way his hands had stroked her neck and how she would really like to be kissed like that again. Eric, in his very English suit and his slightly strange English accent. What would Nottingham be like? She wasn't sure where it was, but he had promised to take her to London one day. The voices of the women opposite washed over her, fading and returning as the train slowed or speeded up. Eric was very interested

1

in Germany, too interested, she sometimes thought; he seemed almost disappointed that there wasn't more marching and flag waving going on in the streets of Duisburg and had wanted to go to Berlin with her to see more of the action. Her parents had strictly forbidden that. When he'd said that surely Hitler was having a very good effect on Germany's economy – look at the roads, look at the building – all Papa would say, and she could feel herself getting cross with him all over again, was that there's far more to that man than he could begin to understand. Well, how could an Englishman really understand? She'd put him right soon enough. And now, now was a chance to go to England, such an exciting prospect and a chance to get away from Germany for a while. All she had to do was get the visa.

"Young woman! Excuse me!" A raised voice interrupted her daydream.

"Oh, I'm sorry. Yes, I was miles away." The train was coming to a halt and the women wanted to get off. Katie moved her long legs sideways and held herself in as they and their bags bustled off.

"Goodbye – and sweet dreams," said one of them and they smiled at each other.

Katie looked out of the window. The women would probably be visiting a family farm, one of many dotted around the countryside. The bags would be full of fresh vegetables when they returned this evening. She used to do the same with her mother several times a year, but they went to visit an aunt who lived near the Dutch border. Doors slammed as the train slowly set off again. Voices, some loud, some quieter, drifted along the corridor behind her. An older couple settled themselves in seats a little way away from her. Twenty minutes and they would be in Cologne, then a walk to the British Consulate; she had checked the route with her brother on a map of Cologne. Heinz had wanted to go with her, but this was her adventure and she wanted to do it by herself. No annoying brothers were going to get in the way. Voices, louder now and closer, alerted her and, curious, she turned her head to look. A mistake. She was just in time to meet the eye of one of two SA, Stormtroopers, who blundered past her talking, laughing, suddenly taking up all the space, all the air in the carriage. She turned her head quickly and stared purposefully out the window. But they had spotted her; one nudged the other, laughing, and they sat down in the seats on the other side of the aisle, legs splayed, brown boots on display.

Katie was furious with herself. How stupid, how stupid to turn round; to look and catch his eye. Now she was in for trouble and she would have to fight to keep her temper. She blocked their conversation out – about girlfriends and last night's drinking. She pulled her dress down over her knees as casually as she could and folded her arms across her chest. But, of course, they noticed it all with the arrogance of nineteen-year-olds who know they can frighten. She glanced at her watch. Still ten minutes to go. Their voices became more intrusive, and she realised they were directed at her. She missed whatever it was they said, her heart beat faster, and she struggled with a mixture of fear and anger. How she hated them with their polished boots and leather belts and buckles, their stupid peaked caps, their ignorant swagger.

"Come on, girl. We can show you around the city! It's no place for a pretty girl to be by herself!"

Katie felt her cheeks flush with embarrassment. How dare they? She stared resolutely and uncomfortably out of the window like a silly schoolgirl, but any comment would be grabbed by them and turned into another attack. Stay calm and ignore them; her father's advice, but these SA, these boys demanded a response, felt entitled to it. One of them leaned towards her, his voice became quieter.

"This is no way for a polite German girl to behave. We just want a little chat. Come on now." The train was slowing; thank God the train was slowing. The couple behind who seemed aware of what was going on began to noisily get themselves up, coughing, talking about the time, where they had to get to, which door to head for. Katie turned her eyes to the boy as the train squealed into the station. She gazed as coldly as she could and held the look until she was sure that he had registered her disgust. She enjoyed the small, small victory as he apparently lost interest, slapped his comrade on the leg and they both got up and pushed their way to the door.

She waited a while before getting up and moving into the aisle. She wanted to be sure they'd gone. Her heart rate was returning to normal, and she was quite pleased that she had managed to keep her mouth shut – she would be able to relate this tale to her parents; she had behaved well this time. She slung her bag over her shoulder and got off the train, walking slowly and checking ahead for brown shirts and peaked caps.

She thought of what she was here to do, took a deep breath and strode towards the enormous arched exit and out into the sunshine. She headed off in the direction of Hohe Strasse and then took a right, but not before turning back to look at the station, a magnificent ornate nineteenth-century building much admired by her father. *Dammit*, she thought to herself. Two Swastika flags were flying from it. One on the central great domed roof and one on the clock tower, the harsh black on red fluttering incongruously against the little turrets and the Kaiser crown that glinted golden in the sun above them all. She turned her back on it and walked away in the direction of the consulate.

*

At the top of the stone steps Katie was asked to show her identification papers. Why was she surprised to see the SA in charge of this? For some reason she had supposed that the British Consulate would be a little island of Englishness but of course the Nazis were here too.

"Why have you come here?" The man was heavily built, older. He glanced at her briefly and his tone managed to be both disinterested and demanding at the same time. She smiled at him. "I'm hoping to visit friends in England sometime soon." She had rehearsed this sentence and even the voice she would use to say it in, slightly flirtatious. She sounded ridiculous.

"Where in England?" He glanced at her again, a little more interested.

"Nottingham, it's in the north." She was pretty sure he would never have heard of it.

"Ah, yes," he covered his ignorance by waving her inside with a shrug and she rewarded him with a wide smile before taking back her papers and walking slowly past him.

There was another one inside. He was leaning against the walls and pointed to the end of the queue when he saw that she was unsure where to go. The number of people caught her unawares; she joined the line behind a small dark-haired man, smartly dressed but shifting edgily from one foot to the other. She didn't think too much about it. She was wondering how long it would take to reach the head of the queue, a couple of hours at least. Near the double doors behind which, presumably, the interviews would take place, sat a secretary behind a desk, who took the name of the next visitor and gave them a slip of paper. The people waiting were quiet, sombre. There was no chatting or light-hearted comment as would be normal anywhere else, or at any other time. Couples occasionally put their heads together and whispered; a child asked his mother how long it would be and was hushed. The silence was disturbed by the SA, who walked briskly towards Katie but stopped just short, looking at the man in front and saying loudly, "You, get behind this young lady – quick now!"

Katie was taken aback, especially when the man was given an unnecessary push, until the penny dropped. He was a Jew. She waited until the SA, satisfied that the man had resumed his place at the back, had turned away.

She half turned towards him and said, "I'm sorry."

"Not your fault." His voice was calm. "I was expecting it."

Katie thought for a moment and leant her head back so she could speak to him without turning round. "How often has it happened?"

"I was first through the doors this morning. And yesterday morning. And the day before yesterday." There was resigned mirth in his voice.

She stayed facing forwards and her shoulders went rigid with the old anger as she thought through the implications of what he had said. This morning's experience on the train had given her courage. The silence was broken by the door ahead opening suddenly; an older couple came out holding some papers and the next person, given a nod by the secretary, went quickly in. Katie watched the SA guard get a cigarette out of his shirt pocket and light up. He blew a cloud of smoke across the room. The secretary, a stern-looking woman wearing black-rimmed glasses, coughed slightly and asked in a voice working hard to remain polite if he could smoke his cigarette outside; she was English and spoke very correct and only slightly accented German. She clearly wasn't going to take no for an answer. Katie was impressed. After a short bad-tempered delay which the secretary ignored he sauntered out, leaving the door ajar.

Katie made use of the distraction. "Get back in front of me." It came out as more of a hiss than a whisper. The man obeyed with alacrity and with two comical side steps he was back where he was before.

Now she could whisper to him more easily. "Listen, you are much smaller than me." He really was, she noticed, by a good head. He conceded this fact with a shrug and a couple of weird sideways nods. She realised that under different circumstances he might have been offended. "I can hide you; don't you see?"

There was a pause where he seemed to be weighing things up. The he turned to look at her and was met with earnest green eyes. He was about her age, around twenty. When she thought about it later, she realised that he had seconds in which to decide to trust her. He gave her a wink and the game began.

He moved slightly to the right so that he was already partially obscured by her. When the door ahead opened, and the line shuffled forward he was at her side. When the SA guard took a walk along the line of people, she carefully turned her body so that he couldn't be seen. They enjoyed the excitement; they enjoyed stifling the laughter as the guard once again walked past, unaware, slightly bored. The double doors were now very close. Another couple walked through and there was only the rather stocky woman, whose bulk had done its part in hiding the little man, standing in front of Katie. Once she had gone through it would be harder to hide him. As the woman went over to the secretary to get her slip of paper Katie looked at the secretary. Keen black eyes glinted behind the spectacles. She looked at Katie and glanced precisely at the young man then back at Katie. She had noticed, noticed everything. The stocky woman resumed her place in front of her and the secretary motioned to Katie to come to the desk. She had chosen her moment. The guard was chatting through the open doorway to his comrade on the steps. She asked for Katie's name and wrote it down on the slip. She was to be No. 27; then placed another slip, on top. On it she had already written: 'a gentleman: No. 26'. This she placed on top of Katie's slip and handed them both to her. "Thank you," Katie said quietly. The secretary gave the briefest nod and the smallest of smiles.

The man's hand was trembling as Katie passed the slip over to him. The adolescent excitement was over, the game-playing was nearly at an end; all Katie could feel was this man's fear. The woman went in and the minutes dragged by; what if the guard suddenly noticed him. They had been lucky so far. Another couple had joined the queue. They both became alert at the sound of scraping chairs coming from behind the double doors. They opened slowly, the woman was having trouble managing them and carrying her bag and papers. Katie said, "Go on," and turned her back on him, making herself large so he could move past her; one more protective gesture. The SA looked over, dimly aware of something not quite right as the Jewish man darted forward and disappeared through the doors. At that moment Katie was aware of a tension that bound her to the secretary; they didn't look at each other but each gave a silent exhalation and felt their shoulders relax.

The doors were polished, dark brown with shiny brass handles and huge push plates. They were all that came between her and her dreams of England, seeing Eric again, but now she was thinking of those trembling fingers that had taken the slip of paper from her. The slip of paper that could mean safety and at last an absence of fear. Her ears were straining for any little sounds from behind those doors but there was nothing but little coughs and shuffles behind her. Then, again, there was the scrape of a chair being moved; she imagined him getting up, one neat movement, thanking the commissioner – maybe they're shaking hands – walking back to the door. More seconds passed, hesitation, quiet voices, then the door handle moved downwards and out he came. Precise steps, one hand pulling the door closed behind him and the other holding the precious visa. There was time only for large smiles to be exchanged between the two of them before he was out, past the guards, gone.

Decades later, walking in London near Covent Garden, she was certain she saw him. She was so sure it was him, the way he moved; there he was – small and neat and safe. Her daughters' eyes showed doubt, disbelief even, but it was him. He had lived his life. He'd got away.

1

Duisburg; a steel town on the River Ruhr; 1923. It was the time of hyper-inflation in Germany. The economy was in serious trouble; war debts, government mismanagement, over-printing of money, were leading to economic collapse. France occupied the Ruhr, the industrial heartland of Germany.

Katie was four years old. She stood on sturdy legs handing her mother pegs as she hung out the clothes. It was a cold, early November morning but the sun shone down on the shared garden with its criss-cross of washing lines. The washing basket had been hauled out of the steamy basement where everyone did the weekly wash. Maria's hands were red from plunging into the rinsing water and feeding the great wringers. Katie loved to watch as the water squeezed out and splashed around her feet – well-protected in brown buttoned boots. Now knickers – large and small – vests, dresses and shirts all hung up still dripping in the cool sunshine.

Through the washing Katie's attention had been caught by something; Maria followed her gaze and saw the little blonde girl. Katie moved forward to get a better look. She was at the far edge of the garden, by herself, poking at the flowerless soil with a stick. "Mama, look." Maria paused.

"Ah! The little French girl."

They had met her once before, at the front entrance to the flats. The two little girls had stared at each other the way little girls do, Katie intrigued by the blonde ringlets that seemed so perfect, the other, slightly older, delighted at the possibility of a playmate. Maria had forced herself to meet the eye of the French woman and had been surprised to see something that looked like fear; the last thing she was expecting.

Sophie had stepped towards Katie and was smiling expectantly. *"Je m'appelle Sophie. Comment t'appelles tu?"*

Katie's eyes grew wide, and she stepped closer to her mother. Maria laughed quietly. "She's asking what your name is. This little girl is French." Again, she looked at the woman. They could never be friends, but she certainly didn't want to be enemies. Sophie had been taken by the hand and pulled away into the building towards her front door on the ground floor while Maria and Katie headed toward the stairs.

"Katie, my name is Katie." She'd shouted it just in time before their front door had closed.

"Maria!" Distracted, they both looked up, shielding their eyes from the sun. Up on the top floor of the block of flats a young woman looked down from the window. "Heinrich is back; come up, come and see!" Heinrich often came home from the office early on Fridays, but this seemed earlier than usual.

"Papa's back already! Come on, Mama, come on!"

Maria blinked up at the window where Lisl still stood, laughing and beckoning. She smiled up at her sister-in-law. Lisl was fifteen and spent more time at their flat than she did at home with her parents. Katie loved her, someone who was always willing to play and found plenty to laugh about.

Maria finished hanging the last of the clothes then picked up the basket, took Katie by the hand and walked back through the damp basement smelling of soap, water lying in small puddles in and around the great cement washing troughs. The basket was put neatly next to a metal tub and they walked through the cellar and out to the stairs, locking the cellar door behind them. Then Katie was allowed to race ahead up four flights of stairs, stopping every so often to catch her breath and check that Mama wasn't too far behind. She looked through the metal staircase and saw Mama's hand on the bannister. She'd stopped. "Come on, slow coach; I'm much faster than you." Katie laughed, delighted. After a few seconds, the hand started moving again and Katie bolted up more stairs and through their front door which was nearly always left ajar.

Maria stopped once more on her way up, smiling to herself at Katie's energy and her own lack of it. The stairs were getting difficult; she would have to make more use of Lisl in the weeks to come. There was noise and quiet laughter coming from the apartment. And the smell of coffee, Lisl must have brewed some for her brother. Maria walked into the kitchen where Heinrich and Lisl stood with their hands on their hips staring at the suitcase in the middle of the floor. Katie stood next to her papa, hands also on her hips since this seemed to be the thing to do.

Heinrich smiled thinly at his wife. "Look at this, Maria."

The suitcase was open and in it were tight bundles of banknotes. Hundreds of packs each one containing hundreds of German marks. They were crisp, new, they could smell the ink. "You'll need a bagful of this junk to buy a loaf of bread," he said, "and by the time you get to the shop the price will have doubled."

Katie squatted down and with two chubby hands picked up a bundle of money. "You can play with them, sweetheart, if you want," said Papa. "Pour that coffee, Lisl." Heinrich sat down at the table and was joined by Maria while Lisl got cups and saucers and poured coffee from a white and blue pot. They watched as Katie built four little walls with the bricks of money. It was difficult for her; the bundles were awkward for her to handle.

"There must be twice as much as last month," said Maria.

"More than that, there's another suitcase full in the passage. They let us finish early so that we could carry this stuff home. It's ridiculous."

"How ridiculous must it get before something is done?"

"The new Chancellor may have the guts to sort something out." Heinrich shrugged his shoulders doubtfully. "We've been lucky, Maria. Our parents have helped us out." He took a deep breath. "As long as the French stay here and take the coal and steel people are going to get angrier. Some families don't know where the next meal is going to come from."

Maria allowed the little lecture and reached for Heinrich's hand across the table. She recognised the tension in his voice and changed the subject.

"We saw the little French girl again just now. Katie is longing to play with her; maybe I should let her."

"Why not?" Heinrich nodded. The family had moved in months before and, aware of the whispering, had hardly been seen.

"I found out who they are, by the way," Heinrich said. "He's a civil servant – just like me, doing his job. Yes, they should get together. She shouldn't learn to dislike people. Whatever the governments are doing we have to stay civilised."

Maria smiled at this. 'Civilised' was one of Heinrich's favourite words. After coming back from the war, he clung to the idea that men had learned from that barbarity and that it should and could never happen again. He would say that Germany must now forget about warfare, think of its great cultural past, join with Europe in the search for peace and progress. His sisters would raise their eyes and call him pompous but Maria, remembering the nightmares, night after night, when she would hold his trembling and sweating body in her arms until he slowly became still again, knew how important his convictions were to him. And, she thought, maybe Katie and Sophie could make just a little progress in French/German relations.

Lisl had been listening as she sipped at her milky sweet coffee.

"Why are you drinking coffee? You're not old enough." Heinrich with his big brother hat on was only half serious.

"I'm fifteen! Of course I'm old enough; even Papa doesn't mind anymore." Lisl, the youngest of seven sisters and one brother, was in everyone's opinion hopelessly spoilt. Maria knew that it was in fact Heinrich, the adored son, who was the spoilt one.

"I've decided something." Lisl, stirring her coffee, took a breath and waited a second or two for dramatic effect. Heinrich and Maria looked at each other. What was the child going to come out with now?

She met Heinrich's eye boldly. "I'm going to go to Berlin as soon as I'm old enough."

"And does Mama know of this new plan?" Last week she had decided on Paris, as the right place for a girl of talent, but considering the fact that French soldiers were marching around the Ruhr and Germans were hardly popular there right now, she had been persuaded against it.

"Why should she mind? It's our capital city and when I'm a famous dancer I can send home loads of money." They all became aware of the money that Katie was busy building into towers that kept tumbling down.

Maria squeezed Heinrich's hand as a little warning not to say anything. Lisl's eyes were shining.

"Johanna and Karoline were looking at a magazine at home; pictures of the theatres and dance halls in Berlin. They didn't want me to see—"

"I should think not!" interrupted Heinrich.

"But I did anyway." She gave him a brief, bold look before carrying on, "The dresses the dancers wore are gorgeous and loads of people go to watch them. Berlin looks so exciting, not stuffy like round here!"

To stop Heinrich, Maria said quickly, "You'll have to become a very good dancer to work there I should think."

"Yes… but in a couple of years I shall be ready." She spoke with all the conviction and confidence of a fifteen-year-old.

Maria knew what Heinrich wanted to say and any minute now he would say it, but Lisl deserved her dreams. Her own young years had been strung out with anxiety, innocence wrung out of her, somehow.

"Berlin may have theatres but it's a dangerous place. Not a day goes by when there isn't fighting on the streets; there are so many groups that hate each other and with the French here they've got more to get angry about…" He stopped himself, realising that Katie had turned to look at him as his tone had sharpened and that Maria had taken her hand away from his arm. Lisl got up and walked over to the window. She folded her arms.

"That'll all be over soon," as if saying it would make it happen. She stared out and with an impatient sigh said, "No-one understands me, absolutely no-one!"

Maria, looking at the back of Lisl's head, her long hair fastened back with a dark blue bow, allowed herself a smile. "You will be a wonderful dancer, Lisl; I'm sure of that." She gave Heinrich a look that said – leave her be, it'll pass. Heinrich glared back but said no more. After a few seconds, some puffing and shoulder wriggling, Lisl turned and walked quickly to Maria. She put her arms around her and hugged her.

"Maybe you understand me a little bit and I do love you. But you," she turned her face towards her big brother, "you are horrible, and I don't like you at all... at the moment." And she went over to join Katie, who, having been listening and finding the haughty expression on Lisl's face very funny, started laughing.

Maria had no doubts about what Adelheid would make of Lisl's latest plans. Her mother-in-law was a woman with certain convictions, one of which was that Berlin was becoming a place of such dubious morality that it couldn't be tolerated anymore and wasn't worthy of being Germany's capital. Nothing good could come out of the place. Too much freedom and too much politics. It was a dangerous mix; there would be nothing but trouble. Adelheid was in a fairly perpetual battle with her daughters about the moral decline of the country. Her fun-loving girls all thought that what was happening was very exciting; people should be allowed to say, write and do almost as they pleased. The days of the Kaiser were well and truly over, and Germany was now a free, grown-up democracy.

Adelheid knew perfectly well that these things were said to provoke a reaction and she rarely disappointed. "What would Father Theodor say if he heard you?" was a common reaction as she fingered the tiny gold cross that hung around her neck. "You have always been such good children and now you are getting wild ideas!" Heinrich would hide his smiles; the thought of any of his sisters as wild was ridiculous. He would pretend to back his mother up. "You're right, Mother. At Mass on Sunday he should be told all about their wild ideas and have a word with them." Father Theodor on more than one occasion had warned his flock from the pulpit against the attractions of the sin-filled capital.

"Well, Lisl, whether you hate me or not you can come with me to spend some of this money right now before it becomes any more worthless. Maybe bread?" He glanced over at Maria, who shrugged and nodded. They were living on preserved vegetables that lined the cellar shelves and her father had sent over a ham that would last a few days now that the weather was colder.

Katie and Mama watched Papa carry the suitcases of money down the stairs followed by a less grumpy Lisl. An hour later they returned with two loaves of bread.

2

Lobberich, a little town near the Dutch border; it was the home of Johann and Adelheid Cremers (Heinrich's parents) and his seven sisters.

"Katie, stand still, sweetheart, so I can get this right and finished before we go to Mass." Maria, putting a couple more pins between her lips, was crouched down next to Katie, pinning the hem of her best dress, making sure it was absolutely level. She turned Katie round slowly and was satisfied. "Right, off with it and I'll get it sewn and ironed." Katie stood in her woollen vest and knickers and watched her mother sew with small, neat stitches. "Look how much you've grown." There was a crease in the material about four centimetres above the new hem. Maria held up her thumb and forefinger to show Katie just how much bigger she'd grown. The dress was rose-coloured with narrow darker red velvet panels in the bodice and a scalloped lace collar. Maria had had a lot of trouble getting the collar to fit properly. She heard the front door slam shut as the others left for Mass. She'd have to work quickly.

Katie had wandered off to the table where Grandmother's electric iron, plugged into the light switch, was heating up. A damp towel was folded up next to it.

"Don't touch, it's very hot."

"I know that, Mama."

Maria snipped off the thread and got up. She laid the dress flat on the thick cloth that covered the table and laid the towel over the hem. Section by section she pressed the iron down; it hissed, and little clouds of steam rose up, smelling of damp and washing soap.

The iron was finally replaced with a clang onto its stand and the plug removed. The dress emerged with a perfectly flat, crisp hem. Maria waved it about for a few seconds in the hope that it would not be too damp to wear but time was running short. Mass was at ten o'clock and she still had to organise her hat. Heinrich was ready. He'd polished the boots the night before. The coats were brushed and laid ready on the little chair in the passage. Their missals with their worn leather covers were on the table ready to be picked up.

He popped his head round the door. "We need to go soon; we'll be late."

The dress was on, hair vigorously brushed, and boots were being buttoned up over pale pink stockings. Maria and Katie went into the passage to put on coats and Maria noticed, not for the first time, that the bottom buttons of her coat didn't do up anymore. She pinned her hat carefully onto her hair; she decided quickly on the brown woollen cloche with a velvet trim, probably more in keeping with Adelheid's taste than the green one with the feathers. Leather gloves were pulled on and the little buttons at the side fastened. Katie's hat was wedged firmly onto her head. As they pulled the heavy front door closed behind them and hurriedly set off, she apologised for the tenth time that morning and Heinrich said for the tenth time that it didn't matter.

*

Katie enjoyed their visits to Lobberich to stay with Grandmother and Grandfather and the aunts. They came by tram on Saturday morning and stayed till after Sunday lunch.

Going to Mass here involved even more attention being paid to clothing and neatness than usual, which annoyed Katie. She liked going to this church, as long as they sat close to her favourite statue of Our Lady, the one with the sparkly bits on her veil and pink fingernails. Katie had studied her very carefully and was quite sure that those kind blue eyes had singled her out for special attention.

But today things were not going her way. First of all, the fuss about her dress. Mama had forgotten about it the night before and then was cross, when she realised that it just wouldn't do, and pulled it off over Katie's head as if it was her fault that she had grown. Mama rarely got cross but sometimes, on Sunday mornings in Lobberich she definitely became irritable, and Katie decided that the best way was to keep quiet, which she didn't like being at all. Now, as they entered the church, she was being pulled in the opposite direction to the statue of Our Lady and, after whispered good mornings, they took their places behind her grandparents, with no chance at all of exchanging smiles with Lisl because she was right at the other end of the row of seven aunts, next to Karoline, the eldest, who could be as severe as Grandmother.

Katie still found the standing and kneeling and sitting confusing and always got it wrong; Mama or Papa would look at her sideways and gently guide her to the correct position. This morning, during the sitting bits, she turned her attention to the fat plaster angels high up on the white columns gazing at the huge cross that hung above the altar. Fleshy babies, with tiny gold wings, which reminded her that there had been talk of a new baby in their house, and if it had wings, with a bit of luck it would fly away. Mama's hand was on her knee. She had been banging her boots together. Grandmother turned round and passed a small card to Maria and motioned that it was for Katie. "Hold it carefully." It was a picture of Our Lady standing on a cloud. She looked lovely – blue dress, arms outstretched and smiling at something far away. Katie was enchanted. She turned it over; there, in heavy black print, was something she couldn't read yet, but she knew it was a prayer. Mama had several of these pictures which she kept in her missal and sometimes she would show them to Katie at bedtime and read the words on the back. Prayers were about talking to Jesus and asking him to look after us and make us good. She turned the card over again, paying attention once more to the mother of God. She had pink cheeks and lipstick which was very pretty and quite apt.

Maria sat behind Adelheid's straight back, unconsciously straightening her own, and tried to concentrate on the Mass, but her thoughts wandered. If only she hadn't forgotten about Katie's dress, but she had been so tired the night before and gone to bed early. She'd had to ask Adelheid for a sewing basket and the iron to be set up. She couldn't leave Katie's dress like that: it was halfway up her thigh. Over lunch the conversation would certainly turn to the new baby. The girls would talk about the things they were making, and Johann would say, not for the first time, that a boy would be just what the family needed. Well, she could understand that; seven daughters and only the one son... however had Adelheid coped with eight pregnancies, possibly more?

She looked again at the slim neck of her mother-in-law, bent towards her missal. She was still intimidated by this noisy family with its opinion sharing and arguing – and Adelheid, who could put a stop to the more outrageous comments from Margarethe and Johanna by tut-tutting and a simple, "That's enough, girls."

She realised she was hungry – she had been too busy for breakfast. The sisters had spent the morning peeling and preparing the vegetables. Normally she would have helped them. A piece of pork was roasting slowly in the oven. Her tummy rumbled very quietly, and she caught Katie's eye in time to stop the giggle. Just then Father Theodor climbed up to the pulpit and began to speak in his slightly high-pitched but very precise voice. Margarethe and Johanna cleared their throats as he started, risking a sideways glance from their mother. Adelheid had unwavering respect for the priesthood, especially for Father Theodor, who had baptised her eight children. She listened attentively to his sermon, which seemed to be trying to square the important need for charity with the injustice of the occupation of the Fatherland. Was it Heinrich's imagination that the priest's own prejudices were hinted at in the extra squeak his voice produced whenever 'our Catholic French brothers and sisters' were mentioned?

Katie didn't like looking at Father Theodor because of the grey hairs that came out of his ears and nose. She had once asked why this was the case in the priest's hearing, which made Grandmother go pink and Papa to tell her afterwards that she had said something unkind. But she had thought it was necessary to point it out in case he hadn't realised it was happening. She couldn't understand why telling the truth was always very important, except sometimes. How was she to know when those times were?

It was time for communion. Row by row people stood up and joined the queue that filed slowly up to the altar. Then they knelt in a long line at the altar rails and the priest popped the host into their mouths. Lisl had explained the process to Katie; it was very important not to call it bread. It might taste like bread, but it most definitely wasn't. Lisl had sounded as if she had had trouble convincing herself about this. Inside, somehow, there was Jesus, so you had to be careful not to chew. What interested Katie most was the way people walked back to their seats. All had their eyes cast down and hands clasped together. Even the big boys looked quite serious. Some of the girls walked very slowly so everyone could see their best clothes. And there was one lady who always went last and walked all the way back with her eyes tightly shut, mangling her hands around and muttering to herself. Papa had told her not to stare.

Then the word – the only word she understood –was spoken. AMEN. It meant 'it's over'. Once again Mama's hand was on her knee to remind her not to jump up yet, not until the congregation had the chance to repeat it with a certain relieved enthusiasm and the priest and altar boys had left.

Outside, the November sun shining unexpectedly brightly into their eyes, there was a lot of handshaking and greeting; Katie was swept up into the air by Grandfather and given a tickly kiss before being handed over to Lisl. After a few minutes of chatter, they headed off down the avenue, the black branches of the huge, leafless trees swaying noisily in the wind, towards the house on the edge of town.

*

They walked home in little groups. Heinrich and his father strode ahead followed by Adelheid, Maria and Karoline. A short distance behind were Anna and Josephine, heads together, each with a hand on their hats. Further back, Margarethe and Johanna, who had pulled their hats off and had Katie between them, giving her huge swings up into the air to make the walk more fun. Katie shrieked every time she was lifted; soon the girls were puffed out and settled to a slower walk and let Lisl and Marianna catch up with them. By the time they reached the house, had hung up their coats, taken off their boots, stowed away their hats, Grandfather and Heinrich were in the sitting room leaning over the card table where the *Frankfurter Zeitung*, the family's preferred newspaper, was spread out.

Maria was in the kitchen helping Adelheid and Karoline with the dinner; she was eager to make up for this morning. The younger ones had shot upstairs to avoid being asked to help but not before Adelheid had called to Anna to help Josephine lay the table and find the extra chairs. Because it was Sunday the huge ceramic stove in the corner of the dining room had been lit that morning, so the room wasn't too cold. Two large tablecloths, one on top of the other, were spread over the enormous table and plates and cutlery arranged. Thirteen could just about fit if Katie wedged between Maria and Heinrich and a couple of the girls managed with a corner each.

Upstairs Lisl was demonstrating cartwheels along the hallway and Katie was trying valiantly to get her own legs up in the air, but they just wouldn't stretch up like Lisl's, which were perfectly straight like stiff sticks.

"Practice," said Lisl, out of breath but enjoying the admiration. "You'll get it in the end."

"Dinner time!" came the call from downstairs. Lisl pulled Katie's dress straight and tidied herself up. She tried to sort out her crooked ribbon, but it stayed off centre and fine tendrils of hair had escaped around her head.

"For goodness' sake, Lisl, can't you stay tidy for longer than a few minutes? You're old enough to know better!" Lisl glared at Karoline who could be very pompous at times.

The serving dishes were being put on the table, Adelheid bringing in the meat platter and placing the apple sauce next to Katie because it was her favourite. She made a fuss because she wanted to sit next to Lisl but was quickly shushed by Maria. There was general chatter and laughter as everyone squeezed in and Grandfather and Heinrich took their places, still talking about what they had read in the paper. Then, at a signal from Adelheid, everyone was quiet, and she said grace. Katie peered at her grandmother's downcast eyes and waited for another 'Amen,' which this time meant that food could be put on her plate, which it duly was.

"I can't understand what the idiot thought he was doing," Grandfather was continuing the conversation he was having with Heinrich as he came in.

"What who was doing?" Josephine looked at her father. She would look at the paper later when he had finished with it.

"A bunch of idiots made a half-hearted attempt at taking over the Bavarian government in Munich."

"Cut up Katie's meat, someone, or she'll carry on eating with her fingers." Maria had been listening, not watching her daughter, but Adelheid seemed to miss nothing. Katie licked her fingers and, chin down, looked half apologetically and half aggrieved at her grandmother while her mother chopped away at the meat on her plate.

"What bunch of idiots?" Josephine looked at her brother this time.

"Hitler and his Nazis," said Heinrich. "The army put a stop to it."
"Oh, that lot."

"Well, 'that lot' have a lot of support. He must have had some grounds for thinking the putsch would be successful."

"Everyone will forget about him now that he's going to be locked up." Grandfather sounded convinced.

"Not so sure they will lock him up," Heinrich muttered to himself.

Katie had been quietly and very carefully spooning more apple sauce onto her plate while no one was looking, but one word had caught her attention.

Quietly she repeated, "Putsch, putsch, putschy, putsch," as she stirred her apples into a mushy puddle. Margarethe and Johanna both laughed and even Adelheid had to suppress a smile. Maria looked over at Heinrich. She knew that this 'little corporal' as he called him worried him, but he was laughing, good-naturedly wagging his finger at his daughter, which of course made her say it loudly all over again.

Later on, Heinrich, Johann and Adelheid left the clearing up to the girls. Maria was told to leave the dishes and come with them into the sitting room and take the weight off her feet, which she was glad to do. Adelheid joined the men in a small glass of cognac, which was her Sunday treat, but it did make her sleepy. Lisl was sent in to collect empty glasses and, as her mother dozed, she ran her finger around the inside of the small round bowl and licked it. Heinrich grinned at Lisl's expression.

"It's disgusting. But," hating to be caught out by her brother, "I'm sure I will grow to like it quite soon."

*

It was already dark when they set off back to Duisburg. Katie watched the lights of Lobberich fade to black as the tram picked up speed through the countryside; her eyelids drooped as she felt the steadying rhythm through the slatted wooden seat, and soon she was asleep on Mama's lap. Maria and Heinrich talked about the day quietly over her head until they reached their stop. Katie woke briefly to see the brightly lit tram rattle away towards the town. She quickly drifted back off to sleep lying over Papa's shoulder as he carried her home, Maria at their side carrying the bottled plums Adelheid had remembered just in time to give them as they left.

3

1924. Duisburg. France was having difficulty accepting the Dawes Plan which was Britain and the USA's solution to the crippling effects the reparations were having on Germany's economy.

Suddenly Sophie was gone. Just like that.

Over the past few months, the little girls had played together, first in the garden as the spring sun hit the damp earth and they had watched the crocuses and narcissi slowly emerge, encouraged by the warmth. Both mothers had called to their daughters to be careful where they trod so as not to damage anything. Small smiles were exchanged but that was all. Maria told herself it was because of the language problem but knew it was more than that; a strange mixture of mutual embarrassment and mutual resentment. It was not comfortable.

The Frenchwoman was very nervous; the first time she came into the garden while Maria was there, she stopped short and turned to go back. "No. Come." Maria had beckoned to her, pointing to her corner of the garden, nodding, and trying to look friendly.

The girls were drawn to each other and Sophie led Katie off to look at a pattern she had made with stones in a bright corner of the garden where the sunshine warmed the wall; she talked patiently and non-stop to the younger girl, clearly giving her instructions which somehow Katie understood. Gradually Katie started to talk back, confident that Sophie would understand. When the stone pattern had been transformed into a miniature garden with weeds draped decoratively over rocks and pebbles, the girls got up for more vigorous activity, chasing each other along the criss-cross pathways, dodging the washing and their mothers. Both women envied their children who had no shared past, no ugly memories. If only it was as easy for them.

Up above, through the open window, a baby cried. "Time to go in, Katie." Katie was pink with excitement and didn't want the chasing to stop. They were getting braver with each other; whenever one caught the other it became a hug rather than a touch, with squeals of delight from both of them. Katie's bottom lip pouted. "Come on; you can play again soon."

Heinz had made his appearance in February and since then managed to spoil most things for Katie. Why did everyone have to make such a fuss, especially for something as noisy as this little red-faced monster – always crying, always hungry? Just because he was a boy. Grandparents walked past her, ignored her, to look and admire the new baby. If she said anything, anything at all, she would be told to be a big girl and not to be so silly or, even worse, not to be so bad-tempered. When she did eventually get to sit on her favourite Opa's lap, and he assured her that she was his absolute number one girl, she wasn't convinced; the cooing and chuckling at any little alteration in Heinz's expression started again all too soon.

Now he was spoiling her playtime with Sophie as well. She would probably never like him very much.

*

Thursdays were Maria's and the Frenchwoman's wash days so whatever the weather Katie was sure of seeing Sophie. If it rained the washing would be hung up inside, around the damp washroom. The girls would stick together, helping one mama by handing her clothes or pegs and then race to the other to do the same. The noise they made was a blessing as it muffled the dense silence that existed between the women. If Heinz was awake, he would be brought down and propped up in a clothes basket, where he could watch everything that was going on. Katie was very pleased to see that Sophie gave him only scant attention; she'd crouched down next to him and gingerly touched his cheek. Then she'd looked at Katie and the two of them had raced off to climb up onto the huge cement sinks and balance along the edges.

Maria was pleased to see that Heinz's presence had a reassuring effect on the Frenchwoman. Her shyness and inability to meet Maria's eye unsettled her more each week. She had ventured over to see Heinz the first time he was brought down, slowly, still keeping her distance, watching for Maria's reaction. The baby's head was turning from side to side with uncontrolled wobbles, his mouth searching for his little wet fist. "*Très joli,*" she said with a hint of a sigh. The women looked at each other properly for the first time.

It was sunny and after the washing was pegged out Maria decided to find a warm place in the garden and feed Heinz; better to feed him before he started to yell. The girls were playing quietly for once and the Frenchwoman was still busy. She found a spot on the low wall near the entrance to the washroom and settled herself and Heinz. She turned her face up to the sun and closed her eyes, enjoying the warmth on her skin; there was the odd buzz from an insect, the flap-flapping of the washing on the line and the distant gentle noise of the girls' chatter. Peaceful moments passed and when she opened her eyes again the woman was standing nearby. She was watching, waiting for a moment to approach. Maria was mildly startled.

"*Pardon, Madame. C'est pour vous.*" She was holding out a little plate. She had to stretch out her arm because she still maintained that distance between them which she must have felt was polite, or necessary. On the plate was a small piece of apple tart and a small fork. It was a perfect square with a shining soft glaze covering.

Maria hesitated but the Frenchwoman was insistent, pointing at Heinz, still feeding at Maria's breast, and saying words that could only mean, 'you need this, you must eat it'. Maria settled Heinz on her lap so she could take the cake. It was perfect. Soft apple, crisp pastry; a hint of lemon. The woman watched her expression anxiously, then, when Maria so clearly found it delicious, smiled with satisfaction.

The girls had come over to see what was happening, surprised at the sudden closeness between the two women. Sophie wanted to give Katie some; her mother shook her head and replied to her at some length with the result that Sophie shot off and came back moments later with something for her friend. It was chocolate. A piece was broken off for her and the rest was given to Maria who broke off a piece for Katie. The creamy, milky sweetness made both girls break into smiles.

A little later as the women got ready to go back in, Maria took the Frenchwoman's hand and squeezed it; thank you very much. Maria had been moved by the gesture of kindness. It must have been hard to do, and she regretted not making a greater effort herself. The woman touched Maria's arm as she turned to go. Maria couldn't make out the expression in her eyes; were they saying, it'll be better from now on, or was there regret, a hint of something ending before it could begin?

Heinrich would be pleased, when told about this, about this little incident in their garden, she thought to herself; *he'll say something like, "You see! Sensible, ordinary people, doing more good than all the idiot politicians."* Meanwhile Katie, her face smeared with chocolate and whose love for Sophie knew no bounds, was busy thinking of all the things she could give her. Mama's biscuits for one, and maybe one of the bracelets Lisl had given her.

Then, they were gone. Pretty Sophie and her golden curls. Gone. Just like that.

4

The French government finally accepted the Dawes Plan and the last of the occupying forces left the Ruhr in August 1925. A large contingent of French colonial soldiers, mainly from Senegal, had been stationed in the region.

E ach of Katie's hands was in the firm grasp of her aunts. "This way, Johanna; I think we can get to the front..." Katie felt herself being pulled briefly to the right.

"No. Look. There's a way through to the front over there. If we're quick..." And Johanna headed with determination toward a gap in the crowd, dragging Katie and Margarethe with her.

"There," Johanna was pleased with herself, "we should be able to see everything from here; they should be coming soon."

Katie was released and for the first time that morning stopped feeling like a piece of string joining the sisters together. They had come to stay a couple of days before to give Maria a hand, and today was so warm and sunny that Maria had told them to take Katie out. She hadn't said specifically not to go into town, everyone knew that the French were leaving today, but the chance was too good to miss. If they made a fuss, they had told each other, they would say it was too important a day to miss, and that Katie should see it too. History in the making; a fresh start for Germany.

Now they stood at the edge of Königstrasse, the road that led to the harbour. There was no traffic; no trams, and policemen were stopping people from crossing the road.

From Katie's point of view, wedged as she was among skirts and trousered legs, there was very little to see. Black dust had been kicked up as people shuffled about and she could feel it in her nose. She'd never been this close to the docks before. Margarethe had promised to pick her up when the soldiers came, and in the meanwhile she wasn't to move, as it would be easy to get lost in the crowd. The crowd was quiet, expectant. She could hear only murmurs and muffled conversation and the words were lost as they made their way down to her. Occasionally there was a rustle, a movement as if something was about to happen, then quiet again. Katie sighed and turned around to see more people arriving, the mass of legs becoming denser, darker. But still they stood quietly, not pushing, just waiting.

A voice behind said, "Listen, I can hear horses." And sure enough a few seconds later everyone could hear the mounted troops come nearer. The French troops would march past on their way to the ships that were waiting in the harbour. Then they would sail, alongside the usual barges full of coal and steel, towards the Rhine, through Holland and eventually back to France.

"I want to see, pick me up." She pulled at Margarethe's hand, but it was Johanna who bent down and lifted her. The sound got nearer and louder and finally she could see them; their heads kept tight on short reins, tails flicking, the odd wayward animal proving more difficult to control, goaded back into line with a clamp of the knees or a sharp jab with a spur. The clattering of their hooves filled her ears, her head; she caught her breath. They passed so close she could have reached out and touched them; she could smell their sweat. They passed in formations of twenty or so with gaps in between. There must have been hundreds. Then the sounds receded, and Katie was sorry as the clip-clopping disappeared altogether. She strained in Johanna's arms to watch the swishing tails, the straight backs of the men. A convoy of trucks followed, slowly, one behind the other, grinding in low gear. Still the crowd watched in near silence.

Later on Johanna thought about this period of silence, as the trucks rumbled away, the canvas aprons at the back flapping and swirls of gritty coal dust kicked up in their wake. She had interpreted it as dignified – people glad that the occupation was over and resigned to an uncertain future – but there was something else: expectancy, an icy tension in the air as well. On the opposite side of Königstrasse there was some movement, a group joining the crowd at the back followed by some pushing and complaining. For the first time it crawled into her mind that maybe it hadn't been a good idea to bring Katie to watch this.

Then all were distracted as the rhythm of marching boots began to approach. Here came the infantry; the same soldiers that had been deployed around the factories and steel plants making sure that most of what was produced headed straight for France. This morning they were marching with their eyes firmly ahead. Rapid steps as if glad to be going home. Light blue uniforms, helmets low over foreheads, glinting brass; Katie's head swivelled as row after row went past.

"Take her for a bit, Margarethe, will you?" Johanna's arms were aching. Margarethe reached for Katie and settled her onto her hip. The rhythm was slowing; there must be a hold-up ahead where horses, trucks and men were crowding into the dock. Slower and slower until the men, marching on the spot for a moment or so, were ordered to halt. The sound of boots stamping on stone had given way to an uneasy rustle as feet settled and rifles adjusted. The soldiers' eyes stayed focussed ahead but Johanna noticed the beads of sweat, the licking of lips. Margarethe nudged her sister. "Look!"

A murmur was heard behind them; Johanna felt pressure from behind as necks craned to see the cohort of Senegalese soldiers, standing still, suddenly vulnerable. There was a sudden and complete silence, the kind that is waiting for something.

"How black they are," Margarethe whispered to herself. And they were. Katie hadn't noticed, but now she did and stared carefully at them. Smooth, shiny, black skin, beautiful. Long, nervous fingers fidgeting with their rifles.

"Why are they black?" She asked.

"Because they come from Africa." Katie nodded, entranced.

There were hoots coming from the back, from both sides of the street, as if an unspoken signal had been given. Margarethe looked back and saw that a couple of men in brown had shouldered their way through the crowd and she heard one of them shout, "At last they're sending their monkeys home!" Nervous laughter and more hooting from the back; monkey noises.

Margarethe put Katie back down on the ground just in time for her not to see the stone hurled over their heads towards the soldiers. People around were getting bolder, shouting, "Go home; go home!" Things suddenly felt dangerous. The sisters looked at each other and knew they had to get Katie away. Margarethe hesitated briefly to look again at the soldier nearest her, to see his eyes flicker from side to side, to see the trickle of blood on his cheek and to hear the swift command to march on.

As the stamp of boots resumed, they took Katie's hands and forced their way through. One man would not give way and Johanna gritted her teeth as she pushed against his shoulder. Katie and Margarethe followed; they made their way to the edge of the crowds and walked quickly away from their swaying backs and turned left towards the post office. Johanna's heart was beating. She was trying to understand what had just happened.

Katie stopped and pulled her hands away and rubbed her eyes furiously. She didn't know why she was crying. One minute they were watching, sunshine bouncing on bright helmets making her blink, blue skies absorbing the stillness. Then suddenly she was down among the boots and the dust, dragged past knees and hips, and there was something else. The noise; it was still there, growing dimmer, but moronic and angry, and it was the anger that was making her heart beat and tears spill, no matter how hard she squeezed her lids together. And behind the tears she could see the wild eyes of the horses, the tossing manes and tails and the cruel jabbing spurs.

"Oh! Katie." Margarethe sank down beside her and put her arms round her. The sisters looked at each other. The infection that had gripped the crowd and that had changed the mood so suddenly had been felt just as keenly by the child; her distress made their own much worse.

Katie's arms were tight around Margarethe's neck and gradually the tears stopped. Johanna found a handkerchief and managed to wipe away the smears of dirt around Katie's eyes and mouth. They both kissed her very vigorously.

"Darling, that wasn't very nice at all, was it?" said Johanna with a look at Margarethe, a look that said, how do we talk about this? *And how do we tell Heinrich about it,* thought Margarethe.

"How about a drink? Would that be a good idea?" Johanna had tight hold of Katie who struggled free and sniffed and nodded. She was suddenly sufficiently self-composed to lead the way towards a nearby kiosk, one of the many in town, and much loved by children as they sold not only cigarettes and tobacco but ice-cream and sweets. After a moment's thought she chose a drink of apple juice and one of her favourite bon-bons, a bright orange stick wrapped in stripy waxed paper with twisted ends. The sisters were glad to see Katie calmer. As she concentrated on her sweet treat, they headed off on the long walk back to Ost Strasse, keeping away from the flat backs of the thinning crowds still watching the marching soldiers, each rehearsing what they were going to tell Maria.

*

The tram jerked and shuddered out of Grünewald stop, the metal wheels squealing as it veered this way and that before settling itself for the ride back to Lobberich. The sisters' summer dresses slid about on the varnished, slatted, wooden seats and they sat close together, looking at the dull brown housing blocks gradually give way to wider streets then open spaces. The tram gathered speed, clattering rhythmically across the flat farmlands, making talking difficult so the women sat quietly, content to watch the familiar sight of men and women bending in the fields and the odd horse pulling a plough or a cart.

Maria, Katie and Heinz had walked to the tram stop with them. It was another warm summer's day and Maria wanted to spend a few hours in the cool of the forest with the children. Maria had hugged both her sisters-in-law warmly. "Don't forget to give our love to your parents and sisters." As the tram pulled away, Katie, in her blue cotton dress, waved vigorously and Maria held up seven-month-old Heinz who was transfixed by the monstrous yellow tram, talking to him, helping him wave with his chubby arm, watching the tram rattle off into the distance.

The tram slowed down to stop at Kempen and in the brief silence

Johanna spoke. She looked past Margarethe at the people on the platform as she said, "I think Heinrich is OK about it all now, don't you? I mean, he didn't say much this morning, did he? Didn't seem angry or anything?"

She looked at her sister who quickly smiled and said, "No, I'm sure he's not angry with us." She felt Margarethe's hand squeeze hers as she gave a relieved sigh and nod at this affirmation.

No, thought Margarethe, *not angry. But he won't forget it, neither will Maria. Poor Johanna, so worried that anyone should think badly of her. She wants the whole episode forgotten about, everything to go back to normal; and maybe it will. After all, Katie seems fine, a little quiet maybe, but behaving normally; and no-one had got hurt, had they?* The tram picked up speed again and she remembered the trickle of blood on the black skin.

*

Maria had said little when Katie and the girls returned from town. Katie crawled onto her lap almost immediately. "Mama we saw horses and guns and, and black soldiers." Her eyelids closed and she fell into a sticky sleep, dreaming vaguely of Sophie hiding, calling and gradually disappearing behind the legs of the crowd. Maria looked to the sisters for explanation. Johanna took a breath and started to speak. She took some of it in; what were they thinking of – taking Katie to watch as the French left the Rhineland? She looked down anxiously at her exhausted little girl then up again from face to face; Johanna, crestfallen, sorry and close to tears, and Margarethe, struggling to find the right words, talking of how the mood had changed, chanting crowds and what? Did she say stone throwing?

Only when Katie woke up, complaining of thirst and hunger, could Maria see that no real damage had been done and then, handing the fractious, teething Heinz over to the sisters, her attention had been taken up with distracting her, letting her talk of the beautiful horses, giving her as much bread and jam as she wanted, watching, listening but not asking too many questions. Then, of course it started all over again when Heinrich came home.

Seeing the anger build in his eyes, Maria had led him away into the small sitting room.

"Of course there was stone throwing! What did they expect?" Heinrich dug his hands deep into his pockets and paced the floor. "Did they think they were just going to politely wave goodbye?"

"They know they made a mistake." She stood in front of him. "They are so sorry. We can't be angry with them."

"Silly girls, such foolishness; they've never thought beyond the end of their noses." And he paced away his anger.

They took their time putting the children to bed. A story followed by bedtime prayers; Heinz thankfully went straight to sleep and Katie made the most of the time Papa was spending with her this evening, surprised that he did go and fetch her a glass of water and then happy to lie and have her hair stroked as she finally became sleepy enough to close her eyes.

Heinrich was prepared with something sharp, something severe to drive home their foolishness, but one glance at their distraught faces softened him immediately. He rubbed his chin, shook his head, and said instead, "Get some glasses," as he sat down at the table where Maria had put the cognac. Margarethe leapt up and went over to the little cabinet, took out four of the pretty glasses given as a wedding present and put them down in front of her brother who poured a modest amount for each of his sisters and substantially more for himself and Maria.

He wanted to hear again what exactly had happened, what had changed. Was it just the appearance of the African soldiers or something else?

"They were an excuse," Heinrich decided. "It's exactly how the brown shirts work. They make sure they are in the right place at the right time and make trouble." He looked into the faces of his sisters and saw they didn't know what he was talking about.

"Well, they, the French I mean, have gone home now so things can get back to normal." Johanna's voice was small, hopeful. Margarethe was quiet.

"No. I don't think so." Heinrich wasn't sure how much he wanted to say, wasn't sure of anything.

"The children," Maria leant forward, "they mustn't see it, this… hatred. I don't want them to see it." Heinrich covered her hand with his. "No, that's right." This was easier, this was a certainty. "We must protect them from it." The 'it' seemed to fill the room, something not yet tangible, something she didn't have words for yet, but Margarethe recognised it; she'd felt it in the crowd.

5

Maria wanted to visit her father, so they all went together to the main station in Duisburg and Heinrich put them onto the train to Mönchen Gladbach before going to work. They would come back in the evening and he would be there to meet them.

It had been a few days since Margarethe and Johanna had left and Maria could now be sure that Katie did not seem to have suffered any ill effects. She knew that a visit to her Opa would prove so exciting a prospect, as it always did, that any residual memories would be banished. At least this is what she hoped. And she needed him, his reassuring bulk, his unconditional love. It would calm her. Heinrich had telephoned him at his office the day before.

They both worked for the police; her father, Peter, as an inspector and Heinrich for the Ministry of Justice, and their respective departments had been quick to install telephone equipment. Heinrich had been very proud of this technological development and her father was beginning to see the benefits, especially when the new-fangled machine brought news of a visit from his grandchildren. He decided immediately to take a day's leave and told Hilde to organise plenty of cake while he would go himself to the butcher for some beef to make a good hot midday meal. Soup – that's what they'd have. Nothing like good soup for those growing children. Then he'd go to the station to meet them off the train.

There was no-one, apart, of course from Mama and Papa, who Katie loved more than her Opa; hard for any child not to love a man who was so exuberantly pleased to see her. He was always pleased to see Heinz too, of course, these days, but she was the one who commandeered his lap with his round, comfy stomach and safe, strong hands. And she loved the way he always cupped Mama's face in his hands when he said hello, his eyes crinkling with pleasure before kissing her on both cheeks.

"There he is, there's Opa!" And off she raced. He'd seen her coming and was bending down ready to grab her with both arms. Round she twirled, lifted high. Opa's face was pink, his grey moustache, as always, carefully curled upwards so that his face was perpetually smiling. Her arms wrapped around his broad neck and she buried her face into the soft flesh which smelt of lavender soap.

"Come on, let's go and help Mama." His eyes were searching for her along the platform and found her as she struggled with Heinz in one arm and bag in the other. He hurried towards her and put Katie down before helping the guard lift the pram down onto the platform. He took Heinz and bobbed and kissed him before depositing him quickly into the pram so he could give his attention to his eldest daughter. He put his hands on her shoulders and gave her a long look.

"You look more and more like your mother."

"Father, you say that every time." But she said it warmly, smiling happily at him.

"Well, it's true." It was Katharina's eyes he was looking into and since having the children they had taken on the same grave expression. The girlishness was completely gone.

"Right, let's go!" he said with determination. "There's dinner waiting for us at home. I do believe it's soup." And, grabbing the bag and Katie, led the way out of the station at a sharp pace. Katie craned her neck back round towards Maria and said with difficulty, because she had to run to keep up with her Opa, but with a huge smile, "Soup, Mama, we're having soup!"

And Maria, pushing the pram behind them, returned the grin. Always soup; whenever they visited it was always soup, cooked with a large piece of beef and today, because it was summer, there would be fresh peas. He was a man of habit, her father, and she loved him for it. She watched his sturdy back and his face in profile as he bent it towards Katie, to listen to whatever she was breathlessly chattering about, and remembered how she and her sister had been led here, there and everywhere at a similar pace. And she remembered her mother, Katharina, laughing and pleading for him to slow down. "Peter, for goodness' sake, they've only got little legs." And just for a minute he would slow down but soon the pace would pick up again and Katharina would have to keep up, kicking against her long skirts.

*

Peter's house was large. He had bought it when the girls were quite young, Mina still a baby. Around the turn of the century a promotion at work had coincided with some inheritance money and he decided the best thing to do was to invest in a good house for his growing family. Katharina had loved the double-fronted house from the start, great rose bushes growing around the large windows and pathways all the way round. And there was a large vegetable garden ready for her to plant.

Katie's strong little legs stomped up the stone steps and everyone helped to carry Heinz in his pram into the hallway. Peter, followed by Katie, went straight into the kitchen to inspect the soup. Maria picked up Heinz, who had greatly enjoyed his race to the house, and followed them.

"Ah, there you are." Hilde, dropping potatoes into the simmering broth, turned towards them. Her mouth straightened into a half smile and her eyes softened a little when she looked at Katie and Heinz.

Katie watched Hilde allow herself to be kissed on the cheek by her mother and wish her good day, and then waited for her to bend down so she could do the same. She sensed the awkwardness of the greetings, which were polite enough but unusually cool for her family, which was good at hugs and kisses.

"Salt!" Peter announced. He'd dipped a finger into the soup and licked it.

"Uh-mm," said Hilde, "maybe." She didn't add any, but began to lay the table, where Maria had already sat down with Heinz on her lap. Maria watched her stepmother; hair pulled back from her face and her stout, short frame encased in an apron. There was little warmth between the two women, but things had got a lot better between them since she had married, and especially since the children had been born. She tried hard not to harbour resentment and she had realised, too late and with some regret, how difficult it was for Hilde to show affection. It was clear that she was fond of Katie, taking delight in holding her hand – when allowed – but there was genuine happiness, open pleasure with Heinz on her knee. Hilde was at ease when playing with Heinz, the precious boy, a reminder of her own sons. Hilde had married her father two years after Katharina had died, bringing her sullen boys with her. Maria had been twelve, Mina, ten. Even now her father didn't know the resentment they had felt towards Otto and Hans; first there was the whispered name calling and then the routine, underhand bullying. Of course, they behaved themselves whenever Peter was around, but Hilde turned a blind eye to all of it, allowing the laziness while expecting the girls to help with all the chores. Heinz was definitely always going to do his fair share, she decided then and there, as she watched him gurgling in Hilde's arms.

After lunch Peter announced that he would go for a little lie down before they went for a walk. He put his face close to Katie's. "Play quietly, sweetheart. I shan't be long. Then we'll go and find some ice-cream." He beamed at her and she beamed back, nodding. The women watched as he got up, patting his stomach, and walked out of the kitchen, heading towards the living room. Maria heard the almost inaudible tut from Hilde as the door closed behind him.

*

Katie explored the kitchen for a little while, being careful not to get in Hilde's way, and watched Heinz, who was playing with some spoons on the floor. He had learnt to sit up by himself and was beginning to take lunges to left and right in his eagerness to move; he had become just a bit more entertaining recently and she was gratified, though not that surprised, that he found everything she did very interesting. After a little while she got bored. Mama and Hilde were talking quietly, and she wondered if it wasn't time for Opa to come back or at least she could go and watch him sleep and wait for him to wake up.

She crept out of the room, down the passage and towards the closed door of the living room. She pulled the handle down very gently and stepped inside.

He was sitting up on the couch where he normally slept, his face in profile and seemingly unaware that she had come in. There was something about the rigid stillness of his back that made her wary of going further towards him. He was staring up at the portrait that hung on the wall opposite him. One of his hands moved to his face and she saw him wipe his eye quickly. The broad shoulders heaved to the rhythm of his slow breathing. Katie backed out of the room on tiptoes and returned to the kitchen.

"I hope you didn't disturb Opa, Katie." Maria could see on Katie's face that that was exactly what she had done. Katie looked guilty, but couldn't explain what she had seen. She nuzzled up to her mother, who kissed the top of her head and caught Hilde's eye.

"So, it still happens?"

Hilde looked down at her hands, knuckles rough from chopping vegetables, washing clothes. "Yes, every so often. I think you remind him, you see…" Her voice trailed off and she looked directly at Maria. Her tone was, as ever, hard and resigned. "It can't be helped." And she raised her upturned hands and lifted her shoulders as if that was all there was to say.

Poor woman, thought Maria. *How hard it must be to live with.* Her father had never, would never get over the death of Katharina. The portrait, painted the year they had married, hung where it had always been and the one time it had been suggested that it could be moved, somewhere less offensive to Hilde, had brought about such a furious reaction that the subject had never been mentioned again. He was intractable when it came to the memory of Katharina, for years unable to accommodate his grief privately, the convulsive nature of it making it impossible for his daughters to express their own. The shock of losing her mother had left her numb; watching her father's undisguised distress made her bury any self-pity. She'd stopped talking to Heinrich about it, because it was clear that he found her father's behaviour self-indulgent, and she couldn't bear to hear him criticised.

And Hilde had to bear this every day and for the rest of her life. Peter had married her far too soon after Katharina died. She was a widow with two boys and was introduced to him by his sister – worried sick because he wasn't coping with his girls, hardly able to get to work. Hilde was a good, Catholic woman who would be able to see to the home and deal with the girls and the female side of things as they got older. It was a rational and sensible move. From Hilde's point of view, it was a gift – security, a fine home, the return of married status – but there had been a price to pay. There was affection between the two. When Maria looked back, she could remember light-hearted moments – hands squeezing shoulders – pecks on the cheek when Peter came home from work. Maria looked at the hard line of her stepmother's mouth. How did it feel to have to settle for gratitude in place of love? In spite of everything she did feel some pity.

Katie's sharp ears heard steps in the hallway and she wriggled free from her mother's lap. Peter stood in the door frame.

"Now then," he ostentatiously patted his pockets, where pfennigs and marks might lurk, with a look of mock concern on his face. "Not sure I've got enough… that ice-cream may have to wait…" Trouser pockets proved empty; the searching with sausage-like fingers continued, Katie watching every move. Of course, this game had been played before and she was pretty sure of the outcome, but maybe this was the time that the necessary coins would not turn up. Then, "Ah, Katie, we are in luck." A shiny mark was produced from his waistcoat and brandished aloft. "Come along, let's go!"

Small hand in large, Maria watched her father march off with Katie to buy ice-cream and walk in the park. No words had been exchanged between him and the women. It was simply understood that this is how it was – and always would be. It wasn't the last time that Katie would see her Opa wipe tears from his eyes, but years would pass before Maria told her and her brothers the story. And she would choose her moment, because it became, small though it was, a tale of complex, confused love at a time when all sense of loyalty and reason seemed to be being blown apart.

6

January 1926. Unusually heavy rain had resulted in the Rhine flooding its banks. The streets of Cologne and Düsseldorf ran with water and Duisburg was also affected.

Papa and Katie stared out of the window. It hadn't rained for days but slate-grey clouds scudded across a blustery sky and the pavement below was slick with ebbing flood water. The road itself was still awash and water lapped against the kerbside as the odd cyclist ploughed his way through.

"I might get home from work with dry socks today, you never know." Papa went off to pull on his rubber boots.

The rain had started in November and continued throughout the month and on towards Christmas. Instead of the usual brisk cold and frost, which fitted the season with its promise of snow, there was damp and endless leaden skies. The odd dry day became a rush against time to wash and shop, find a Christmas tree before the next deluge. Maria had hauled as much wood as possible up from the cellar to keep a fire going in the kitchen, where clothes seemed to hang forever trying to dry. Christmas itself was quiet, families unwilling to put on galoshes and raincoats and leave warm living-rooms. Maria insisted on one visit to her sister, Mina. She, Albrecht and little Friede had recently moved to an apartment in Grünewald and, as long as the tram was running, they could get there. So on the day after Christmas, a Saturday, off they went, clad in rubber boots, Heinrich with his enormous umbrella, to pay the visit Maria felt had to be made as it was their first Christmas in their new home. The children played together with Friede's new toys, mainly dolls, which Heinz maltreated, making Friede cry and complain. Heinz was swiftly removed and entertained by his uncle, who could always make him laugh. The wet journey home was delayed as long as they dared, and as long as Heinrich could bear. He found Maria's sister superficial, and Albrecht could be pompous, but he put a brave face on the visits.

After New Year the flood waters had got so bad that a few enterprising boat owners had set up ferrying services which Heinrich used to get to the office in the town centre. For a few days the flood waters were high enough to flow down their own street, near the forest and furthest from the Ruhr. The stairs and landings in the building were piled high with the contents of the cellars which slowly filled with cold, grey water. The occupants had to step over jars and bottles, crates and boxes until the water receded and the cellars could be cleaned out and allowed to dry a little.

This morning water still covered the lines, but the trams were able to run slowly through the town. Heinrich had missed only two days of work, when the downpours made it impossible, but he had managed to wade through twenty centimetres of water and then use the boats to get to the office, much to the amusement of his colleagues, many of whom stayed at home from mid-December till well into January. Each morning he changed into dry shoes and left the galoshes to drip under his desk, damp trousers clinging to his legs for most of the day.

But these were good days at work. Though cautious optimism was something he had buried in the battlefields in Belgium, he couldn't help but share his sisters' excitement at living in a young democracy. When with his family he maintained a dignified cynicism when talking to them, as befitted a big brother. With a twinkle in his eye, he would take his parents' side; they lamented the loss of the Kaiser and feared for his well-being. Women had been given the vote in 1919, the year of Katie's birth, and he remembered Margarethe holding her, it must have been in the summer, and saying what a lucky girl she was to be born at a time when women would be taken seriously and of course he'd made some joke about the impossibility of anyone taking any of his sisters seriously. Inflation had been brought under control and American loans were easing the burden on government and business. The mines and factories were hard at work again. Laws were relaxing; even here in Duisburg, in his department, at the regional office of the Ministry of Justice, there were new instructions coming from government that there were now employment possibilities for not only women and Catholics but even Jews. There was freedom in the very atmosphere, even the air he breathed felt fresher. Yes, it was a good time, a hopeful time.

This morning all but those stranded in the north of the city were back at work. He was pleased to see that Claus, who tended to get into work as conscientiously as Heinrich, had already arrived. He had the *Frankfurter Allgemeiner* spread out on his desk and shouted his greetings across the room; Hermann and Franz hadn't shown up yet. Claus was young, had missed the war and had unbridled enthusiasm for the new democratic Germany. He trusted Heinrich and made use of their times alone together in the office.

"Morning, Heinrich!" He slapped at the newspaper. "Have you seen the latest from Berlin?"

Claus, like him, was delighted with the recent changes made by the government. But, unlike him, was such a thorough optimist that Heinrich immediately became wary and found himself arguing and trying to bring him back down to earth.

"Are you talking about the latest street fighting or the latest election? It's hard to keep up with it all." Heinrich had just noticed that he really did have dry socks and wriggled his toes contentedly in his shoes.

Claus glared at him good-naturedly. "Things will settle down, Heinrich. Now that people have the promise of work the street nonsense will stop." He looked out of the window and grinned at Heinrich. "And it's even stopped raining! It's a portent!"

"Don't be ridiculous..." Heinrich was just about to explain, for the fifth time, how the Communists and the Nationalists were never going to get together and govern sensibly but was stopped by Hermann's arrival.

Both men straightened themselves very slightly and Claus quietly folded the newspaper and laid it down at the side of the desk. They had only once spoken of their political opinions in front of Hermann, naively imagining that he and Franz would be as enthusiastic as they were. Hermann, a large but carefully contained man, finicky about his work, clipped with his speech, had reddened – his starched, white collar glowing against his neck. The present regime was an insult to the memory of the fallen, he had said in a voice tense with restrained anger. The Reds were getting more powerful and what good could come of that? Germany needed strong government if it was ever to get its self-respect back. Heinrich listened to this man, who had gone through the same experiences in the trenches as he had, but whose deep and furious sense of betrayal, he couldn't understand, and resolved to be more careful in assuming that conversations could be had as casually as they were at home. He should have known better. Claus, he remembered, couldn't hide his shock, and had he not been so aware of his friend's tight silence he would have given an angry reply. Here was a man you couldn't argue with.

The men pretended to forget the incident, in the interest of office *bonhomie*, so this morning, like all the others, after the genial early morning handshaking Hermann settled his bulk behind his desk, positioned closest to the Director's office, an indication of his rank, and the three of them got on with their work. Franz came in fifteen minutes later, addressing his apologies to Hermann with an unnecessary explanation of the difficulties of his journey and, receiving no reply, sat down limply at his desk, adjusted his glasses and started to gently move papers around, casting frequent glances at Hermann. Heinrich thought his nervousness dated from that outburst when they had all learned what could be spoken about and what could not. Poor Franz, so eager to please, who jumped when asked to perform a task, who glowed when praised. Claus would hide his mouth, and its inclination to grin, behind his hand and Heinrich would give him warning glares. Poor, harmless Franz. Both men agreed that he would be a pen-pushing clerk for the rest of his days. No chance of promotion for that one!

7

"Your sister?" Claus was, to put it mildly, taken aback, and the bottle of beer that was heading towards his mouth was momentarily suspended, mid-air. "But you have so many, my friend; which one did you have in mind?" The beer found its mark and Claus took a large gulp, an eye firmly on Heinrich and a smile playing around his mouth.

Claus's suitability as a potential brother-in-law had come to Heinrich not so much in a flash, more as a dim and yet to be considered idea at lunchtime that day. They had squelched their way to a small park to eat their sandwiches. The sun had brought out office workers and they were lucky to find a dry bench to sit on. As Claus innocently ate his salami, cutting off chunks with a penknife and tearing at a lump of heavy bread, looking with the usual envy at Maria's carefully prepared lunch complete with gherkins and cubes of cheese, it occurred to Heinrich that this principled young man would undoubtedly meet with the approval of his younger sisters. Karoline, the eldest, was sure to announce her engagement to Helmut soon, a man with the potential to bore them all to death. And Josephine's declaration that she wanted to become a nun had become ever more insistent no matter how much her sisters cried at the idea. But the younger ones...?

So now, in the pub, a friendly establishment on the corner of Tulpen Strasse, on the way home for Heinrich although in completely the opposite direction for Claus, who didn't mind at all if it involved a couple of beers, Heinrich, having thought about it, decided to put it to him.

"Marriage, generally speaking, is good for a man," is how Heinrich had begun and stopped when he realised how pompous he sounded. Claus played along and adopted an overly serious and attentive expression. Heinrich cleared his throat and decided to be more direct. "Have you thought about getting married? Is there anyone... erm... around at the moment?"

Claus, sensing that Heinrich had something to say and lacked the skills to do so, waited a moment, enjoying his embarrassment. "Well, Heinrich, there are lots of girls *around* at the moment; there's Trudi who lives in the apartment upstairs, and the barmaid in my local, she's..."

Heinrich cut him off, "OK, OK, but anyone serious?" He decided to launch straight into it. "I think, I really think that you would get on well with one of my sisters." This was when the beer bottle stopped mid-flight. "She's, she's bright and, well, pretty." He was flustered and nearly added, 'I suppose', because he'd never thought of his sisters in those terms. Both men took large gulps of their beers.

"Johanna," was the answer to Claus's question. Heinrich said it limply as he heard the amusement in Claus's voice and was wondering why he had started all this. But any silences would be worse, so he ploughed on. "There would be no harm in meeting her – would there? We could arrange it at our flat, a sort of accidental thing – she often comes over with Margarethe..." Johanna was his choice. Thoughtful, principled; she would be a good influence on him.

Claus smiled kindly. "Heinrich, what are you thinking of? How could I possibly marry anyone? I've only had my qualifications for a year." He had moved from his parents' home in Cologne to work for the Ministry of Justice and rented a room off Mülheimer Strasse.

But his tone suggested that he wasn't rejecting the idea. Heinrich felt confident once more. "No-one's thinking about marriage yet," he lied, "just a meeting; come over for a coffee or something, we can invent an excuse; see if you like each other."

And so it was that Claus, unable to offend his friend and just a little curious about the pretty sister, agreed to be invited to their apartment on a Saturday afternoon a few weeks later when Johanna and Margarethe were there on a visit.

Maria was very excited at the notion of matchmaking and agreed that Johanna could certainly be ready for such an introduction; she also realised how important it was to make the whole thing look accidental. So Claus arrived, bearing 'papers' that Heinrich had forgotten and that he would need to read before Monday morning. Introductions were made and coffee produced along with some biscuits that Maria had happened to make the day before. Katie fell in love immediately and insisted on showing him all her toys one by one, in order to get as much attention as possible, until told by Heinrich to leave the poor man alone. She took another biscuit from the table and threw herself onto the sofa in a sulk. Heinz, now three years old, was busy constructing a railway network in the bedroom. The noises of engines and monumental crashes drifted through from time to time.

The plan was a success. But not in quite the way that Heinrich had planned. Claus was charming and played the part of a man surprised and delighted for the chance to meet his friend's family. It didn't take long for Maria to see where the real attraction was. Johanna was shy with the lively Claus; Margarethe was dazzled but not into silence. She made Claus laugh a couple of times and even Heinrich noticed the two of them catch each other's eye. Heinrich made a mental note to have a chat on Monday about appropriate behaviour, especially when he noticed what could only have been a wink, aimed at Margarethe, when it was time for him to leave and the family crowded around the door for handshaking and goodbyes. Claus told Katie she could come with him, if she promised to be very good, and she got halfway down the third flight of stairs before losing courage and running back up where everyone was waiting, grinning. "Maybe next time, Katie!" Claus shouted up before the front door crashed shut.

Katie looked seriously at Maria. "I don't think I want to leave you just yet, Mama." Maria picked her up. "No, not just yet, darling, I'd be very sad if you left."

*

It was nearly three years later that they married. Margarethe was determined to train as a typist, and worked briefly for a small publishing firm, and Claus set about diligently preparing for the next level of civil service examinations, which he passed. They saved carefully and both sets of parents contributed so that they were able to set up home. Claus got a position in the Ministry of Justice in Düsseldorf and it was there that the couple took up residence in May 1929 after the wedding. And six months after the birth of Hansgünther, Maria and Heinrich's third child. Claus and Heinrich remained firm friends, meeting often, and over too many beers discussed the painful progress and ultimate disintegration of the short-lived German republic.

It had been a difficult pregnancy for Maria and the birth left her weak and reliant on help. During the first few weeks the aunts took turns to come and stay but soon Maria became stronger and with Katie's enthusiastic help things settled down, much to Heinrich's relief.

Katie had never been much interested in dolls but this real, live baby to play with was altogether more to her liking. She was allowed to take him out for walks in the pram, as long as she stayed in the street so that Maria could catch a glimpse of them out of the window. She was also asked to keep an eye on Heinz, who played football with Matthias and Benjamin from across the street. If the ball bounced anywhere near the pram, endangering little Günther, she would yell at them all and kick the ball halfway down the street.

8

By January 1929 the young republic was in trouble. The national debt was rising and there were nearly two million unemployed. Adolf Hitler was in firm control of the Nazi Party and was ready to exploit the devastation caused by the Wall Street crash when it came.

Katie's tenth birthday was approaching, and the entire family was invited to celebrate. A tenth birthday was a big event and Katie was beside herself with excitement. As luck would have it, January 5th fell on a Saturday so everyone could come except Aunt Josephine, the second oldest, who was now living in a convent in Kassel. Adelheid had been her only ally while she was making her decision to become a nun; the rest of the family were at first appalled, then realised there was no stopping her. Johanna, angry and tearful, took every opportunity to say that so much more good could be done, by using her talents in the 'real' world rather than running away. But Josephine, her serious blue eyes helplessly registering her sister's hurt and concern, remained steadfast in her decision.

Katie had started school four years earlier and it had become a glorious place of freedom and excitement. She approached it all with passion, loving some of the teachers and loathing others even though Maria said sternly that it was unchristian to hate anyone.

"But Mama, Herr Drexler is disgusting. He spits when he talks to us. Well… shouts; he always shouts," adding, "I HATE maths."

Or on another occasion, breathless, excited,

"Guess what, Mama? I've been picked for the school athletics team. Fräulein Kästner, oh she is SO nice, says I'm the fastest girl in the school and really good at the high jump. I think I'm better at long jump, actually. I can jump further than Rolf and he's in the boys' team AND older than me!"

Maria learned not to comment on all the proclamations that were made by her daughter on most days after school. Rather to accept them as evidence of a girl happy with everything school had to offer. Anyway, as well as the new baby, she had other worries. Heinz had developed asthma around his fourth birthday and there were daily anxieties around his welfare. Now, as his sixth birthday approached, she became more concerned about his ability to cope with the rough and tumble of school life. Heinrich was keen that he should not be mollycoddled, no way to treat a boy, he said, but secretly he worried as much as Maria.

Both Heinz and Katie were oblivious of this worry. Heinz was as boisterous as ever and was looking forward to starting school and Katie only pandered to his affliction when her parents were watching. She had seen him struggle to get his breath and it was very frightening. The first time, she'd hidden behind Maria watching his face turn blue and heard the strangled wheeze as his body fought to suck some air into his lungs. When he at last relaxed and the breathing became easier, she took great gulps of air into her own lungs for him and felt the pain in her hands where she had clenched her fists too tightly. But then, after a while, he would be back to his normal annoying self, getting in the way or throwing things, and she very quickly realised that he was using his asthma to get what he wanted and she wasn't going to let him get away with that, even if Mama and Papa turned a blind eye to most of his crimes.

Because of the party, Heinz had to subdue his excitement at the thought of his first day at school, with its promise of the traditional school cone filled to the brim with chocolate and sweets. Watching the preparations brought out the worst in him and in the end, after repeatedly nudging Katie, while she was carefully decorating place names for everyone and ruining them, he was sent to his room and told by a hot and weary Maria not to come out till Papa came back home.

She wore a new dress, pale blue with a lace edging. The table filled with food that Maria had prepared and that the grandmothers and aunts had brought. There was boiled ham, tiny meat balls called *frikadele*, sausages of various kinds, potato salad with gherkins, open sandwiches with cheese and thin slices of spicy beef and two enormous chocolate cakes smothered with cream. Claus and Margarethe came, and Katie had to hear for the hundredth time how she had nearly eloped with him when she was seven. There was an armchair that was filling up with gifts which she wasn't allowed to open till after people had eaten and drunk a toast to her. Her cousin Friede came, and the girls did their best to behave in a way fitting for ten-year-olds. After a couple of glasses of wine, Aunt Marianna sat at the piano and played some jazz she had taught herself. It was a song called 'Where did you get those eyes', a huge hit from the year before. Then she managed a few faster numbers and Lisl, looking lovely in a pink and white dress, demonstrated the Charleston and Papa, who had had quite a few beers by then, joined in, much to Maria's delight. Katie and Friede could bear it no longer and joined in with abandon, dragging the others to their feet until Adelheid, pretending to disapprove, began to fear for the furniture and ornaments.

Birthday candles were blown out and at last it was time for the presents. Each gift was opened, and the giver given a kiss. There was a watch from Opa and Hilde with tiny gold numbers on its face and which came in a small purple velvet bag; a gold cross on a delicate chain from Adelheid and Opa Johann; a pair of earrings from Karoline, small pearls on silver chains. Katie looked at them and then at her mother. It must mean she was going to be allowed to have her ears pierced soon, something she'd wanted for a while. There were books from Lisl; one an atlas and another about the United States of America. She was keen that Katie broaden her horizons. The gifts were passed around, examined and approved of by each member of the family, with many interjections of "What a lucky girl."

Finally, as guests were beginning to find coats and hats and the long ritual of goodbyes began – Katie, crumpled and very happy, ready at the door to shake hands, kiss and thank everyone once again – Opa produced, from nowhere it seemed, a large parcel which he loudly declared was for his eldest grandson on the occasion of his first school day. Heinz, who had managed, just, to be 'big' and 'good', in spite of the ridiculous attention paid to his little brother as well as to Katie, suddenly swelled with surprise and pleasure. Inside the package was a shiny leather satchel which he put on and refused to take off till bedtime.

"Now you are ready!" Opa beamed as he planted a kiss on the top of his head.

9

*German state schools accepted children from all denominations
but Catholic and Protestant children were taught separately.*

It wasn't just that the boys went into school by a different entrance
than the girls that was confusing; the Catholic boys went in by
a different door to the Protestant boys. Katie had described the
system to him but had no explanations.

"So Matthias can't line up with me?" Lining up was a difficult
enough concept as it was.

"No, he has to go in the other way."

"Why?"

"Because he's Protestant."

"But why can't he come with me?" Heinz was not satisfied.

"Because he isn't Catholic."

"And how about Benjamin?"

Katie knew that Jewish children weren't Protestants but there
were definitely only two ways into school. "He'll be going in with the
Protestants." That's what Marthe had to do because she was Jewish.
After they became best friends, they used to jump and wave and
shout at each other from their lines before the teachers came out.

"Why can't he go in with me?"

"Because he isn't Catholic." She was running out of patience. "He
has to go in the other way."

"But why? It's stupid."

"It's just the way it is." Her voice rose to signal that the conversation
was over.

There were quite a few Jewish children in the flats opposite. Some came to their school and some went to another school closer to the synagogue. Thank goodness, Heinz thought, Benjamin was coming to his school. He was very good at football and shared his interest in cars, spiders and boxing.

There were, of course, many things that were ridiculous at school. Being quiet, sitting still, being told to listen, with the occasional "You aren't like your sister, are you?" Well! Of course not!

Playtime was best; then he could play with Matthias and Benjamin because everyone could mix up in the playground. And sometimes there was fighting. He knew he was going to be good at that although some of the big boys were very big indeed and he thought he might wait a bit.

After the first couple of days Katie kept her distance from her brother. He played happily enough with his friends and she wanted to spend time with her own. Marthe's collection of pictures of film stars was more extensive than Katie's and the girls loved looking through them. She wasn't sure whether she liked the German or American stars the most. She wanted her hair cut just like Louise Brookes as soon as Mama would let her. She was fighting to be allowed to see her in a film but both Mama and Papa had refused. She loved the funny ones she went to see with Lisl, or sometimes Claus and Margarethe, but she longed to see her screen heroes and heroines. Marthe loved Rudolph Valentino, but she preferred Douglas Fairbanks, who seemed to be more exciting and daring.

Gradually Heinz began to enjoy school. He was clever and responded well to the teachers he liked. Maria and Heinrich were relieved to read the fairly positive school reports and were pleased that he was coping well in P.E. lessons. There were just a few comments criticising his behaviour and Katie was resentful that she seemed to be getting the blame for this.

"Katie, we've told you to watch him at playtime. Whether he starts it or not, rough play is bad for him. You know it might start an asthma attack." At least Papa was conceding that he might start the trouble sometimes. Mama never did. And anyway, it NEVER triggered an attack; they seemed to start all by themselves.

"But I can't watch him all the time, why should I?"

"Because you are ten and it's what big sisters should do." It was so unfair.

Whether it was Heinz's predisposition to seek out trouble or his extreme ability to feel injustice, particularly towards himself, Katie was from time to time kept busy coming to his defence or dragging him away from potential trouble. Occasionally she had to concede that he was absolutely right in his objection to something and then it was difficult to decide what to do. Although she found him a pest generally, she did take her responsibility seriously and more than once became aware, after spitting onto her sleeve and wiping the blood from his nose or knee so that Mama wouldn't know about that day's misdemeanour, that she did love her difficult and brittle brother.

10

After the world economic crisis in October 1929, the young republic found itself in free fall. Already in trouble, the financial crash dealt the final blow. In 1930 unemployment stood at nearly 2,000,000.

A round about this time Katie began to become aware of differences between her classmates at school. She hadn't really noticed the bow legs before, or the shaven heads, or how tiny Emmi and a few others were.

"You mean they are like that because they haven't got enough to eat?"

"Some families have been struggling for years," Maria told her, "since the Great War."

"But that was ages ago, everyone should be OK now." Katie absentmindedly stroked her own arms, contemplating the plump firm flesh. "It's not fair."

"No, it's not."

"Maybe I could share my lunch with Emmi. She is so small, and she smells, so no-one plays with her." Katie was confused by her own feelings of disgust and pity. She never joined in the name-calling but had never done anything about it either. A new sensation of guilt seemed to creep into her bones, sticky and unpleasant.

Maria said gently, "But then you would grow thin. I could put an extra little sandwich in your box…" Katie looked up as if that might be a good idea but after thinking for a minute said, "But then there is Trudi and Wolfgang. Mama, he hardly has any hair, and his scalp has blood on it. Herr Schmidt makes him sit by himself in a corner."

Katie seemed destined to take the injustices of the world to heart. God help her, thought Maria.

She knew of the Pankowskis, Emmi's family. They lived round the corner in Handel Strasse, in a rundown block of flats full of families that seemed to have lived in semi-poverty forever. And it was getting worse. The churches and synagogue on Landwehr Strasse did their best with collections of food and clothing but, Heinrich said, without proper government and with rising chaos it would always be the poorest who suffered most. Emmi's father was in, then out of work. The pattern had been constant since the end of the war. The steel works had briefly recovered but now stood idle for longer periods of time with some lucky men employed merely to stop the great hulking mills from seizing up while waiting for supplies of iron and coal. Emmi's father, who seemed a kindly man, sought solace in the pub; his children played in the streets; his wife gave up all pretence of dignity after unemployment payment was cut and queued outside both synagogue and church to receive food parcels.

*

Later that day Maria walked into the kitchen to find the contents of the food cupboard on the table.

"There's lots here we don't really need. The coffee for a start. Then this tinned milk – it's horrible anyway. Maybe this raspberry jam…" Maria's preserves were lined up and Katie's fingers lingered over the strawberry, her favourite. "We could keep the strawberry jam – we'll need something."

"All right, then." Maria decided not to argue. Since hearing about the food collections handed out after Mass Katie had pleaded to be involved. She'd sorted out some of her own clothes that could be given away because they were too small or because "I'll never ever want to wear that again." Heinz's clothes were all destined for his brother, so they had to be kept, apart from a pair of trousers still good save the patched knees. She gave Katie a bag so she could put the food into it although later on she removed the coffee – Heinrich would object, too expensive – but then decided to put a few spoonfuls of the fragrant beans in a little paper bag and added it to the other items in the parcel.

On Sunday morning they carried the two bags to church and added them to the dozen or so already there at the side door where the priest came in and out before Mass. Katie was full of worthy excitement. She was looking forward to handing over the parcels, imagining the happiness on the face of the receiver, her gift transforming misery into joy.

But this was not to be. A couple of members of the Church Mothers' Committee came from behind a pillar, gathered the parcels quickly and efficiently and disappeared behind that mysterious heavy door. Maria felt Katie's righteous disappointment. "That's how it works. The parcels are handed out this evening and they are in charge of it all." She had been invited to join the Mothers' Committee but had made an excuse. She found their pious superiority unpleasant. "Don't worry; there will be a family tonight very happy with what you have given."

Katie nodded slowly. She was struggling with the feeling of having the whole experience spoiled. She was uncomfortably sure she shouldn't be feeling this way.

"Imagine how happy Emmi's mama will be when she finds the jam," Maria said, and she put her arm around Katie. It could only be Emmi's mama.

"Do you think they will like the tinned milk?" Katie was comforted at the thought of the food and clothes safely in the hands of the Pankowskis.

"I'm sure they will. It tastes good with coffee and bread and jam."

"Mm." She sounded unconvinced but was unwilling to puncture the happy image. She felt better now and later realised she was looking forward to seeing Emmi at school the next day. Emmi would seem different somehow and she would watch her and keep and hug her happy secret to herself. Yes, that's how it was going to be.

11

Autumn 1930

Heinrich slipped the little key into the post box at the foot of the stairwell. He glanced absent-mindedly at the two envelopes in his hand before starting to climb the steps. How glad he was that he had managed to secure this flat for his family. It was brand new. Part of the government's house-building drive before the crash brought everything to a halt. He hadn't thought twice about using his position as a civil servant to jump the queue and having a third child just nudged him to the top. A few weeks ago, as the last of the snow melted away, and with the help of Anton's truck, they moved from Ost Strasse to Kammer Strasse, Number 164. A move of only five hundred metres but it felt to them all a world away.

The substantial metal and wood banister was smooth and unscratched and the passageway still smelled of paint. Heinrich's shoes scratched and echoed as he made his way to the top flat, under the eaves; hard work for all of them, especially Maria with Hansgünther to manage, but worth it. And as soon as an apartment on one of the lower floors became available, he would apply.

He flung the letters on the table when he came into the kitchen. Maria was washing her hands and wiping Hansgünther's face and hands; he was propped up on the draining board and laughed when he saw Heinrich come in.

"We've been in the garden. Your son has been very helpful."

"Yes, I can imagine." Heinrich picked him up and swung him into the air just as Katie came in.

"I'm doing my homework." She glanced at her father as she said this. "Maths." She gave Heinrich a quick kiss and a half-hearted hug before she disappeared back into the bedroom she shared with Heinz; soon a little bed for Günther would somehow be squeezed in as well.

"She hasn't really forgiven me yet, has she?" Heinrich said, sitting down and absent-mindedly stroking his son's black curls for a few seconds before adding, "But it was the right decision."

Maria didn't say anything. Once Heinrich had made a decision it became 'right' and everyone had to accept it. She had learnt that he would listen to her but rarely change his mind. And, in any case, she had become convinced, that this particular decision was for the best, although she was surprised at how Katie's resentment had lingered.

She had at first been taken aback by Heinrich's rather brusque announcement. Proud of her bright daughter, her enthusiasm, her joy at every achievement, such a contrast to her own fractured education, disrupted by her mother's death, the arrival of stepbrothers. Why not encourage her? Why not the grammar school? It would cost a little money every month, but her father would help. But no. Grammar school was going to be for her brothers only. They would be the ones who would have to support families; she, in all likelihood, would marry and have children and be better off with a more practical education. His tone had been matter of fact. He'd caught her eye briefly and noticed the doubt and chose to ignore it. Of course, he would never take money from her father.

For Katie it was a bombshell coming out of nowhere. She had taken her sunny vision of the future for granted. To have this bedrock shaken, disturbed, was unfamiliar, what was going on? She looked from one face to the other. They seemed to have gone blank.

"But everyone I know is going to St. Mathias..." she said eventually, as it sank in and that her life would be ruined. As she thought of her Marthe the tears came.

"Nonsense," said Maria. searching and failing to find words to make things better, "you'll make lots of new friends..."

For the first time she felt a sense of betrayal. It was a catastrophe, and she would never forgive them.

That was three weeks ago. And although it was by now less of a catastrophe the unvoiced and unacknowledged acceptance that she was less than her brothers took seed and rubbed away at the lustre of her life. Grammar school cost money, she'd discovered. They were worth it, she wasn't.

*

Heinrich lowered a wriggling Günther onto the floor and reached for the letters on the table. One he recognised as the monthly request for the rent. The other, with a pale blue envelope, was addressed to both himself and Maria. He opened it first.

"It's from the school," he told Maria when he saw the headed notepaper. "Could we please come into school at the earliest opportunity and at our convenience? The school would like to discuss a matter of some urgency."

Maria raised her eyebrows. "Does it say anything else?"

He quoted: "It will be easier to explain the details at the meeting." Maria was thinking of Heinz's bruised shins, ripped back pocket. Whatever had he been up to?

Heinrich looked grim. "Heinz," he shouted, "come in here. Now!"

Heinz appeared from the living room where he had been lying on his stomach engrossed in a book about cowboys. Katie stood in the doorway, not so involved in her homework, it seemed, to ignore the interesting tone in her father's voice.

"It's no good telling me it's all someone else's fault," Papa was saying.

"But…" Heinz was ready to launch a case for the defence.

"Don't dare interrupt!" Papa looked very angry. "You have to keep away from trouble and the troublemakers! When are you going to learn? Now we all have to go together to see the headmaster. This is your responsibility and whatever punishment the head has in mind your mother and I will be fully supportive." Maria, watching Heinz's bottom lip quiver and the tears start, wasn't too sure about that –

she'd always thought that Herr Nagel had a mean streak. She clasped her hands together to stop herself putting her arm around Heinz's shoulder.

"Why do we all have to go?" Katie sounded quieter than usual.

Heinrich was in no mood to pay attention to Katie. He was still glaring at Heinz "It's a family matter and we all go. That's that."

*

The next morning, after Hansgünther had been deposited into the welcoming arms of Auntie Botha at Uncle Anton's garage, Maria and Heinrich, with Katie and Heinz a step or two behind, set off to the school. Uncle Anton sold cars and fixed them. For Heinz the garage was probably the most exciting place on earth and recently he had been allowed to spend Saturday afternoons there. He was learning to recognise the different tools and was sometimes asked to pass them to his uncle while he was either peering at the engine or lying underneath a car. He was also learning to recognise the different models of cars. Loved the way they all had numbers for names. The B14 and B15 from 1925; then the C4 and C6 in 1928; the big six-cylinder C61 in 1929; all Citroens.

But today there was to be no helping Uncle Anton, not even any joking or happy banter. Heinrich explained curtly what the matter was. Katie and Heinz shuffled about, eyes downcast as Auntie Botha took their brother and then they were marched off.

They entered the school via a side door that was only used by people who were either very important or, the children had decided, were very bad indeed. They had only ever seen Herr Nagel use it and here was their father boldly going in as if he did it every day. If Katie and Heinz could have felt any more awed, any more fearful, this was the moment, as they stood on the highly polished lino outside the office door. As the door slowly opened, Heinz, uncharacteristically, reached for Katie's hand. She squeezed it gratefully.

"Ah, Herr Cremers, Frau Cremers, please come in." And he stood to the side to allow the four of them to walk past him. They remained standing and Herr Nagel took up his position on his side of the desk.

He looked serious, Katie noticed when she dared look at him, but not vicious. This was perhaps a good thing. But she was shocked to see that Fraulein Schulz was also in the room, standing back a little. Her lovely, kind Fraulein Schulz whom she adored; what on earth was she doing here?

"Thank you, both of you," Herr Nagel said, smiling sadly at Maria, "for coming so quickly to see us. You obviously understand the urgency of the situation. The solution, I'm sure, is to nip it in the bud and that is why we decided that your children should be present at this meeting. It's not normal practice, I can assure you." At which he nodded gravely first at Heinrich, then Maria and then, briefly and with a hint of a glare, at both children. Heinz moved imperceptibly closer to Katie.

"Herr Nagel, I can't tell you how often we have spoken to the boy about his behaviour. Again and again we have tried to impress upon him the importance of controlling his temper, of keeping out of tr—" Heinrich was cut short by the Headmaster's raised finger.

"Oh, I think your hard work is paying off. We've noticed a definite improvement in Heinz's behaviour over the past few weeks." He paused, just long enough for the figures in front of him to feel an element of confusion in four very different ways. "I'm afraid it's Katie we're here to talk about."

Maria looked at Heinrich, who clearly hadn't begun to process this idea. She had an inkling of what was to come. Heinz's hand slipped from Katie's as Herr Nagel's words sank in and he relaxed into the unfamiliar glow of an unexpected reprieve. Magnanimously he once again found Katie's hand, keen to support his sister in this moment of need.

It's Katie we're here to talk about. Blood rushed to her ears in great thumps and heat flooded up into her neck and face. She looked over at Fraulein Schulz but couldn't bear to catch her eye. What was this about? But, despite the blurring panic, she knew what this was about. The tiniest suspicion had planted itself when the letter came but everyone was so sure it was to do with Heinz, she buried that worrying notion very quickly. Even before Herr Nagel started talking again, and to her great fury, tears brimmed over and gushed down her cheeks. She pulled her hand out of Heinz's to wipe them away and gave a great sniff.

"It seems that Katie has been, shall we say," he glanced over at Fraulein Schulz, who had silently moved a little closer to the group, "a little over-zealous in defending her brother."

Maria wanted badly to look at Heinrich, who seemed to have been turned to stone; he didn't even appear to be breathing. For her part Maria found she wasn't as surprised as she should have been. After all, she had watched her daughter often enough out of the window, guarding the pram like a ferocious bulldog.

"Perhaps Fraulein Schulz can explain what happened?"

Fraulein Schulz stepped closer to Katie and touched her arm briefly before she began.

"I'm sure Heinz will have told you that there are a couple of the bigger lads who do cause trouble in the playground. The teachers are aware of it but cannot monitor every moment. The children are asked to report incidents when they occur and of course to keep out of it but... well... that doesn't always happen. On this occasion, Rolf, one of the lads in question, picked on Heinz, or according to some it was Heinz who said something to Rolf," Heinz looked a little sheepish at this point and his ears went pink, "but whatever it was, a tussle followed – pushing and shoving and Heinz ended up on the ground." Heinz gave a small grunt at the humiliating memory.

Katie remembered it all too well. Heinz had fallen on a patch of gravel where the ground had become worn with the play of a hundred hobnail boots and dozens of games of football. She'd been watching from a distance and was pretty sure that her playtime was about to be spoilt once again by her brother, who was at that moment facing up to Rolf – and it really was up, since he was taller even than her and she was one of the tallest. Rolf had a mean look on his face and his friends, lolling about behind him, were laughing and egging him on. There was a jab in the shoulder and a push and down went Heinz, into the sharp gravel. His cheek was grazed, tiny pinpricks of blood appearing. Katie looked at Rolf who had turned to acknowledge the admiration of his pals. He looked excited, angry, not done yet and she walked over quickly, ready to get between him and Heinz.

Squinting into the blue sky behind Rolf's big face Heinz shouted, "You're a pig, nothing but a fat pig!"

As she got nearer, she saw Rolf's foot pull back, ready to deliver a kick as another boy said, "Go on, Rolfie! Teach the little bugger a lesson!" The next thing anyone knew Katie had launched herself onto his back and was thumping him as hard as she could – his cheeks, his ears, his hair, anything she could reach, at the same time calling him a thug and a bully. Rolf managed to shake her off just as a teacher came running to put a stop to it. Rolf, humiliated by a girl, had to stand shamefaced, as the teacher shouted at the three of them, and put up with the giggles from Heinz and Katie's classmates.

"It was quite an assault, actually," Fraulein Schulz was saying, clearing her throat before finishing with, "and, of course, Rolf is a very big boy, and no damage was done."

Heinrich's mouth had actually fallen open. He was at a loss. His daughter was certainly lively but to do something so... well... so unfeminine, so violent? Maria had found herself biting her lip during Fraulein Schulz's description; there was something in the teacher's tone that was not all condemnatory. There was a touch of admiration there and Maria couldn't help but feel it herself. Of course, she couldn't let it show.

Neither parent found the words needed at this point and Katie found the silence so unbearable that she broke it with great heaving sobs and incomprehensible words that might have been apologies. Maria wasn't sure whether she should put her arm around her or wait a little longer. Fraulein Schulz did it for her.

"I know, I know... it was a moment of great silliness and quite unlike the Katie I know so well." Her tone was kind but resulted in another bout of sobbing, at which Maria could bear it no longer and gathered her daughter into her side where she cried and sniffed into her brand-new navy-blue wool jacket.

Finally Heinrich managed to say, looking at the rumpled head, "Katie, Katie how could you?"

"Looking after little brothers is, of course, an admirable thing to do," Herr Nagel's voice was matter-of-fact. He wanted to move things on. "But," and he looked very deliberately at Heinz, "I don't really think Heinz needs much help. Do you?"

Heinz wasn't sure whether to answer or not – and what the right answer could possibly be. He gave a very uncertain shake of his head.

"Because I believe you are going to be very well-behaved from now on," Heinz nodded slowly, "and Katie will have nothing more to worry about." At last the headmaster's gaze left Heinz and he dared once again to breathe.

"Nothing excuses what Katie did." Heinrich wasn't ready by any means to move on.

"No, no. You are quite right. But I think this lack of self-control may well have been a one-off and now that we have all confronted it and bearing in mind what Fraulein Schulz has told me of her usually exemplary conduct, we should perhaps draw a line underneath it. Katie, I hope you are listening." Katie turned a blotchy wet face towards Herr Nagel. "Are you listening, Katie?" Katie nodded miserably. "No more heroics in the playground. And we have spoken to Rolf. He knows he is being watched very carefully."

Katie pushed a damp fringe out of her eyes and face. The agony she felt was not one of remorse. What she was feeling was the agony of being found out, shown up in front of Mama and Papa and, above all, Fraulein Schulz. She'd never be sorry for attacking Rolf. Without raising her eyes, she said in a small voice, "He's really not nice, you know," and her bottom lip began to quiver as a fresh bout of crying threatened.

Maria heard a plea for understanding but for Heinrich it was plain stubbornness. He kept the thought that his daughter was insisting on having the last word to himself.

Herr Nagel ignored her and said, "I think it's time these two went to their classrooms now; Fraulein Schulz, can you take them, please? You both need to think carefully about this, especially you, Katie, and I hope I never have to ask your parents in to see me again." He'd resumed his stern tone, but the interview was clearly over. The children left the office with Fraulein Schulz who did her best to tidy Katie up before she joined her class.

"I'm absolutely sure it won't happen again," Herr Nagel said as he shook Heinrich by the hand.

"You can be sure of it."

Maria couldn't share either Heinrich's shame or his certainty. This would need careful handling at home. Of course, what Katie had done was unacceptable, but she didn't want Heinrich to overdo the condemnation.

"She clearly feels terrible about it." Maria had linked arms with Heinrich as they walked slowly towards Anton's garage.

"I should damn well think she does. What an appalling thing to do!" Heinrich shook his head for the tenth time.

"Yes!" Maria shook her head in synch with his. "Can you imagine – jumping on the back of such a big lad!" Heinrich looked sharply at her; did he detect just a touch of sarcasm in her voice? Brown eyes looked up innocently into his. Yes, there was a hint of a twinkle there. He squeezed her arm against his chest. "Maria, Maria, she cannot be allowed to think that it is acceptable to use violence."

"Of course not."

"And she's a girl, for heaven's sake!"

"A brave one." She could tell he thought the same but wouldn't admit it.

"She has to learn to control herself."

"I'm pretty sure she will."

After a while he said, almost to himself, "God help anyone who touches a hair on Günther's head when he starts school!"

Maria relaxed and smiled to herself. Katie and Heinz both had a fatherly tirade coming and certainly deserved it. But it would blow over and normal family relations would resume.

12

A fifteen-minute bike ride from Kammer Strasse was the district of Wedau, a large, flat area far away from the dirty industrial heartlands of Duisburg. It contained half a dozen small, interlinked lakes where people could swim or sail boats and canoes and spaces for football, handball and gymnastics. It was built for the workers, and very popular at the weekends and during the holidays. Katie, Marthe and Lili pedalled along the quiet cycle tracks, swimming costumes on under their skirts and blouses and towels in bags around their shoulders.

It was Katie's last holiday before secondary school. Marthe was going to the grammar school and already there was a change in their friendship. Less to share and talk about, both sad that they couldn't make plans, but they loved to go swimming together and went two or three times a week. Lili was going to go to the same school as Katie and was one of the few who could keep up with her in the water. As they pedalled along the broad tree-lined road that led to the lakes, Katie noticed how dry the ground was, how little tufts of dying grass and gorse poked up through cracks in the pavement, grainy dust lying in still little pools. The holiday was nearly over. Soon it would be time for the new school. She and Mama had gone there once last week so that Katie was sure of the walk, but it had that dead look that schools have during the holidays and she didn't want to think or talk about it.

They swung their bikes off the cycle track onto the dusty pathway that led to the cycle park. Metal slots for dozens of bikes and the girls expertly slotted theirs into them, bounced off the bikes and headed for the turnstiles that led to the lake. Once through they linked arms and walked down the slight slope to the water's edge. They saw that their usual spot by one of the trees was taken by a family who were busy setting up camp, spreading out towels and carefully putting pairs of shoes on the corners to designate territory. Bottles of water, paper bags and a pile of plums were laid out and the boy, a handsome lad about their age, was searching for something in his rucksack while two girls ran off to the water. He pulled out some small flags and said something to his mother, who smiled and nodded. He carefully pushed a flag down into the sand on each corner of their space. The little swastikas fluttered gently, and he stood to admire them for a second before racing off to join his sisters, while the parents settled their ample bottoms on the towels and watched them.

Katie felt Marthe's arm tighten as they passed the family and she looked at her. "Let's go over there," was all she said, pointing to the diving board, a simple wooden structure that jutted out from the shore. It was broad enough for two or three to jump off at the same time as well as practice untidy dives. They set out their towels then slipped off their clothes and folded them carefully into little piles. They stood, Katie with her hands on her hips, looking at the lake. It twinkled at them; no boats today and there was only the gentlest of lapping of water at the edge. Their slender, still shapeless bodies were brown from the hours spent outside in the summer sun. Lili, fastening her pale blond hair behind her ears, set off for the board and the other two followed. The board was bleached and dry; they must be the first on it this morning. Lili, then Marthe dived off, breaking the stillness of the water and disappearing for a second before both heads emerged a few metres out, laughing and blinking away the water from their eyes. Katie watched and waved as they shouted to her to join them. She stood for a moment, quite still, feeling the sun on her back, closing her eyes as the heat hit her. With all her heart she wanted the world to slow down, for the summer not to end, for Marthe not to go to another school. She sat down on the edge of the board then pushed herself forward until her toes reached the water. Slowly she lowered herself down, sliding into the coolness, down and down, hair lifting and floating, nose and ears filling with water until toes felt the soft mud on the lake bottom. Weeds slithered against her calves as she held her breath for as long as she could, then with strong kicks she rose up and offered her face to the blue sky.

She swam on her back, fingers straight, arms slicing the water, watching the odd cloud high above, then stopped to see where she was. Lili and Marthe were small dots in the distance, the shoreline and diving board like pencil lines marking the water's edge. Her arms and legs moved about lazily then she thrust her face into the water and struck out towards the girls, breathing and turning her head as her arms pushed and pulled and her legs kicked up a rhythm just enough to keep her passage straight and smooth. As the water sluiced over her, her skin, her muscles loosened. The ease of it sent bubbles of pleasure to her throat and she smiled as she breathed. Past Marthe, past Lili, on towards the opposite bank. She didn't want to stop.

"Hey! Wait for me," Lili laughed and started to chase. She was strong too, but no-one could catch Katie once she got going. Then she remembered that Marthe wouldn't chase, so she circled round and after an underwater somersault popped up near Lili and they both made their way back to where Marthe was floating on her back.

The girls twirled their hands about to keep afloat and kicked their feet gently. They were in deep water here but knew exactly how far they would have to swim to touch the muddy bottom.

"I'm going to the cinema tonight," announced Marthe. "Mama and Papa are taking me to see *Emil and The Detectives* although I think I'm far too old for it. I really want to see *Anna Christie.*"

"I'd love to see that. Greta Garbo looked so lovely on the poster." Lili pushed herself away from them causing little ripples to catch the light around their faces.

"Papa won't let me go to the cinema anymore." Katie's voice sounded resigned.

"Why ever not?" Marthe looked across at her friend who promptly disappeared under the surface and reappeared behind her.

"Because…" Katie took a deep breath and ducked under again, popping up next to Marthe, grinning. "Because of the newsreels."

"That's silly. The newsreels are important. At least that's what my papa says."

Katie didn't really want to talk about this. She felt she had got Lisl into trouble the last time she had been taken to the cinema just a few days ago. It was a comedy and Maria had decided it was suitable for Katie. There was a short cartoon first and then came, as always, the news before the main film. Papa had overheard her telling Heinz about the cartoons but suddenly interrupted her, demanding to know what the newsreel was about. Well, they were all about Herr Hitler, shaking hands with people, looking stern but somehow friendly. Always standing in the middle, centre stage, calm, in charge.

"Oh, for goodness' sake, Heinrich, it was just the news." Lisl was exasperated with her brother, who overreacted every time Hitler's name came up. Papa said she understood absolutely nothing, and Katie was never to go to the cinema again, before disappearing behind his newspaper.

"He'll probably change his mind." Katie wanted the conversation to stop. Marthe was no longer listening. She was looking over at the family and their little red and black swastikas, a frown on her face.

Lili broke the silence. "I'm starving; let's have our lunch." And all three headed for the shore, dragging themselves out of the water and, dripping, throwing themselves down onto their towels and enjoying the heat of the sun for a few minutes before scrabbling about in their bags for slightly squashed bread rolls and lukewarm bottles of water. Everything tasted delicious.

As they ate, they became aware of the boy with the flags walking slowly along the shore. He was looking for something or pretending to look for something. He glanced occasionally towards them and slowed down so as not to pass them.

Katie stopped munching, surprised to find herself noticing his nice shoulders. "I think he's looking at you, Lili." Lili was very pretty, and her curls were already dry and catching the light like a halo around her forehead. Marthe, who was engrossed in examining a scratch on one of her big toes, looked up and said, "No, it's you, Katie. He was watching you swimming earlier on," and added slyly with a sideways smile, "he's probably in love with you." All three shrieked and Katie pushed Marthe so hard she toppled over. By the time they looked over to the shore again the boy was hurrying away back to his family, much to Katie's relief. She wasn't ready for love. She jumped up, laughing, blushing, needing to move. "I'm going in the water again." Marthe and Lili stayed where they were, giggling. She jumped onto the diving board, heat bouncing off it, and ran hard, feet thumping on the wood. Marthe shouted something but it was drowned out by the splash as she hit the water, smiling hugely at something she didn't quite understand.

13

September 1932. There were now six million unemployed in Germany. Hitler was increasing his power base by manipulating the Chancellor, Von Papen, an intellectual light weight who believed the Nazi Party could be controlled.

Heinrich often walked back from the office these days. Gave him time to think. Things weren't the same without Claus, no-one left to laugh with, although things had gone beyond mockery. What idiots they had been. Fooled into imagining real change was possible. Not now. Not with Hermann Grühl as the director, sitting behind the door and communicating chiefly through Franz, the booby, the yes-man, the no-hoper, who scuttled in and out of the big man's office and laid directives on everyone's desk, sometimes grinning as he emerged holding an imaginary phone to his ear. "Berlin!" he would whisper loudly and nodding as if he were party to some vital and secret piece of information.

He wanted to spit in the street at the thought. How had it come to this? The local Ministry of Justice had never taken orders from Berlin. Now all they cared about was rooting out 'Reds' and disrupting legitimate street demonstrations, happy to enlist the help of the Nazi thugs and turn a blind eye to their excesses. Real crime was being ignored. Robberies, even murders, unsolved, undetected. Claus told him it was even worse in Düsseldorf. How he missed him. But... today was Friday and he was due to meet Anton for a beer or two and he cheered up at the prospect.

He crossed the road near the station, dodging men and women eager to get home and off the streets – everyone was learning to keep off the streets – and turned into Kammer Strasse. He dipped his head into the first pub on Tulpen Strasse as if he was looking for someone. Well, he was, but Anton would have done the same thing and not gone in either when he spotted the four or five men drinking noisily in the corner. Recently it had become a favourite with the Brownshirts. A shame. Used to be a nice place. He turned slowly so as not to attract attention and headed for the pub opposite, on Harald Strasse. It had, he realised, shaking his head, become second nature to avoid being near them. He'd got used to the unease they caused.

'Die Weisse Blume' was nearly empty, waiting for the teatime customers, and Heinrich sat down opposite the door so that Anton would see him. He took a sip of his beer and took out the folded newspaper, noticing another hole in his pocket where his fingers caught and ripped. He wouldn't tell Maria about it. She was busy enough patching and mending the boys' trousers. No spare cash for a new coat this year. He spread the paper out on the table and gave an involuntary grunt at what he saw. There he was again! Looking meaningfully into the near distance as Von Papen whispered into his ear. He had them all where he wanted them. Even the *Frankfurter Zeitung* had his picture in the centre of the front page. Just then an overflowing glass of beer was set down with a thud directly onto Hitler, soaking into the paper, slopping over the headline that another election was inevitable.

"Forget about it, Heinrich." Anton scraped the chair opposite back a little way to accommodate his ample frame. "You know it's not good for your health to read the papers at the moment." The men smiled at each other.

The summer election had made Hitler kingmaker but not yet king. "No-one's health will benefit when that man takes over."

"Please God it won't come to that." But Anton's tone implied that it inevitably would come to that.

"He's got too much on his side. Von Papen is an idiot who wants to hang on to power and he thinks Hitler will help him." Heinrich's tone had gone up a notch.

"The old man might be able to do something to stop him." Anton meant Hindenburg, the old war hero.

Heinrich couldn't help the look of disgust. "Bah! The man's senile. It's too late, my friend. Too late."

They both contemplated their beers silently, aware of the ticking clock that hung behind them on the dark panelled walls and breathing in the comforting smell of hops and cigar smoke. Heinrich realised that it was his fault that the evening had been pitched into gloom. He folded the paper in half, then again, and once more and finally slapped it down firmly on the chair next to his.

"You are right, Anton, as always! There are better things to talk about." And he called to the barman to bring two more beers.

He could feel Anton's relief at his change of mood and listened as he gladly launched into a tale about a customer who wanted to buy a new Citroen barely a year after buying the previous model. There was clearly still money about for some. The man was a Jew, good with his money. Thank goodness. It was good for business. It was still a struggle though. And he prattled on, eventually asking after Maria and the children and Heinrich was pleased to tell him how well Heinz was doing at school nowadays. Anton nodded. Yes, he was proving to be a clever boy. He had hoped briefly that he would come and work in the garage one day, but he was clearly destined for greater things. Of course, for Botha there was no-one quite like the little one. Little Günther was the apple of her eye. So quick, so funny.

There was a tension in Anton's voice, speeding up the steady, merry flow of words. Heinrich wanted to stop him. "How is Botha?" he said gently. "Maria mentioned something about the doctor."

Anton's face straightened and he pressed his lips together. He moved his beer glass around to avoid looking directly at Heinrich. "Not so bad, you know, women's troubles," he shifted about on his seat, "but she is strong, healthy... so... maybe..." And his voice trailed off. They had waited years for children; there had been hope a couple of times but always disappointment. Heinrich didn't know what to say. He had no words for such personal sadness. He leant forward and gripped his friend's arm. What he believed was that some things are entirely in the hands of God, but it wouldn't help his friend to say it.

Anton's eyes were moist as he said, "It's so difficult for her. I have work to keep me busy. Poor Botha." He took a quick breath and seemed to give himself a little shake. "I'll have to get back soon. Dinner will be on the table." Heinrich smiled at him. He needed to get back as well, back to Maria who would be peering through the curtains, down onto those uncertain streets, trying not to show her anxiety. But he didn't want Anton to go straight away.

He sipped his beer slowly and changed the conversation to the subject of his sister, Marianna.

"You have too many sisters, Heinrich," laughed Anton, "which one is she?"

"One of the older ones."

"Ah," said Anton, not much the wiser.

"Turns out she's a talented milliner, good enough to set up her own shop." Heinrich watched his friend's face. He was listening, interested.

"In Düsseldorf," he continued, "doing very well, apparently."

"Yes, I can imagine. Money for that sort of thing in Düsseldorf."

Heinrich, calling for more beer, noticed with relief and pleasure Anton resume his business face. He asked a few questions. Where was the shop? Did Marianna employ anyone? The mood lightened.

"You're right, Anton, there is still money about." The men laughed and agreed it was a shame not enough of it was coming their way.

Outside it was still light, still warm, but the street was almost empty. Two weeks ago there had been a fight near here, between some Brownshirts and a group of communists. They were all drunk, shouting at each other across the street. One man had been beaten almost to death before his comrades had carried him off.

They heard the singing coming from the pub opposite, raucous and out of place in this quiet, forlorn little square. "Time for home," said Heinrich and he shook Anton's hand.

"Take care, Heinrich." And where the road forked the men parted company and set off home.

"I will, Anton, I will."

14

October 1932

Katie lay on her back, listening. It was so still, so silent. She stared up at the straight-limbed trees, crinkled with lines of dry, dark green moss snaking around peeling bark while her fingers played with last year's leaves, scrunching them into powder. There was the occasional quick rustle high up, a squirrel maybe, or a disturbed pigeon, then silence again. Midday in the forest and the creatures slept. She'd fallen on a flat piece of earth near the path and the sun was shining on her face, finding a gap in the canopy of leaves high above. She noticed that some of them were changing colour already, there were spots of brown and yellow.

She turned her head and saw her bike lying on its side, the back wheel just about ceasing its spin. Her hip felt a little sore where she had hit the ground, but she thought she was all right. The path had been uphill, and she hadn't been riding very fast. She must have gone over a root or something. Her eyes closed, breathing the motionless air in and out as she dimly remembered that there was something she should be doing, that she couldn't stay here, although the ground felt soft and the sun warm on her skin. She lifted her head but felt immediately a little sick so lay back down again. Somewhere there was the muffled buzzing of an insect. Far away there was another sound, a voice, a few voices. Bickering, indistinct and anxious. They sounded familiar and she struggled to make them out. She turned her head gently in the direction of the voices; they were coming towards her up the path. She still couldn't see them.

"She must have come this way," a girl's voice, "I'm sure she rode away on this path."

"She better turn up soon because I'm hungry. We'll have to leave her and get the police to find her. Before it gets dark, of course, because that's when the wolves come..." and then another sound, a quiet but insistent wailing. "Oh, shut up, Günther, for heaven's sake. I was only joking."

The girl's voice was beginning to quiver. "If you hadn't been so mean, about finding all the treasures, she would never have gone off like that. It's all your fault and now we might never see her again." At which point they saw, first the bicycle, then Katie lying on the ground.

Katie still felt sick but raised her head for a second to see Heinz and Friede dragging Hansgünther between them before closing her eyes.

"Oh no! Is she dead?" *Friede can be so silly sometimes*, thought Katie, as the fog inside her brain started to clear. She looked at the three of them and lifted herself up onto one elbow. Other bits of her body began to hurt. Her mouth felt dry, making it hard to force any words out.

"You're bleeding." Heinz sounded interested rather than sympathetic as he pointed to Katie's head. She lifted her hand. It seemed to take a long time to reach the side of her head where she felt a sticky warm mess clotting her hair. Friede came to help her up. Hansgünther had stopped grizzling, pleased to see his sister, but still fairly miserable.

Katie stood up carefully. Her head and hip ached but she wasn't going to say anything.

Heinz looked at her carefully. "I'll push the bike home. You shouldn't ride it now."

Katie managed to register surprise at Heinz's uncharacteristic insight. But they had been getting on better recently. "Thanks," she said, watching him pick it up and give the back wheel a small kick to straighten it. Friede, very concerned and eager to help, linked arms with her, and Günther, holding tightly onto Katie's hand, set the slow pace home.

They had come to the forest after breakfast to finish the game of treasure hunting that they'd invented that summer. Friede had come to stay for a few days, and they'd shown her how the game worked. It took place over two days. On day one they took small toys or things Mama would let them have and found places in the forest to hide them. They did it together and watched where things were buried. Each took care to disguise the spots with moss, earth or leaves. The next day, or sometimes two days later, they went back and had to find the 'treasures'. It was hard because by then the trees all looked the same, the little bumps and mounds on the ground that they tried to memorise seemed to disappear or move. But Heinz was really good at it and Katie had got better.

The forest was a fifteen-minute walk away from home and the children had spent most of the summer there, under the strict condition that they didn't go further west than the end of Ost Strasse and kept well away from the tramlines which cut through the forest to the north. They were familiar with their patch. They had been taken there almost daily since babyhood and now enjoyed hours of uninterrupted, unsupervised time with their friends. There were play areas and a sand pit where Günther would happily dig for hours but Heinz got very bored and wanted to play deeper in the forest away from the paths. When their little brother was left at home, they could do this and that's when the game was invented. That morning they had to take Günther with them, so that Mama could go to the market on her bicycle which she'd load up with groceries for the week.

The arguments began when Heinz wouldn't let Günther 'find' a treasure. Heinz had an almost uncanny ability to remember where he and everyone else had hidden things. He'd already retrieved a couple of pegs and a cotton reel and Günther was thrilled every time something was unearthed. Katie thought it would be nice for him to find something for himself. Of course, he would have to be led to the treasure and shown where to dig it out. Heinz couldn't see the point of this at all. If he knew where something was, it was by rights his. He wouldn't even put something back into a hole and let Günther discover it for himself. Katie got so angry she had got on her bike and raced off down a path to get away from him. Friede had stared at her cousin, never having seen her in such a rage, and watched her disappear. Friede didn't know how to get really angry. At home she mostly got whatever she wanted and there were no brothers to mess things up.

*

Friede and Heinz carried the bike down into the cellar while Katie and Günther trudged up the five flights of stairs. The little boy had a small rusty toy car clutched tightly in his hand, one of the treasures, which Heinz had given him on the silent walk home, a belated acknowledgement of his earlier attitude. Katie felt absent, her head woolly, and her hip was becoming much more painful.

Maria was laying the table for lunch when they trailed in. She didn't look at them, just shouted that they were to go straight to the bathroom and wash their hands. Then, surprised that no-one moved, looked up. In a moment she had switched off the gas stove and pulled Katie to her to examine her.

"What happened? Why are you bleeding? You are very pale."

Günther, worried once again, remembering his own fright, said, "She's OK now." And, as explanation, added, "She got cross."

Maria ignored the last comment. "So you hurt your head. Does anything else hurt?" She had hold of her shoulders and was scrutinising her face. Katie's eyes seemed dull.

"My hip. A bit." She noticed the dry lips, the blood in her hair.

Heinz and Friede had crept in and were standing very still by the door. She dismissed them with a tense, "Go and wash your hands!" The children darted away and into the bathroom. "And be quick. I want Katie to get into the bath." This took a little while as the boiler had to be lit and the water trickle into the tub. While they were waiting, and to put a stop to the bickering between Heinz and Friede, Maria put lunch on the table – mash potato, chopped cabbage and chunks of smoked bacon all mixed in one pot.

While they ate, and after they had been warned to be quiet and to keep out of the bathroom, she helped Katie get into the bath and knelt down next to her, pouring water over her hair to wash away the blood. It stung but Maria gently persevered until the water ran clear. A bad graze but it would heal. She looked at her thirteen-year-old daughter's long, skinny body, bruises beginning on her shins and hip, and smiled. Still such a girl. The changes would come soon enough.

"I'm all right, Mama," Katie yawned widely. The warm water was making her sleepy. It felt very nice being washed.

"Mmm. Well, you're going to lie on the settee where I can keep an eye on you, and we'll see what Papa thinks when he comes home."

*

Heinrich brought down the book called *Practical Suggestions for Family Health* which was consulted whenever any of them showed unusual symptoms. It was kept on the bookshelf in her parent's bedroom, but Katie had discovered that she could just reach it if she stood on a chair and Heinz held it steady. They loved looking at it because it showed pictures of bits of their body they didn't know they had and which they were pretty sure they weren't allowed to talk about.

That evening Papa laid the heavy book on the kitchen table and several pairs of eyes watched as he turned to the pages entitled 'Injuries to the Head'. Heinz and Friede were either side of Papa, Hansgünther was on his lap, while Katie, on the other side of the table where the settee was, leaned against her mother's shoulder, annoyed that she couldn't see properly but her hip hurt if she moved so she was stuck. And anyway, she was quite enjoying the status of invalid.

"Hmm," Heinrich stared first at the page then at Katie. "The following should be ascertained before treatment: does the patient have a headache?" All eyes turned to Katie.

"Not really… well a bit." She was trying to work out what level of drama to aim at.

Papa's finger hovered over what must be a list of questions. "Does the patient suffer from blurred vision?"

In response to Katie's confused look he stretched his arm across the table and told her to watch his finger carefully as he moved it from left to right, up and down. "All clear?" She nodded. Friede giggled.

Heinrich maintained a very serious demeanour and returned to the book. "Does the patient feel an overwhelming desire to sleep?"

"I've had a sleep, but Mama woke me up."

"Quite right too. Next… does the patient feel an overwhelming need for Mama's almond biscuits?" There was silence as Heinrich lifted his eyes from the book and raised his eyebrows, looking quizzically at Katie while Heinz looked very carefully to find the word 'biscuits' in the tiny print near Papa's finger.

Katie's laughter broke the silence. "Yes, I would love an almond biscuit." She was the star in this pantomime and relished it. She was thirteen now and proud to be part of the grown-up play acting, understanding the nuance that was beyond her brothers and even Friede. It was a new feeling, to see the world from a distance, to see that she might have a part to play in it.

"Splendid! But first of all we have to address the wound." And he turned the pages once again where various methods of bandaging a head were on display.

"Step one," he read, "shave around the affected area." Katie and Maria both gasped and Katie's hand flew up to her head. "Oh, Papa, no!" Play-acting forgotten.

"Well, it helps stop infection. We could use my razor. What do you think, Maria?"

"I can fetch it," Heinz said helpfully, getting up.

"Stay where you are!" said Maria firmly. "I think that would be quite unnecessary. The antiseptic lotion has already done the trick." Katie grimaced at the memory. The bottle of brown liquid stood on the kitchen dresser, ready, she knew, for another stinging application.

"Very well." And with a smooth movement he rose, deposited Günther on the edge of the table and took from next to the bottle a huge roll of bandage which had been kept ready in the cupboard for just such an eventuality. He told Katie to sit up and with a certain relish started to unroll the bandage until metres of the stuff snaked about the table-top in peaks and troughs. He cut a small piece off and folded it into a pad which Katie had to hold in place. Then he wound and wound the bandage around her head and told Hansgünther to tell him when he thought it was enough. This took a little while.

When he was satisfied with the enormous egg shape that used to be Katie's head, Heinrich pinned the bandage into place, and everyone could at last have a biscuit.

At bedtime Maria, as she reorganised the bandage to more manageable proportions, told Heinz and Hansgünther to share a bed that night so that Friede had somewhere to sleep. Usually Günther shared with Katie, but not this time as Maria wanted her to be undisturbed. He complained for a while, but eventually the boys settled down.

"Are you feeling OK?" whispered Friede. She had been genuinely upset at Katie's fall. She was easily rattled.

"I'm all right, I think." She could see the shape of her cousin's body in the dim autumn half-light as her eyes closed. "Don't worry, I'll be all right."

*

Heinrich and Maria lay close together in bed. Heinrich's thoughts went back to Anton as he wrapped his arms around Maria's soft body. He wished he'd been able to find the right thing to say; why was it so hard to find the words? He began to drift off to sleep, breathing in Maria's comforting warmth. Every night this warm body made the day slip away, made words unnecessary.

"She's too thin." Maria's voice was a whisper, as if she was talking to herself. She was lying very still but her head was full of Katie's unfamiliar silences, her pale bruised body, the recent darkness under her eyes.

"Mm. She's growing very fast." Heinrich could only manage a mumble.

"Too fast. She needs to eat more. Tomorrow I'm going to make a big pot—" "Of chicken soup, don't tell me..." Heinrich smiled in the dark as she gently nudged him with her shoulder at the interruption. "Well, you know it's the best thing..."

"For absolutely everything, yes I know, I know." Another deep sigh and he was asleep.

Maria lay awake a little longer, struggling to remember what it was like being thirteen. She had had to live with her father's endless despair and the non-stop small cruelties inflicted by the stepbrothers. And there was the war. She and Mina had done their growing up with their husbands. Sometimes she thought Katie was almost refusing to grow up, fiercely hanging on to childhood and fighting off what she didn't understand with all that furious swimming and cycling. But right now, she had to deal with the shadows under her eyes and those thin limbs.

*

The next morning was cooler, bringing a hint of autumnal frost with it. First Hansgünther rolled out of bed and joined Maria in the kitchen, leaving Heinz to stretch out his limbs in the warmth before heading off sleepily for the toilet. Friede got up and looked at Katie's face. She was fast asleep and looked a bit pink. She turned and bumped into Heinrich who wanted to look in on Katie before going to work.

"Morning, Friede," he said. "Your mother is coming later on this morning to take you home, so I'll say goodbye now." And he ruffled her pale red hair gently as she squeezed passed him. He knew she was a little wary of him. He wasn't the walkover that her father seemed to be.

He bent over Katie and felt her forehead and said, in a voice aimed at being just loud enough to wake her up, "Good morning Katie; how are you feeling?" She was too warm, and it was unusual for her to be this sleepy in the morning. Maria came in and sat on the bed. She had been up during the night to check on her and noticed the rise in temperature then. They looked at each other.

"I'm glad you've taken off the bandage." The cut was healing. Maria had pulled the sheets away from Katie's face and neck and she had a flannel in her hand that she'd wiped her with.

"It must just be a reaction..." They nodded together but Maria's voice was uncertain.

"Let's see how she is this evening."

"OK. But if she gets worse, I'll go and see Dr Beckmann while Mina is here."

Katie was awake, listening, but couldn't quite open her eyes. Her lids seemed to have something lying on them. She forced them open enough to see her parents looking at her and pushed herself up the bed using her elbows and noticed that places were hurting that hadn't been hurting yesterday. When she asked for some water, her throat prickled, and she didn't bother saying anything else.

15

Another election was held in November 1932, destined to be the last free election. The results showed a small drop in support for the National Socialists but Hitler and his Party henchmen pressed on.

The next day Dr Beckmann diagnosed a severe throat infection which would have to run its course. *What could that mean,* thought Maria. Keep her cool and give her plenty of liquids. Gargling with salty water helps. She's a strong girl and would recover in a week or so. *No, she's not strong;* Maria felt like a taut string listening to him. *Can't he see how thin, how pale she is?* The cuts and bruises from the fall were nothing serious but it was possible that the infection caused a lapse of concentration that perhaps led to the accident. *Yes, yes, that made sense.* To be on the safe side keep the other children away from her, he had seen three or four other cases that week – it was the season for throat infections – and clean everything with disinfectant. Contagious infection can spread just by touching a doorknob. Maria and Heinrich glanced automatically and in unison at the shiny brass handle on the children's bedroom door, hung on and swung on by so many small hands. The doctor left with a promise to return in five days and an assurance that there would be great improvement by then.

*

But there was no great improvement. Just the opposite.

This infection, like all infections, was slow to incubate but when it showed its ugly nature it took root. Invading by stages. Punches to soft tissue followed by phoney periods of recovery. Hopeful peace, then panic as pain increased. It crept through the highways and byways of muscle to the bones, to the centre. It sneaked along the veins and arteries dispersing tiny poisons as it made its stealthy way to the heart of things. This way, that way it hunted, seeking out tiny forgotten healthy cells until all were contaminated. Pink flesh became inflamed and tortured making it impossible to speak, impossible to swallow. Words were strangled before they moved from thought. Thoughts themselves imprisoned in the boggy heat of sickness. This infection, like the infection attacking the country, sought out every nook and cranny searching for the place it could do most harm and when it found it, that pulpy core, it lingered and lingered, determined to damage and not be forgotten.

*

There followed days of family upheaval which Heinz at first took to very badly.

"But why do I have to sleep with Papa and Günther? It's a disgrace that I have to share a bed with anyone. I'm ten!" Everything was a 'disgrace' at the moment if it stopped him doing what he wanted.

"You know why, Heinz. I don't want you catching Katie's infection." Maria was on her knees washing the floors. The doorknobs had been wiped hours ago. Heinz was now back from school to find himself turfed out of his bedroom and his world in disarray. She looked up at his petulant face.

"Katie is seriously ill and you are going to stop being such a selfish boy!" She got up, wrung out the cloth and flung it at Heinz. "Finish that corner now! There's not a lot left." She had had enough. Hansgünther had been cross because he couldn't go near Katie. Katie wouldn't even drink, let alone eat. She was hot and slept the whole time. She absolutely had to clean everything; she was imagining danger crawling over every surface.

Stung into silence he knelt down to attempt to wipe the corner of the kitchen floor. Mama never threw things. He knew Katie was ill but really! Sleeping with Papa and Günther who would wriggle and kick all night! He made plans for a camp bed. They might not object to that.

Maria went into the children's bedroom where she was going to sleep until the infection passed. Katie was propped up on a couple of pillows and there was a glass of water on the floor next to her. Maria sat down and stroked her head. Her eyes were closed but she was awake.

"Let's try a little water." Katie nodded and took sips from the glass held to her lips. Maria saw how dry and cracked they were. "Good girl."

"It hurts, Mama."

"I know. It'll get better soon but you must drink. The doctor said it's important." A few more sips were obediently taken.

"Open your mouth, let me have a look at your throat." Katie, wincing, did her best. And there they were. Tiny yellow spots bright against the red flesh. "Oh, that does look sore, my poor girl." There was a noise, a hesitant shuffling and Maria turned to look.

"Mama, can I come in now?" Hansgünther asked pleadingly. He was poking one foot through the doorway, daring to dab his toe on the forbidden floor as if tempting danger.

"Afraid not sweetheart, Katie's got yellow spots in her mouth and when they've quite gone you can come in again."

Günther looked thoughtful. "But I'd really like to see the yellow spots."

"They sound disgusting," Heinz had appeared behind his brother. "If I get my binoculars, I think we'll be able to see them from here."

Maria sighed, "Not now, Heinz. Katie can hardly open her mouth, maybe tomorrow."

"Great. I'll go and find them. I'm pretty sure the magnification will be good enough." And he went off to find them in the hall cupboard closely followed by Günther who, as always, was impressed by Heinz's knowledge and ingenuity.

Katie closed her eyes again and felt the fuzz of infection weigh her body down into the bed. Vaguely aware of her mother's hand stroking her forehead she slept and fell immediately down a hill, a familiar hill in the forest, rolled down and down till something hard broke her fall, something hard and shiny. Twigs caught at her neck and scratched at her. She tried to pull them away, but they wouldn't move. There was a noise, a clattering. It was a tram. She was near the tramlines, where she wasn't allowed, and it was coming but she couldn't shout because the twigs were catching at her throat and her lips wouldn't open. The tram loomed and she woke, gasping and saw Papa, lowering himself down to sit next to her.

"Papa." First she closed her eyes, in relief, then opened them quickly to make sure he was really there.

"It's all right. A bad dream, that's all." He wiped her face very carefully with the damp cloth. "You were trying to speak."

"I couldn't..." Her voice was a painful whisper.

"That's no surprise, child," his hand rested on her shoulder, a comforting weight. "Best not to talk." And Heinrich sat quietly with her until she drifted back to sleep.

16

D r Beckmann came a week later and said the infection was definitely going. Maria watched him examine Katie's arms and legs, bending them and moving her feet from side to side. She wanted to know what he was doing. Sometimes an infection like this is followed by a few little joint problems but she seems fine. Maria looked at the limbs, even thinner after a week of barely eating. She didn't look fine at all. Encourage her to do a little walking; lots of milk. He would be back in a week. He signed the insurance form and was gone.

*

Katie now spent her time in the kitchen on the settee behind the table. It was a solid settee covered in hard leather and the end flipped down so that if someone lay at one end, head propped on pillows, legs could be stretched out. Maria was relieved that her appetite was coming back, and she was eating small meals again. Chicken soup was nearly always on the stove. She even managed a little dumpling today, Maria told Heinrich, with chopped parsley hidden in it. And she would drink milk with ground almonds cooked into it and sweetened with sugar. That had to be good for her. Adelheid had told her about that. She'd made it for all her children whenever they were ill. The boys were allowed back into the bedroom. Katie was beginning to look forward to going back to school.

*

Maria told herself it was her imagination. If the doctor hadn't mentioned problems in the joints, she probably wouldn't have noticed anything, but Katie wasn't walking properly. Everyone said it was because of spending so long in bed; her muscles were weak. That was to be expected. Katie tried hard, pushing herself off the settee, or out of bed and stumbling about the flat. It got worse. Her shoulders and elbows hurt so that she couldn't lever herself up. The swelling had spread to all her joints and her hands would jerk all by themselves. Maria noticed pale red patches on her arms and tummy.

*

Just as rheumatic fever was diagnosed Heinrich heard that a flat on the third floor was to become vacant. They could apply for it if they were quick. Maria listened distractedly to Heinrich saying they couldn't possibly lose this opportunity even though Katie was so ill. They would have so much more room. Maria couldn't bear to think about it, the disruption, the upset. But Heinrich was determined. It would be better for everyone and he went ahead with the application. In fact, the move became a way of helping Maria cope and entertainment for Katie. If she lay very still it didn't hurt, and she could watch the boxes being packed. On moving day, any men they knew who were not at work came to help. It took four of them to carry the settee and the kitchen cupboard down the staircase into the new flat. Heinz and Hansgünther were given small packages to take down, which was fun for a bit. Claus volunteered to carry Katie once her bed was ready and he did it very gently, one step at a time. She found it hard not to giggle all the way down although her knees were swollen and red and hurt with every movement.

Once in, boxes unpacked and the beds made, Maria had to admit that Heinrich had done the right thing, but it would be a little while before she admitted it to him, grumbling instead that she didn't know where anything was and that the living room curtains were too short for the window and that the cupboard door under the sink wouldn't close properly so could he please fix it now. Heinrich, sitting on the settee in the new, large kitchen, with Katie's head on his lap, grinned at them all contentedly.

17

January 1933. The progress of the National Socialists was unstoppable. Throughout the country Communists and Socialists were arrested and sent to concentration camps.

The family celebrated Christmas in the new flat and the New Year slipped in with muted celebration. Maria made a point of knocking on her neighbours' doors to wish them well and Lisl, looking lovely in a fur-trimmed pale-beige coat stopped by with her new young man, Manfred, on the way to a party. The boys asked to be taken downstairs so they could see his car, an American Ford, which made Manfred the most glamorous person they knew. Lisl sat with Katie and told her about the play she and Manfred had been to see in Düsseldorf and promised to take her the minute she was feeling better. Katie sleepily inhaled her perfume as she kissed her goodbye.

Since Christmas Katie had stayed in her bedroom. She wanted to sleep a lot, and nobody expected the boys to be careful all the time. Heinz was shocked at the change in his sister and even took it on himself to read to her sometimes. Maria thought that if any good could come out of this it would be that her eldest son had learnt to consider others. Hansgünther asked daily when Katie would at last be better: she'd always been around for him, a willing playmate; he felt bereft.

"Not for a while, darling," Maria would say. "This might take a long time to go away." Eventually he stopped asking. He took his pencils and crayons into her room and made himself a little corner for drawing. "Everything I draw here is for Katie. This way she won't forget what it's like outside," said the wise five-year-old.

In fact, no-one really knew how long it would take. Maria tried hard to stay positive and not imagine the worst. The swelling was very bad, and the doctor had given Maria a bottle of medicine to help with the pain but told her to use it sparingly. On good days Katie would chat and eat small amounts and on bad days she slept and the grey around her eyes darkened. Even when she was alone Maria didn't allow herself to cry about it. She felt she wouldn't stop if she did that.

Of course, there were visitors. The aunts came with tasty morsels, which Maria promised to give her but which usually got eaten by Heinz and Hansgünther. Adelheid, no longer very well, came and promised to pray for her and get Father Theo to offer up a Mass. Mina's visit had to be cut short. She had come without Friede, in case there was still contagion lurking about and had burst into tears when she saw Katie, declaring the child could be in a wheelchair for the rest of her life. A door had been slammed but Katie was only dimly aware of the commotion. When Opa came he always brought a piece of beef for Maria to cook. The broth would be good for Katie, he said, but he was as concerned for Maria, who looked worn out and permanently worried. He would lower himself into a chair next to Katie and as carefully as possible take hold of her hand and wait for her to open her eyes.

*

On the last day of the month, while Opa was sitting there like that, Heinrich came in and spoke quietly to his father-in-law.

"That's it. Hindenburg has made him Chancellor. The old fool's been duped." Katie was aware of their voices and the rustle of the newspaper.

"Maybe he's not such an old fool. Maybe he'll make use of him and then kick him out."

"How the hell do you get rid of a man like that?" Papa's voice didn't sound normal. They thought she was asleep.

*

It had been snowing for a couple of days and the streets were covered. Maria opened the curtains for Katie to see the thick flakes licking the window and, when the sun shone again, the treetops shimmering white. She was propped up on two pillows and was wearing a blue woollen jacket knitted for her by Karoline, Heinrich's eldest sister. They saw very little of her and her husband, Helmut, but she had made the journey from Cologne just after Christmas to see Katie. The jacket was lovely but why did Karoline's eyes fill with tears when she said thank you? Anyone would think she was never going to get up again. She wished people would stop being so serious. At least her brothers were normal around her. Hansgünther knew he shouldn't climb on the bed, but he got as close as he could and asked her questions which were hard to answer or showed her his pictures. Heinz was getting very good at telling jokes, but she had to laugh carefully, because it hurt her chest. He'd also learnt how to wink, which became a secret sign between them when visitors were being particularly grim.

*

When Claus and Margarethe came it was never serious. They always remarked on how much better she looked and that "it won't be long now." Margarethe and Maria, sitting either side of Katie on the bed, gossiped about the aunts and about Adelheid's health. She was losing her famous vigour and was reluctant to leave the house; Johanna, who still lived at home and seemed to be content to take care of both the house and her parents, was worried. Maria was about to ask a question when Papa's voice was heard. Angry. He and Claus were in the kitchen.

"You weren't stupid enough to join them, for heaven's sake?"

"No, no…" A chair scraped and a door closed. The voices were still raised but muffled.

"What are they talking about?" Katie asked, looking at both the women in turn. They exchanged a quick glance and before Maria could say anything Margarethe said, "She needs to hear, Maria. She needs to know. There's going to be so much more…" her voice drifted, became calmer. Maria nodded reluctantly, warily, not quite sure where this conversation might be going. Her eyes fell on Günther's latest drawing, pinned up on the wall opposite, where Katie could see it. Trees and clouds and Katie, smiling, on her bicycle and Papa, hand on hips, smiling next to her.

"Two days ago, the Parliament building was burnt down. You know what that is, don't you?" Margarethe looked at Katie.

"Of course I do."

"Herr Hitler is blaming the Communists—"

"Well, it was a Communist," Maria interrupted.

"Yes, but not all of them. Now members of the CommunistParty are being arrested."

"What's that got to do with Papa and Uncle Claus?"

"Papa was worried in case Uncle Claus had joined the Party." Maria wanted the talking to stop now; Katie couldn't possibly understand all this.

"But he hasn't," Margarethe drew breath. "He thought about it, but it would have caused difficulties at work." Probably the sack, certainly victimisation.

"What happens if you are arrested?"

"You are kept in a cell – for a long time." *And kicked and punched and beaten. Tortured and often killed. The stories were everywhere.* Maria pleaded with Margarethe with her eyes. *Stop now. I know you are angry but stop now.*

"But that won't happen to Uncle Claus?"

"No!" both women said in unison.

"Why would Uncle Claus join the Communists? I thought they were bad."

"They are all as bad as each other." Maria didn't believe this herself anymore but what could she say in front of Katie?

"But Maria, someone has to make a stand, haven't they?" Margarethe's voice was sharp, her cheeks flushed. "It's not good enough to just keep quiet and go to church!" Not looking at either of them she got up quickly and left the room. They heard the kitchen door open and close. It was suddenly very quiet.

Katie reached out painfully for her mother's hand. She couldn't squeeze it, but she wanted to make contact. She knew it was a serious matter. Only serious things would make them shout. Maria looked at the thin hand and the swollen wrist and at the pale face on the clean pillowcase and allowed the tears to roll down her face. Distressed, Katie whispered, "It'll be all right, Mama. It'll be all right." She heard the faintest of sounds coming from the kitchen.

Then a few moments later Papa, Claus and Margarethe came in carrying coffee including a very milky one for Katie. Papa and Claus were laughing at something and Margarethe put her arms around Maria's shoulders and kissed her, then bent low over Katie. "It's alright, darling," she said kissing her gently, "you see?"

All was forgiven. Katie sighed with relief.

18

March 1933. A weak government, manoeuvred by Hitler, called for another general election.

D r Beckmann eventually told Maria to beat an egg yolk into a spoonful of cognac and give it to her every day. Opa had suggested this months ago but Maria was sure that the alcohol would do harm.

"The alcohol will be good for her circulation and the egg will build her up," Beckmann had said, signing the insurance form. "Give it to her every evening."

Then it was the day before the general election and the green beginnings of daffodils were poking themselves through the wet earth in the gardens. Mama had opened the window of Katie's bedroom for a little while to let in some fresh air but closed it again after a few minutes because of the noise in the street.

"I'll be glad when this blasted election is over, then maybe we'll have some peace and quiet."

Mama and Papa had both been bad-tempered all week. With each other in particular. Mama wanted to vote. Papa thought it was too dangerous and there would be too much intimidation in the street. Katie told Heinz to find out what intimidation meant and then decided that she didn't want Mama to vote either.

The conversation had been going on all week, on and off. Today, Saturday, the family sat in Katie's room after breakfast. She was getting up occasionally and wobbling around the room, holding on to the furniture, but it still hurt. Now she lay, as usual, in bed. Mama had a pair of Günther's trousers on her lap and she was threading a needle ready to sew a patch onto the knee. Papa, legs crossed, one foot twitching, listened to the loudspeakers outside, the muffled bellows and clatter of boots as the Brownshirts marched past yet again. The boys, sensing that serious talk was imminent and that they had done their duty as far as Katie was concerned, soon went off, Hansgünther to find something to play with and Heinz to the bathroom. They were forbidden to look out of the window when the Brownshirts came electioneering, but he had discovered that, if he opened the bathroom window and stood on the toilet seat, he could just about see what was going on. He needed to know and he needed to tell Katie, later.

"I'm coming with you tomorrow, Heinrich," Maria spoke quietly as if she knew what Heinrich wanted to say. She didn't take her eyes off the needle.

Katie looked at Papa. She had noticed that they didn't leave the room anymore when the talk turned difficult. She was half pleased that she was being treated like a grown-up and half fearful. A few seconds went by.

"You know it's all a waste of time. It's too late." He spoke quietly as well, as if resigned, and laced his fingers together. He was looking at the top of Mama's head with a small smile playing around his lips. Maria's body tensed slightly; her voice was sharper.

"And you know that we would never forgive ourselves if we didn't vote against that godless man. That noise outside is meant to stop us. Well, it's not!" And she stabbed the needle into the patch with unnecessary force. Katie was impressed. Then she turned her head painfully, her shoulders were hurting today, and looked at Papa.

"But what about the intimidation?" she said, pronouncing the new word carefully.

Eyes still on Maria's bowed head he said slowly, "We'll walk around it." She looked up, catching his eye.

"Or through it," said Mama. Katie watched that lingering look and knew she was witnessing something secret or private. She swallowed and turned her eyes towards the window. There was more incomprehensible bawling on a loudspeaker, followed by singing. And the boots, always the sound of boots.

There was a noise coming from the boys' room and Maria put down the trousers and went to check. Papa stayed. He moved to sit on the edge of the bed and took Katie's hand. It was Katie who broke the silence.

"You will be all right tomorrow, won't you?"

He straightened. "Most certainly we will," Papa sounded very sure. "Your mother, as usual, is quite right. We must vote – it's our democratic duty." He was quiet again, scanning the wall above her head. Günther's latest was a winter scene, snow, Mama wearing a red scarf.

"You said it was too late." She wanted to get to the heart of things. Papa paused then took a deep breath and kept his voice steady.

"It is, Katie. Too many people believe in simple solutions. They've decided to believe him. But that's why it's important that we vote tomorrow and not be frightened by noise and threats. Show Herr Hitler that we are not all fooled."

*

Oh, but he was frightened. Katie, doing her growing up in pain, learning about the darkest side of life while still a child, mustn't suspect it, but he was frightened. Every time the front door of their house slammed shut behind him, he could feel, taste, the tension, it seemed to come up at him from the pavements. His own fear wasn't born of uncertainty but of the inevitable. People walked, shopped, posted their letters as usual but there was no chatting in the queues, no shouting greetings across the street. They were fearful of letting an opinion or a view slip out, so public spaces became sullen, deadened. Yesterday he had walked past the Town Hall which had been filled with the din of a broadcast speech exhorting Germans to "Awaken". Old soldiers, women with children, young men listened to the hate-filled words. Some, like him, hurried past, dodging the swaggering Brownshirts. A dull anger gnawed at him when he thought of his children, their future being ripped up and his inability to do anything about it.

*

Next morning Heinrich got up early and, on the pretext of fetching some bread rolls from the baker on the corner of Sternbuchweg, walked swiftly around the block to the polling station, which was already busy, Brownshirts lolling against the building, shouting "Heil Hitler!" tucking their revolvers more firmly into their belts to draw attention to them as they gave out leaflets. As he walked past, he saw three of them surround a man and haul him over to the other side of the street. He was pushed hard and kicked from behind, then kicked again when he tried to recross the road. When he thought better of it and retreated down the street the men laughed. "Communist pig," said one and spat into the gutter as they sauntered back to take up their positions.

He decided the day would get uglier and he and Maria should go soon rather than leave it till later. Maria was dressed smartly when he got back, ready for Mass. Her hat was on the hall table.

"We'll vote before church, Maria. Let's have some breakfast first. We'll come back for the boys when we've voted."

They ate in silence. Maria tried hard to keep the nervousness out of her voice as she gave Heinz copious instructions as to what to do while they were away. He was to clear the breakfast things and make sure his brother got his boots and coat on; the buttons were fiddly, and Katie couldn't manage them yet although her hands were a little less swollen. Then they would wait with Katie until they got back. They shouldn't be more than forty-five minutes and Heinz was quite old enough to cope for that length of time.

"I'll see to everything," said Heinz, rising to the occasion. He was wearing his best jumper over a shirt and his hair was flattened down with a bit of Papa's hair cream.

"Good boy," said Heinrich, not sure if his heart was breaking or swelling with pride at the sight of his son, too aware of what was happening, his childhood slipping away.

Heinz and Hansgünther watched as Mama fixed her hat with a pin and then as the apartment door closed with a click; the bobbled glass panels transformed them into disappearing phantoms as they turned away together towards the staircase.

*

Katie fell into a dream. It happened all the time while she was ill, a sudden, brief but violent disappearance into another space. As if the vivid images which crowded her head while she slept were making up for the barrenness of her days. She was trying to reach something, but her legs were sluggish, held back. She was trying to move across moorland, thick tufts of uneven grass that spread out in all directions. Shades of undulating grey, no light coming from anywhere, no stars, no moon but she knew that ahead of her lay a path, pressed onto the land, like a great flattened worm. The path was wide and crept over the dead landscape. She needed to reach it but her muscles strained with the effort; she looked down and saw that her feet were bare, felt the cold and wet for the first time. The heavy slate sky sucked the air from her. She wasn't going to get there, and it was important; she could feel the panic rising in her chest, stopping her breath. Her head lifted off the pillow in time to see Mama, back from voting, bending over her. Slowly, slowly her heart quietened and slowly Mama's voice made sense as she asked if there was anything she needed before they went to Mass. No, no she would be fine, just fine.

*

Heinrich felt buoyant after voting. They had walked arm in arm, not looking to right or left and through the door of the voting station. Maria had wondered briefly whether their party, the Catholic Centre Party, would be on the ballot paper. Election posters had been ripped off the walls and the candidates had kept a low profile. A meeting that had been held last week at the church had been interrupted by the hooting and braying of Brownshirts outside and the intermittent kick on the bolted door. But all twenty-one parties were there on the ballot sheet, the National Socialists at No. 10, their party at No. 3, neat little circles next to each to receive the cross. Even the Communists, banned for weeks now, were there. They each made their crosses – it would be the last time for twelve years – and folded the scrap of paper into quarters. As Heinrich turned to leave the booth, he found his path blocked by broad shoulders. The man stood still for a long moment, looking at the slip of paper in his hand then at Heinrich who, heart beating, managed to hold his gaze. There was an alien arrogance in that look before he moved slowly aside to allow him to post it into the black locked tin. As they left, they saw the long queue of people walking quietly and solidly into the polling station. Maybe, just maybe… but by the time the family returned from Mass the feeling of elation was giving way to something else, something closer to the certainty he'd felt before, that the results, due to be announced tomorrow, were a foregone conclusion.

19

How to keep this fractured and splintered world, where all previous notions of goodness, moral certainties, ambitions were suddenly rendered meaningless, how to keep all this away from his children, out of his home? During the weeks after the election, as he pounded his way to and from work, head down, past the greening trees of Kammer Strasse, crossing the cobbled side streets, acknowledging the occasional greeting, he determined to plan his way through this uncertain and hazardous future. It would be a matter of constant vigilance, constant countering of the new assumptions and new order. Exhausting because this vigilance would have to be secret and private; and exhausting because it would have to take place within a chest-tearing, explosive silence, the only safe way when anyone not noisily supportive was suspect. Surely if he planned and prepared, the worst of whatever was to come could be kept away.

So Heinrich fretted and thought of how he could keep this poison out of his home. But events were unfolding fast, and the claws of the new State were reaching ever further into the crevices of people's lives. By the time spring had turned into early summer opposition parties were banned, trade unions neutralised, and local government brought firmly under the control of Berlin. But still, still, there must be a way to protect, to continue, to preserve their lives. He left the office promptly these days, glad to escape the stifling atmosphere, walked home quickly, kicking at loose stones as he thought of another possibility and grunting to himself, as yet another obstacle occurred to him.

*

Maria was watching. Watching as Katie grew steadily a little stronger; watching Heinz as he came back from school each day, listening carefully to what he had to say and watching Heinrich become in turns distracted and then enthusiastic over some new project. One day he came home with a shoe last. He had spotted it at the market and now the three-pronged, black, cast-iron anvil sat in the middle of the kitchen table. He had struggled getting it home and up the stairs and was still hot and sweaty from the effort.

"Now we can fix their shoes ourselves, it can't be difficult to hammer new soles onto the bottom of the boots." Heinrich was convinced of the need to save money. "We should be able to pick up some pieces of leather and the nails. Heinz – you can help me by holding the nails in place." And he looked slyly in Maria's direction, knowing she was thinking of the possibility of smashed fingers and thumbs.

On another occasion he brought home extra preserving jars although the cellar was full of them. "Concentrate on vegetables this year, Maria, the children need plenty of vegetables," he said as he helped her squeeze them onto the shelves. And manuals. Manuals on plumbing, electricity and how to repair gas cookers which Maria vowed would never happen. "No problem whatsoever. You just have to remember to switch the gas supply off." And he slammed the book shut and added it to the small library on the kitchen shelf.

A drawer became the receptacle for numerous mysterious tools which he accumulated; a small mirror for examining teeth, lengths of string, measuring jars, a variety of tapes and a box of putty. Maria knew it was a way of coping; as his workplace became increasingly alien he would double efforts to be in control at home, be ready for any eventuality, do away with the need to ask for help.

*

Meanwhile Katie was recovering, growing stronger. She was moving around the apartment and had been given gentle exercises by the doctor to practice three times a day and Hansgünther helped her with great enthusiasm. One day Lisl and Johanna came to visit. They had packages with them which they tipped out onto the table in front of Katie who was having a mid-morning cup of milk and bread roll, part of Maria's strict regime of small meals to build her up. The promise of short walks outside now that the weather was warmer made her obey every command.

"Then Papa will fix my bike and I can go out properly." Katie beamed at her aunts who pretended not to notice the thin pointy chin and the dark circles which refused to disappear. Lisl hugged her hard.

"Oh, darling, it's so good to see you up and eating! Wait till you see what we've brought you but first stand up and let's have a look at you."

Katie stood. "I have grown a bit," she said, looking down at her toes.

"Oh, definitely," said Johanna. "And your hips are getting rounder."

"Are they?" Katie sounded surprised.

"Well, of course. You are becoming quite the young woman." Katie smiled, blushing, at Lisl, enjoying the small, unfamiliar glow of pleasure. Maria caught Johanna's eye. The women knew that her periods would be delayed because of the illness and her bosom was still non-existent.

"Look what we've brought!" Three dress lengths of material were spread out on the table. One a silky pale grey – very grown up – one a lilac covered in darker tiny flowers and one a blue geometrical design. "Very fashionable at the moment," Lisl assured her and brought out a magazine which the women pored over, choosing hem lengths, sleeve shapes, collars and buttons. After measurements were taken and scribbled down the cloth was packed away. Katie was delighted. Three new dresses all at once! "You've grown out of everything. Of course you need them. I can't wait to see you in them – you will look just gorgeous." *Gorgeous*, thought Katie. Only Lisl would say that. The family were very keen on clean and tidy but to look gorgeous was never the goal. Katie savoured the idea.

"I'll take the grey," said Maria. "I think I know exactly what to do with it."

After lunch, and while Katie slept and Lisl read stories to

Hansgünther, Johanna told Maria how worried they all were about their mother. Adelheid was growing thinner and weaker but would never admit that there might be something the matter. She was persuaded to see the doctor but would not tell anyone what he had said.

Johann was also pretending nothing was wrong. "She's just a little tired – that's all. It's to be expected at her age." She was sixty-two. But there were times when she couldn't disguise the pain, in her side, her back. She would sit down abruptly, trying to maintain that straight posture of which she was so proud. Then Johann, forehead creased with worry, would put his arm around her and say, "Come, come Mother. A little lie down is what you need," and help her gently to her feet and put her to bed.

*

And the following spring, in April 1934, Adelheid, mother of eight children, Katie's stern and distant grandmother, died. After the funeral in Lobberich, as the family walked slowly out of the church, there was a pause because Josephine, allowed out of her convent for the occasion, was being greeted particularly warmly by the priest, standing by the great wooden door to commiserate with the mourners. Lisl was sobbing on Margarethe's shoulder; Johanna and Marianna walked arm-in-arm with their ashen-faced father; the older sisters with their husbands. Heinrich glanced at Katie and Heinz, looking uncomfortable and bewildered. And he felt a stab of grief, the first in all the days since Adelheid had died. So resolved was he to armour himself against this new world that even his mother's death had failed to penetrate. He felt his throat tighten and gulped down the sadness. Maria, her arm linked with his, felt a softening, watched a tear fall and was glad of it.

20

1934

"Be careful. Be watchful." Every morning before Heinrich set off for work Katie and Heinz would listen to his serious voice, look at his serious face and hear a variation of this warning. Because it was a warning. He had to do it – to prepare them for what they might hear, read and learn. If he warned them enough, he could save them from believing the bile that they were fed.

Heinz didn't want to be careful or watchful. He wanted to learn interesting things and play with his friends. The trouble was that Herr Vogtländer, his favourite teacher who had told wonderful stories about the Wild West, had left the school and now they had to listen to Herr Richter, who made them do the Nazi salute every morning which he knew Papa would hate, so he tried to do it a little differently from everyone else. He tried various tactics: twisting his hand in the wrong direction which hurt a bit; or spreading his fingers out just enough not to get noticed. Not lifting his arm high enough didn't work because Herr Richter would see the lack of symmetry immediately and flick Heinz's arm with his stick till it achieved the correct height and rigidity. Lots of the best books were gradually removed from the little school library and replaced by books about The Leader. Adolf Hitler. Or stories about Germanic tribes and heroes.

When he mentioned the lessons about 'race culture' to Mama

she had said, "Oh dear God," under her breath and made him repeat every detail to Papa when he got home. About the ugly pictures and drawings of Jews and black people and how Herr Richter had said that they weren't really people at all. He had turned to look at Benjamin, his friend since forever, great footballer – so quick and clever with the ball – now always on the back row, red-faced, close to tears, and felt shame. He didn't tell Mama and Papa this bit – how no-one played with him anymore. Mama sat listening with her hand clamped over her mouth while he talked; he got more nervous, began to stutter, as he watched the colour drain from Papa's face. Why was this so bad? School didn't make such big mistakes, surely?

Papa was quiet for a minute, which frightened Heinz more than any outburst of anger. In fact, Heinrich was fighting with himself and mustering his self-control in order to say the right thing.

"Do you think that's right, Heinz?" His voice sounded tight, strange.

He looked at his boy, at his soft skin, soft baby mouth. At his messed-up hair and grubby jumper. Ten years old. He stared into the confused and frightened brown eyes and kept his voice as gentle as he could.

"Is Benjamin a human being, Heinz?" His voice sounded like dull thunder coming from far away.

"Yes, of course." His face flushed and tears stung at his eyes as he remembered Benjamin cornered in the playground while a couple of boys shoved him about, called him names, "You're a dirty little Jew," and he had watched, not helped, just watched. He felt sick at the thought. The teacher had done nothing, turned his back.

"And his parents, Herr and Frau Linzmann, are they human beings? You've been to their house many times."

Yes, he had. The best cinnamon cake in the world. Herr Linzmann would say this every time with a wink directed at the boys and Mrs Linzmann would laugh as she poured milk and coffee. Benjamin loved him coming over after school so he could put off his piano practice. He hadn't been round there since before Christmas.

"Yes," he roughly fisted away the tears that insisted on falling, "and, and they're really nice."

"I think you know what your mother and I think about Herr Richter and his lessons, Heinz." Heinrich stopped speaking. It wasn't easy for him, but he stopped. They had decided that short counter-blasts to the poison worked best. They hoped it would give the children time to think and process and maybe ask questions.

But it was very difficult for Heinz. The only question he wanted to ask was why he couldn't do what all the other boys did. He'd become angry when both parents refused point blank to allow him to go on the camping weekends with the Hitler Youth Organisation. He would be laughed at if he wasn't allowed to go. It was going to be so exciting. There would be drills, just like in the army, marching practice. They would sleep in tents, cook on fires, eat from tin plates and mugs. They would climb and conquer mountain peaks. Karl, a new friend, knew this because he had seen a film at the cinema called *Hitler Youth in the Mountains*. There would be gymnastics and games and singing.

Maria voiced her objections even more strongly than Heinrich, which took everyone by surprise. The Catholic Youth club, run by the church, had survived till October 1933 and then been forced to close as part of the Reich's battle against religious establishments. For Maria this was the last straw. And it was when she found her voice. How dare they attack her church, her faith? And now this godless crew wanted to take her son and do God only knows what with him. This struck so closely to what she held most dear that for the first time she was moved to real anger and felt the power of it. No, he was not going and that was the end of the matter. Anyway, there was his asthma to consider.

Heinz had to bear it and it was only after Karl told him about the trip that he stopped feeling aggrieved. He had come back with bleeding feet because the marching had been so relentless. They had been bullied and harangued by boys only a couple of years older. The gymnastics were a waste of time, the food was awful and there wasn't enough of it. The campfires were quite good, but he had fallen asleep during the singing. His mother had complained to the leader of the group and then been laughed at for not wanting her boy to learn to be a good German. He was never going to go again, and Heinz should consider himself lucky.

*

Maria decided to fight her own little war against the regime. Heinz's asthma was a useful weapon and was used as an excuse to take days off at uneven intervals. He was always quite surprised to be told that he sounded wheezy, and that Mama would be much happier if she could watch him for a day or two. The asthma hadn't been a problem for a couple of years now and was certainly never used as an excuse but suddenly Maria declared loudly to anyone who might be listening that it had definitely flared up again over recent months and she was quite worried.

Katie was also given as many opportunities as possible to miss school. At the first sneeze or snuffle Maria would insist on a day at home to check that it did not mean a return of the terrible rheumatic fever. Katie was in fact getting stronger and healthier-looking by the day but Maria, after two seconds' thought, decided better to be safe than sorry. Opa and Oma Hilde were also used as an excuse. Katie was needed to run errands to Mönchen Gladbach quite frequently. After all they weren't getting any younger. Of course Katie loved these visits, almost as much as Opa did, although Hilde was getting grumpier. Sometimes she stayed overnight and the following day Opa would take her to the station, stopping at the butcher's and baker's, to buy a few 'little things' to take home for Mama.

Katie's return to school had been difficult. There were obvious changes, like different teachers. There were only a couple of female teachers left at her school in accordance with government policy of restricting the employment of women. Thank goodness Fräulein Meyer was still there – needle work being very much a female preserve. Most lessons were soured by the constant insertion of Nazi ideas and references to The Leader. Katie grew watchful, noticing which teachers were more casual about this requirement and who were more enthusiastic. As time went on, she became more guarded with her friends as well, noticing changes in what they talked about. Lili had become firm friends with a group who had all joined the League of German Maidens and when Katie had said she didn't want to and anyway her parents wouldn't allow it, Lili had frowned at her and said it was every girl's duty to demonstrate how patriotic they were and how much they loved their Leader. It sounded like something she had read and learnt off by heart. With that pretty frown still creasing her forehead she had added, "Don't your parents love our Leader?" and she'd squeezed her eyes up at Katie, running off without waiting for a reply. Katie thought about this conversation on the way home from school. She was uncomfortable about Lili talking about her parents. Better not talk about them at all in future. She would have a word with Heinz about this as well.

*

Uncle Anton had bought a new camera, and, in the September of 1934, he stood Hansgünther in front of the block of flats and immortalised his first school day. Hansgünther beamed into the camera, carrying his enormous paper cone stuffed with sweets and pencils before the family trooped off to school to wish him well, Auntie Botha wiping away tears. How could he already be six years old and going to school? At lunchtime, once Heinz was back home, the family celebrated with a cold lunch plus an enormous cheesecake – Hansgünther's favourite. Opa came with a school bag and Opa Johann bought him a fountain pen which he had to keep safely until he had learnt to use it.

Maria hid her fear well that day. She watched her little boy, brown curls long since cut off, short trousers a size too big held up with leather braces, well-polished boots over long socks as he marched proudly down Kammer Strasse walking alongside his Opa and Heinz, excited, expectant. Maria laughed and joined in the banter and told Heinz that he would have to watch out for his brother now just like Katie had for him. And as she watched him, small and vulnerable walking into the school yard, Heinz doing as he had been asked and holding his hand, showing him where to stand before joining his own line, she joined the others in waving and shouting, "Good luck! Work hard!" and waited till the line of giggling children were silenced by Herr Mueller – thank God, it was Herr Mueller, she knew him to be a good man – and led into the school.

At lunchtime, through a mouthful of potato salad, Hansgünther talked enthusiastically about what he had done, some drawing, some counting, lots of playing and Maria allowed herself to relax a little. It had been a happy day, a normal day, one to remember. Our Leader hadn't been mentioned. But give it time, give it time.

21

But Katie missed her little brother's big day. Heinrich and Maria had noticed how unhappy she was at school. It wasn't just the illness that had extinguished something in her. When she came home from school, she was quiet, sullen even, shrugging off questions and snapping at Heinz. Gradually they realised that she was never going to settle back into a school system that had changed so radically.

One Sunday, after Mass, Heinrich took a leaflet, lying in the entrance to the church, entitled "Ensuring the future for our young women" and put it absentmindedly into his pocket. He'd forgotten about it by the time he got home and only found it again later that afternoon while he was searching for a few pfennigs to give the boys to go and buy some ice-cream. As they clattered off down the stairs, he spread the leaflet out onto the table and told Maria to come over and have a look.

It was a cleverly worded leaflet although it took a little while for them to work it out. The language seemed to mirror the language being used by the Reich when describing the perfect education for its young people. In this case girls and young women should learn the domestic crafts of cooking, housewifery and childcare in a safe and comfortable environment geared to producing morally well-adjusted young German women for the future. Maria noticed how few references there were to the Catholic Church until they saw at the very bottom of the double-sided sheet in tiny italics that all courses were run by the Sisters of the Convent of St. Francis in Elberfeld and overseen and approved by the Holy Father Pope Pius XI.

The germ of an idea was tugging at Heinrich; this could be a way for Katie to get away from school, from the pressure and the isolation she was feeling. Maria was less sure. School might be difficult but for her to leave home – and for a whole year? She was barely fifteen. But that was exactly why it would be so good. Heinrich was convincing himself. A year away from the city, from the endless propaganda, from the League of German Maidens! Maybe when she got back... no, no, things would be just the same or maybe worse when she got back, but this way she would have a precious year away from it all. He would ask Margarethe to get in touch with Josephine and find out about the place.

Margarethe, agreeing wholeheartedly with her brother that getting away from school would be a good thing, thought she could do better than that. She offered to go there herself and make enquiries. That way Katie needn't know anything about it, until they were sure. But, Maria had said to her, we need to be sure the place is sincerely run on Catholic values. For her this was code for being anti-Nazi and, on this occasion Margarethe didn't repeat the well-known fact that plenty of Catholics, including priests, had become enamoured of Hitler and were joining the Party. Maria was still too naive for her own good in her opinion. Josephine helped her get an appointment with the Mother Superior and Margarethe set off on the train to Elberfeld, a little town mid-way between Düsseldorf and Essen. She would find out about this place for herself.

*

The two women took stock of each other across the heavy oak table. Mother Hildegard sat still for some time, hands motionless and hidden behind her white scapular, before asking some general questions about Katie. What sort of things she was interested in, her love of sport, her recent illness. She didn't ask why Katie's aunt had come rather than her parents.

"Since being ill, she's found school quite... difficult," said Margarethe. They were both choosing their words carefully, watching each other's reactions. Seconds passed.

"Yes, in these modern times school can be... difficult." Mother Hildegard had hooded grey eyes, very bright, behind wire-framed spectacles. Her voice was gentle but the tone was measured, saying just enough to make her meaning clear.

"We want her to be happy, and… and well… safe." Margarethe felt she was expressing herself poorly and was relieved to see a glimmer of a smile in Mother Hildegard's eyes.

There was a short pause before she said, "We are all children of God, are we not?"

"Yes, we are," Margarethe agreed more emphatically than was strictly necessary. Unspoken was the implication that we are not the children of the state, of the Reich.

"And as such," continued Mother Hildegard, "our duty must be to each other. Here," and she emphasised the word with a slight movement of her head, "we believe that being kind and compassionate to each other brings about true happiness."

Margarethe's eyes wandered to the large wooden cross hanging on the wall and the statue of Our Lady standing solitary on the heavy oak cupboard at the side of the room. Crosses and statues were being removed from schools all over the country.

Her eyes returned to the woman sitting opposite. "Her parents would agree absolutely with that philosophy."

Mother Hildegard smiled and said, "I'll look forward to meeting them one day."

There was a silence while Margarethe struggled to find the right words for the question she needed to ask. Mother Hildegard gave her time.

"Do you… are you able to… do your work without… interference?" She looked urgently into the nun's eyes. They remained steady.

"Interference comes in many forms. But, with the help of God we deal with it. The welfare of our children always comes first." The tone was even, the eyes calm. Margarethe was sure.

"Now, you must be hungry and since it is our lunchtime maybe you would like to join some of the Sisters in the dining room. It will give you a chance to have a look round." The interview was over, and Margarethe was shown the dining room, where some very young nuns were eating, in silence. They greeted her with smiles but waited till the meal was over before talking to her.

*

Katie took a little persuading, but Margarethe was so enthusiastic that she began to think she was being offered a long holiday and her sense of adventure was tickled and tempted.

"But I don't want to leave you all." She had to say this and anyway it was true. She couldn't imagine life without Mama and Papa.

She sat at the table with her chin cupped in her hands and thought about what Margarethe had told them. About the beautiful house, the forest nearby where they were encouraged to walk and cycle. About the prospect of good new friends. The orphanage where the girls worked and played with the children. The nuns didn't seem strict at all, they were all so friendly. Mother Hildegard was, she was quite convinced, a good and kind person.

"We would come to visit you and you can come back here every holiday. A year isn't so very long." Papa wanted to sound encouraging; it sounded like a long time to Katie.

Maria looked at her daughter's conflicted face. She suddenly noticed how pretty she was becoming and thought that maybe a spell with the Sisters would be a good thing. "I will miss you very much, darling, but I have a feeling it will suit you down to the ground."

*

"I'm surprised you've come round to the idea so quickly," Heinrich said after the children were in bed. "I know how hard it's going to be for you... for me too."

"But it will be such a relief to know she's safe, away from everything," she said. "You were quite right. The year will pass soon enough, and we have the rest of our lives to be together – in one way or another. She's growing up fast. The nuns will be good for her."

"Maybe they'll be able to control that headstrong nature of hers. Aren't these schools meant to turn out compliant young ladies?" Heinrich smiled and raised his eyebrows questioningly at Maria.

"Mm... well, I wish them the best of luck with that!"

And while her parents were dreaming about the return of a

ladylike daughter in twelve months' time, Katie lay awake, heart beating, both scared and excited at the thought of this new, unexpected turn of events. A whole year. A different place, new faces, new things to learn about. Under the bedclothes she pulled up her knees and hugged them, smiling into the pillow, enjoying a brief, uncluttered moment of anticipation.

*

Hansgünther was for a short while inconsolable. Heinz listened silently as they were told about Katie's imminent adventure with the serious expression that he reserved for momentous family news. Hansgünther was not silent. After listening and digesting the information and having discarded everything except the unimaginable fact that Katie was going away for a whole year the tears started to roll down his cheeks and Maria braced herself for a lengthy period of misery.

The questions came out as howls. "Why, WHY does she have to go away?" Answers went unheard as his face got redder.

"It's not fair! I need her! She promised to help me when I start school." This new thought prompted further noisy crying and furious glances were hurled at Katie, who looked crestfallen. Liberal use was made of his sleeve to wipe away the snot.

"I don't understand it at all. How could you DO this," he held his hands in front of him, palms up, pleading.

Where did he learn to do that? thought Heinrich.

"How COULD you?" The rest of what he said was fairly incomprehensible, words muffled and buried under gulps and intakes of breath. Heinrich decided to put an end to it. He raised his voice enough to be heard above the racket.

"Enough. For heaven's sake stop that and pull yourself together!" Hansgünther stopped breathing completely for a few seconds then made a huge and dramatic effort at self-control.

It was Heinz who broke the silence. He stepped towards Hansgünther and put an arm very lightly and a little self-consciously around his shoulder. He bent his head towards his brother. "We'll manage," he nodded gravely, slowly as he spoke. "It's not as if she's going away forever, is it?" Hansgünther looked unconvinced. "And we'll be able to visit. On the train." This was clearly better news; Hansgünther looked hopefully up at Mama for verification. She nodded. "It'll be fun."

And so it was that Katie missed not only her little brother's first day at school but also the visit from Mina, Friede and Albrecht which laid the foundations for decades of distrust and dislike, both buried and overt.

22

By the end of 1935, the Reich was digging deep into people's lives. Soldiers were swearing unconditional loyalty to Hitler and the cult of 'The Leader' was being promoted in every town by the Party. Schools and universities had been transformed. Trade Unions banned.

"It must be costing you and Heinrich quite a lot of money to send her there."

Was it a statement that Maria could safely ignore or was it a question? Mina's eyes glittered with curiosity. How could she look so like their father and yet be nothing like him?

They were in the forest. It was a warm late September day and the sisters walked arm in arm, hatless and in their summer dresses. Friede and the boys had gone on ahead; Heinz had his hands in his pockets. Heinrich and Albrecht were some way behind.

"It's not so expensive. The Sisters try to keep the cost manageable." Maria knew she would have to say more. "You're right, of course, we couldn't manage it by ourselves. Luckily Father and Johann are helping out." Both men had been more than happy to help send Katie off to the nuns for a year.

Mina's "Aah," was long drawn out. Maria could feel the wheels of resentment begin to turn. Then, as an afterthought, Mina said, "It's not really the sort of thing people like us usually do, is it?"

The phrase hung in the air for a second before Maria said, "You mean because it's expensive?" Surely this wasn't about money. Their father had probably helped Mina and her family more than anyone else. Maria waited to see where her sister was going with this.

"We think that girls can learn everything they need to know from us, at home." Mina gave a small nod as she spoke, sure of her ground now. "What on earth was wrong with staying at school here anyway?"

"You know what's wrong with school, Mina; doesn't Friede tell you what's going on?" Maria had told her many times how unhappy Katie had been since going back to school. Mina's face remained blank. There wasn't the usual agreement that Maria was used to when she spoke to Heinrich's family or to her father. Now she'd raised her voice and wished she hadn't. The silence remained for some seconds and unconsciously the sisters' arms dropped to their sides and a distance opened between them.

"You are both being ridiculous about all this." Mina clearly had more to say, things she and Albrecht had talked about. "Look how safe the streets are now. Life is so much better. At long last we can begin to be proud to be German again!" A prepared little speech. The same one trumpeted in the newspapers, on the radio, over the loudspeakers.

Maria stayed quiet, keeping her eyes lowered, looking at her shoes as they stepped and crunched over tiny dried-up twigs and cones that had fallen from the pine trees, and succeeding in not showing any outward expression of what she was feeling. This was her warm and dear sister who had never had an opinion about anything in her life. Harmless, affectionate, silly even. And now Mina was talking like a Nazi. Or was she? Was she jumping to conclusions? She kept quiet.

Mina risked a nervous glance at her sister before continuing, "I… we… just can't understand why you feel so strongly about it."

It, thought Maria, *it – such a tiny word. I don't want to hear what you're going to say, Mina, don't say any more.*

"Hitler is a strong leader. Just what we needed," Mina ploughed on. "We must give him a chance."

"A chance to do what exactly?" Maria's voice sounded harsh. The silence between them was brittle. Then, out of habit, out of kindness she softened her tone. "Mina, what are you saying? You know what sort of a man he is."

Now it was Mina who kept quiet. She could never argue with her sister; it was quite something that she had said what she had but she was worried, worried that Maria would one day do something, say something foolish and get them all into trouble. Albrecht was never very specific about this, but people did get into trouble these days.

Hansgünther was running towards them, grinning and shouting, "There's a new kiosk, look," and he pointed at the little wooden shack that lay ahead, just where the path they were walking on emerged onto Lothar Strasse. "Can we have a few pfennigs to buy some sweets, please Mama?"

The men had caught up. They were walking in silence. Was there tension there too? Maria sensed there was. Albrecht, always the jovial uncle, was first to delve into his pocket and find a five-pfennig piece for each of them and the children ran off towards the kiosk. The walk home was uncomfortable: some small talk about Friede's exams; she'd had to sit the final year again and was still finding the work difficult; the women talked about their father's health and who was going to visit him next. They had coffee together before Mina, Friede and Albrecht set off, with an air of hasty relief, for the tram back home.

*

"Do you know what he said? He said, 'It will end in war, Albrecht, you realise that don't you?'" They were sitting in their little room that evening, simply furnished and very clean. Albrecht's foot was twitching in mild annoyance. "I mean, for heaven's sake, what is the matter with the man?"

Albrecht and Mina had been intent on convincing them of the error of their thinking that afternoon. It was their duty. Both to their family and for the greater good. That had been how Herr Scholz, his superior at work, had put it when Albrecht had mentioned that his brother-in-law was one of the few that he knew who was less than happy with the new government. Scholz had shaken his head in kindly commiseration.

Scholz and Albrecht worked for the Ministry of Transport; their work involved co-ordinating and making improvements to train and tram timetables across Duisburg. Scholz was adamant that Hitler was doing great things for the Ministry by simplifying the system, doing away with layers of bureaucracy, making his life, for one, a lot easier. "Our department may be humble, my dear Albrecht, but by God, we can make it efficient and get Duisburg moving again!" Scholz seemed to puff up; his eyes glowed at the prospect. It wasn't hard for Albrecht to become infected with his zeal.

"War?" Mina tutted and reached for her neat pile of mending. "Of course there won't be another war!" Friede's stockings had holes in the heels; the girl really needed to start looking after her things a bit better. "The Führer would never allow that to happen." She tutted again with a little shake of the head as she threaded the needle.

"What did he say when you mentioned joining the Party? I didn't even get that far with Maria." She was concentrating, squinting, as she jabbed the thread into the eye of the needle. Albrecht didn't answer.

Scholz had asked where his brother-in-law worked. "Justice, eh? Well, they'll demand loyalty, that's for sure." Albrecht had assured him it was only a minor department in the Ministry. "Doesn't matter, co-ordination is what counts now. And co-operation. In fact, no such thing as a minor department – we are all important – we all have a role to play!" Scholz suggested, as a friend, and as a concerned German citizen, that Albrecht explain this to Heinrich.

"He asked me about the Rosens," continued Albrecht after a thoughtful pause.

"Who?" Mina frowned across at him.

"Apparently Katie was friends with Marthe Rosen."

"Oh, the Rosens," Mina nodded over her stitching, "had the dress shop on Sternbuch Weg."

"Jews."

"Mm… lovely clothes," she remembered the elegant displays. Then, tightening her mouth a little, "Of course they were a bit out of my range – money wise."

"Heinrich asked me why they had left, not where they'd gone, mind you, but why." Albrecht sounded put out. "Apparently they've gone to Holland. They've relatives there and…" he shrugged his shoulders, "Heinrich just wouldn't let it drop – 'why, Albrecht? Tell me why they've gone?' He just kept repeating it."

"Rich Jews, they'll be all right."

"That's basically what I said to him. If they want to go, let them." Albrecht decided to bring the conversation to an end. He reached over for his little cigars and lit one. He leant back, looking fondly at his wife's strawberry blonde hair bent over her mending, then puffing a cloud of smoke over her head. She loved the smell of them and lifted her head to smile at her husband. As she stitched, first one heel, careful little under and over stiches, then the other, she thought of Maria and that concerned look of hers. Why always look for problems? She loved her sister, and it really didn't matter anymore that she had always been her father's favourite, but sometimes she just couldn't see sense. She snipped off the thread neatly.

"There," she said, holding the stockings up and giving them a little shake. "They should last a few more weeks at least." And she put the needles, the thread and the small, sharp scissors carefully back in the little drawer next to her chair.

*

A little earlier, in Kammer Strasse, and just after Mina and Albrecht had left, Maria had to endure an hour of pacing and muttering.

"Dear God! I don't know how I managed to stay calm when he started to lecture me on Hitler's genuine vision and – this really got to me – his famous 'humble' origins – as if we aren't all aware of *that* particular fact – the man never stops banging on about it." He glared at Maria who was trying to imagine Heinrich staying calm. "It was only the sight of you and the children that stopped me giving him a piece of my mind."

The boys were safely out of earshot, having been sent to Anton's garage to help 'tidy up' and were probably now eating cake with Botha.

"It won't be long, Maria, it won't be long before the man is wearing the Party badge, mark my words!" Heinrich's hands were dug deep in his pockets as if he needed to keep them under control. "He told me the only way to get promotion was going to be by joining the Party! As if I give a hoot about promotion right now!" He stopped suddenly and sat down next to Maria.

"He's right of course." He paused for a few seconds, leant forward and laced his fingers together. "There will be no promotion. Do you mind?"

Maria was surprised to hear uncertainty in his voice. And that he needed her – well what – consent, affirmation?

"Heinrich you know how I feel."

He looked at her sadly. "I don't want to let you and the children down."

"There's more than one way of doing that." She took his hand. "You will do the right thing, Heinrich. And that is what the children will see."

Heinrich squeezed her hand. "And what do we do with that sister of yours. Albrecht knows exactly where I stand now, I'm afraid."

Maria sighed. "I don't know. Wait and see I suppose."

Heinrich paused before saying, "If they join the Party, I don't think I can tolerate them coming here."

She paused then said, "If they join the Party they won't want to come." She was suddenly sure this was how it would be.

23

1936. Laws designed to purify the German race had been established by the Nazis. The handicapped and mentally ill, gypsies and African-Germans were all considered inferior, incapable of working or fighting for the Reich.

At the beginning of January, the snow began to fall. It covered the pit heads and blast furnaces from Duisburg to Dortmund. It fell on the lumbering coal trucks, holding yards and creaking railway lines, still rusty, still waiting in anticipation of Hitler's Four-Year Plan when they would power into action. It covered and transformed the church spires, the houses and the streets of the cities, creating brief beauty before turning into grey slush under a thousand feet. The farms and forests that cradled the cities were silenced by the shining white powder that fell and fell for days, keeping the cattle in their steaming barns and the pigs, disgruntled, in their sheds, crystallising overnight into a glittering crust, cracked open at dawn by heavy-footed farmers carrying pails of feed.

If anyone had been passing the walls of the convent in Elberfeld they would have stopped and tried to peer through any cracks they could find to locate the unearthly sounds of screaming to be heard coming from somewhere in the grounds; seconds later they could walk on, fears laid to rest, as the screams gave way to hoots of laughter, shouts and screeches of delight. But the scene would have been worth seeing.

Sister Benedictus, veil flying behind her, feet sticking out either side of a toboggan was the one responsible for most of the screaming. She was flying, almost literally as the wooden sledge skidded over bumps, rising in the air before eventually coming to rest safely at the bottom of the slope. She threw herself off and lay in the snow, red-faced and laughing, laughing almost as much as the girls that raced down the hill to help her up. Katie grabbed one arm and Karin the other, giggling as they helped her shake away the snow from the folds of her habit. Karin pulled the toboggan back up the slope where Sister Francis was shouting that it was her turn next.

Above them, at a window overlooking the convent grounds, Mother Hildegard, attracted by the sounds, stopped on her way to the kindergarten at the back of the building, and smiled down at the girls – because they were all girls, the Sisters barely nineteen, Katie and Karin fifteen. Then she tidied her wimple, running her forefinger under the front of it where it pressed against her forehead, pulled the black cloak firmly around her shoulders and headed towards the staircase that led down to a side entrance. The path that led to the orphanage had been swept clear and she hurried along it, past the cherry trees, branches drooping with snow, through the courtyard where the children played come rain or shine. But not today. Today the Inspector was coming, and she wanted to make sure she got there before he arrived.

Katie and Karin heard the bell that signalled the beginning of the day's duties and walked quickly up the slope to the path, where they had to step aside for the Mother Superior. They bobbed in unison and said, "Good morning, Mother Hildegard," and were briefly surprised that she swept past them with only the briefest acknowledgement. "Come on, quick," Katie pulled Karin through the door where they kicked the snow off their boots, took them off and replaced them in the neat row that ran along the wall. "She was in a hurry," said Katie as they hung up their coats. Karin, who always knew everything, said in a mock scary voice, "The Inspectors are coming. They've been talking about it for days. I'd say she and Sister Joseph are quite tense."

"What do you mean?"

"You do know what 'tense' means?"

"Yes. Of course I know what it means." Karin often made her feel foolish. "I just don't see what they've got to feel tense about."

The conversation was cut short by Sister Benedictus bursting through the door. "You are going to get us into trouble, hurry up!" She watched them as they put on their soft-soled indoor shoes. The girls scrambled to their feet and ran along the corridor. "And next time you can help us put the toboggan away!" Too late, they were gone, up the stairs to the dining room where they were responsible that morning for washing up the breakfast things.

Katie and Karin were work partners. Partners changed once a fortnight. Today was Friday and the timetable was as follows:

9-9.30	Kitchen duties
9.30-12.00	Orphanage/kindergarten
12.00	Prayers in chapel
12.30-1.30	Lunch
1.30-2.30	Arithmetic
2.30-3.30	Prayers and singing in the chapel
3.30	Coffee and cake/free time
5.30	Post/letter writing
6.30	Evening meal

It was always the best day of the week, and today had begun especially well when Karin had dared to ask Sister Joseph if she and Katie could go out tobogganing while the other girls finished their breakfasts. Sister Benedictus, a particularly lively soul, had overheard and volunteered to accompany them. Sister Francis had appeared out of nowhere and declared that she had half an hour to spare, and could she go too? She bit her lip almost immediately. Spare time wasn't something that nuns ever had… but she needn't have worried. Sister Joseph, second only to Mother Hildegard in the chain of command, usually so thoughtful about all decisions, said, "Yes," surprisingly quickly, adding only, "Don't be late back," as a distracted afterthought before hurrying towards Mother's office, veil and skirts flapping.

Now, kitchen duties done to the high standards of Sister Julian, whose eye would spot a drop of water on the scrubbed and bleached draining board from across the room, the girls set off for the orphanage. Under their arms they carried their cloth bags, each of which contained the timetable, an ironed handkerchief and a pencil and small notebook. The cloth bags had been embroidered during their first needlework lesson with Sister Francis; Katie had been commended on the neatness of her cross stitches. But then so had Eva, whose attempts were anything but neat and who stuck her tongue out between her teeth as she sewed.

They weren't allowed to use the outside path during winter so they made their way along one of the main corridors, rows of windows placed high up so no-one could see in, and no-one could see out, up a flight of stairs, along another narrower corridor towards a winding staircase. They were used to the smell of polish by now, and the sight of the odd nun bent low over her task. They also hardly glanced at the pictures on the walls, pictures of holy saints, of bleeding hearts of Jesus, of the Mother of God, pale-skinned, dressed in blue, eyes uplifted. There was a cross in every room. This particular staircase was only wide enough for one person at a time and a wooden rail, worn smooth with use, ran along one side of it, to help some of the more ancient nuns haul themselves up. The steps were steep. The girls had soon learnt that, so long as no-one was looking, they could lean on the rail, lift their feet and slide around the bends. Once at the bottom they passed through a vestibule, down another corridor until coming to the heavy, wooden door that led to the orphanage.

The girls knocked once then walked straight in, as they had been taught to do. The door seemed to signal the entrance to something very grand but in fact it led to a small room, once possibly an office but now used as a storeroom for toys, easels and other equipment brought out for the children. Little prams, scooters and some recently acquired toy cars were stacked neatly around the room. There was a small window on the right and Katie noticed a large car parked in the area usually full of children playing; she wondered where they all were. They walked into a larger room where a dozen or so young children were playing. A few of them immediately ran up to the girls and threw their arms around their legs. Katie and Karin bent down to hug them back, laughing, nearly toppling over in the process.

"Ah, there you are, girls." Sister Joseph looked relieved to see them. "Now then children, go and play, they'll be with you in a minute." She waited while the children, three little girls dressed identically in dark blue pinafores and blue ribbons in their hair, ran off, then said in a forced bright voice, "It's a special day today because the Inspector from the Education Department is paying us a visit. I'm very glad that two such sensible girls are helping us this morning."

Karin made a strange noise in the back of her throat which Katie knew meant 'I told you something was going on', before both of them bobbed and said, "Thank you, Sister."

"Mother is talking to Herr Brockmeyer at the moment," and she glanced nervously over towards the office where the children's records and reports were kept. "When they have finished, he would like to spend some time with the children. Then he has another appointment but will return later this afternoon to see the older children when they return from school." There were eleven older children who were marched each morning to school in Elberfeld. Sister Joseph took a deep breath and straightened her shoulders and seemed momentarily to become lost in thought. Her mouth became a thin, hard line.

After a moment's silence Katie said, "Shall we get the easels ready for painting, Sister, or take the children outside? They'd love to play in the snow."

"The easels, Katie. We will wait until a little later before we take them outside. And make sure there's as little mess as possible." She was moving away from them.

"Very well, Sister."

"By the way, you're staying here until 2.30 today. It's been arranged." And she headed towards two boys who were squabbling over some building blocks.

"Great!" whispered Karin as they dragged the easels out of the stockroom. "We'll miss Arithmetic."

The office door had been left open – no nun could be in a room with a man with the door closed – but all that could be seen was a corner of the desk and a cabinet against the back wall. Every so often Herr Brockmeyer's voice was heard, indistinguishable grunts and responses. Mother Hildegard's voice, of course, was never raised above the level tone she used on every occasion. The open doorway seemed to exert a power over the room and Katie, like everyone else, was drawn to glance toward it at intervals and modified her own voice as she helped little Theo put on his apron. The children, usually so boisterous, noticed the change in the grown-ups and the weight of it stifled them. Once there was a flash of Mother's habit as she got something out of the cabinet and everyone, including the children, was silenced until she disappeared once more behind the desk.

*

Mother Hildegard had prepared carefully for the visit. The small office was tidy, the desk organised. The filing cabinet was in order. A chair had been placed behind the door ready for the visitor. The new Inspector – the old Inspector of Children's Homes had unaccountably been dismissed – would have no trouble examining the paperwork that was kept for each child. Two of the files had given her cause for concern and she had sat up late that night over the typewriter making the slightest of alterations. She had consulted God most fervently about this and prayed for guidance but the change of Inspector at such a time left her in no doubt. A doctor's opinion had been removed here, a mother's details there. No sin in that, she was sure; if there was, she would take the consequences. And now Herr Brockmeyer was sitting opposite her, taking occasional sips of his coffee, looking at the neat pile of folders on the desk, not very interested in the nun opposite, obliterated as she was in her black and white habit, enthusiastic in his new role, keen to prove himself. All this she noticed. She assumed a position of moderate authority, elbows on the edge of the desk, fingers laced together, back straight. She lifted her chin slightly, ready for him. Behind him and visible to her beyond his shoulder, a cross hung on the white, empty wall and she concentrated on it as she prepared to speak.

"It doesn't seem long at all since our last inspection. Herr Bauer was here, let me see now, last March, wasn't it?"

"Yes, he was." Brockmeyer didn't bother lifting his eyes from the files; he was flicking through them quickly and thoroughly, pausing only to note the names on the front of each brown folder by stroking his long index finger under each one. His tone implied she would have to wait till he was ready for the conversation to continue. She wasn't going to let that happen.

In a pleasant tone she said, "Herr Bauer gave us a very good report, especially on the improvements we have implemented in provision for the youngest children."

Brockmeyer's mouth twitched in annoyance and he was forced to look up. "Yes, yes, that's as maybe, but there is never room for complacency, is there? Herr Bauer could be a little lax in his assessments."

Mother Hildegard's expression remained relaxed and non-committal as she looked at the young man, fair hair cut short, bright grey eyes noticing her for the first time. He clearly did not intend to be lax. She wondered where poor Herr Bauer was now, punished as he was for his kindliness and habit of turning a blind eye.

She let Herr Brockmeyer continue. "These youngsters," he said and tapped the files with that long finger, "are going to grow up in a new and vigorous state. A state that is paying for their upkeep. They need to be worthy of that privilege."

She held his gaze for a second before saying, "And every one of these little souls is indeed worthy."

"I'll leave their souls entirely to you. To tell you the truth I'm not that interested in their souls. I am interested in their potential as citizens, in their health – both physical and mental. The Reich needs able bodied, loyal workers and your duty, as is the duty of all educational establishments, is to produce them."

Brockmeyer pushed his chair back slightly so he could straighten his legs. He was pleased with himself. He wanted this woman to know exactly what her function was whatever grandiose opinions she might have had in the past. He took out a packet of cigarettes and lit one, silently daring her to object.

Mother Hildegard ignored it. What a child he was! As he leant back, the cross behind him seemed to nestle momentarily on his shoulder before being obscured. She leant forward slightly.

"Since you bring up duty, Herr Brockmeyer, mine and my Sisters' remains, first and foremost, to God, as you surely know." She smiled at him.

Brockmeyer heard the steel in her voice but the smile made him choose a conciliatory tone. "As I say, I'm happy to leave their souls to you and I'm sure you want them to be a credit to Germany. Our country is changing direction, moving forwards."

A second's pause and she said, "Our aim is for our young people to be a credit to themselves and to God. I'm sure that's the same thing, aren't you?" Again the annoying smile. He tapped cigarette ash into his saucer. He was going to get nowhere with her. These religious types were all blinded to what was happening.

"I'm interested in where the children come from," he insisted. "Herr Bauer wrote that there had been an increase in the number of foundlings brought to the convent."

"A few years ago, that was certainly the case. Some were taken by adoption agencies. Those we cannot find good homes for stay with us."

"And why would that be? Feeble-mindedness? Unknown heritage?"

"No child would ever be turned away, Herr Brockmeyer." Straight away she regretted saying it. Maybe she had implied, too soon, that she knew his true purpose. She should stick to God – he didn't like that, and it was always for the best. "All children are the same in the eyes of God, after all."

He didn't respond to the challenge to reply. Instead, he breathed out heavily and leant forward to stub out his cigarette, which he did messily in the saucer.

She said, "Quite often there are no suitable parents for the children we have. Few want to adopt older children; it's always been the same."

Brockmeyer stood up. He was very slim. The dark brown suit hung on him loosely, wide around his legs. The small badge glinted in his lapel. "I'm sure you and the Sisters provide a valuable service to the state. Now I think I shall have a quick look round to get a feel of the place. I'll take these with me." And he picked up the files.

"Of course." And Mother Hildegard rose neatly and pushed the door wide open, momentarily trapping him and forcing him to squeeze around it in order to follow her out. As they stepped through the doorway she stopped and turned. "Our young ladies come every day to help with the children. It's part of their programme. You are very welcome to talk to them if you wish." He gave a non-committal nod in response before she added, "A Sister would be present, of course." And he was finally allowed to step into the room.

*

Theo was pointing out of the window. He wanted to be out there but today the big doors remained shut and he had to stay inside. He watched a robin chase a sparrow across the path where a dish of crumbs had been placed that morning. The sparrow, on rapid little legs, raced in a wide circle around the dish and watched from a safe distance as the robin, red chest puffed out, guarded the crumbs and finally took a piece in its beak and flew up into the hedge with it. Katie was kneeling beside him, watching as well.

"What a cheeky fellow that robin is, eh Theo?" And she looked at his face as he smiled broadly at her. She said "Look, look! The sparrow is coming back. Let's hope he gets something this time." They both watched the sparrow approach the food and, once he was quite sure it was safe, grab a crumb and proceed to peck and eat it up before taking another piece. Theo looked at Katie again and smiled.

"Thank goodness, Theo, at last he's getting some breakfast." Theo nodded gravely. "I wonder what you had for breakfast this morning?" She said it gently, not expecting a reply. "I'm guessing it was hot chocolate…" he turned and grinned at her, "and perhaps a bread roll…" another grin, "which you dipped in the chocolate when Sister wasn't looking?" This time huge, silent laughter and Theo put his hand delightedly over his mouth and Katie mirrored his action, their heads close together. Then she pulled up his socks which always fell in pleats around his thin ankles and said, "Come on, let's find something to do." And they both stood up and turned to see Mother Hildegard and the Inspector standing at the far side of the playroom. Theo didn't notice straight away. His head was still happily full of sparrows and hot chocolate but when he did his grin faded and he stopped and reached for Katie's hand.

Brockmeyer was standing near a group of girls playing in the little model kitchen complete with table, chairs, pots and pans. He stood with his hands clasped behind his back, looking intently at the children, searching for what he was sure he would find. The books he had been reading were clear that the purity of the race depended on weeding out the weakest. It was common sense. It was simply a matter of identifying hereditary malformations. He would take careful note of what he saw today. A place like this was a God-given opportunity. After a moment he crouched down near the girls, who were told to say 'Good morning' to the Herr Inspector, which they dutifully did. He replied briefly and asked Mother Hildegard for their names.

"I'm sure the children can tell you themselves," she said, watching him carefully as Brockmeyer looked at each face as it turned towards him, his eyes sweeping from left to right, up then down. Some kind of measure being taken.

"I'm Irmgard."

"I'm Lisbeth."

"I'm Anna." All three smiled as they spoke, small proud voices, first at the stranger then at Mother Hildegard, who smiled at them encouragingly.

"Can you stand up please?" They pushed themselves off their little chairs and made themselves as tall as possible, grinning at each other, comparing, enjoying the attention. Brockmeyer looked for their files and slipped them to the bottom of the pile. At that moment both he and Mother Hildegard had the same image in their minds. The same page of drawings and statistics and measurements which outlined the perfect head shape, distance between the eyes, position of the chin, desirable in the Aryan. Of course, they had read, small variations were only to be expected but larger differences were almost certainly indicative of major hereditary malformations.

Mother Hildegard had sent off for the book, written by some learned Swedish professor, keen to understand how the notion of 'Racial Purity' might affect their small charges. Then, as the convent slept, she and Sister Joseph turned the pages under thin, cold electric light and shuddered as they looked and read and understood.

Brockmeyer, disappointed but keeping his expression neutral, stood up and surveyed the room. Somewhere among this little group of the unwanted he would find the evidence he was looking for. Evidence was important; policy should be based on scientific fact, and as he thought of the acclaim he might receive, by adding to the Reich's body of knowledge on the subject of racial cleansing – a phrase that gave the young Inspector not a second's disquiet – his gaze fell upon the girl and little boy standing stock still over by the window. The white light behind the boy outlined his small frame and, as Brockmeyer made to approach them, he noticed his slightly bent stance. Maybe, probably, a spinal deformity.

Both Mother Hildegard and Sister Joseph had spotted the direction Brockmeyer was taking. He walked slowly, looking with pretended interest to left and right, and to the nuns the walk seemed to make time freeze. They had prayed this would not happen, that Theo, their most vulnerable, most loved child would not be of interest. Sister Joseph, her heart fluttering, caught Mother's eye and saw her raise her forefinger and make a gesture that said, 'be careful, nothing rushed, leave them.' Sister Joseph finished speaking to two boys who were vigorously filling small bowls and buckets in the little sand pit and moved calmly towards Katie and Theo so that she would be just within earshot.

Now, then, Katie, Mother Hildegard's innermost thoughts were directed equally towards Katie and to God. *Do the right thing, say the right thing. I don't know what that could be, but I think you can do it. When the devil comes into our midst perhaps the most innocent have the most power.* Brockmeyer, his back to her, had reached them and was signalling down at Theo with his fingers, saying something. Katie was very still, looking at Brockmeyer, appraising. *Good girl. Think. Think. Work him out. Your instincts will help you.* Was she taking too big a gamble? Brockmeyer would believe nothing the nuns said. She would watch and hope.

Katie had learnt a lot about the Herr Inspector during the last couple of minutes. Nothing put into words, of course, but she had processed the information. Theo's grip on her hand and refusal to move had forced her to look carefully. The man was walking towards them, looking at other children but not seeing them, his gaze always locking back onto Theo as if there was something drawing him like a magnet. And she had seen him with the little girls, intense and cold. He reminded her of some of the new teachers at school, the ones she had to be wary of. As she watched him and felt the pressure of Theo's little hand, she became aware of the old sensation of suspicion which had, up to now, left gratefully at the convent door. It felt familiar, icy in her throat. He was very close now. Fifteen-year-old Katie didn't like him and as Theo leant more closely into her skirt, she straightened her mouth into a smile, gave the customary bob and said, as she and Karin had been instructed by Sister Joseph, "Good morning, Herr Inspector." She glanced at Sister who was comfortingly close and noticed the subdued nod of permission.

Brockmeyer gave the girl a cursory glance of acknowledgement and the briefest of smiles and said, as a pair of very clear green eyes met his, "And who do we have here?"

For a second, she was confused. Did he want to know her name? But when she saw his eyes first linger on Theo and then his long fingers hover over the files he was holding, she said, "This is Theo. Theo Schaubel." He found the file and flicked through it, reading quickly the bland and useless details Mother Hildegard had chosen to include. His favourite food and how he slept well after stories read by Sister Benedictus. How much improved his general demeanour had become over the past twelve months. He closed the file and looked at Theo from above. Five years old and he looked like a three-year-old. A cranium that was suspiciously narrow. The shoulder stoop was definitely spine-related.

"He's very small, isn't he?"

He didn't seem to be addressing her particularly, but she decided to answer as well as she could. She didn't say – well what do you expect when for the first three years of his life he was hardly given anything to eat. The policeman who found him said he was living on scraps he found lying on the floor – no, she decided not to tell him that. Instead, "He's grown a whole two centimetres since December," she tried to make her voice sound girlishly jolly. "We are very proud of him." He looked at her directly for the first time.

And then she suddenly crouched down, leaving Brockmeyer first staring at nothing then looking at the two heads below him. He heard Katie say, "Theo, I want you to go to Sister Joseph now. I think she has your favourite car for you to play with." They looked earnestly at each other and Theo's grip on Katie's hand relaxed. He wanted to go away from this man and Sister Joseph was quite close. Off he went, with his strange little lopsided walk.

Katie was relieved to see him safely with Sister Joseph and Brockmeyer was glad of the opportunity to see him walking. He imagined the girl had engineered the move for his benefit. He looked again into the clear, expectant face, momentarily disconcerted because he noticed what a pretty girl she was. But only for a second, then his fingers tapped the file and he said, "He walks badly, why is that? Can you tell me?"

"Because his leg was broken twice before he came here."

"Ah." *Dammit*, he thought, *that's not what I wanted to hear.*

"By his father," continued Katie who, now that Theo was out of earshot, and hearing a hint of disappointment in his voice, decided to explain in more detail. "The bones never healed properly." And, especially for him, "That's why he doesn't like men, why he was frightened of you. I'm really sorry about that."

Brockmeyer failed to register that she didn't sound very sorry. He was busily thinking that there must still be an hereditary cause for the boy's disfigurement. Looking over to the child, who was silently pushing the toy farm truck with its load of cows and horses, he said, almost to himself, "But the head, the head shape is… not right."

Katie didn't say, 'Neither would yours be if someone had slammed it against a wall.' It was Sister Benedictus who had told her the terrible story of Theo's early life. She hadn't minced her words. Sister Joseph had simply said that Theo was 'rescued' and left it at that. Katie adopted an innocent but horrified expression and said, "His father was a brutal, brutal man."

Brockmeyer sighed; he had to say something to the girl. "That is a shocking thing to have happened." Katie nodded gravely while he thought that he might still send one of the specially trained doctors, trained to identify hereditary disease, to examine the boy. Mother Hildegard was suddenly and silently by his side.

"Herr Brockmeyer, I think you have time to visit the bedrooms and the dining room before you go, and perhaps the bathrooms as well...?"

Brockmeyer declined the invitation with a distracted shake of the head. He was looking at the files and deciding on a course of action. "Maybe when I return this afternoon, when I've met the older children." He handed them reluctantly back to her. "I'll return at one o'clock."

"Would you like lunch? Perhaps you could eat with the children?" Mother Hildegard had guessed that such a proposition would be very distasteful to him.

"That won't be necessary." And with a brief nod he said goodbye, took his coat which had magically appeared in Sister Joseph's arms and left.

The two nuns and Katie stood in a line, watching as the door closed behind him. Sister Joseph said, "The man didn't even notice that Theo doesn't speak."

Katie said, "He was interested in his legs, and his head, I don't think he had a chance to notice that he doesn't speak." She dragged her eyes away from the door and looked shyly at Mother. She hoped she had conducted herself well.

"That's good, Katie, otherwise he would have found out that Theo has never spoken a word in his life and in our strange new world that would have been a golden opportunity for our new Inspector." Mother was still looking at the door as she spoke. She tucked her arms into the sleeves of her habit before turning to Katie and smiling at her. "I am proud of you, Katie, there are people in the world more difficult to deal with than we would like." And on that note, she asked her to rejoin Karin and prepare the children's morning drink. Katie, confused and pleased with herself at the same time, did as she was told.

*

"Do you think Theo's safe now?" asked Sister Joseph.

"I think we have bought a little time. That's all we can be sure of."

Both nuns sighed deeply. Mother Hildegard went on, "He'll be fast asleep when he comes back this afternoon so safely out of the way. And we must think about Maya." Dark-skinned Maya, brought in ten years ago by her mother, weeping, desperate, ashamed. Unable to care for the child of a black soldier. "Make sure she is at the back during singing, where she won't be noticed, and afterwards she can help clean the nun's dormitories. He won't want to go there. I'll rely on God for inspiration if he asks questions. That is if He forgives me for inventing a German war hero as her father."

*

When Papa came to bring her home at the end of her year at the convent, Sister Benedictus pressed a folded piece of paper into her hand. "Write to us, Katie. We would love to hear from you." Excited about going home, letter writing was the last thing on her mind. But she did. First out of childlike duty, then, during the decades that followed until Sister Benedictus' death. The annual letters became precious, a valuable reminder and link between a world that was both horror-filled and one full of affection and her own carefully crafted safe haven. The letters would provide an opportunity to describe and justify her life to someone who would never judge but would encourage and bless her decisions.

That morning, as she waited for Papa to finish a conversation with Mother Hildegard before they could head off to the tram stop, Katie didn't expect to see any of the nuns again, or Karin or Eva, despite the tears and promises made the evening before. As she pushed the piece of paper, a short letter wishing her well and the address of the convent carefully printed underneath, into her jacket pocket, she was thinking of home, Mama, brothers, the future. She felt expectant, grown-up, ready. She was sorry she was leaving; she had loved her time there but that's what happens, things come to an end, people leave, go away, sometimes without explanation… like Marthe… She struggled to keep hold of hope but felt her resolve weaken. Theo's eyes would haunt her. They could tell her more than the other children could with their chatter. When Katie had told him that it was time for her to go home now, they had filled with tears but quickly and sadly accepted it, as if it was his lot in life to lose things. His thin arms had clung fast around her neck as she kissed his hair.

She looked over at Papa, who was shaking Mother Hildegard's hand. Then he turned, smiling, and walked over to her. Katie had grown; she was nearly as tall as him, plumper, a young woman. Heinrich's smile was one of pride. He picked up the suitcase and offered her his arm. "They've been saying very nice things about you." But he wouldn't tell her anymore. He wanted Maria to hear it first.

On the tram, as it jolted through Wuppertal, past the sluggish Ruhr, which was being widened and dredged, warehouses built on either side, northwards towards Duisburg, thoughts of the Sisters, of Theo, of the other girls jostled with the excitement of going home, of what might lie ahead. Her hand slipped into her pocket and she felt the piece of paper. Of course she wouldn't forget them all. Through the window she saw the trees of the forest, their forest, and felt deep pleasure at the familiarity. The apartment blocks, the shops she knew so well. A short walk and she would be back with Heinz, Hansgünther and Mama. She smiled at Papa and took his arm.

24

*During the 1936 Olympic Games there had been a pause in the
street violence. But as soon as they were over the intimidation
resumed and rafts of laws were brought in by the Nazis to make
life for the Jews so intolerable that many emigrated.*

Katie raised her eyes briefly and looked around at the bowed
heads of the small group of women, all concentrating on
their stitching. It was unusually quiet even though talking
was frowned upon by Frau Wettmann when her girls were busy on
their garments. This afternoon they were all straining to hear what
was being said in the small dusty room where Frau Wettmann kept
the orders and talked to customers.

In spite of their best efforts the whole establishment remained
dusty. Every action – cutting, measuring, pinning, tacking, sewing –
seemed to send tiny featherlike particles by the thousand up into the
air which remained there, sometimes invisible and sometimes visible,
dancing in the murky sunlight, breathed in by the lungful and not
only defying every effort with brush and duster but exacerbated by
them.

Luise had been summoned into the room by a very sober-faced
Frau Wettman and the door had been firmly closed. That morning
a woman had walked into the workshop and asked to speak to the
owner. She wore a brown suit and the badge declaring she belonged
to the National Socialist Womanhood was pinned on one lapel
while the swastika sat on the other. Luise had shrunk into her seat
while Bettina blushed her response to the woman's perfunctory 'Heil
Hitler' which was delivered again on her way out. It was March 1938.

When Luise emerged, she was deathly white and holding a piece of paper. She stared at them all. "That's it. I have to go." She took her jacket and hat from the coat stand and put them on while they stared at her silently. She folded her certificate with a harsh slide of her fingers and put it into her bag. Katie wanted to go towards her, she had known her for two years, but now there was ice between them. "Well, one less Jew for you all to worry about," said Luise, and gave one last look, at them and around the room, before quietly leaving by the front door. She hesitated for a second, faltering, looking down at her shoes, as if not sure whether to turn left or right before setting off in the direction of Graben Strasse.

"I had no choice." All eyes turned to Frau Wettmann, who stood at her office door looking out of the window at Luise's retreating figure. "You know what they do to people who employ Jews." She sounded resigned rather than sorry. "At least she has her certificate. I'm sure it will come in useful. Eventually." She turned back into the office where she pondered the difficulties faced by small businesses when it was forbidden to have Jewish workers. She had hung on to Luise, easily her best seamstress. Customers returned demanding that their clothes be made by her and now she would have to disappoint them. A damn nuisance.

*

Katie walked home a couple of hours later nursing the hard stone that had lodged itself somewhere behind her throat, pushing down the anger, stifling the tears. She came to the marketplace in Neudorf. The stalls had packed up hours ago and apart from a couple of men sweeping up the remains of the morning's activity, it was deserted. She sat down on a bench near the church and wrapped her coat more firmly around her neck. It was cool but there was still enough of the spring sunshine around to warm her face a little. Sometimes she would go into the church on her way home and sometimes it even helped.

But not today. How could Luise say that – 'one less Jew'? They had been friends, laughed together, giggled at Frau Wettmann behind her back, complained together at being given yet another menial task in the early days of their apprenticeship. But she hadn't said anything; just like the others she hadn't said anything. The ugly stone in her throat grew, guilt-shaped, and tears stung her eyes although she knew she had no right to them.

It would have been Bettina who reported Luise. Or maybe she reported Frau Wettmann for employing a Jew. Bettina, who had befriended Katie on her first day, showing her the ropes, helping her with the machine when it wouldn't cooperate, sharing gossip and jokes and finally inviting her to her home for an evening meal. She wanted her to meet her family; there were things she wanted to show her. Katie shuddered at the memory, but she had been flattered; at last one of the crowd, no longer the awkward newcomer. Last autumn they had cycled to the large house by the forest and left their cycles at the side of the building and walked round to the back where a garden lay in gloom, towering oaks blocking the sun and beginning to throw their leaves onto the ground.

She was introduced to her parents and offered wine to drink with the meal. The conversation was polite, but Bettina was clearly in a hurry to finish. Something was on her mind and as soon as Katie had finished, she took her by the hand and said, "Come on, Katie, I have something to show you." She looked excited, flushed, as she hurried to her room at the back of the upstairs landing.

The room was in darkness and Bettina raised her hand as if to tell her to stop and wait. Suddenly a light was switched on and Katie, blinking, saw at first only red; red curtains blocking out the light, red drapes over a table slightly raised against a wall, a rug in front of it. And above it a giant picture of Hitler. It was a well-known portrait, three-quarter profile, the merest hint of a smile, eyes, pinpointed with light, gazing into the distance. Bettina had flung herself onto her knees and then lay prostrate in front of the image. Katie watched speechless, looking first at the makeshift altar with candles waiting to be lit and small swastikas on sticks arranged in vases like dead and dying flowers, and then again at Bettina, who was now sitting back on her knees, tears streaming down her face. "Isn't he magnificent?" said with adoration, with passion. Katie realised her mouth had fallen open. "I love him so much." And the tears started to fall again.

With every fibre of her being Katie wanted to run, to get away from this pathetic, dangerous girl, but some long-held, residual need to leave politely made her find some words, "No Bettina, I don't... I can't..." She was backing away towards the staircase. Bettina seemed to come to her senses and got up, following Katie out and closing the door behind her. "I see," was all she'd said, her mouth a thin, grim line. They'd walked silently downstairs, and Katie took her jacket and bag from the coat stand and left by the same back entrance. She'd steadied herself for a few seconds, bile rising in her throat, holding the handlebars before pushing the cycle out of the driveway, jumping on and riding home as fast as she could.

*

Katie, remembering all this, feeling the chill as the sun dipped behind the houses, got up and walked home. How had madness become so normal? It was something her father said often and there was no answer. He had become quieter recently which worried her mother. He pored over the newspaper, the one he still trusted, occasionally flinging it across the table with a single word, "Idiots!" Not aimed at the government but at the British and the Americans. "They understand nothing, nothing!" At which point Maria, with a disapproving glare, would take the paper and hide it in the sitting room.

She climbed the three flights of steps and let herself in with the usual shout, "It's me!" She was met with a shout from Günther and the smell of a peppery goulash. "Dumplings!" was all Günther had to say as he swung around the kitchen door, grinning. And the grin made her decide not to mention Luise. Maybe later, maybe just to Mama, maybe not at all. She hung her jacket up on the row of coat hooks and went into the kitchen, where her brother had returned to dropping the little floury balls into the stew pot, carefully, without splashing. "Smells lovely, Mama," she said, while an unbidden image fleeted across her mind of Luise, in her mother's kitchen at that moment, with news that would be both disastrous and not unexpected. "It'll be ready in half an hour. Go and see what Heinz is doing and keep the door shut." Doors were often shut, shut on whispered conversations between her parents, on exchanges between mother and daughter, and on adolescent boys breaking the law.

Back in the little square passage which led to all the rooms in the apartment she heard the crackle of the radio. The radio had pride of place in the sitting room. It had arrived months before and now sat in the corner on a small table that was covered by a cloth that Katie had embroidered at the end of her first year as an apprentice dressmaker. Maria was heartily sick of the steady diet of popular music and skewered news broadcasts on the cheap 'Peoples Receiver' which Heinrich had bought back in 1933. Gradually the dramas she had enjoyed, and classical music broadcasts had been cut in favour of Party-approved programmes. Heinrich, never very keen to spend money unnecessarily, used the excuse to find a radio which would pick up foreign stations and, with Uncle Anton's help, finally bought one, well wrapped-up in a box one dark evening. They were pretty sure that no-one had seen them carry it from the car to the front door and they had met no-one on the stairs. Buying the radio wasn't against the law but listening to foreign stations was. Which is what Heinz was doing at that moment. He glanced at Katie, as she came in and closed the door behind her but returned his attention quickly to the vertical red line which magically searched and found, amid the bleeps and hisses ('static' he had informed her knowledgeably), languages and music from across the globe. This ability to tune into the world was so exciting that to stop his children from using it would have been impossible, so Heinrich had given them a lecture on the importance of keeping it a secret. It had been a risk, and Maria wasn't sure that Günther would be able to keep quiet, but so far, so good.

"I think I've found another English German-language station." He wrote a number down on a piece of paper. "The Russians are broadcasting in German as well, but I haven't found them yet." He kept his ear close to the set because the volume was turned down low. She studied his profile for a moment. He was changing fast, as tall as her, nearly, and good-looking, already popular with the girls at school.

"How do you know that the Russians are broadcasting in German?" She crouched down next to him and watched his fingers slowly twist the tuner. None of the family had tired of listening to languages from across the globe suddenly materialising in their sitting room.

He winked at her. "I just do," he said. After a minute's fiddling he added, "They seem to be as interested in us as the British after Austria."

Then they both said, in unison, "At last!" And laughed together because that is what their father said whenever a foreign power suggested that Germany was perhaps getting out of control.

Heinrich had put Heinz in charge of searching for foreign radio stations that sent out broadcasts in German. Heinz hadn't been able to disguise his excitement when the German army had walked into Austria unopposed. The reports and pictures of confident, smart and smiling young soldiers being cheered in the streets were hard for fifteen-year-olds to be unimpressed by. "Find the stations – British, Swiss and anything else that's out there – and listen to what they say." It was a wise move; it played to Heinz's strengths and was a much-needed bonding exercise between father and son. Strict rules applied, which made it even more exciting for Heinz. Volume to be kept low, never do it when anyone else was in the apartment, keep the door closed and always, always tune back to the official German station before switching it off.

Heinz did that now as they heard the front door bang shut. Papa must be home. They listened for a few minutes to an enthusiastic German news reporter describe the humiliations suffered daily by the Sudetenland Germans who lived in Czechoslovakia, apparently starving and experiencing violence on the streets. The reporter's voice rose a level to proclaim, "Every one of them, to a man, longs to be part of the Great German Reich. When, oh when will their wishes be realised." The door opened and closed behind them and Papa said, "Found anything interesting?"

Heinz told him he hadn't managed to find the Russian station yet. "But I will; it's just a matter of patience." A reply guaranteed to please. The radio was switched off.

"I know you will, my boy. Now here is something I was given today at work." And he took out of his pocket an orange rectangle, the size of a postcard. There was a hole, the size of a radio knob, cut out in the centre. He held it so that all three of them could see. Across the top was written in large print: THINK ABOUT THIS. Then beneath 'Listening to foreign broadcasts is a crime against the national security of our people. It is a Führer order punishable by prison and hard labour.'

"Well, we know that already," said Heinz, a little uncertainly.

"Yes, but clearly some people aren't taking any notice!" Papa's voice had taken on a mock authoritarian tone. "Hang it on the radio, Heinz. And remember: THINK!" Heinz slipped the bright, not to be ignored card on the volume knob, a perfect fit. Smiling conspiratorially at each other they left the room, closing the door behind them.

*

The brief feeling of unity dissipated a little during the evening meal. After the prayer was recited each settled into their own thoughts, filtering out the events of the day that couldn't be shared. Günther ate his goulash heartily and chattered about school, and how he was in great need of a bow and arrows so he could be like the red Indians in his cowboy books. Maria and Heinrich responded amiably, saying they would consider it when it was his birthday. Or maybe even before if his school reports were satisfactory, and they watched him count up the long months before he would be ten. Heinz listened but was thinking about the orange card now hanging on the radio, how he felt about disobeying the Führer, about how he might look in a soldier's uniform, and whether Ilse would catch his eye again on the walk home from school. All these thoughts muddling around together in his head but not getting in the way of his appetite.

Katie wasn't listening; she pushed her food around and put small pieces into her mouth. As she chewed slowly, she tried hard to remember the little Luise had told her about her family. Was there a brother, older? He had been studying at Cologne University but been sent back. Now they had no income at all; soon would have no home. Her food stuck in her throat. Most difficult was that last look, before she left, lumping them all together, making them all guilty when Katie would have done anything to help. But of course, she hadn't; she couldn't, could she? Now they would have to leave but that was getting harder – and would cost money which they didn't have. Her throat constricted and she coughed, covering her mouth.

"What's the matter? Drink some water." Katie did as Papa told her. *Nothing was the matter.*

And Heinrich, choking back the anger he felt daily at the pollution engulfing his workplace and determined never to bring it home with him, tried to focus on his children, Maria, the meal. But through the filter of Hansgünther's chatter, the tinkling of the cutlery, thoughts dragged themselves back to his office, his branch of the Ministry of Justice, still enshrining the ancient laws of the land. Still upheld, still admired unless, of course, there was a call from Berlin, reinterpreting, upending, overturning all that he held dear. The call would be obeyed without a murmur, dissent was unthinkable. Flurries of activity, papers to be checked, signatures sought. He was rarely involved, and his desk had been moved nearer the door, the equivalent of a demotion, his work reduced to the most mundane of matters. But he was noticing that even the mundane was becoming infected.

Maria's voice broke into his thoughts.

"Heinrich?"

"Oh, yes, just a little more, please." Meat and gravy were spooned carefully onto his plate, a dumpling onto Günther's and the rest for Heinz.

*

Maria's daily routine brought with it its own secrets. Things she saw perched on her bicycle on her rounds of the butcher shops and the vegetable market. The Jewish chemist shop, which she had been going to for years, run by Herr and Frau Liebermann, first boarded up and a week later reopened by a smiling couple freshly moved up from Koblenz. The hardware store in the market smashed to pieces in broad daylight by brown-uniformed men and little Herr Winkler left bruised and weeping and spat upon. The placards, she had seen

two more today, emblazoned with the proud declaration of loyalty –
'Jews Not Welcome Here' – outside a restaurant, and a boot maker.
And when she got home, putting things away, making a cup of coffee,
asking herself why she didn't feel more, feel the anger enough to speak
out, to scream out. What was happening to her?

Now Maria watched Katie pick at her food and force it down.
She would ask her later what the matter was. She'd ask her to help
clear the large table in the sitting room ready for a visit from Johanna
and Lisl tomorrow, who had managed to get hold of some lengths
of fabric to make some summer dresses. Katie had groaned at the
thought of more sewing, but Maria had reassured her that she needn't
be involved – just choose and advise. She would ask her then what
had happened. Try and soothe the anger which sometimes consumed
her eighteen-year-old daughter. Concentrate, concentrate on her
children, anticipate what might come next although anticipation was
always exceeded by reality.

Her father, Peter, had died quite suddenly a year before.
Dropped dead at the feet of the wife he had never truly loved. Hilde,
not the hysterical type, had taken her coat and gone to inform first
the doctor and then the priest, asking him to telephone Heinrich at
work who had then to rush home and deliver the news. The entire
family had gone, devastated, on the tram to Mönchen Gladbach. It
was the blackest week, the January weather matching their mood.
She had only collapsed when they returned home, unable to keep
up the pretence of control any longer, closing the bedroom door and
weeping into the pillows, for her father and finally for her mother,
whose memory she had managed to bury until now. Heinrich forbade
the children from disturbing her.

And now she was clearing the dishes, passing them to Heinz to
dry, thinking of Katie's face, too thoughtful, too pale, and wondering
where to buy bow and arrows. And in the silence of the evening a
solitary truck rumbled past in the street below, alternately grinding
its gears to slow down then noisily speeding up, as if to make people
aware of its presence.

25

August 1938. Threatening noises were being made towards the Sudetenland and Czechoslovakia. Italy's dictator, Mussolini, had declared support for Hitler. Britain and France were on alert.

"Who is going with you?" Katie and Heinrich were in the cellar making last-minute adjustments to her bike. Heinrich wanted to be quite sure it was roadworthy before Katie set off on her trip tomorrow.

"Jens, Jens Lehmann is coming, and I think Bernd, you know – Anna Schneider's brother, they are both coming." She gave the bolt that fixed the front light on a final twist with the spanner. "I won't need this light, Papa; we'll always be stopping before it gets dark."

"Ah yes, the Schneiders. A nice family. Yes, Katie, you do need it. You never know. You don't want to find yourself on a road in the pitch dark, in the middle of nowhere."

He was concentrating on checking the brakes, making sure the pads grabbed smoothly when the pedal was pushed backwards. But Katie wasn't fooled.

"Papa, I've known them all since I was five years old. They are all nice or I wouldn't be going on holiday with them." Her voice was calm. She'd let him continue the gentle interrogation. She knew what was coming.

The group she was going with were all from the church. Church youth clubs were now banned but the friends met regularly and informally either after Mass on Sundays or at one another's houses. This trip, to Heidelberg along the Rhine and then to Frankfurt, had been planned around their kitchen table, amidst much noise, a few beers and sandwiches which Maria managed to set down alongside the spread-out map, and Heinrich's well-meant interruptions which were finally halted when Maria dragged him onto the balcony to help with the plants, telling him to leave them alone for heaven's sake, they knew what they were doing.

"And Otto – is Otto going as well? I hear he has exams after the holidays." Heinrich was looking intently at the rear brake pad.

There it was. It hadn't taken long. He really wasn't very good at this casual cross-examination.

"Mm, yes Papa, he's going too. I need to adjust the seat, it's a little low." She loosened the seat bolt and handed him the spanner to hold. He took it from her absentmindedly.

"I would've thought he should be revising if he wants to get into university. To study Law I think you said."

Why should he think she was interested in Otto? Was she making it so obvious? She had bumped into him last year and he had transformed into a handsome, beaming man almost unrecognisable from the skinny boy she'd sat next to at school. He had recognised her and shouted across the street, made her blush. She was definitely interested.

"He needs a break from the studying and anyway no one really knows what's going to happen, what may lie around the corner." She fixed a stray lock of dark blonde hair behind her ear. "Do they, Papa?" And she gave the seat a little tug upwards before taking the spanner back. She was surprised that she had shut him up so easily.

Have I made her too anxious? he thought. Every time Hitler opened his mouth it became more obvious that he wouldn't be satisfied until there was war. It was an obvious truth but maybe he should tone it down a little.

"But you young people must still think about the future, when this… this is…"

"What? Over? It'll never be over, Papa!" She pressed her lips together with the effort of tightening the bolt.

"It will, Katie, it will," he told the lie as gently as he could before adding, "I'm glad you are all off together. Don't forget to take an extra puncture kit." And he took the spanner from her and gave the bolt an extra turn to make sure.

The next morning, early, around seven o'clock, Katie's friends gathered outside the dark brown front door, propped open so that her bike could be wheeled out and her brothers and parents could come and go, say goodbye, hand out titbits for the first leg of the journey, check the saddle bags and rucksacks and generally make a noise until Jens said they should make a move if they wanted to get past Düsseldorf by lunchtime.

"Four weeks, Mama, then you can send out the search parties!" Katie called over her shoulder, laughing and steadying the bike, getting it under control with the extra weight in the bag and on her back. Finally, the five of them disappeared around the corner of Sternbuchweg and the only sound was the rustling of the trees which by now had grown so high they were blocking the light into their apartment windows.

*

They aimed to get to Kaiserswerth, a pretty old town about thirty kilometres away, as soon as possible and put the steel mills of the Ruhr well and truly behind them and after a few hours they were sitting on a couple of the town's benches near the river and tucking into their cheese rolls, bikes leaning against one of the large chestnut trees that lined the riverbank. Katie took a long drink of water and looked around for somewhere she could fill up before setting off again. Otto pointed out a little water fountain set into an old high wall, roses tumbling over it and weeds poking out of the cracks and gaps, just off the road behind them and they both walked over to it. Katie felt warm and strong and free, her arm brushing against Otto's, watching the water flow over his brown fingers as he sluiced it over his face, laughing, telling her to do the same, which she did.

Then all of them back on their bicycles and off towards Düsseldorf and the first of many youth hostels earmarked along their route.

*

Once Cologne was behind them the land opened out and they passed fields and gentle hills on their way to Bonn. After that the going got tougher. They kept to the left side of the river and the roads were steeper. High above them they glimpsed the turrets of the Drachenberg Castle, but they had decided not to stop here too long but press on to Remagen, where there was a bridge, the Ludendorff, which Jens, the budding engineering student, was interested in. Katie listened absentmindedly to him explaining how this railway bridge was built in the First World War by Russian prisoners of war to supply troops on the Western Front. Otto, Jens and Bernd went off to look at it while she and Anna sat on the riverbank. Every so often they heard a train rumble over the huge iron construction.

"It's ugly," said Anna and Katie had to agree. At the far end of the bridge were two enormous brick towers with slits at the top for, presumably, machine guns to fire on any enemy troops.

They continued looking for a minute or two then lay down on the grass, closing their eyes against the sun. Katie was thinking of Otto's strong back ahead of her as they pedalled up and then down the slopes along the Rhine.

"What are you going to do after the holiday?" Anna's voice broke into her thoughts. Katie sighed, remembering the dressmaker's stuffy workroom. "Continue my apprenticeship with Frau Wettmann, I suppose," she shrugged. Didn't want to think about it. "I need to earn a bit of money. What else can I do?"

Anna, a clever girl, who had watched career paths for women disintegrate before her eyes, was now training to be a nurse and about to do her final year in Cologne.

They sat up, contemplating the future, listening to the sounds around them, the hoots from the river barges, the odd truck behind them on the road and then, in the distance, a faint rhythmic crunching. They looked towards the bridge end of the road and saw first Otto, Jens and Bernd cycling towards them over a slight incline then slow down and come off the road, jumping off their bicycles. They stood still and looked behind them. The girls watched as the sound came nearer, louder.

There were thirty, maybe forty of them, their age, maybe some younger. The sergeant gave an order, and they broke into a run, keeping the rhythm, eyes firmly ahead, back packs bobbing. The five friends watched silently as they ran past, boots kicking up dust in the hot sunshine.

"Well, maybe that's what we should be doing, eh, Otto?" said Bernd with a wry grin on his face.

They waited as the young recruits, red faces wet with sweat, panted down the hill and out of sight. A few seconds' silence as each of them for the hundredth time banished the thought that this was their real future, and that their plans may be just fantasies they were clinging onto with a blind desperation.

"Not for me," said Jens, throwing himself on the ground next to Anna.

"Otto's thinking about it though, aren't you, my friend?" Bernd laughed and gave Otto a push from behind.

"Don't be ridiculous," Katie said, as if it was the most unlikely idea ever. But Otto hesitated a fraction too long before speaking. She looked up at him, surprised, waiting.

Otto glared at Bernd then said, "I just think we should be prepared, that's all."

"What for, exactly?" Katie's voice was incredulous. "To die for Hitler?" Soldiers took their oath of loyalty to Hitler these days, not to Germany.

"I don't want to die at all." Otto looked calmly at her. "That's the point."

They looked away from each other and gazed across the river, over three hundred metres wide at this point, calm waters carrying cargo, the odd pleasure boat. Further back was the bridge, its steel arch black and heavy against the blue sky.

"You can't possibly be a soldier, Otto." Anna had jumped up and was getting ready to get back onto her bike. "Remember what we said. One lawyer, one nurse, a baker, a dressmaker and an engineer. Between us we have the world sorted!"

Katie was still sitting; she had pulled her knees tight up to her chest, rubbing her chin against her knees, watching Otto.

"We need to be realistic, that's all," he said quietly with a slight shrug of the shoulders.

"Come on," Bernd, never happy when the atmosphere turned sour, always the first to steer away from conflict, "let's get to Westerwald, away from this damned road."

As they set off Jens gave the bridge one last admiring look over his shoulder. "Built to last, that one," and he pushed down hard on the pedal to catch up with the others.

26

Duisburg

"How is he really, Maria?" Margarethe spread out the damp tea towel on the edge of the sink to dry. They had had lunch together, sausages and red cabbage, washed up, wiped everything while she told Maria about her and Claus's move to her father's house and Maria told of the boys' exploits and Heinrich's latest hoarding fad. Pieces of leather, small sheets of rubber, balls of string were all accumulating in the cellar; Maria wouldn't tolerate any more in the apartment. And tins of milk and fruit came home in dribs and drabs. "Look! They were going cheap, Maria."

Now they were sitting on the little balcony that opened out from the kitchen on two cushioned wicker chairs and surrounded by geraniums and pots with lettuces. Margarethe lit a cigarette and watched her sister-in-law's brows form a hint of a frown. There was a long pause. Margarethe knew Maria well by now; they would be honest with each other.

"The nightmares have come back," Maria hesitated then met Margarethe's blue eyes, so like Heinrich's, "for the first time in years and years." Both women looked over the wall of the balcony across the gardens where the tops of apple and cherry trees could be seen, fruit ripening.

"A lot of people are having nightmares. Does he tell you what's going on at work?"

"Sometimes," Maria looked down at her hands. Work was an agony for him. Invisible barriers, secrets, backs turned, sudden silences all had to be endured; every area of work contained poison.

Margarethe noticed for the first time the little flecks of grey that were appearing on her black hair. Both women had taken Lisl's advice and had their hair cut and permed into waves that spread across their heads in shiny ripples and bounced gently around their cheeks.

"There's something else..." Maria looked at Margarethe. Margarethe knew there was something else and patiently drew on her cigarette, turning her head to blow the smoke across the balcony wall.

"It's probably nothing but he falls asleep so easily in the evening and forgets things – he forgot about Anton last week, completely forgot that he had arranged to meet him at the garage." Margarethe laughed and said that Claus fell asleep every evening and he would remember nothing if she didn't remind him. Heinrich was behaving like a normal middle-aged man.

"Mm. Maybe... but Anton..." Anton had been concerned, noticed something, something other than the usual stress and worry. Maria sighed. "I'm sure you are right." And she lifted her head and smiled. They sat in silence for a while, enjoying the warmth, watching a bee nosy its way past the geraniums and settle on the rocket, past its best and coming into flower.

Maria took a breath and, as if she had decided that something needed to be cleared up, leaned towards Margarethe.

"He just can't do what Claus did, he just can't."

Margarethe realised that she had misunderstood and was angry with herself.

"Of course not. You have children. We never expected..." Her voice trailed off. So that was it. Heinrich was battling with himself over whether to stay at work.

"Maria, it was so different for Claus." She had been right behind him when he announced he would have to resign. Before he was kicked out. To his boss, who was glad to see him go, he used the excuse of moving back to Mönchen Gladbach with his wife, who wanted to help Johanna take care of their father, but the truth was that the big house meant they had somewhere to live and made it possible to give up the job at the Justice Ministry in Düsseldorf which had become more and more under the domination of the local Nazis.

Maria, watching Heinrich fret and frown at the news, had said that their decision had been easy. No children, somewhere to live rent-free; they could indulge in the luxury of keeping their hands clean.

"There's room at the house for all of you, you know that."

"He would never give up our home, Margarethe. And you know that!" Maria felt anger but it was gone in a second.

"He's a proud man. But you are the one he listens to." Margarethe was suddenly smiling at something. "Do you remember the time you sewed sandpaper into his trousers?" She leaned forward to stub her cigarette out in the ashtray on the floor.

Maria laughed at the memory. At least fifteen years ago and the story had entertained the children time and again. Heinrich, so proper and well-mannered, so disapproving of coarseness in others, had the atrocious habit of scratching his backside in front of Maria, which she decided she couldn't stand any longer. She had cut a two-centimetre square of sandpaper and using the tiniest of stitches sewed it very neatly into a part of his trousers where it would cause maximum discomfort. He had spent an excruciating day at work, unable to do anything about it; walked home in record fast time and rushed into the bedroom to tear them off. It had been a while before he could laugh about it and the bad habit didn't go away entirely. Could there really have ever been a time when they could be so light-hearted? Margarethe saw the smile die on Maria's face.

"Claus hasn't found a job. He reckons the ultimate irony will be when he gets called up."

"Heinrich thinks war is only months away. Surely Claus is too old. What is he – thirty-eight?" Margarethe nodded and shrugged her shoulders. There were no certainties now. Who was too old, too young? Maria closed her eyes and thought of Heinz – sixteen next birthday – desperate to shave the soft, dark fluff from his upper lip – she couldn't bear to think about it.

"Katie will be having a wonderful time with those friends of hers," Margarethe smiled mischievously. "When is she supposed to be getting back?"

Maria remembered how years ago it was Margarethe who would stick with the difficult truth, like a dog with a bone, not let her off the hook until she had confronted it. Now she was the careful one, changing the subject to safer ground.

"In a couple of weeks, I hope. I never thought I would miss her so much."

"I'm told that that Otto is extremely good-looking." Margarethe put heavy emphasis on the 'extremely'.

It took Maria a minute to realise what she was suggesting. "They are all good Catholic youngsters and know how to behave themselves," Maria said with emphasis and a firm look. Lisl, she thought, it would have been Lisl enjoying the gossip and making something out of nothing. "I wouldn't say he was all that good-looking," she said, remembering the handsome face turned towards her as she offered sandwiches, "and anyway he has exams and is going to university soon."

Margarethe was determined to persevere with this. She had been furious at the decision to send Katie on the dressmaker's apprenticeship. She had a brain – she could have done anything! She and Heinrich had had a row, a noisy one, Katie shut herself in her room crying and Maria had to calm everyone down. College would cost money; they had the boys' future to think about. It just wasn't possible. Maybe, thought Margarethe, a clever aspiring lawyer was just the right thing for Katie.

"Mothers are often the last to be told about a romance," she said gently.

"I think she would tell me," said Maria, just as gently, just a hint of doubt, and looked down at her fingers. And then, coming from somewhere, a barely heard warning whispered to them to stop. Plans, fantasies about the future, normally a right, a joy, were not theirs to have. Wiser to avoid disappointment, wiser to concentrate on the present. They lapsed into silence and thought of Katie, both hoping in their hearts she was grabbing at life while she could.

27

P ast Koblenz, where the Moselle and the Rhine meet, they slowed down. The August sun beat down on the vineyards, fruit ripening and shrivelling in the heat, and on them. Their skin had become brown, muscles harder and the soft hair on their arms had bleached white. They took every opportunity to swim in the river, clambering down banks and slipping on the large boulders at the river's edge before throwing themselves into the deliciously cold water, then drying in minutes lying on the grassy slopes, faces to the sun, eyes closed.

Just outside Bingen, after a long and welcome swim, the friends were discussing whether they could afford a meal in one of the restaurants that lined this part of the river and buy a couple of bottles of the local wine to drink with it. It was Jens's birthday, and some sort of celebration was necessary. Otto and Katie lay side by side, both of them laughing at something Bernd had said, their arms touching and the sensation made them turn and look at each other. Otto's fingers were creeping along the dry, tickly grass to find hers.

"If we are going out tonight, I need to find a shop and buy some face cream." Anna sat up and addressed Katie. Otto's hand retreated. "The skin on my face is turning into leather. Are you coming, Katie?"

Katie ran her hands over her face. The skin across her cheeks was bone dry and flaky. She smiled at Otto before sitting up. "Yes. I could do with some too."

They arranged to meet outside the hostel in a couple of hours and rode off into town.

*

The girls left their bikes against a lamp post and bought themselves an ice-cream. They sat on the kerbside nearby to watch Bingen waking up after the lunchtime hiatus, when all good folk ate lunch together and if possible, had a cat nap before afternoon business got under way again. They looked up and down the narrow road, searching lazily for a pharmacy. Shutters were being lifted and the street fluttered with awnings, some striped, some plain. There was the odd flag. Somewhere off a side alley a dog gave a half-hearted bark. There were few people about, but an elderly woman passed by and greeted them without a smile, asking where they had come from. Anna shielded her eyes against the sun to answer her.

"Duisburg."

"Uh! Muck and wealth go together." As if it was an indisputable truth and Anna and Katie were the embodiment of it. They watched her walk off and raised their eyebrows at each other.

"I think that might be a pharmacy," said Katie, pointing with her ice-cream at a shop on the other side of the road, some way off. They got up and sauntered over to it. The shutters were up and the shopkeeper, a Herr Schiller according to the sign outside, was behind the door turning the card to signal that he was open.

"Come on in, young ladies, what can I do for you?" The groups of cyclists that passed through from spring to autumn boosted trade no end and his greeting was greasily warm. He took his place behind the counter. Katie spotted the little tins of Nivea and asked for one.

Herr Schiller looked at them both and smiled broadly. "Now then, if you just give me a moment to find them, I have something that may interest you. Came in this morning and I haven't had time to put them out yet." He disappeared through a door behind and there followed brief sounds of rummaging, a parcel being ripped open.

Katie's eye had caught a small display of lipsticks and she wondered about buying one. Maybe the dark red… or would that be too dramatic?

"Here we are!" Herr Schiller re-emerged looking pleased with himself and carrying half a dozen little round tins. "This will put you ahead of the game! I'll bet no other young ladies have had a chance to get hold of one of these yet!" And he put the tins carefully in a row on the low counter and passed his upturned palm across them as if introducing an extra special guest. It was Nivea remade, repackaged for their delight and approval. The slogan 'for home and sport' still danced above the brand name, which was written in simple large letters and beneath it the same gentle instruction 'to care for the skin'. But this was so much more than that; this was Nazi Nivea; a dark blue, almost black, tin had replaced the Mediterranean blue, gold lettering twinkled at them in place of the simple white print of old.

The silence that greeted this display told the experienced shopkeeper that he might have misread the two tanned young women in front of him. He carefully laid the tins next to the others on the shelf and said, "Of course the price is exactly the same."

Anna, more diplomatic than her friend, said, "They are very striking, aren't they, Katie? But I think I'll take a blue tin."

"So will I," said Katie quickly. All thoughts of lipstick, dramatic or not, had fled from her thoughts.

They paid and Herr Schiller threw their money into the till, watching them leave. As the shop door clicked shut behind them the heat smouldering in the paving stones flung itself back up into their faces.

*

Jens, Otto and Bernd were peddling up the hill to the hostel.

"Why are hostels always at the top of hills?" laughed Bernd, panting, a question asked by one of them every time they got to this bit of the day's journey. Today had been very hot and their muscles were feeling the strain.

All three were standing on their pedals to avoid slowing, sweat ran down their arms. Otto was at the back and was surprised when, out of the corner of his eye, he found himself being overtaken. The man was grinning and managed to say, as he gradually passed him, "See you at the top." American. His rhythm didn't break, and he passed both Bernd and then Jens, who tried to chase but found he couldn't increase his pace. Another two hundred metres and they were through the gates and onto the gravel driveway that led to the hostel, a large white building, shutters closed to keep out the afternoon sun.

The American had slipped his bike into a stand, rows of which were bolted into the ground, and was drinking from his water bottle as the three pushed their bikes towards him. He wiped his mouth and grinned at them. "Name's Russell," he said in German and shook hands with each of them. Names exchanged, Bernd complimented him on his bike and Russell managed to explain that it was hired and indicated its expense by the universal gesture of rubbing his thumb and fingers together. The impressed nineteen-year-olds nodded appreciatively.

The sound of tyres on gravel made them turn their heads, expecting to see Katie and Anna but it was three other men, who greeted Russell loudly in English and said something that must have been, Otto thought, about Russell always having to be first. More introductions and handshaking. There was another American, Leo, a Frenchman, Olivier and Eric, an Englishman whose handshake was less vigorous than the others. It wasn't the first time they had encountered foreigners on their trip, but these seemed particularly friendly and keen to talk. Both Olivier and Eric spoke passable German so they could ask where they had come from that day and where they were headed.

It seems they had met two days before on the road and had decided to ride together for a couple of days. Eric and Olivier were headed for Frankfurt before starting the journey home. Russell and Leo were in Germany for longer and not sure where they were going after Frankfurt, maybe Munich. The noise of the men's talk drowned out the sound of Anna and Katie's bikes as they pushed them along the drive.

*

"The Americans are probably spies," Bernd had been thinking it over. "They weren't as keen as the other two to tell us where they had been and where they were going."

The five of them were sitting on a terrace, glasses of wine in front of them. Down in the valley, past vineyards heavy with grapes, the Rhine flowed smoothly on, evening sunlight catching and glinting on the surface of the water. They had carefully chosen the cheapest things on the menu and were content to wait while customers with deeper pockets took precedence.

"Maybe they are," said Katie, excited by the thought.

"Or maybe they're Nazis," this was Otto's suggestion, "they have quite a following in America, I've heard."

"Nonsense," said Anna, who had become smitten with Russell the minute she had set eyes on him but was determined not to let it show. "That's just propaganda. The Americans have got more sense."

"I wouldn't be so sure," said Jens, who wasn't fooled by Anna's sharp tongue and sensed her interest in the American. To his surprise he found he was jealous.

Katie sipped at her wine and realised for the first time how good it made her feel. It was a perfect evening, and she allowed her mind to drift. She was looking forward to seeing the foreigners again although they had apologetically refused the invitation to join them for the birthday celebration, saying they wanted to explore Bingen and have a few beers before getting an early night. That afternoon, as they had sat in the courtyard of the hostel, leaning against a shady wall, waiting for it to open, Katie had noticed how the Americans had kept their distance, friendly enough but preferring to talk quietly together whereas Olivier and Eric had been very keen to get to know the young Germans. She liked the way the Englishman leant forward to listen to what they had to say, and the way he pushed his spectacles up his nose.

Her hazy daydream was interrupted by Jens's laughter. Anna had been telling them about the Nazi Nivea. Otto was telling them to keep their voices down and they automatically scanned their neighbours to see if anyone had taken any notice of their conversation. But they were much too content, too comfortable with the wine and the food, and the sight of the powerful river with the hills, grey-green in the distance, to bother listening.

"At least there was no Swastika," said Bernd.

"Give it time," said Anna. "If there's money to be made, they'll appear everywhere."

"They are everywhere, in case you hadn't noticed." Jens was watching hungrily as the couple nearby were served something with dumplings.

"Maybe you shouldn't have bought it at all."

"I'm not going without my skin cream," said Anna firmly, taking a large gulp of wine.

"Dear sister!" Bernd smiled fondly at her, "principled, almost to the last!"

"Do you think we might be riding with the foreigners tomorrow?" There was sudden silence as four faces turned towards Katie, who had asked the question, before laughter broke out again.

"Well now Katie, and which of the foreigners would you like to ride next to, eh?" Bernd grinned at her.

"No, I don't mean that." She was aware of Otto's eyes on her, "It's just good to talk to people who are... who have..."

Anna came to her rescue. "A different perspective, maybe?"

"A different point of view?" offered Jens.

"An interesting accent?" Bernd. Only Otto kept quiet. Katie blushed and told them all to be quiet. They were being childish. Obviously, it was interesting to talk to people from abroad. To hear what they think of what is going on.

"We know what they think," said Otto quietly. "They think the country has gone mad."

"Then at least we can tell them we are not all the same." Katie's voice had risen.

A waitress finally brought them their food, substantial portions of sausages in gravy, new potatoes and vegetables, with a buttery sauce to go with it.

They realised how hungry they were, raised their glasses to wish Jens a happy birthday and tucked in with relish.

"I wonder if food tastes this good in England." Bernd looked into the distance as if he was thinking out loud.

Jens paused in his eating. "What do they actually eat in England, anyway?" Everyone except Katie pretended to think very hard about this.

"I think they boil everything," said Anna. "Of course the French, now they know what to do with food."

"I refuse to join in with this conversation." Katie hoped she had put a stop to it. Of course, she hadn't. During the course of the evening, oblique remarks were made about the allure of foreignness, the romanticism of the French and the stalwartness of the doughty British. Katie laughed with them, but something had moved inside her, something had ignited. She found their accented German exciting and listening to the Americans thrilling. She wanted to touch these other worlds. It was the most intense sensation she had ever experienced, intensity born out of the sure knowledge that time was running out. No time for leisurely decision making. For her there wasn't the luxury of planning adventures that were sure to be realised in some distant, positive and assured future. Her future was going to be snatched away from her before she could even imagine fully what it could be.

*

The next morning Olivier told them that Russell and Leo had set off very early and maybe they would meet up in Frankfurt. Anna just managed to hide her disappointment as they busied themselves packing up their bikes. Bernd caught Jens's eye and mouthed the word, "spies', and raised his eyebrows with an exaggerated 'I told you so' expression.

"But I hope we can ride together today," Eric smiled at all of them. His German really was very good, thought Katie, nodding enthusiastically.

"Great idea," said Otto and couldn't resist adding, "Hey Katie?" which everyone had the good grace to ignore.

There followed discussion on which route they would take. Katie noticed how Eric and Olivier tactfully left this to the Germans, listening and nodding as they consulted the maps and pointed into the distance. It was decided that they would climb the Taunus hills before heading down to Wiesbaden. A hard climb but worth it. Otto took the lead and Olivier pedalled next to him for a while. The others followed on, taking turns to ride with each other. A couple of hours later, hot and sticky, they were looking down on the river, suddenly small and winding far below them.

As they made their way down the roads that would take them just beyond Wiesbaden, a little spa town, they promised themselves a swim and a beer; Katie felt confused and excited and exhilarated by the attention she was getting from both Olivier and Eric. She watched Otto's back, broad and relaxed as they coasted downhill, but was aware only of Eric, just behind her now, and she knew that if she turned round, he would be grinning at her. Otto's beauty and grace were growing dimmer, unable to compete with the glamour of the foreigners. He knew it, of course; she didn't bother once to catch up with him and something told him it was for the best. He was certain what the future held for him; it became clearer every time he read his father's newspaper.

*

Eric was twenty-five years old. He lived in the city of Nottingham which was, he told them, in the middle of England, surrounded by hills, and a centre for textiles. He worked in the same factory as his father and was training as a manager. Katie imagined a picturesque town full of well-mannered easy-going Englishmen. He and Olivier were keen to quiz them about the present state of Germany, which they quickly noticed made the young people uncomfortable and, for the rest of their time together, they kept their questions to a minimum. But when Eric was alone with Jens or Otto they did talk about the possibility of war. Preposterous, said Eric. England didn't want it and Germany surely didn't want to take on enemies on all sides, not when the economy was on the up. Otto, listening and making guarded comments, wondered whether this enthusiastic Englishman was deliberately unwilling to understand what was driving the Nazi regime or whether there was something else, something harder, in the bright gaze behind the spectacles. He decided not to argue. Why break the spell, the happy illusion of continental harmony?

After Wiesbaden they went together to Frankfurt where they were delighted to find not only that the hostel was, compared with the others they had stayed in, unexpectedly luxurious – hot showers, comfortable beds – but that Russell and Leo were still there. Bernd had spotted them first and walked over to greet them.

"When are you off again? We didn't expect to see you." The Americans smiled their wide smiles and promised to get together that evening. They would probably be leaving tomorrow morning, not quite sure where to yet.

Later, sitting at a long trestle table in a noisy beer garden, Leo said to Otto and Jens that they seemed to be getting on very well with the Englishman and the Frenchman. Jens nodded and said yes, they were having a good time together.

"You probably have a lot in common," Leo's German was hard to understand. Otto watched him carefully, picking at what he was saying, curious as to what he was implying.

"You know, they really admire what is happening here." Leo was looking down at his beer and inclined his head towards Eric and Olivier. He seemed to be choosing his words with care. "The hard work, the drive, you know?" He lifted his head, dark eyes narrowing.

Jens shrugged and took in a large mouthful of beer to avoid saying anything. Otto was aware of something that sounded like a warning and looked over to where Katie and Anna were laughing with Russell, Eric and Olivier joining in. No, it can't have been a warning; the idea was dismissed before it became conscious. Such a cliché – Germans working hard! But Leo wasn't quite finished.

"The progress you have made, dumping old ideas. Very exciting." His tone was flat, and his eyes held Otto's. Otto picked up the sarcasm.

"Of course, not so progressive if you're Jewish, like me," Leo added, eyes never wavering.

Anything that Otto had wanted to say froze in his throat. His neck flushed pink, and he felt ashamed. He looked once again at the group at the other end of the trestle table and to cover his embarrassment he raised his glass. "Well, let's drink to us, at least," and added, to his own surprise, "and to survival." But this last little phrase was drowned out as they all clinked glasses, spilling a little, laughing and shouting 'prosit, prosit' to everyone in turn, everyone flushed and happy, Otto watching Katie's eyes light up when she looked at the Englishman.

*

And on the road again, homeward bound, Otto battled with the worm of doubt he felt about Eric, or was it jealousy, gnawing at his heart. At Koblenz they said good-bye to the Americans who said they were heading for Belgium and then England before going back to the United States. Invitations to "Come over any time! You'd all be most welcome," rang in their ears, Anna fighting her sense of loss, Jens standing firmly next to her, waving them off.

Eric and Olivier stayed with them. They both wanted to have a look at the Autobahn built as an experiment by the Mayor of Cologne, Konrad Adenauer, to link his city with Düsseldorf back in 1932. Hitler had had publicity photos taken of himself, man of the people, shovelling spadefuls of dirt as the project began. They all laughed at that. Then, in Düsseldorf Eric and Olivier took their leave of them; they were going to Paris together by train, after which Eric would return to England. He would write to Katie. She had his address.

28

*Duisburg, September 1938; Prime Minister Chamberlain and
Hitler were resolving the Sudetenland crisis.*

In Munich the sun shone down on the combined heads of the
desperate maintainer of peace and the wily champion of the
Sudetenland. Meanwhile, as they talked and made their promises
to each other, Hansgünther was walking home in one of the heaviest
downpours that summer. The morning had started bright and warm,
and he had walked over to Werner's house and from there to the
forest, where they had spent a happy few hours playing soldiers,
constructing camouflaged shelters, lining up, standing to attention
and 'sieg heiling' a bit because it seemed right, dying and being reborn
time after time. The trees gave good cover and both boys, by the time
hunger called them home, felt they had fooled the enemy, alternately
British, French or Russian, and killed a sufficient number of them.

It had suddenly become quite dark, and they were glad to get
back onto the forest paths. The rain fell first in fat drops then in a
torrent that broke through the canopy of trees and quickly drenched
them. The novelty of warm rain after the dry summer made them
slow down and watch as the brittle undergrowth took on a shine and
the smells changed around them. They came to a little bridge that
took them over a stream and stopped for a while to see the water
speed up, stepping down to put their hands in and scoop up some
leaves and twigs that offered themselves and kicking at the muddy
bank to see what would happen. The kicking became quite vigorous
as they noticed how certain angles produced a far-reaching muddy
spray although most landed on their legs and trousers.

The rain had eased a little, but they could feel water dripping down their backs and when they wiped the water from their faces, they noticed with delight how they had been transformed into very authentic-looking blackened commandos. Their boots had thick mud on the soles and up the sides almost to the laces. Two very grubby boys emerged onto Lothar Strasse and by the time they got to Gneisenau Strasse and saw the car they were in a very sorry state.

It was enormous, bigger than any car he had seen in Uncle Anton's garage, long, black and sleek with two small swastika flags, wet and bedraggled, perched on either side of the massive front bumpers. It was parked outside a small building which also displayed two limp dripping flags above the door. A couple of men in uniform, their boots as black and shiny as the car, were huddled in a nearby doorway, smoking, backs to the street.

The boys crossed the road to get a better look at the car. "It must be Hitler's." Hansgünther was absolutely certain that such an impressive vehicle could only belong to the Führer. Werner saw no reason to disagree. Confusingly, magnificent as this machine was it also became an immediate object of loathing as it belonged to his father's sworn enemy, although he must never, ever disclose this fact to anyone. It was top secret.

Hansgünther glanced at the soldiers then put his hand on the back door handle of the car. Oiled and polished, it gave without a sound and opened.

"What are you doing?" Werner asked, getting worried.

"We could have a look inside?" At that moment the rain resumed with a fury, clattering down on the pavement and car, drowning out sound, forcing the two soldiers deeper into their narrow shelter.

The two boys with their sodden, filthy trousers and their boots oozing mud climbed into the pristine car, admiring with the eyes of artists their improvements as their hands trailed over the backs of the front seats and their backsides slid across the impeccable brown leather upholstery. They climbed silently out the other side.

"Again, let's do it again!" Because they could; the enemy was stupid, hadn't noticed a thing. They crept around the car, re-entered, this time taking care to scrape as much mud onto the carpeted floor as they could in the remaining seconds allotted to them before Hitler came out.

The car doors clicked shut behind them. They crossed the street, adopting a casual walk, hands in pockets, until they passed the shop that stood on the corner of Kammer Strasse. Then, whooping with joy and pent-up excitement, they raced for home and the wrath of their mothers.

*

Luckily for him it was Katie he encountered first. She was unlocking their letterbox as her mud-smeared little brother came through the house door. Eric would have been home for a couple of weeks now and she was hoping for a letter. Nothing had arrived yet.

"For heaven's sake! What has happened to you?"

Hansgünther beamed. He was so pleased to see her. "Me and Werner have just sabotaged Hitler!" Good word that. Sabotage.

"Mm, unlikely, as he's in Munich telling lies to the British Prime Minister."

"Oh." His brown eyes filled with disappointment. "Well, it must have been someone important." His act of heroism can't possibly have been in vain.

"What exactly have you done?" Katie was standing with her hands on her hips, but he was undaunted. She would be proud of him, he was sure.

The stair well was empty, so she let him tell his tale. Halfway through she told him to keep his voice down.

When he'd finished, she noticed that he was cold, beginning to shiver. "Let's go upstairs and get those clothes off you." And he trudged up the stairs in front of her, exultation slowly ebbing, while she watched his back, boyish shoulder blades visible through the rain-soaked shirt and smiled with pride.

"Go straight into the bathroom," she told him as they walked in. Then she raised her voice and aimed it at the open kitchen door. "I've got a very muddy boy out here, Mama. I'll get him sorted out."

Maria popped her head round the door and said, "High time

he was back, what on earth has he been doing all this time?" then disappeared back to her cooking.

"Wash – properly! I'll get you some clean clothes. You can tell everyone about your adventure afterwards." He looked at her, confusion and disappointment at a lack-lustre response written all over his face. She noticed and smiled encouragingly. "They'll listen more carefully if you are clean." He nodded. *That made sense*, he thought as she closed the door on him.

*

The response was mixed. Heinz gave a loud hoot and clapped him on the back. "Brave boy! Mind you, when the Gauleiter comes to call I will wash my hands of you. I dread to think what happens to insubordinates these days."

Maria's "What on earth were you and Werner thinking of?" was met with, "It was my idea, not Werner's. He'd never dare…"

"Never mind whose idea it was." Heinrich had his arms folded and was leaning back on his chair. The plates were still on the table and Hansgünther, despite the concentrated gaze of his family, was running one of his fingers around his plate to lick up the remains of the gravy.

Maria and Heinrich were thinking the same thing. If anyone did see him and knew who he was, someone, probably some sixteen-year-old uppity youth, would come to call. They could handle that, but it would put their household on the map, make them objects of interest. It seemed unlikely, though. The weather was so atrocious… no-one about. And it was Saturday, so all the shops had shut up for the day.

"How much muck, exactly, did you manage to spread?" Katie's tone was that of an inquisitor, but her brothers recognised the opportunity for some fun.

"Yes," said Heinz thoughtfully, "I would say any punishment would depend on the quantity and consistency of the deposits, especially on the seats where they would have the most impact." Hansgünther beamed at him and he eagerly started to explain.

"Well, the second time we went through," this was new information, and his parents exchanged a look and raised their eyes, "I managed to walk across the seats, so there was loads of mud and some grit..."

"Maximum damage then," Heinz nodded approvingly, "the sentence will have to be severe."

"Enough!" Heinrich wasn't angry but his boy would have to be warned. "Clear the table, I'll speak to you later." And as Hansgünther noisily and gratefully gathered the plates and knives and forks together Heinrich said quietly, "And you two for heaven's sake don't encourage him. Men are being shot for less."

"Papa!" Katie knew it was true but there was no need to frighten him. He returned her stare but said nothing else.

Hansgünther filled the sink with hot water, rolled up his sleeves and started on the washing-up while the family sat in silence until Maria, unable to keep still, got up to help him. She put her head very close to his and whispered, "Promise me you will never do anything like that again, promise me!" Hansgünther looked up at her, his brown eyes showing no hint of remorse. He was too full of his brother and sister's admiration. "I mean it! If the wrong people saw it... it's simply too dangerous."

He shrugged and said, "All right, I promise. But it was only a joke, it was only mud," and, unable to resist, "nice and sticky!" And he looked over his shoulder at Katie and Heinz who started to laugh and then up at his mother who could never be cross with him for long and who now pressed her fingers on her mouth to hide the smile.

"Oh, for goodness' sake!" Heinrich scraped the chair back as he got up and headed for the door. "You are all hopeless! I'm going down to the cellar." It was his favourite retreat. He would inspect and rearrange his collections of food and emergency items. It helped to keep him calm.

"I thought Papa would be proud of me." Hansgünther held up a plate and let it drip for a second before stacking it on the wooden draining board.

"He is proud of you but he's also worried that you'll get into trouble. And trouble for you means trouble for the rest of us; we've tried to explain that to you before."

He thought about that for a minute. "I see. Sorry, Mama," and he leant over to her. She kissed the top of his head and they finished the washing-up in silence.

*

Heinrich contemplated the well-stocked cellar shelves with satisfaction, but he needed to clear an extra space for wood. Deliveries had been made as usual, but he was sure they would need more. There was a pile of newspapers which he pushed to one side; he had been saving them for the past twelve months, he needed to learn how to turn them into bricks for burning. Kindling would never be a problem with the forest so close by. Bundles, stacked against a wall, were drying out. Enough for one winter but how long could a war take? Maria had done well this summer in the garden. There were rows of bottled beans, peas and a sack full of potatoes. Even jars of white asparagus, one of his favourites. Apples wrapped in newspaper as well as preserved pears and cherries. On one of the shelves he had put a wooden box with a lid. He wanted Maria to start buying extra flour and sugar to store there. Hopefully the mice wouldn't be able to get at it. Stacked next to the box were six little tins of Nestlé's evaporated milk. Heinrich smiled thinly. She's getting the idea, he thought.

Back upstairs, the whole family listened to the radio as it broadcast Prime Minister Chamberlain's return to London. The broadcaster reported on the bobbing of umbrellas, the waving of hats and the cheering, muted because of the rain, and the little piece of paper held up in modest triumph. Katie watched her father's face grimace as Peace for Our Time was declared.

*

November 9ᵗʰ, 1938

Hansgünther was looking over Heinz's shoulder as he skimmed through the newspaper that their father had left on the kitchen table.

A banner headline read: ***Anniversary of 1923 Munich Putsch to be Celebrated Nationwide.***

"What was the Putsch?" Hansgünther really wanted to get back to his room to finish a drawing he had started of an aeroplane flying over a mountain; he hadn't got the shape of the wings quite right and it was bothering him. But the word 'putsch' caught his attention. Heinz swivelled his head round and gave his brother a hard look.

"You obviously haven't been paying attention at school, have you?" Hansgünther shrugged. "It was when our glorious Führer tried to take control by conquering a beer hall. Chances of success were slim. The police caught him, and he went to prison."

"Why did they let him out?" It seemed a sensible question, so he was surprised to hear his father, busy polishing shoes by the sink, give a derisory snort behind him.

"Because they didn't want to lock him up in the first place… and," he paused briefly, for dramatic effect, thought Heinz, who had heard it all before, "it was more of a two-year holiday than a prison sentence – special food, visitors whenever he wanted, writing materials, and *armchairs* for heaven's sake!" Heinrich's polishing became more vigorous as each of Hitler's perks was listed.

"Well, that's ridiculous," said Hansgünther, shoving his hands down into his pockets and heading for the bedroom, pleased to hear himself sounding very much like his older brother. As the kitchen door shut behind him his head was already busy with the problem of how to use his pencil to show the blur of the propeller of the Russian fighter plane as it flew over the mountains of Northern Spain.

"By the way, I don't want you going anywhere this evening." Heinrich had his back to Heinz; he was washing his hands at the sink.

Heinz straightened his back, annoyed. "What do you mean?"

"There'll be too much drinking going on. Hitler's virtually declared it a public holiday, the streets won't be safe." Heinrich turned, drying his hands on a towel, to meet the hostile glare of his son.

"But I was going to meet up with Tomas," and with Ilse, with a bit of luck. Heinz could tell that his evening was about to be ruined. His father shrugged and shook his head; it couldn't be helped.

"But I'll be letting him down, I can't let him know…" and Ilse was so pretty.

"I'm not talking about this anymore, Heinz. You're not going anywhere."

Heinz pushed the chair noisily backwards and stomped out of the room, bumping into his mother in the passage on his way to the bedroom. "The man is completely unreasonable," he shouted, red-faced and furious, before slamming the door as loudly as he dared.

Maria looked questioningly at Heinrich. "I told him he couldn't go out tonight," he said.

"It won't be that bad, surely."

"Not taking any chances."

Maria sighed and wondered how long she should wait before going to talk to Heinz.

Katie, rereading her letters from Eric, was barely aware of the commotion.

*

But it was that bad. As Heinz fumed in his bedroom and Hansgünther worked on the shape of the fighter plane wings, down in Munich, where, in a great smoky beer hall the hierarchy were attending the anniversary meal, celebrating the failed *putsch*, phones were busy. Lines buzzed with messages to the regional Gestapo to expect outbreaks of violence directed against synagogues and propertied Jews. Telex and telegrams sent on Hitler's personal order stated that on no account should the Gestapo organise such attacks, but they should never be discouraged. Goebbels, always the patriot, declared that care should be taken to minimise damage to German property and businesses. Party activists, already enjoying celebrating the 1923 uprising, set to with relish and in the early hours simultaneous fires, hellish in their intensity, burnt down synagogues across the country, Jewish businesses were smashed up, windows exploded in the heat and by morning streets were littered with a layer of broken glass. Little notice was taken of the looting ban.

And why this flurry of murderous activity? Well, by great good fortune and extraordinary coincidence, on November 7th a Polish Jew by the name of Greenspan, angry that his parents, who lived in Germany, had been deported, had walked into the German embassy in Paris where he was living at the time and killed the first man he saw. What an opportunity this was to ignite the growing anti-Semitism, now so embedded in the minds of Germans, especially the young, into an act of full-blown hatred. As Goebbels sipped his champagne late into the night, he smiled at the thought of the righteous mayhem taking place across the Reich.

*

Heinrich listened to the foreign news reports the next evening with his head buried in his hands. The synagogue in Duisburg on Landwehr Strasse had been virtually destroyed. The family had slept through it all.

29

After the taking of the Sudetenland, there followed the inevitable annexation of Bohemia and Moravia in March 1939, and then the annexation of Memelland in Lithuania in the same month. Now Hitler had his eyes on the Polish Corridor, a stretch of land on the Baltic, outrageously dividing a portion of northern Germany.

Duisburg, July 1939

Katie was staring at the contents of one of her bedroom drawers when Lisl put her head around the door and, smiling, walked in and gave her a hug. Then, holding her at arm's length said,

"So you are really going?" Katie nodded without looking up and turned again to the drawer.

"I don't know what to pack. It's summer but England is different, colder, I think. My new suit for best, a raincoat. I only have one suitcase." Suddenly she sat down on the bed and burst into tears.

Lisl sat down with her and held her close. "It's the excitement, it gets to you. I was like this before my wedding," and she sighed at the memory. Katie shook her head and tried to wipe her face. Lisl found a handkerchief in her bag and gave it to her.

"I want to go so badly but I hate the thought of leaving everyone, especially Hansgünther. He's only ten."

"It's a holiday! You'll be back by Christmas!" She took the handkerchief and dabbed around Katie's nose. Katie pulled her head back and gave her immaculately dressed aunt an arch look.

"I don't know how you can be so sure of that."

"My brother has been wrong before, you know!" Lisl had driven

Heinrich into a rage when she'd stated that Hitler might 'have unpleasant ideas' but no-one could deny that Germany was a truly great nation once again. Maria told him it was how most people thought. When he heard that Lisl and Manfred were thinking of moving to Berlin he muttered, "Good riddance," into his newspaper accompanied by much foot twitching and paper rattling. The move had been delayed several times.

"Papa is very keen for me to go."

"They like Eric, don't they?"

Katie smiled at the mention of his name. "Yes, they do."

"You must follow your heart. You must go."

Katie stood up and went back to the drawer and grabbed a handful of underclothes which she threw into the overflowing suitcase lying on the floor. Then she knelt down with a thud next to it and began to furiously fold and neaten the assorted clothes.

"It's not because they like him that they want me to go, you know." The tears were gone; here was something she needed to get off her chest. "Nothing to do with my heart or my happiness," she put mocking emphasis on the last few words, "it's to get me away, out of Germany. They've got the crazy idea that I'm going to get myself into trouble." The look she gave Lisl then, over her shoulder, was one of complete bafflement.

Lisl met her gaze. "But you want to go?"

"Yes!" Katie snapped back.

"And you did get yourself into trouble."

"Oh, for goodness' sake, they were just boys!"

*

Young, maybe, but not boys. After Katie had come back from Cologne, her travel visa secured, she felt invincible. She was getting away, out, to England, the land of calm and reason. She'd written to Eric to tell him that she would be able to travel in August, after she had finished her contracted time with Frau Wettmann. It had been a dull year but the letters from Eric and his visit at Easter had made it fly past.

She had been in the town centre shopping for things to take to England; gifts for Eric and his family, two pairs of stockings for herself. It had been fun, discarding and selecting, spending her own money. Now she was walking home in the late afternoon, swinging the small shopping bag and daydreaming about the journey ahead of her. She walked through a short tunnel where the wallpaper of their lives plastered the concrete pillars. Huge swastikas, portraits of Hitler and posters exhorting the young to love the Reich above all things. She had learned to ignore them but today she took note, enjoying the notion that she would soon be gone, leave it all behind.

Once through, she crossed narrow streets of little houses occupied by railway workers. It was a dull afternoon, the sun disappearing behind clouds and buildings, heavy, still air promising a shower. She heard a shout, a whoop as she approached Melchior Strasse. Sounds intruding on her thoughts, muted then louder. She looked and focussed, her mind rearranging itself to witness the present; she saw the men in brown laughing and painting a Star of David on one of the windows, then another on the door. She froze and stopped. She saw the words 'Jew house' already daubed on the wall in red paint. A few seconds passed as the pit of her stomach lurched at the fuzzy memory of Marthe, her beautiful friend, disappeared. Luise, humiliated. Her head, her body were overtaken with a purple fury. No thinking, no making a decision. Her legs moved toward them.

"Why are you doing this?" Now she was next to them, close enough to see their faces, smell their beery breath. The three of them stopped what they were doing and looked at her, surprised.

"They've all gone! Why are doing this?" A veil of angry mist obscured the men, and she didn't see the arms rise and the fists clench. "These are people's homes! Men, women and children live here!" Someone was screeching. Was that her voice? "They've gone, all gone!" And her face was wet with tears and through them she saw them laughing at her, coming towards her, poking and pushing her backwards.

"Little Jew-lover, are you? Sorry to see the back of the rats, are you?"

For a moment their faces blurred together into one ugly sneer then one of them shoved her so violently that she fell down. She scrabbled to pick up her bag, to get up and move away from them. Now she was frightened. She pushed the hair out of her face and tried to look defiant as she stared back at them. The street was deserted.

"What's your name, Jew-lover?" One of the men stepped towards her.

"Katie Cremers." Her knee hurt. Little drops of rain were beginning to fall. "Where do you live?"

"Kammer Strasse." No point in lying.

"Go home, bitch. We've got work to do." He motioned her away with his head. She turned slowly to move off, straightening her skirt.

"We'll remember you," he said.

"We certainly will," said another with a leer. They all laughed.

She prayed they wouldn't notice how she was beginning to shake. Around the corner, off towards Kammer Strasse, the walk seemed to take forever. Only when she reached Bismark Strasse did she turn her head. No-one was following. The only sound was the gentle movement of branches overhead, the delicate sound of raindrops hitting the leaves. A dog accompanied her across the road, nose assuredly pointing forward, tail optimistically upward. It kept a discreet distance ahead of her until she reached her front door.

As it slammed shut behind her, she felt her legs buckle. She held the handrail and sank down onto a step, hunched, keeping close to the wall. In the semi-gloom she concentrated on controlling her breathing and noticed her torn knees. No hiding them, she thought, or the rip at the bottom of her skirt. She took a breath then began the climb, preparing what she would say to her parents.

*

After Lisl had left, Maria came and helped Katie. Everything was taken out of the suitcase and arranged in piles on the bed. Some things discarded, some added. The unspoken dilemma was that no-one could be sure when she would return. Would she need her winter coat? How about at least one warm skirt? The questions were all code for 'when will war be declared?' In which case would she be coming home at all? Maria couldn't face that, wouldn't allow it to be said. Instead, she declared that another suitcase was essential and would go to see Aunt Botha, who had an array of smart leather cases she and Anton used when they went on one of their driving holidays. A second case would solve the problem.

*

At his desk, by the door, Heinrich listened to the talk in the office. As he dealt with small fry sent from the courts, misdemeanours, divorce settlements – oh look, here there is a Herr Müller successfully divorcing his wife (née Sussmann and complete with her own little yellow star) – all of which needed transcribing, recording, filing, he listened to chatter about the Führer's legitimate claims on Danzig. And why not, after all, the whole of Poland? He was right, surely, to begin to make positive overtures to the Soviet Union, a powerful nation to have as an ally; the spineless western leaders were a waste of time. Some kept quiet during these infrequent and snatched observations, maybe nodding and making muffled noises. Heinrich, largely ignored, took his time, organised the paperwork meticulously, watched the clock.

Walking home past enthusiastic last-minute shoppers, cafés and bars just opening, welcoming groups of young people, children hurrying home from sports halls, he thought how normal everything looked and felt. How could human beings delude themselves to such an extent? Claus had laughed when they'd talked about it. Of course they can, he'd said, anything else would be to think the unthinkable. Thank God Katie was going to get out. He'd been angry with her after her incident with the Stormtroopers, angrier than he'd meant. But she could have jeopardised her trip to England, imagine that! Soon she would be safe, no matter what happened, she would be safe.

*

And now she was on the boat train. It was the eighteenth of August 1939. Suitcases were stored above her, checked and double-checked by her father. He'd jumped down onto the platform just as the whistle blew, doors slamming, pistons hissing. He had held her close, something he hadn't done for a long time, but he hadn't been able to speak. He tried to but coughed instead as he stroked her cheek. Slowly, slowly the train pulled away and she saw her mother's distraught face smiling bravely, Günther standing alone, confused, unhappy. All faces were upturned to the passing carriages, white and blurring together, a hand raised here and there, mouths slightly open. And ghosts, did she see ghosts? Did she imagine Theo, waving, Otto, giving her a sad thumbs up, Marthe, smiling her knowing, ironic smile, Luise, turning away?

She looked around her. Superficially normal. There were women with baskets on their laps heading for local destinations and smartly dressed couples and families ready for a longer journey. Soon people started to search and find their tickets, identification papers and visas. The ticket inspector was making his way down the aisle and any chatter there had been, was silenced as he checked, frowned, hesitated and moved on. Documents were stuffed back into pockets and bags amid silent sighs of relief. Conversations restarted, children were given apples to eat, and all watched as the buildings gave way to green fields and the train sped on to the Belgian border.

At Aachen everyone had to get off and change trains. Children and suitcases were carried and dragged to the opposite platform and the train for all stations to Ostend arrived promptly. As Katie settled herself once again, cases stacked with difficulty above her, she saw a large contingent of soldiers on the platform beyond the railway tracks. Their helmets were strapped to their rucksacks. Officers, some in black, were standing some distance away. All were noisy, smoking. All looked up when the guard walked down their platform shouting "Berlin, Berlin! The train to Berlin is arriving in three minutes!" Cigarettes were shoved into the corners of mouths, the sergeants began shouting commands, and rucksacks were hoisted onto shoulders. And then they were obliterated from view as the train, enormous, deafening, spewing steam, rolled in to take them to the east.

Katie looked around at her silent companions. The women with baskets and the men in work clothes were no longer among them. Left were the travellers, like herself, wary of last-minute delays, eager to get across the border, watchful as the Belgian guards and ticket inspectors got on board, holding their breath until the whistle blew and the wheels turned. The train, now a refuge of sorts, a means of escape, seemed to exhale an audible sigh of relief. Conversation remained guarded; a habit not easily broken. Some mention of family in Brussels, a possible trip to Paris. Katie said little. She leant her head back and closed her eyes, allowing thoughts of home, of family to drift and be replaced by the prospect of seeing Eric again, of his arms around her, his body pressed close. She smiled sleepily at the memory of his visit three long months before, her parents' delight at his Englishness, her father's quizzing on the state of British politics, confusion at Eric's assertion that Germany was the more 'mature' nation from which Britain had much to learn. Well, maybe not just now, Heinrich had said, and they had all laughed it off. Maria was impressed that he spoke such good German. Her brothers were in awe of this foreigner, unsettled by this interloper, and kept their distance. Eric had borrowed Heinz's bike and they had gone on rides in the forest, where they learned a little more about each other's bodies and planned her visit to England.

At last, they reached Ostend. The corridor that ran along the compartments was packed with people, so it took a while to get off the train. Finally, jostled and pushed by others who seemed to know where they wanted to go, she found herself on the platform and herded towards the exit and the signs for the boats. Dover! There it was! A minute's searching had her heading in the right direction. Around her she heard English spoken and occasionally French. It felt delicious, the excitement of last summer all over again. The cases were heavy, her bag was strung around her shoulder and she moved forward awkwardly. Suddenly they all had to stop and queue to show passports, tickets, boarding documents and visas. Families, couples, individuals shuffled forward, scrabbling for the paperwork, pushing suitcases with their feet. Then, waved on by the Belgian controller, she went through enormous gates which led to the dockside and the ramps leading up to the ship, already groaning with people. She could smell the sea, seagulls squawked overhead.

As she clambered up, holding tight to her cases, she watched, as, at the other end of the ship, cranes loaded swinging baskets of luggage on board, dockers shouting and yelling to each other. She spotted a cello case wedged in among one of them, strong arms steadying the basket as it was lowered.

The deck was wet and slippery, and she followed the people in front of her as they made their way to the narrow iron steps up to the middle deck. Any benches had long since been taken and she finally found a place near the front of the ship, where people were setting up little territories for themselves using suitcases as demarcation zones. She used one of hers as a seat, past caring what might get squashed, and the other as a prop to stop it moving about. Then she spotted a small space next to a bench and moved her cases. Now she could lean against the painted wall and felt altogether more secure.

Again sitting on a case, she pulled her skirt around her knees, keeping her feet in, and watched as more people managed to squeeze themselves into any vacant spots. She had exchanged a glance and a smile with the two women sitting on the bench next to her and now realised they were speaking English. She could understand nothing of what they said and thought about how she would manage when she got to England. 'Don't worry. Just show people your tickets. They'll help you.' Of course, Eric was right, English people were nice. There wouldn't be a problem. Suddenly she was aware of a voice directed at her. One of the women was bending towards her and saying something. Katie turned to her and immediately the woman laughed and said, in perfect German *"Ach, natürlich! Sie sind Deutsch! Entschuldigung."* Katie laughed back and apologised for not understanding. They were in their thirties, she guessed and well dressed. Greys and creams. So English, she thought admiringly.

"I was asking if you would like a cigarette." She noticed for the first time the open packet being offered.

"Oh, no. No thank you. I don't smoke." She watched them light up and blow smooth plumes of white smoke into the air and decided that she would start soon.

"Going to London, are you?" said one.

Their faces were powdered, small, neat mouths lined in red. She felt her own must look young, unsophisticated and naked in comparison.

"Well, actually I'm going to Nottingham," she pronounced it carefully, giving definition to each of the three syllables. "My friend has invited me." The women's faces remained impassive and watched her carefully.

"Difficult time for a holiday," said one. Katie nodded, unsure how to further this conversation in the wake of such a self-evident truth.

"My name is Madge, by the way," said Madge to lighten things.

"And I'm Valery, call me Val," she stretched out her hand in true German style to shake Katie's, who realised she had missed this little formality to set the scene for continued talk.

"My name is Katie Cremers and…" she was going to say it was the first time she had travelled by boat when the funnel which happened to be directly above them let out an immense gush of steam and the accompanying noise made talk impossible. She desperately wanted to watch as the ship left the harbour, and the women yelled and indicated she should go to the railings and they would watch her luggage. By the time she had found herself a space the *Prince Leopold* was leaving the dockside, men were pulling in the ropes, a couple with a young boy were waving wildly and Katie thought how much Hansgünther would have loved this; her heart lurched at the thought of him, of Heinz giving her an awkward adolescent hug. She squeezed her eyes tight shut to stop the tears and opened them to see the oily water broaden out between her and the land, the grey expanse becoming wider and wider as the ship gained speed, and above the gulls screeching ceaselessly. No going back! No going back!

When she clambered back to her place Madge was sitting by herself on the bench and motioned to her to sit next to her. "Val's gone to see if she can find something to drink," then, looking around, "I've never seen the boat so full. Not surprising, I suppose." Katie looked more carefully at the people, bulging bags and suitcases, children draping themselves over them being organised by their parents. Some were Jewish, she could see that now. French, Dutch,

Belgian. She thought of the young man in the consulate in Cologne.

"They're getting away," said Katie and when she looked back into Madge's face, she found herself being scrutinised, the blue eyes turned hard.

"Yes, they are," Madge's voice was sombre. Then, after the briefest pause and eyes still on Katie, she laughed and said, "So are we! Redundant as from last week!"

"Oh?" Katie looked at her quizzically, not sure if it would be right to ask questions.

But Madge was happy to talk, the jolly tone restored.

"Embassy staff were told last week to pack up and go home. We were both in Berlin and travelled to Cologne two days ago. What a rush!" She smoothed down her skirt and lifted one foot to examine her shoe as if worried about her appearance. Katie thought she looked perfect.

"Look what I found!" It was Val holding three small bottles of beer. Katie jumped up and sat back down on her suitcases. "Thanks," said Val, giving them each a bottle and settling herself back on the bench. "And that's not all," she added, and took out of her pocket a miniature bottle of whisky and waved it triumphantly aloft.

"Splendid," said Madge with feeling. "I could definitely do with a drop of that."

They clinked bottles and Katie dared to say, "Cheers," in English as Eric had taught her and the Englishwomen laughed and said she was on the way to mastering the language. Then Val unscrewed the whisky bottle and offered it to Katie.

"In England we call this a 'chaser', is there a name for it in German?"

Katie had the little bottle in her hand. "I don't think so," she thought of how Papa would describe it, "just something like 'another little sip'," and she took a very small sip, warm and comforting in her throat. She began to watch a family sitting nearby.

Madge smiled. "Always room for another little sip," she said, taking a hearty slug before passing the bottle to Val, who did the same before screwing the top back on.

The woman was getting something out of her shopping bag,

rummaging and talking to herself. Two children were sitting expectantly side by side, silent, coats buttoned up to their chins against the possibility of sea breezes. The mother finally found some bread and she gave a piece to each of them. They didn't speak; the mother resumed her distracted rummaging.

"Well now, Katie," Madge broke into Katie's thoughts, a hint of the official in her voice which Katie vaguely picked up, "first time on one of these steam packets? First time in England?"

Katie nodded, her eyes dancing. It felt like the first time she'd breathed so deeply, the first time she was coming into touching distance of so many possibilities. A sudden spray of water shot over the railing and made a group of children squeal with delight. She took another sip of her beer and noticed the salty taste when she licked her lips. She smiled happily at the women who were both looking at her.

"What do you know about Nottingham?" It was Val this time, leaning forward, waiting for an answer.

"Not very much." She thought hard, through the beer and whisky. "It's a pretty place." What had Eric told her? "Good for cycling."

"Yes, I believe it is." Val sat back and crossed her legs.

"But it is a funny time to come, Katie."

Madge had mentioned this before, hadn't she? "Well, hopefully I will be home by Christmas…" it had always been wishful thinking, something to keep Mama from breaking down. She looked directly at Madge. "I don't really want to go back right now."

"No." Madge nodded and her face relaxed. Val had rolled up her jacket and put it behind her head as a pillow. She was ready for a nap, she said. Conversation seemed to be at an end.

*

Leaning over the railings, gulls wheeling around her, she saw the famous white cliffs that Eric had told her to look out for. People were gathering themselves onto the deck ready to disembark. Katie was practicing the words 'Liverpool Street Station' to herself, her next destination. Madge and Val were a little ahead of her in the queue and as they shuffled forward towards the gangplank Madge came to say goodbye.

"Good luck, Katie. I hope everything goes well for you."

"Thank you. Thank you very much." Excited, still dazzled, Katie had to shout back above the din around them.

"Just take care – and always tell the truth!" Madge squeezed her arm and gave her the kindest smile before hurrying to rejoin Val, who gave a little wave.

What a funny thing to say. As if she would ever do anything else.

Off the boat, towards passport control, the two women were ushered rapidly through and were gone. Katie joined the queue for foreign nationals. It took some time.

30

Eight months later. May 1940. The rapid fall of France and the Netherlands led to fear of an imminent German invasion of Britain. In the panic toleration of foreigners gave way to intense suspicion.

She had been put on a train with the police officer. Yes, that's right, she struggled to remember exactly, the man had sat beside her all the way from Nottingham to London. Bareheaded and a grey mackintosh raincoat. She must remember all this so she could tell Eric when he came down to see her, which wouldn't be long now, she was sure. The man had been kind and bought her a cup of tea at the station, which she couldn't hold properly because she was shaking so much. Vaguely aware of it being put into her hands. One minute she was outside No. 32 staring wildly, first at Eric's mother and then at Elsie, who was crying and shouting at the policeman, who was shouting back, and the next she was bundled into the car. Eric wasn't there. He was at work, he had to go to work.

Mrs Clarkson was wearing her pinny – such a nice word – the one with the little blue flowers on it and leaning against the door frame. Her skin looked grey. The car door slammed, and Elsie's face appeared at the window. Distraught, eyes frantic. What had she said? Don't worry? Was that it? Then her face disappeared, and the door was opened, just long enough for a bag to be shoved onto her lap. A large linen laundry bag – there it was now, next to her on a chair – someone must have run and collected some of her things. Then there was Arthur's face, hot, sweating, he must have run, heard somehow about the arrest and belted round, shouting through the window as the car was pulling away from the kerb. His mouth was opening and closing. He looked like Eric, but it wasn't Eric. She wanted Eric not his brother.

The train. What happened on the train? There was the rush of steam, the heavy thigh of the policeman which he moved self-consciously whenever it drifted too close. Sometimes the train stopped. People got off, got on. When she closed her eyes against the looks from the other passengers, she saw Elsie's tear-stained face and something else. Olive, by the neighbour's wall, chewing her fingernails and Vinnie next to her, excited, watching reactions. Oh Eric! It might have been Vinnie! She never liked me, did she?

She sat, trapped, by the window. The glass was grimy, and her head banged against it sometimes, as the train jolted. Occasionally she caught a glimpse of her reflection, skimming along the countryside, sunken, cast down. Then movement and the talk around her was of arrival and she saw huge letters roll past the window. St. Pancras. Brakes screeched. The policeman made her wait till everyone else had got off and then told her to go. He carried her bag. She stepped down onto an emptying platform, looked at the hurrying backs of the travellers heading towards the barriers, even noticed the giant Bovril advertisements telling her that it 'helps prevent that sinking feeling'. She looked up at the vast vaulted ceiling. Eric, you told me about this, one of your favourite buildings, you should be here.

Briefly the din and racket of London hit her then she was in another car, doors slammed, the noise ceased, and they were off. To Holloway Prison.

*

And now she was sitting in a small room with pale yellow walls, her bundle of clothes beside her, looking at the heavy metal door that had been locked just moments before. She expected it to open any minute; someone was going to come and say she could go now. This was all a mistake. She could go back to Eric or maybe home to Germany. The thought of her parents made her eyes sting, but she was frozen, her body tight and rigid.

When the warder unlocked the door and walked in, she saw a straight-backed girl sitting very still, raised eyes suddenly hopeful and expectant. "Right then, let's get you sorted."

Her bundle was taken from her and she was given clothes to change into. Beige-coloured shirt and overall. Then photographed and fingerprints taken. Questions were asked, "Why did you come to England?" She was listened to as she told them the truth. Always tell the truth, the woman on the boat had said. My boyfriend lives here. He'll be here soon. And I hate the Nazis and what they are doing to Germany.

"Well, anyone could say that, couldn't they?" But the woman wrote it down anyway.

She was taken to her cell. Every footstep set off a dull reverberation, a sad murmur along the long metal corridors that radiated the vast space, three floors high. Her room had a bed, a toilet, a table. On the table were a beaker and some toiletries. On the bed a grey cotton nightdress. Someone brought her a sandwich and a cup of sweet tea.

"You can 'ave your tea in 'ere tonight. Tomorrow you'll 'ave it in the dining room with everyone else." The door clanked shut and a key turned in the lock.

No light switches. The lights were turned off by someone, somewhere and she lay in the dark, sleeping, dreaming and waking. The darkness was so intense she was unsure whether she was awake or asleep. A dream where she was being pulled and pushed off a train gave way to noises close by, crying and shouting that stopped abruptly. She felt her face, her cheeks were wet. She could hear shouts and sobbing coming from the rooms nearby. She stared into the darkness and thought of Eric, after all they had done together, spoken about, promised each other. He would come and sort it out. He must come. Her eyes closed. More dreams, this time in the kitchen of No.32. Eric's mum and Elsie, both looking at her; someone was behind her, but she didn't know who. Someone was laughing.

*

The lights were switched on and Katie got dressed. The door was unlocked, and she was led to the washrooms and met some of her fellow prisoners for the first time.

"Another bloody German."

"I don't want nuffin' to do with no bleedin' German."

"Don't be bleedin' stupid, she looks terrified."

"Probably can't speak a word of English."

"Be quiet, the lot of you. You've got five minutes then breakfast." The warder brought the talk to a halt.

Apart from being terrified Katie was trying to understand the English these women were speaking. Every word sounded completely different to the friendly Nottingham sounds she had got used to. They seemed to speak high up, through their noses and it was difficult to work out where one word ended and the next began. There was only time to throw some cold water over her face then the women were told to go to the dining room.

She knew what porridge was. At the first hint of a chill in the morning air it had been put in front of her, grey and steaming, and she watched Eric and his sister, Alice, pick up their spoons and eat it up eagerly. She had put a little in her mouth and tasted, well, nothing. But the conjunction of soft lumps and granular pieces sitting on her tongue was very difficult. Eric saw her face and took pity.

"Don't think Katie's ever eaten porridge before, Mam." Mrs Clarkson looked astonished. How could anyone get through winter without it? Alice sprinkled more sugar on it and a splash of milk.

"Try now." It was still awful, but she persevered. By December she was almost enjoying it.

The porridge that sat in front of her on that first morning in Holloway, lukewarm and sugarless, the din of scraping chairs and cutlery, the subdued talk of watched women, all brought about such a feeling of despair that she felt somehow hollowed out and despite the pain of it she still couldn't cry, still couldn't talk. Someone took her porridge and ate it.

At night more dreams, vivid and violent. She was on the boat to England but had lost her suitcases. She searched and searched, she must find them, no-one helped. Panic woke her up. Then she was banging on her parents' door. She could hear them all, Heinz,

Hansgünther, could hear laughter, smell cooking. They were all there, she knew it, but the door remained closed against her pounding. She was shocked into consciousness by the lights and the bell, sweating and exhausted, her fist clenched.

*

There were Germans in the prison. She heard them, was aware of them as she was led from cell to bathroom to dining room. Who were they? Were they like her or Nazis? She didn't want to find out. Not yet.

*

On the third morning, staring once again at the porridge, Katie registered that the woman sitting next to her had spoken. To her. Had addressed her. The voice had stood out from the dull murmuring, it was close. She turned her head.

"It would be a good idea if you ate something." Her voice was calm and matter of fact. Katie listened. "No-one eats when they first come but it's gone on for long enough now." She looked about forty years old; pale skin, pale hair pulled away from her face. Another accent, different, but clear as a bell.

"No point talkin' to 'er. She's German," a woman opposite said.

"Bleedin' Germans," offered another.

The pale woman took no notice of them. "Do you speak English? There are plenty of Germans in here, some speak very good English." The tone remained calm. She wasn't pushing for a reply. But Katie wanted to hear her, she felt herself waking up a little.

"You shouldn't be talkin' to 'er, Mary."

The woman, Mary, turned her head slightly in the direction of the woman who had spoken but kept her eyes on Katie.

"I'll talk to whoever I want to, Freda." A moment's pause and Katie could have sworn she could hear Freda's jaw clamp shut. Whoever she was, this woman had power.

"I do speak English."

"Thought so," said Mary. "It's Saturday. At weekends we get toast." And sure enough, there it was on the table. "How about it?" There was some margarine and runny jam as well. Katie ate two slices.

"Some of the Germans are Jews, are you Jewish?"

"No, I'm not. But why are they locking up Jews? That's as bad as in Germany!" Katie registered surprise.

"Ah, well now, the English are a suspicious lot when it comes to foreigners, you'll have discovered that for yourself by now."

Oh, she had. She thought back to the look on Vinnie's face whenever she and Eric had met her in the street. Eric said she was jealous, she'd get over it. And there was Cousin Olive who they met at Arthur and Elsie's wedding. She refused to even meet her eye. "But Cousin Olive doesn't like anyone," Elsie had said, out of breath and happy, hanging onto her young husband's arm as the four of them walked in Sherwood Forest. They had all laughed.

Suspicious was a new word. Yes. It explained a lot.

Mary's grey eyes looked steadily at Katie who had by now registered the accent as Irish. She had met some Irishmen in the various pubs that Eric had taken her to. She had marvelled at their capacity and enthusiasm for drink.

"Where are you from?" asked Mary. "I mean, in England."

"In Nottingham, I was staying in the house of my boyfriend."

"Naughty girl," said Freda slyly.

"No, no," said Katie, "it is the house of his parents. They are there too."

"Now, that's a shame." Freda wanted to keep this thread going and Katie found, to her surprise, that she was blushing, and an urge to smile made her mouth twitch.

Trays were being rattled; the warders were calling out. Breakfast was over.

"There's a library. Ask nicely and they'll let you use it. I'm in there most days," and Mary managed to add, before being led off in a different direction, "Oh, what's your name?"

Katie told her. Then she, with Freda close behind her, trailed back, along the long open corridors, to their cells.

"She done 'er old man in," Freda had leant forward and whispered into her ear. Then, realising that Katie hadn't understood, said in a low voice, "Mary, murdered 'er hubbie."

Katie stopped dead and turned to stare at Freda.

"Said she was sick of being beaten up." Freda shrugged her shoulders.

"How?" Katie couldn't help the question.

"Plenty of knives in the kitchen, aren't there?" Freda was enjoying herself.

*

Katie did ask to go to the library. She was told they would see what they could do. Prisoners were given jobs, cleaning and there was a sewing room. But most of the time they were in their cells. Two days later her door was unlocked, and she was taken to the small badly lit room with a handwritten sign on the door 'Prisoners' Library'. Mary was sitting by the window with a book open on her lap. She looked up and saw the uncertain expression on Katie's face.

She sighed and said, "Not much of a library, I know, but better than nothing. Take a look round." Katie moved cautiously towards the bookshelves, keeping a distance between herself and Mary. They were surprisingly well-stocked although the covers were old and worn. Mary watched her and sighed; Katie's uncertainty stemmed, as she understood very well, not from the surroundings but from being in the room alone with her. She spoke quietly, almost to herself.

"Well now. Freda's obviously been talking to you." Mary looked down at her book and after a pause continued steadily, "This," she waved her hand around the room, "was set up by the last governor, a good soul who wanted to change things. The war's put paid to that unfortunately." Katie fingered the books on the shelf, not really focussing on them.

"The door's not locked, by the way, and a warder looks in from time to time. They don't let just anyone in here, you know." Katie looked at her in surprise and realised she was expected to decide. Walk out and find the warder or stay. It didn't take long. She chose a book at random, sat down and waited.

"Good choice," Mary nodded at the book in Katie's hand, *A Study in Scarlet* by Arthur Conan Doyle. "It will help your English."

"What is it?"

"A detective novel."

"Oh." Katie smiledrelaxing. "A good choice for this library."

"It is indeed." They smiled at each other. Mary's fingers tapped gently on the edge of her book. Katie could tell it was poetry. Her curiosity about this woman must have been written all over her face.

"It helps. Poetry. W.B. Yeats. I've been here a long time and it helps. The old governor understood that and brought more in for me."

Should she ask questions? Katie didn't know how to. Mary closed her book and hugged it to her chest. She turned to look up at the window, which was small and dirty and just high enough to make it difficult to look out of.

"Sometimes you can be sorry and glad about something at the same time." Katie caught her breath. What was she going to say? Was she really going to talk about it?

"I can't regret it. I'm glad he's gone. He would have started on my babies. Without a doubt he would have hurt my babies."

"Oh. I see." Of course, she didn't. She was shocked, horrified even. Mary had children. Where were they now?

"Like war, Katie. Like war. Sometimes bad things have to happen."

Her father had said the same, Katie thought later. There must be a war. The only way.

"By the way, the word is out that we are being moved to make room for more Germans." Mary's eyes were on the door. Her voice had dropped a tone.

"More?" said Katie.

"Hundreds more."

*

Within days the remaining prisoners were moved to Aylesbury. One more furious, "Bleedin' Germans," aimed in Katie's general direction from Freda, as she and the others filed out of their cells, many of them excited at this change in their endless routine, and they were gone. Katie hoped that Mary would have access to her poetry books wherever she was.

That day the prison was eerily quiet. In the canteen the women seemed to divide themselves into groups. Some talked in English, some in German. A woman sat next to Katie and declared this whole charade would be over very soon once Hitler invaded. She was British with an accent that Mrs Clarkson would have called 'posh'.

"What makes you so sure?" Katie tried to keep her voice cool.

The woman looked around and said quietly, "The government here is run by mice, not men. It won't take long," and with a smile at Katie added, conspiratorially, a reassuring, "don't worry." At first Katie said nothing. Then realising what she was implying picked up her tray and stood up. She bent down over the woman's rather startled face.

"I am no Nazi, and you have no idea what you're talking about!" Her heart beat fast as she slammed her tray down on an empty table. Please God, she thought, glowering at her plate, let her be wrong. But getting angry did her good; her brain seemed to go into a higher, clearer gear.

*

The next morning brought an end to single-cell occupancy. A mattress was brought into Katie's cell and she had to help rearrange the furniture to accommodate it. To her surprise the cells were left unlocked and remained that way. In the afternoon they started to arrive. A woman of about forty was brought into Katie's cell. Next door were two younger women who talked quietly together. Every so often more filed past and were allocated a cell.

Her cell mate was called Lottie, married to an Englishman, so obviously all this was a ridiculous mistake. Alf was about to join the Air Force. They both loved England, why on earth would anyone think she could be an enemy alien? She had to go home again to look after the children, their youngest was only ten; at which point the tears started to fall and further information about her family was rendered incomprehensible. Katie put an arm around her and said that without a doubt she would be released soon and meanwhile to make herself as comfortable as possible on the bed, she would sleep on the floor. Lottie calmed down a little and talked about meeting Alf in Berlin in 1922. It hadn't been a hard decision to move to London to marry him.

After an hour or so Katie felt she could leave Lottie for a while. She was tempted by the unlocked door. The corridor was quiet, only the door at the very end was locked and warders could be seen standing around and chatting. Once in a while one would unlock the door and walk up and down, peering into the rooms. The two women next door were domestic servants and arrested after their mistress had decided to get rid of them. Further up the corridor was a group of five or six sitting on the beds and on the floor. They looked up, concerned and silent, when she greeted them. Because they were Jews, and she was not. She pretended not to notice their suspicion.

"If there is anything I can do? I've been here over a week now," she said awkwardly as if it gave her some sort of expertise.

A younger woman sat red-eyed on the bed. She looked up and whispered, "They have taken my baby away."

An angry voice explained, "Prison is no place for a baby, apparently, but it's all right to tear their mothers away from them."

"How could they do that?" said Katie.

"You should know." The angry voice again.

Katie was stung but it would be worse to walk away. "I just don't understand why you are being arrested too." She was speaking to herself. The situation these women found themselves in appalled her. The self-pity she had been fighting now gave way to an anger she could justify to herself.

"Something you can tell us, when do we get fed in this place?" This was said by a round-faced woman sitting on the floor. The tone was conciliatory.

"At five-thirty. But I'm afraid the food is horrible."

"Why doesn't that surprise me?" The woman's hollow laugh was echoed by a couple of the others. Katie smiled apologetically and moved on, past a small group of British fascists, smoking furiously, and another group of German speakers who also wanted to know what time they would get a meal. She walked slowly back up the corridor to the barred door and called to one of the warders. A burly woman, annoyed at being disturbed, heaved herself up off a wooden chair.

"What do you want?"

"Would it be possible to see the governor, please?" While Katie had been learning English, she had gone to great lengths to learn how to ask for things politely. Eric and Arthur had laughed at her insistence on this.

"I don't think that would be possible, no I don't." The warder mimicked her tone and looked at Katie with distaste. "I don't know who you Germans think you are, I really don't." She seemed to be working herself up into a state of thorough negativity. "You must be the third one in the last hour, demanding this, demanding that. No, you can't see the governor. She's very busy, what with you lot arriving all at once."

"I would just like to see her when she has a moment. It's important."

"Add her to the list, Edith," came a voice from behind her bulk. Edith tutted and reached for a clipboard lying on a small table. "Name?" Edith sighed as she asked the question.

"Katie Cremers – c-r-e-m-e-r-s." Edith seemed to find the writing of a German name a physically painful act. But it was done. Katie returned to Lottie and waited for teatime.

*

"What can I do for you, Miss Cremers?" The governor pronounced it Miss Creamers, in a tone that was both flat and hard and she didn't look up. This was the fifth German she'd had to see this afternoon and she was beginning to get tired of their whinging. It was four-thirty already and her tea had grown cold. She glanced at it, a greyish film had settled on top of it, and finished filling in the details for Enemy Alien No. 579 who arrived yesterday. She was dressed in a severe tweed suit buttoned over a shirt and tie. Katie noticed the cold tea and the overflowing ash tray and waited for her to finish what she was doing, rehearsing for the final time what she wanted to say. Finally, the governor put down her pen and reached for her packet of Senior Service. Katie cleared her throat and said,

"I thought that you could explain to me why there are Jews being imprisoned here? It doesn't seem right considering what is happening in Germany."

"Quite frankly, young woman, it's none of your business." She lit her cigarette with a large silver lighter and inhaled deeply, looking at Katie for the first time. She picked a bit of tobacco off the tip of her tongue. Katie decided to plough on.

"Some of the women here have children. They cry all night. Some are old. It's not right."

"As I said, it's none of your business."

"And why am I here? At my Alien Tribunal they came to the conclusion that I was no threat and classed me as a Category 'C'. So why am I here?" There was a new, higher note in her voice and Katie suddenly realised she didn't like it. She was pleading, as if she was more important, and it wasn't at all how she wanted to sound but it was too late. She said no more and waited.

The governor flicked ash towards the ashtray and missed. She took a breath and said, "You have every right to ask to see me, but I am under no obligation to say anything to you, let alone give you reasons for your or anyone else's incarceration." Her eyes were implacable, she wanted to say more. Instead, in an act of deliberate self-control she picked up her pen and resumed writing. "Go back to your cell." Katie, feeling humiliated, turned on her heel and headed for the door. This granite-like rebuttal made her eyes sting. Self-pity made it impossible to see the driven logic behind what was happening.

She was escorted back to her cell, passing on the way a noticeboard on which was pinned the front page of that day's *Times* newspaper. The headline was 'We will fight to the end,' as proclaimed by the newly appointed Prime Minister, Winston Churchill. He was reeling, angry at Hitler's easy victories in Holland and Denmark. Now France. The country was panic-stricken.

31

June 1ˢᵗ, 1940. As the Germans advanced through Belgium and France, 340,000 troops were evacuated from the beaches at Dunkirk. By mid-June France had surrendered.

"So you went off on your bike without this Eric of yours?"

"Yes. He had to work that day and it was so nice that I thought I'd go out onto the moor. We'd been there together a lot with the cycling club."

The women were on a train. They had learnt of their destination as they got on it.

Liverpool? Where on earth was that?

Katie was sitting next to Lisebette, who had arrived at Holloway only a week ago. She had come to London from Vienna a year before to learn English and had not wanted to go home. They had found each other, kindred spirits, relieved to be accepted without suspicion. They had been exchanging stories since they met. Katie was explaining why she had been arrested, five long weeks ago.

"Aliens like us aren't allowed to wander about on bicycles by ourselves, you should have known that." Lisebette looked seriously at Katie.

"Yes, but I didn't think it would matter. How would anyone know I was a foreigner?"

"We look different, apparently."

"Oh. Anyway, I went on the Mansfield road then turned off towards Sherwood Forest."

"Ah! Robin Hood!" Lisebette had certainly never heard of Mansfield but had read the Robin Hood story while still in Austria. A great favourite.

"Well, I didn't get very far, because I spotted a parked truck, absolutely enormous, with two anti-aircraft guns on it. The truck had some sort of army regimental sign on the doors. Sherwood Foresters, Eric told me later on. I had to have a look. Guess where the guns were made?" Lisebette shrugged.

"Essen! They were made by Krupps!" Katie still found the fact extraordinary.

"So you went home and told everyone what you had seen?"

"I told Eric, and his mother, and Arthur, a bit later on... I suppose other people would have heard about it." Like Vinnie and Olive. "A couple of days later the police came and told me I was suspected of spying and that was that."

"Have you heard from Eric?"

Katie paused then said, "One letter. He was so shocked when he got home that day. He never thought it would come to this." She looked out of the window as the train rattled through the Midlands, close to Nottingham. If it did 'come to war' it would be over in a jiffy. By the end of '41 at the latest, then she could go back. Arthur had once said to her that his brother didn't have the same take on the course of events as the rest of the family. Loyalty and love had stopped her from asking questions, from even imagining that there might be questions to ask.

"Someone will have told him not to write. Dangerous business, consorting with the enemy." Lisebette leaned back in the seat, thinking of the friends she had lost in London.

"But they know me! They know I am no enemy!"

Lisebette looked at her with a slight shake of the head. "Oh, Katie! Wake up!"

The train pulled into Lime Street station a couple of hours later and they were surprised to see women, many Jewish, with their children on the platform. They must have reunited them at some point.

The stay in Liverpool was short and Katie would remember almost nothing about it except having to sleep on the floor. Then, on a perfect summer's morning, they were taken to the quayside, where ferries had been organised to take them all to the Isle of Man.

They left Liverpool under a clear sky, the Liver building basked in sunshine, the boats on the Mersey honked their farewells. The crossing was calm, the sea a deep blue. The sudden screaming from a hysterical woman disturbed the peace; heads turned. She was trying to wrench herself free, pulling against the strong arms of a couple of men, her face was distorted, head up. Katie and Lisebette looked on with interest.

"Let me get off; don't lock me up, don't hurt me." Each phrase strained and muffled. She was held tight and forced down onto a seat. Apparently, she had been caught trying to jump overboard. Someone brought water. Guards stayed with her for the rest of the journey. It was all over in a minute, but the atmosphere changed, became uneasy.

"A Nazi, I dare say. They should be frightened," said Lisebette. "I wonder where they are going to put them." The question hung in the air.

The ferry arrived at Douglas, the long promenade stretching out to the east and they were marched towards the waiting trains. Lisebette had tight hold of Katie's arm. "Let's try and stay together," she said. Katie looked around. Every woman had a tag around her neck. It stated name and nationality but nothing else. They were walking close together, maybe six abreast. Who was she walking next to? A Nazi, a British fascist, someone like her?

The atmosphere was calm, there was laughter, she saw a guard pick up a toddler who was crying and comfort him and his mother. But she was suddenly apprehensive. Ahead lay the road and a crowd of people, watching, waiting.

"Here we go," said Lisebette.

"What?"

"Last time I was marched along an English road it wasn't very pleasant. I didn't think the British went in for shouting and swearing but I was wrong. The spitting was the worst." Katie had heard about this but not experienced it herself. She and Lisebette hung on to each other, bracing themselves.

But here there was no shouting or spitting. The faces in the crowd were unsmiling, curious. The women walked on; the crowd looked on. All were silent. They turned into the station where several guards stood on the narrow platform to usher them methodically into the carriages of the waiting train. It was tiny, almost toy-like and once full and the whistle blown, chugged south, down the coast of the island, green and lush on one side, sea sparkling on the other, the prettiness somehow at odds with the vague disquiet felt by the rows of women, bags on their knees, tags around their necks. There was some murmuring; most sat quietly looking out of the windows where the lowering sun shone. She closed her eyes for a moment and let it warm her and was suddenly in Victoria Park with Eric, lying on her back, one arm flopped over her face, shielding her eyes against the late September sunshine. They had escaped the family one Sunday afternoon and gone for a walk. There were other couples clasped together on the slopes under the trees, some men were in uniform.

"Will you join up?" All the men were talking about it; it was only a question of when.

"Doubt they'll have me. Eyesight." He grinned, pushing his spectacles further up his nose.

He was very short-sighted. She remembered him lying there, propped up on one arm looking at her, stroking her hair before bending down to her ear. "It'll all be over in a jiffy, my lovely *deutches Mädchen*," he whispered, "then the world will be ours," and kissing her so that she couldn't think of anything except wanting him. She remembered the heat of his back, through the cotton of his shirt.

"All right ladies, stay in your seats, please. We'll get the families off first." Daydream broken. The train had arrived at the little town of St. Mary's. Another short, narrow platform, clean and neat with plant containers at intervals. They watched as women and their children got off and were led away.

"But they're not sorting us out," Katie said as they stood on the platform. They had been counted and put into groups of twelve, randomly, although the guards consulted each other and their clipboards. "Just stay close to me. We can't do anything about it." Lisebette was right. Group by group the women, Jews, Nazis, Austrians, Germans, were marched towards the boarding houses overlooking the sea which would house them for the foreseeable future. The southern peninsula of the Isle of Man was now an internment camp for these alien women who were penned in between the Atlantic Ocean on one side and a brand-new barbed wire fence stretching from Fleshwick to Gansey on the other.

Katie, Lisebette and four others were told to stop in front of a terrace, paint flaking off around the rusty numbers telling them they were outside Number 24. The guard checked their name tags before indicating with his head that they should climb the steps to the front door. Greyish net curtains fluttered nervously before the door opened.

32

Duisburg, 1941. Hitler had banned all correspondence to and from enemy states on the outbreak of war. Some post arrived from the Red Cross.

What would I tell you if I could, my lovely girl, while I lie awake here next to your father who has finally, finally gone to sleep? We think about you all the time – are you safe? I think the answer to that is yes and we thank God for it. I so want to tell you what's happening here. I'd start with the good news first. Hansgünther passed his piano exam. We were all very pleased and Papa admitted it was worth the agony of getting Opa's piano into the apartment after all. Do remember that day? My goodness! Claus and Papa both had backache for a week and Margarethe and I nearly died laughing. Of course, that didn't help. And there is news I am not so happy about. Heinz has been called up. It was inevitable. He will join the Wehrmacht and probably be sent to France. His training starts in two weeks. He is eighteen.

We have food, you need to know that. There are the odd shortages, but we get by. I go every couple of months to see Aunt Anna on the farm and get a few sausages, some butter, and a piece of pork, if I'm lucky. She has to send so much to the war effort but manages well. Lisl's Manfred has been sent to the East. She says very little about it.

I had a letter from Heinz today so I can tell you that he is fine. French girls are very pretty, apparently, and there is very little to do in Paris. I must say he looked very handsome in his uniform. The population just want to get on with their ordinary lives, he says. Of course, Papa had plenty to say about that – "For God's sake they are occupying a foreign land! France!" He screwed the letter into a ball and threw it in the bin. I took it out. He is eighteen!

I wish I could hug you. Stay well my darling.

*

Not a day goes by when I don't thank God that you are no longer living in this blasted country. Probably best if you never come back although it'd break your mother's heart. I can't imagine how we can recover. You'll remember the Meyers who live on Harold Strasse? We've known them for years. Well, I bumped into old Georg yesterday. They got a visit from the SS who threatened the family with three months in a concentration camp if they were caught sympathising with Jews. Goebbels isn't satisfied with the effect the yellow star is having. Some Germans, instead of shunning them, are actually being nice! Can you imagine?

That fool brother of yours has been called up. Inevitable, of course. Thinks he looks the bee's knees in his uniform. That's the end of his education, maybe the end of everything. I told him before he left – no heroics! Above all, don't volunteer for anything. He's safe enough in France, I suppose, for the time being at least.

At work I'm asked almost daily where my loyalties lie. With God, Germany of course, and my family, I reply. To be loyal means to wear the badge, to join the Party which, as you know, I refuse to do. I expected to be sacked but now I think they need the old fellows like me. The younger ones are being called up; young Lorenz left, only last week, poor devil. He certainly isn't soldier material. I continue to carry out the tasks I am given and suffer the poisonous atmosphere in silence. Friedrich and the other Jews sacked long ago. You'd tell me to pack it in, wouldn't you? No Katie. I am going to watch and listen and pray for the day when Grühl and the rest of them get what they deserve.

We have seen pictures of what we have done to London. I have nothing but admiration for the English for not giving in to it. We will never be forgiven.

*

Heinz is coming home on leave. It's wonderful to think I'll be seeing him in a few days. I'm saving the meat rations and will buy beef. Günther is very excited, he can't help being proud of his big brother. And – you would want to know this – Friede is marrying Karl next month. Mina came while Heinrich was at work, especially to tell me. I found a couple of tablecloths for her to take back as a wedding present. I doubt I can persuade your father to go to the wedding. What a pity, what a pity.

Yesterday, a letter. A letter from you! We couldn't believe it. There it was in the post box downstairs, stamped to within an inch of its life and with a large red cross over everything. Front and back. You are in a safe place and you are with good people. I had the best night's sleep I can remember.

*

Your mother confessed to me that she had given Mrs Pankowski a bag of food, vegetables mainly. She had seen her walking back from the market empty-handed and followed her towards Ost Strasse. When she was sure no-one was looking, she caught up with her and put the bag down at her feet. She was in her usual shabby coat and the yellow star was sewn in place with big irregular stitches. No word was exchanged.

Now we have no vegetables and no shopping bag! I think I'll make her a new one with the length of canvas I've got in the cellar.

Heinz will be sent to Russia, no doubt about it. Our dynamic, insightful and vigilant leader believes that is where victory lies.

New laws for the Jews! They aren't allowed to use public transport in the rush hour. They aren't allowed to visit museums. They cannot buy flowers. They cannot buy shaving soap. They cannot own fur coats or woollen blankets. They cannot eat in restaurants or sit in deckchairs! Needless to say, they are hardly allowed to eat.

It is madness but with a purpose. I fear it is a prelude to much worse.

Isle of Man 1942

They were being moved. From Port St. Mary's where they had been for two years to Port Erin. Lisebette was glad of it. Staying with Mrs Bradley and her children and her laundry had been hard work. They had both felt sorry for her, husband called up, four children and the laundry to run. And she was tiny. A strong wind could blow her over. And then she was forced to billet six aliens, strangers from countries she knew nothing about, except that a monster was waging war on them all, and her husband in particular.

"We can help you." Lisebette and Katie were strong, willing and it would be the only way to make life with her bearable. The laundry was behind the house and local guest houses brought their washing to her in huge canvas bags. Mrs Bradley, nervous at first, showed them the great metal boilers, the rinsing tubs and the ironing room and, as she saw them set to, capable, quick to learn, she left them to it, grateful to be able to spend more time in the house and with her children.

Now they were being moved. The last few weeks had seen a lot of changes. After two long years of petitioning and waiting for the Home Office to come to a decision the Jewish families were to be released. Katie was very glad for them but would miss those she had come to know. The teacher who was helping her English, the pianist who gave concerts.

With fewer internees it was decided that they could all now be accommodated in Port Erin. Lisebette and Katie packed their cases and were taken with four others to a large boarding house on the promenade in Port Erin, a couple of miles away. It was spacious and rather grand and run by a formidable lady called Mrs Berry.

*

Darling Mama and Papa,

I will write a letter and pray the Red Cross can get it to you. I've heard nothing from you yet – maybe next month. Our new home here in Port Erin is very nice. It overlooks the sea and there are palm trees in the garden. We take it in turn to do the work while Mrs Berry indulges her passion for bridge. I remember Opa trying to teach me once. He'd be proud of me now! We all have to learn so that there are always enough people to make fours. There is a Catholic church here and I can get to Mass every Sunday. I think the priest is rather glad that the number of Catholics on the island has grown so much.

We hear very little about the war. I pray you are all safe.

We are so lucky to have Frau Semberger with us now. She is Austrian and a marvellous cook! It's amazing what she can make out of the little we have. She asks the butcher for the meat no-one else wants and makes the most delicious meals. Mrs Berry looked a little worried at first but even she enjoys the meals now. The English always seem to eat the same sort of things. Some are very good of course – like the smoked fish called kippers – but some don't taste of anything much. Frau Semberger asked to go mushroom hunting. What a difference mushrooms would make! But she was refused. They probably thought she wanted to concoct poisons! People don't collect mushrooms here. Strange.

Hug Günther for me. Maybe he is too big for hugs now. I love you all, Katie.

*

Duisburg 1942

This is how it goes, Katie, this is how it goes. You don't know about it yet. I'm glad of that but one day soon you will. Claus told me what is happening because he has talked to the wrong people. Or the right people depending on your point of view. He takes risks, not like me. The trains come into the shunting yards in the evening and wait, hidden, like hungry beasts watching for their prey. No-one knows their business. No-one wants to know. The trucks arrive in the streets in the middle of the night. The soldiers, so brave, have their long lists of men, women and children and wake them with bangs on the door, shouts and bellows. They are given minutes to pack a suitcase and told to leave and climb into the trucks. Babies and small children are handed up to the parents. They do as they are told, Katie, these people without rights, without friends, without anything. The trucks drive quietly through our streets, those same streets you used to play in, with the chestnut trees and the cracks in the pavements and speed up to get to the shunting yards some way out of town, where the Jews are asked to get onto the trains, trains with seats – quite nice. Let's not cause panic, say our brave soldiers, we don't want a riot. But later they are taken off those trains and put into trucks used for transporting animals. So many more can be squeezed in this way. Hundreds and hundreds of them. The suitcases need to be left behind. Dumped in piles on the platforms. The trains set off, towards the borders in the east, Poland, we think, where a fate awaits them that not even Claus knows about. But one day we will all know and how will we live with that, Katie, how?

*

Isle of Man, autumn 1942

Katie was sitting on a rock staring up at Bradda Head. She had been up there a couple of times in the previous year and once she and Lisebette had been lucky enough to see the hills in Northern Ireland, grey-green in the distance. But the winter had been harsh, windy and cold, like today and she was going to make use of her free time walking on the beach with Max and rereading the letter she could feel in her pocket. Her fingers curled around it, felt the softened paper, a small miracle to be savoured again and again. It was from Heinz. Somehow it had found its way across Russia, across battered and terrified Europe, to her. Max, a mix of collie and something else, was having the time of his life racing the length of the beach and back. The seagull population had long since left for safety, perching on the cliffs, waiting for the dog to leave them in peace. When the women had arrived on the island, they were allowed to send one letter, to an address of their choosing. She had thought of sending it to Eric but then felt her parents really needed to know she was safe. That would be how Heinz would know her address.

The letter was already months old. Most of it had been blacked out, leaving just the odd morsel of precious information. He was able to write to their parents and he got the odd letter from them. The weather was still holding out, but they were worried about the winter. She tried to imagine him so far away, in such a vast country but failed. It was enough to have this scrap of paper in her hand, warm in her pocket, a little bit of him. Tears stung her eyes. She missed her family, missed them all. She stood up quickly and set off at a smart pace away from the Head and towards the sea. She needed to hear it, hear the waves pounding the shore, let their din drown out the pain she was feeling. It would pass, she knew that. Max was suddenly at her legs, wet and panting. He had a stick between his teeth and was looking hopeful. She crouched down and rubbed each side of his damp head. "OK, couple of throws. Then we'll have to get back." She grabbed the stick and threw it with all her strength along the glistening beach then watched as Max's four legs churned up sand and spray and took heart from his unbridled joy, unfettered freedom.

*

Nottingham, February 1943

"What are you doing, Eric?" Eric was on his knees dragging a box out from under the bed. He turned his head towards his brother, pushing his glasses back up his nose but remained silent. "Getting rid of the evidence?"

Arthur looked at the magazines and leaflets spilling out of a large bag, each with its lightning flash symbol on the corner. Eric continued pushing the paper into the bag. When he'd finished, he sat on the bed and kicked the box across the room, the room they had shared as boys.

Arthur looked at his brother, a disappointed man, whose ideas for a new Europe were being kicked around as surely as that box.

It had been a mystery to him how his younger brother had become beguiled, then excited by the fascist movements in Germany and Italy, as well as the half-baked one in England.

"Have you written to Katie yet?"

"What could I possibly say to her? Anyway, you know I'm seeing Flora now."

"You could tell her the truth."

Eric was staring at the bag stuffed with bellicose nonsense, obscene lies and false promises. He turned toward Arthur and said, "We all make mistakes, don't we?"

"Katie wasn't a mistake." Arthur's voice had a hard edge. "She was lovely."

Eric's shoulders slumped. He squeezed his forefinger and thumb over his eyes.

"I know. That's why I can't write. Anyway, she'll have forgotten me already." He looked at Arthur, in his uniform, ready to be sent to the coast. Embarkation for France could be at any time.

"She's not that kind of girl." Arthur turned to go, back downstairs to say goodbye to his mother, back to his Elsie. He paused before clattering down the stairs and pointed at the bag. "And for God's sake burn those."

33

May 1943. Waltham airfield in north-east Lincolnshire. Arthur Harris has been in charge of Bomber Command since late 1941. Its capability has been transformed.

The pilot and bomb aimer both stirred their tea slowly, staring at the milky liquid before throwing the spoons on the table and reaching for their packets of cigarettes. Johnny, the pilot, looked out of the window.

The Lancasters were being fitted with their bomb loads, and refuelling trucks were careering down the runways towards them. Men were up on the planes checking the turrets; someone was leaning across the nose working on the forward-facing machine guns. They had twenty minutes.

Doug, drawing deeply on his Woodbine, was familiarising himself with the list of co-ordinates he'd been given for tonight's hits. His foot tapped on the floor as he concentrated. Johnny looked at his friend's face, serious and unshaven. Doug was the fidgety one, first in to see the flight officer, first into his position on the floor in the nose of the aircraft.

Lucky so far. It was their twentieth mission. Their first had been over Essen back in March. The rest of the crew had joined them a couple of weeks back when the raids continued over the Ruhr. Lucky so far. He looked at the clock on the wall. He stood up and adjusted the fastenings on his Sidcot suit.

"Time, Doug. Let's go and do some damage." He kept his voice confident and light, the voice the crew needed to hear. Doug gave a nod, scraped his chair back and ground out his stub under his boot.

They threw their waistcoats over their heads, grabbed the rest of their kit, and walked through the flight officer's room, past his abandoned desk – he had joined the crews outside – air still thick with cigarette smoke.

A huge board above the desk gave the destinations for tonight's attack. For Johnny and his crew and the other Lancasters taking off from Waltham the destination was a place called Duisburg. A name as unfamiliar to them as Bochum, Dortmund, Wuppertal and the other cities that made up the Ruhr, the heartland of German heavy industry, ship building, mining and arms manufacture. Squadrons based along the east and south coasts had had a busy few weeks as they combined to inflict as much destruction as possible on these blurry shapes scudding past beneath them at 20,000 feet, breaks in the cloud revealing occasional glimpses of black, coiling snakes of river.

The other crew members were checking each other's waistcoats, life savers if they had to ditch into the Channel, adjusting goggles and leather helmets, before climbing into the plane; the flight engineer sat low down next to Johnny, eyes fixed on the fuel selectors and gauges on the control panel, navigator in position in the centre and the three gunners in their turrets.

Before crawling into his narrow space, Doug said to Johnny, as he always did, "Home for breakfast, Johnny." If he didn't say it, it would be bad luck and he didn't fancy trying to bail out of his narrow escape hatch with his parachute on. No matter how you looked at it he wouldn't fit. Once in, lying on his stomach, bombsight controls on his left, bomb release selectors to the right, he checked the radio then pulled on his sheepskin-lined gloves. They'd have to come off when he got down to business, but for now he wanted to keep his fingers warm. Beneath them all, in the belly of the plane, lay a 4000 lb 'Cookie' and incendiary bomblets, sweetly named, housed in six SBCs, the bomb containers.

The four Rolls Royce Merlin engines shuddered into life and the plane shook. "Beautiful," said Johnny, as he did every time. The faces of the seven men, average age twenty years eight months, were obliterated by helmets, goggles and radio masks. Underneath their flying suits, secreted in their uniforms, next to their hearts, a cross, a talisman or a lover's letter kept them safe. Their bones shook as the plane gained height. Then for a short while they could relax, talk to each other and wait until the Belgian coast came into view. Dusk turned to starlit night and to either side dozens then hundreds of aircraft joined them. The moan and drone of engines filled their world.

Below, grey cloud merged with black with the odd dull orange glow. Doug listened for information. He knew the bomb load and target position, now he needed the wind direction, speed and altitude in order to calculate the bombs' trajectory. The Mark XIV bombsight was a huge improvement as it did the calculations automatically and ensured greater accuracy; he kept his right hand on the bomb release selector and watched the sighting glass for the moment when the target was in the cross hairs.

"OK, get ready," said Johnny.

Ahead the Pathfinders, Mosquitoes mainly, shot out flares into the blackness to light up the sky and illuminate the city. Through the cloud, sprawling, untidy Duisburg lay exposed with its docks, its factories and railway lines, its dirty river, all suddenly vulnerable. Johnny flew lower; now they were nearly within range of the anti-aircraft guns. Doug released the Cookie. The German night fighters had located them and were keeping the gunners in the turrets busy, Browning machine guns firing in all directions. Air thick with flak. Doug was sweating now; the noise was deafening. Time for the incendiaries. On the railway lines. On the blacked-out houses.

Suddenly Johnny veered away and south over the city. Deep black below. "Get rid of it, Doug. Now!" He heard Johnny above the racket and pressed the final release button. The last incendiary went down, who knows where. It had to go. Its weight would hinder their journey home.

"Just look at that, will you." Johnny's voice again and they all looked down as fires sprang up instantaneously, coal depots becoming part of the inferno. Widely scattered explosion after explosion showing gold; red-hot metal thrown hundreds of feet into the air, an endless inverted firework display. A fighter had followed them, and the undercarriage took a hit. Johnny lifted the nose of the plane and headed west and south. "Home for breakfast, Doug!" Doug, shaking, at last aware of the cold in his bones, closed his eyes.

*

Duisburg, May 1943

We are all exhausted. Falling asleep on the trams, at work, even standing up in the queues for food. Teams of people are clearing up the debris, including some Russian prisoners of war, released from their work in the railway yards. Barefoot, for God's sake. Can you believe it? Nerves are shredded. Some cannot stop shaking; some children have stopped speaking. Last night's attack seemed to split the sky wide open, split our brains; the noise was indescribable, by far the worst yet. Your mother's ears bled and she is in great pain. And yet our building still stands, close enough to the forest to avoid direct attack. Hansgünther, who takes an interest in these things, tells us the planes are Lancaster bombers capable of dropping enormous bomb loads. He, like a lot of the children, has become expert in recognising the sound of the bombs, which ones are the incendiaries, which ones the high explosives. We've sent him to Anna's farm for a few days.

Katie! I wonder how you are on your little, green island. We have found it in the atlas! We keep it open on that page and, like a pair of old fools, talk to you by looking at it!

*

I took Günther to stay with Aunt Anna last week, before the very worst of the air attacks. What I haven't told your father is that I had a little incident with the SA on the way home. Anna gave me a beautiful pork and garlic sausage. She wrapped it up in newspaper for me. I only wanted half, but she insisted. Well, I was waiting for the tram to get me back home and could see the guard walking towards me. Now, we are all hungry, but I was not about to share my sausage with this particular gentleman! I opened my coat and shoved the sausage, under my skirt and down my knicker leg. He watched me do it! Still, he swaggered up and asked, "And what have you got there?"

"What business is it of yours?" I was angry. How dare he?

More people came to the tram stop and I suppose some sense of decency stopped him searching an old woman for a sausage! I must say no sausage has ever tasted so delicious! We will have to make it last. There is very little food to buy.

*

Our office had a wall blown out, but we are able to continue on the far side of the building. No-one talks to me anymore, but I am still useful. After a day of clearing and reorganising, the work of the Ministry continues. Herr Grühl is as fanatical as ever. Hitler will think of something, he says. In the city on the other hand there is a lot of grumbling, not against the British but against our government! A bit late! Goebbels is doing the rounds, trying to cheer us up. I won't be there to greet him. I heard one man say, 'Why don't the planes carry on and drop their loads on Berlin?' Good question. This is the price we must pay to get rid of the plague, but your poor mother! The doctor thinks her hearing will get a little better but the damage is certain to be permanent.

Some cousins from Essen are coming to stay with us. Emmi, Johann and their daughter. Their house was flattened. Anyone who has a spare square metre is expected to offer shelter.

*

Oh! Another story that I think can wait a little before your father is told. You know how he is. A few weeks ago, a prim young man, all of sixteen years old, came calling. He looked very smart in his Hitler Youth get-up. "Frau Cremers, it's time, wouldn't you say, that young Hansgünther did his duty for the Fatherland and joined us?" It was the way he lolled against the doorframe that made me see red.

"Who sent you?"

"No-one sent me. It is my job to find the shirkers. My job to do something about them." Shirkers!

"We are at war, Frau Cremers. All Germans must serve the Führer as he would want!" What a pompous little idiot, Katie. The world is falling down around our ears and he comes out with such rubbish. I moved towards him so that he had to take a step backwards, out of my home.

"My son is doing his duty." I tried hard to keep calm, but I was angry. Margarethe taught me that anger can give you strength.

"My son is working very hard on his aunt's farm producing food for the Fatherland." It was a lie, God forgive me, I hadn't taken him yet. At that moment he was in the bedroom with his ear pinned to the door. I moved a step closer and could feel my shoulders square up to him. "Don't you dare come here telling this family about duty! I have a son fighting for his life in Russia!" It was all I could do not to stab him in the chest with my finger.

He was edging backwards, towards the stairs, looking worried, I'm glad to say. Well, I didn't want him to fall down and crack his head open, so I grabbed him by the arms, turned him firmly round and pushed him on his way. He said nothing, little coward. I slammed the door shut and leaned against it, my hand clamped against my mouth. What had I done? Günther came out and looked at me, eyes as round as saucers.

"Don't tell your father," was all I said. A couple of days later we went to Anna's.

Oh Katie, so much to tell you when you come back. Let's hope my ears are better by then.

34

1944

H einrich had acquired two potatoes. He held the precious
bundle close to his chest as he climbed the stairs to the
apartment. It was getting harder. He was fifty-eight and
walked like an old man. He turned the key and walked straight
toward the kitchen, where he expected to see Maria but she wasn't
there. Emmi, Johann and their daughter Sissy would be out searching
for food, either at a food queue or at the black market. This was a
dangerous business. The location changed daily, and they risked
arrest if discovered. Hunger makes you reckless. Trinkets, clothes,
anything could be sold there, sometimes there was even tinned meat.

He heard a sound coming from the bedroom and went towards
it but not before trying the gas on the cooker. A hiss emerged from it.
Thank goodness. Something warm could be cooked tonight.

Maria sat on the bed holding a telegram. He looked at her thin
face, dry-eyed but grim with sadness. "Heinz has been shot. In the
lungs," she held the telegram up.

"Oh dear God, Heinrich!" He took it and sat down beside her
and held her as he read it and the tears finally flowed.

*

Heinz was in a hospital near Magdeburg, recovering sufficiently to be able to smoke again. His fighting days were over, however, and he prayed his thanks daily while waiting to be sent home. He had kept a diary of his experiences in the forests of Belorussia and the rock-hard terrain that transformed itself into mud lakes after a rainstorm. The soldiers had been sent towards Ukraine and then, realising they had been duped by the Russian generals, trudged back north again towards Minsk. Holed up in destroyed villages or terrifyingly dark forests, they awaited the onslaught. Their numbers were too low to withstand the unlimited numbers of Soviet troops.

As he lay on his bed the pain in his chest and back, where the bullet had ripped through, weighed him down and he could still taste the fear that had engulfed him in those forests as they stumbled, tripped and crawled their way through the darkness. He had thought only of the men on either side of him. Wolfgang, Rudi; he would die for them. They would die for him. Nothing else mattered. Just stay alive. Keep them alive. At night every crack, every snap of a branch had them ready, had their hearts beating in their throats, always a false alarm. Until the evening when it wasn't; when the heat of the shot pierced and tore at him and he felt the blood trickle warm onto the earth.

He regained consciousness briefly in the truck, lying on blood-soaked wadding. Then again in a field hospital near Warsaw. Here they patched him up. No bullet to remove, it had passed straight through. Some damage to the soft tissue but he would mend.

On the way to Magdeburg, he and the other injured soldiers joined the growing numbers of refugees heading west. Loaded cars and trucks, families on foot pushing prams and wheelbarrows, some on bicycles. Later the cars and trucks lay abandoned on the roadside alongside suitcases, clothing, boxes and baskets. Now there were just people, hundreds then thousands; endless lines trudging from land stolen for them, desecrated for them, away from an army who would stop at nothing to exact revenge. So many women; carrying children, dragging children. Of course, Heinz realised, the men were either fighting or dead. The Russians were weeks away from Warsaw, they were pushing towards Berlin. Nothing would stop them.

His shoulders tensed as he thought of Wolfgang and Rudi and pain shot through him. He wasn't due for painkillers till this evening and then only if he could catch the attention of the nurse. His friends would be killed, probably already dead. And he lay here between dry sheets.

And then came the order for all those able to be moved to go home, to Duisburg, to his parents. He had to think about them now and thinking about them made him cry. Great sobs that he tried to suppress, to push back. He covered his face with his arms, ashamed, out of control. The heaving tears threatening to split his chest in two. No-one must see this. No-one. The man in the bed next to him watched him and waited for the sobbing to subside. He had lost a hand and part of his right leg.

"Relief and guilt, lad, relief and guilt." He said it in a matter-of-fact tone. "Might as well get used to it. Probably be with you for the rest of your life."

*

March 1945

Hansgünther was almost relieved to get out of the house. There was a truck waiting outside with four other young recruits, that was what he was now, a recruit, and they were to be taken to a makeshift barracks near Düsseldorf for two weeks' training before joining the rest of the army tasked with pushing back the Americans.

A soldier, a man of about fifty, dishevelled, day-old grey stubble, one of the newly formed Home Guard, had arrived yesterday saying that all sixteen-year-olds were now required by the Führer to join up. No ifs or buts. He wasn't officious, spoke with tired determination. He would return for him at ten o'clock sharp the following morning. Since then there had been pandemonium. Mama's 'not over my dead body' was followed by plans to hide him. Papa said there was no time and Heinz said it was pointless to try and get out of it, they would find him and anyway in the East people were being shot for any act of disobedience, out right in the street, in their homes. It wouldn't be long before it happened here. Then Mama began to cry, "Have I got one son back only to lose another, a boy, a child?" Hansgünther said loudly that he already knew basically how to use a gun and he would come back safely, just watch.

Once in Düsseldorf training began, which was difficult because there were no guns and very little uniform. Sergeant Hoffe, a weary man, tried to give demonstrations using his own rifle but there were no bullets, so it was cut short, and the boys were shoved into a truck and taken on a trip. They were hungry all the time and the fact that everyone was didn't stop the moaning. But it was an interesting trip, a ringside view of the Führer's latest and last great plan to thwart the enemy. As Hansgünther sat next to Werner and Horst, who looked not a day over thirteen, fingers clenched around the wooden seat, trying to prevent his teeth shattering as the truck lurched and bumped its way over pot holes, craters and rubble, Germany's finest military engineers were racing towards the mighty Rhine, their pockets stuffed with explosives. The master plan, a stroke of genius, was to blow up the bridges straddling the Rhine before the Americans could cross them. Those cold, dark waters had kept so many enemies at bay in days gone by; they would surely save the Reich now.

Sergeant Hoffe drove along the banks of the river and cocked his ear. If you listen carefully, lads, you may hear a muffled 'Puff!' coming from the north, from Wesel. Such a pretty place, standing on important crossroads, bombed into dust. And now its bridge destroyed by our own hands. The river, startled by the interruption, took stock momentarily and then continued its relentless journey to the sea.

Then in Düsseldorf, the Hamm Bridge, straddling more than eight hundred metres. Pop! Gone in seconds. Next, the Duisburg Railway Bridge itself, pride of the steel workers with its mighty struts and girders. Bang! It was merely wreckage, fast-flowing waters spilling over it.

And as the boy warriors raced south to save the day, towards ancient Cologne, its proud cathedral spires standing above the flattened city, what did they hear? Dimly, in the distance? Phut! The Hohenzollern Bridge. No more. No use to the Ammies now. We'll have the last laugh yet, lads. And Sergeant Hoffe smiled encouragingly. Let's stop for some soup. By a miracle there was some soup, lentil and something green. It must be the Führer's doing, see how he thinks of us.

There is one bridge left. The Ludendorff at Remagen. Once that's gone, we can wave at the Ammies across the waters. But what's this? The officer in charge had had one too many glasses of schnapps the night before and mistakes seem to have been made. The detonators failed. It did finally collapse but not until thousands of Americans had crossed over. Hansgünther heard the fighting while hunkered down near Cologne, an arm around Horst, who was sobbing. Sergeant Hoffe was waiting for orders.

One evening, a week or so later, the Ammies found the boys, hiding in holes near the ruined riverbank. They had been out earlier looking for food.

"Jesus Christ, what have we got here?" A huge man with blond stubble across his chin and grey dust ingrained into every line in his face reached out his paw of a hand and pulled the boys out.

"*Wir sind Soldaten,*" said Werner foolishly, trying to stand straight.

"Oh yeah?" The big American looked doubtful but cocked his rifle anyway, causing sharp intakes of breath.

He went over to his friends. "What the fuck are we going to do with them?"

"Shoot 'em, Sarge. Easy."

"Look at them, for Chrissake, they're kids."

"Nazi kids. Shoot 'em."

The men turned their exhausted gaze onto the boys. The big man got up and stared down at them. He fished out a pack of cigarettes and tapped one out. He stuck it between his teeth, sighing deeply. Hansgünther felt a glimmer of hope at this point. He thought he would try his luck.

"*Wir haben hunger.*" He said it very quietly. Their bellies ached and their throats were dry. Horst was leaning against him. He had stopped talking some time ago.

They hadn't eaten for two days. Before leaving them – he'd realised his number was probably up – Sergeant Hoffe had given them what he had left, a chunk of hard bread and a piece of cheese.

"*Dieser Junge muss nach Hause gehen.*" He'd promised Horst with all the fervour of a sixteen-year-old that he would get him home.

The big man, not understanding the words, took it all in, the sunken eyes, the young, buckling limbs.

"Where do you come from?" No response till he reeled off a list of places – Dortmund, Cologne, Duisburg?

"*Ja, ja! Duisburg!*" The brown-eyed boy with the face of a tired angel spoke. "*Meine Mama wohnt in Duisburg!*"

"Your mama, huh?" The American sucked on his cigarette. He had to get rid of these kids. "Get some food going, for fuck's sake, will you, Marko? Hot!"

"But Sarge…"

"Do it. Just fucking do it, Marko."

The next morning, still licking their lips from their breakfast and with dried meat and chocolate in their pockets, they were crammed into the front seat of a Jeep headed north and east where it was considered safe enough to dump them and send them on their way.

The boys watched the Jeep disappear. It was the end of March and little tufts of green were poking through the grey earth. There were figures moving on the horizon, alone, bent. The silence was profound and all they could hear was their own breathing and the sound of their boots rasping against the turf. Like animals they lifted their faces to locate the river, its direction and home.

35

1945. England

It was just a question of time. The newspapers said it daily. A question of time. The Russians pouring in from the east, the Americans from the west. Bridges blown, and then mended, people starving, people desperate, millions on the move. Months, maybe weeks. Time had become a physical force for Katie. For years it had been like an empty well which needed to be filled with menial work, with English lessons, discussion groups, and above all supporting one another. Now it seemed to be racing towards some sort of an ending, a cliff edge, certainty for some and complete confusion for others.

The Ministry of Labour had suddenly realised that a handy workforce was sitting idle in the internment camps and sent out directives for them to be put to use wherever there was a need. Letters like the ones Katie and the others now held eventually found their way to the inmates on the Isle of Man.

"They want to know our last address. Then what skills we have that can be of use." Lisebette was hunched over her form, sitting at the table in Mrs Berry's sitting room, tapping at the form with her pencil. She started to write.

"God! I can't wait. Back to London. Life! Men! No offence – I love you all, but I miss men!" Everyone laughed.

Katie listened to the excited chatter, the jokes about what

they would do with the first handsome man they met and laughed along with them, but her thoughts were pulled inevitably towards Nottingham, towards Eric. No choice now but to face it. She had to go back. It was the only place she would be allowed to go. The silence, absence of letters, spoke for themselves but now she would find out for sure. Occasionally she allowed herself the fantasy of imagining he was waiting for her; she even imagined she still loved him. With a resigned sigh she completed the form and left it on the table for Mrs Berry to collect and take to the warder's office.

*

The goodbyes were harder that she expected. At Liverpool Station she and Lisebette clung together, sobbing into each other's collars. A couple of guards stood a discreet distance away; their job was to see the women on their way. The din of the place was shocking, exciting after the peace of their camp. Lisebette had to raise her voice.

"I can't imagine you not being there, Katie. I'm scared to death." Katie knew it. For all her brave talk! They were all frightened.

"You'll be all right," Katie smiled at her good friend. "No-one is as capable of being as all right as you are!" Lisebette laughed and wiped at her face.

"Come to London! As soon as you can – you know, if Eric…" Even Lisebette indulged Katie in the hope that there might be a happy ending.

Katie gave her a half-hopeless smile and said, "We'll see. Anyway, what on earth would I do in London?"

"Believe me, it's the best place in the world!"

"Even for us?"

"Well, I'll find out and let you know!" Lisebette's train was due. They let go of each other. Neither woman was smiling. "You've got the address. Streatham! South of the river." Katie watched her disappear into the crowds. Then, suddenly sick with loneliness and trepidation, turned to find her own train to Nottingham.

*

At the far end of the platform stood a woman with a child at her side. Katie walked towards her, not sure at first. Then, when she smiled, quite sure. It was Elsie.

Katie smiled shyly back.

"Oh, Katie! I can't believe it." Older, thinner but as kind, as gentle.

"Neither can I. It's so good to see you." There were tears in their eyes as they searched for each other's hands, searched each other's faces. The little boy was pulling at Elsie's shabby coat and holding something up. Both women looked down.

"This is George. He has something for you." Katie looked quickly at Elsie, a look that said, 'your son, Elsie – he's beautiful, just beautiful,' before crouching down so that she was on a level with Arthur's boy. George held out four little daffodils wrapped in some newspaper. Bright yellow with orange trumpets. "Hello George. Thank you so much." George looked seriously at Katie, worried by the unexpected tears streaming down her face. Elsie spoke quickly.

"I remembered the flowers you brought for our mam the first time you came. And you said that giving flowers was important in Germany... I thought..." Katie stood up, wiping her face.

"They are the most beautiful flowers I've ever seen." George, appeased, smiled up at her and manfully took her hand.

"Come on," he said, "we're going home now."

"You're staying with us. Arthur's not back yet."

Katie, alarmed, said, "Is he all right?" She had wondered about them all so often. Did she even have a right to ask?

"Yes, I think so. In Holland last we heard." There was a restrained tinniness in her voice and her head inclined a little towards George as she said it.

They walked out of the station. Elsie linked arms with Katie, who stopped for a moment when she saw the piles of rubble, neatly cordoned off, traffic moving around it.

"The German bombers did that," George informed her. Katie nodded, freezing a little.

"Worst attacks were in '41. Nottingham didn't get hit as badly as other cities." Elsie squeezed her arm gently as she explained.

A bus took them to Alfred Street. Mrs Clarkson was by herself and welcomed Katie with a hug. "We've all been through it, luv, haven't we?"

The room looked much as Katie remembered but dowdier, still clean and tidy but the fire was unlit. "Glad you're staying at our Arthur's. You will be company for Elsie."

Later on, George tucked up in bed, Elsie said, "Katie, there are things I need to tell you. About Eric."

Katie nodded and sighed. "Yes, I expect you have."

*

I can't stay much longer. These people are so good, it's not fair. How can they be so kind to me when the newspapers show such horror?

"But we know you, Katie; we know what you're like." And Elsie turns the pages quickly so as not to upset me, but we have to get upset, have to know. I turn them back. Auschwitz, Buchenwald, Belsen, Dachau; one by one the photos appear, taken by a shaking soldier's hand, grainy yet somehow distinct. Limp white bodies melting into each other, piled, heaped. There are no words. The opposites of 'love' and 'goodness' and 'justice' have lost their strength. Elsie held me tight. "Didn't you know?" Her little boy is lying upstairs, fast asleep.

What did I know? How can I answer that? To say 'I knew' makes me as guilty as the men and women who did it. Doesn't it? To say 'I knew' means I can imagine the same atrocity these people dreamt up. How could I 'know' this?

What did I know? I knew what I could bear to know. There was evil around me, around the people I loved, it had been allowed to creep out then to explode. But this was beyond evil. There are no words. How often would I be asked, 'What did you know?' For years? Forever?

*

She was put to work in a factory making demob suits for the soldiers when they came home. The factory was run by a Jewish refugee from Berlin who had come over in 1937. They got on well; talked in German together and he appreciated her hard work. The rough woollen cloth made her hands sore as the material flew through her fingers, but she hoped one of the suits would be for Arthur, due back any day now. It was a relief to be busy. The machines clattered away around her and, eyes down, it gave her time to think.

To think about Eric, who was quietly planning his wedding to Flora. She had bumped into him at his mother's. It was brief and awkward but what she saw was someone who knew he had made a mistake and had been made small by it. There was a brief moment of pity, when she saw how cold Elsie and a couple of others were towards him. Elsie thought Arthur would never forgive him. But he would. This family didn't harbour grudges.

She looked at the growing pile of trousers to her right, about to be taken, matched to a jacket and packed into boxes. On her left was another pile of trouser legs, cut and ready to be stitched. Each to be given to a returning hero, a loved and missed conqueror, a beloved slayer of evil. She had not gone to the street parties in May; she celebrated Hitler's death by volunteering to sew the buttons on dozens of jackets, Germany's surrender by machining the buttonholes on scores of trousers, her foot poised on the large grid-iron pedal of the machine, guiding the cloth through, needle hammering. She remembered the beautiful buttonholes she had been taught to hand sew at Frau Wettmann's, each one done with shiny waxed thread. When would a letter come from home? When? The needle slowed down as the machine manoeuvred the buttons. She watched, hypnotised – up, down, criss-cross. The racket made from the endless pounding of needles through cloth was deafening. Hair fell over her face as she bent low, suddenly overcome with such grief that it almost choked her. Outside in the streets, as she volunteered for extra shifts, old and young laughed and sang, celebrating an ending and she knew there would never be an ending for her.

And, on the walls she walked past daily, hung red posters shouting 'Vote Labour' for prosperity, for security. The war had been won, now win the peace. The future was thick with hope.

*

In the end she needed to be free of their kindness. It was suffocating her to be so considered, so endured.

Lisebette's letters had said 'come, COME!' London was still the best place in the world, and "*Ich vermisse dich!*" Oh, I miss you too, thought Katie, deciding immediately that the time had come. I miss being with someone I can feel comfortable with, say what I like to and whose eyes don't cloud with suspicion when they meet me.

So she finished the last of the demob suits, folding it with care, lapels flattened, before putting it into the box. She wrote to her parents and told them to send letters to Lisebette's address in Streatham. She sought permission to travel to London and bought her ticket. Parting was tearful but there was a certain relief in the smiles as they wished her well and waved her awkward presence off. As she got on the train and blew her last kisses to them, Arthur shouted, "Don't forget to write!" How could she forget? They wrote every Christmas for decades to come, news of births, house moves and, sometimes, deaths.

36

September 1946. Streatham, South London

"D o you think they'll let me come back?" It had occurred to her suddenly in the middle of the night as she lay awake thinking about what to take with her.

"The real question, Katie, is do you want to come back?" Lisebette took a sip of the horrible chicory-flavoured coffee that she insisted on drinking first thing in the morning along with smoking her first cigarette. Katie preferred a cup of tea; she was happy to wait for the real thing. She looked out of the little kitchen window. Her train left in three days' time. Soon she would be home.

Did she want to come back? She had encountered little difficulty buying her single ticket to Duisburg. Restrictions on travel were easing all the time. Trains running again in Germany, sort of. Once there she would have to apply to the British authorities for her return ticket. But did she want to come back? To London, to Streatham, to the dingy workshop where she was churning out cheap skirts, dresses and blouses by the hundred on unreliable machines next to girls who took every opportunity of going outside for smokes and gossip and screaming laughter, leaving her side-lined, ignored?

"I thought you were going to see that chap you met at Richard's party, what was his name…?"

Katie met Lisebette's eye directly. "Lisebette, I haven't time now. I've got to go home, to see them all, see things for myself. Anyway," she said with a note of regret that didn't pass Lisebette by, "he'll have forgotten all about me by the time I get back. If I come back." Lisebette could see by the set of Katie's mouth that her mind was made up.

"Right! Let's go to Pratts." It was Saturday; they could do whatever they wanted. "We'll look at the things we can't afford and see if there is anything in the sale." Pratts, the department store on the High Street, proudly open since 1850, had continued trading throughout the war, escaping both the Blitz and the V2 rockets. Katie nodded. Maybe they would have something she could take for her mother, her cousins, her aunts.

That evening she decided not to go dancing with Lisebette. Lisebette would go with Richard, junior doctor, amateur cellist and love of her life and other friends she had met at the hospital where she worked as a secretary. Katie loved the dance bands at the Locarno but often felt shy, awkward, too tall! And nervous of talking to dance partners. That dreaded question, "Where do you come from?"

The letters from her mother and father lay on her lap. She'd read them many times, but she wanted to look at them again. *We are OK but we have nothing*, they said confusingly. *If you come remember you can get anything with a couple of cigarettes.*

The small pastel-coloured, flower-shaped soaps she had bought in Pratts lay next to her in a scented cloud of lemon and lavender. She would wrap them individually in newspaper later. She had also found a tie for her father. Dark blue with a tiny red pattern. Very English, he'd appreciate that. She stroked its silky smoothness. Any money she had left was for cigarettes.

She ached for home. Longed to see her mother, hug her father, laugh with her brothers. All these years she had carried with her images of the kitchen with its ancient family sofa behind the table where so many dramas and discussions had taken place, the smell of familiar food cooking, of the carefully kept sitting room with its tiled corner stove, lit for visitors and when the winter cold was too unbearable. Like a precious book of beloved photos to be looked at in secret. Be careful, she told herself, be careful, remembering the other photos of ruined cities, piled up bricks, sunken cheeks.

Whatever happens, don't even think of coming home yet. We live amidst rubble. No food. This from her father shortly after VE day once mail was allowed to flow freely again. *It's too dangerous. Gangs roam the streets.* Everything would be different, she told herself, forget those cosy memories.

And from her mother a month later: *Not much food. So little transport I can't get to Anna on the farm. They won't have much either of course. Heinz goes to the Black Market. I'm very nervous of it.* Katie felt sick with guilt. She was working, had her ration card – no questions asked – just as many foreigners in London as ever, not much food but always enough.

A few weeks later from her father: *The Tommies are well behaved and respectful. Every time I see one, I thank God they are here. Heinz had to report to them and hand his uniform in.* He swapped two cigarettes for half a cabbage on the way back.

All these snippets of information left her with more questions than answers. From her mother: *Since Hansgünther came back he has been very quiet. All he wants to do is draw and talks of Art School.* Back from where? Where on earth would her little brother have been? And why was Heinz already at home? She needed to be with them, what on earth was she doing here?

The newspapers spoke of 4,000,000 German prisoners of war. They also spoke of the millions missing, lost children, desperate parents, starving families on the move across the continent. Many returning from the stolen territories in the east, the innocent mingling with the murderous.

*

The train rumbled through Belgium painstakingly slowly. Faults on the line, signal failures, inexplicable halts. It inched its way past shattered towns, roofless warehouses, destroyed factories. On the roads that ran parallel to the railway lines were the odd jeep, truck or bus. She saw small, isolated groups of people with somewhere to get to. Katie tried to stay awake, she wanted to see it all, but she was tired, and her elbow kept slipping off the narrow window ledge, jolting her out of half-sleep. Past fields and she saw a man alone harvesting the wheat with a scythe. As the train passed, he paused and stretched out his back.

Then the border. English soldiers climbed on board, peering into the carriages, followed by unarmed German guards with strange uniforms, some very young, checking the passports and tickets. Katie noticed the soft skin of the boy who handed her documents back to her and she glanced up, hoping to exchange a smile. But his face was stone. A year ago, he would have been scrambling around in the rubble, playing soldiers, hoping to kill an Englishman for the Führer.

Then all was quiet while they waited for the train to lurch off again. There had been little conversation between the other passengers, all German, all busy with their own thoughts. Katie had told them that she was going home for the first time since the beginning of the war, but no questions had been asked. They seemed uninterested, hugging their own stories to their chests, their eyes, brown-shadowed and tired, looked away when she spoke. At last, the train did move, clanking over the points, hissing its way towards home.

*

It was evening when she stepped down onto the platform, cool enough for her to put on her coat, the same one she had taken with her six years earlier. There was a strange feeling of space around her, and when she looked up she saw the bare metal skeleton of the roof, all that was left. And when she looked behind her, she had a clear view across acres of grey towards the river and the docks where ships lay on their sides. She stood still a moment as people around her hurried off, heads down, disappearing into what passed for a city. She buttoned her coat and picked up her case.

She had tried to prepare herself for what she would see. Almost every landmark was gone. Layers of grey rubble stacked neatly along the side of the road. As she turned towards Kammer Strasse, this stretch of it just a grey, anonymous strip of scarred concrete and cobble, she was aware of figures lurking behind the stones, lolling against a still-standing doorway, as if it had always been like this. The figures scuttled along keeping up with her, clever predators who had spotted their prey, keeping cover, dowdy clothes camouflaged against the dusty rubble. She kept tight hold of her case and walked more quickly towards what should have been the Blumen Strasse junction with its four corners, where the bars her father had sometimes gone to with Anton had stood. Only one was left, damaged but somehow resolute in this sea of tidied devastation, its summer awning flapping sadly. The ghostly figures had lost interest and disappeared into the dusk.

Straight across, finding Kammer Strasse once again, as it wound its way towards the forest, buildings began to reappear. To left and right pock-marked apartments were standing, some shutters hanging loose but many screwed back on and holding fast. Windowpanes replaced and there was even the odd pot plant struggling hopefully on a windowsill.

Across her path lay Sternbusch Weg, a wide road, where trams had rattled, and coffee shops been busy throughout the day. This evening there was nothing, just someone on a bicycle turning away out of sight.

Nearly there and by some miracle there was one dim streetlamp shedding light where the trees used to be and where the wall still was behind which were the vegetable gardens her mother helped tend, where she had played as a girl. She stopped by the corner shop where she had been sent a hundred times to buy rolls, or butter, or some of that good mettwurst. Frau Edelman had always given sweets along with the change. Ahead a door slammed. She lifted her head and peered into the half-dark. She knew that sound. It had slammed behind her as she had run off towards the forest to play, as the family had gone off to Sunday Mass in their best clothes, slammed as she had struggled with her bicycle down the cellar steps or raced up the five flights of stairs ahead of her brothers. Her heart lurched as she saw a figure approach, stop dead, then run towards her. Heinz. She dropped her case and opened her arms.

"I was meant to meet you. I'm so sorry. I got stopped..." he babbled on about being stopped by the Tommies, a regular occurrence apparently, and bent to pick up her case. She was only half listening, busy looking at his thin face, more handsome than before. He couldn't stop smiling; neither could she.

"Mother is going out of her mind, thinking of you walking home by yourself. Come on. Supper fit for a queen is waiting for you! Well, as far as rationing will allow… Katie, what's the matter? Come here." They were standing in front of the familiar old brown front door with its little window and the push buttons on the right which would signal their arrival. She stopped Heinz's hand from pressing the one marked 'Cremers'. Tears were pouring down her face, uncontrolled relief and joy to be here, to see her brother, to know what a welcome was waiting for her.

"Wait a minute, Heinz. I can't go in looking like this." She dug her hand into her pocket to find a handkerchief and wiped her eyes and her nose.

"OK?" He smiled at her, serious concern in his eyes. She nodded. "But let me press the bell." She pressed, and after a pause the door clicked open.

37

S he heard Hansgünther before she saw him. Not the clattering footsteps of a boy but the precise, quick tread of a man. As tall as Heinz, same tender face, thinner of course. The large brown eyes took a second to appraise her, recognise her, then the wide smile.

"Katie!" He took the last steps down towards her three at a time and, not sure quite what to do, took her hands in his.

"Oh, look at you! So tall and grown up." Where had her little brother gone?

He smiled again and looked at her from under his eyebrows. "And hungry! We have meat! Mama found a piece of BEEF! Only small but it smells very good. Come on." His voice was deep, but she laughed at the familiarity of her brother's obsession with food. The three of them climbed the final flight of stairs, the apartment door was open, and in the hallway, watching and waiting were Mama and Papa.

*

I'm shaking, shaking like a leaf and I can feel my heart race. If I let go of Heinrich I might fall. Will she look the same, my beautiful girl? What will she think of us, shrunken, poor? Damn these ears of mine. I so want to hear her voice, clear, like I remember. And what will we say to each other? There's so much she cannot possibly understand, and so much I don't want her to know. The last year was worse than even Heinrich imagined. And God knows I'm luckier than many. We are all alive and now – together. I can hear them, the three of them, just like before, coming through the door, starving hungry. There she is. Oh, don't look shocked! I know how we look. That's better. A smile. Come here my darling. Come here. Let me hold you.

Katie held Maria tight. Her back was narrow, the soft roundness gone, she felt like a bird that might break. Over her shoulder she looked into her father's eyes for the first time. Weary eyes momentarily alive and happy with relief. Katie rocked her gently and drew away, allowing herself to be scrutinised, hair to be stroked, a small voice saying, "You look well. Doesn't she, Heinrich? She looks well." A moment later, "Her hair is blonder, don't you think, from the summer sun? Very pretty." Maria didn't take her eyes off her daughter's face, her smile getting wider.

"And in the meantime, some of us are getting very hungry." Katie laughed at Hansgünther and Heinz scowled at him. "Maybe you could think of someone other than yourself for once!" Hansgünther scowled back.

Then there was embarrassed shuffling in the little hallway as her case was taken into her old room and her coat was hung up and she was ushered into the kitchen and generally treated as a special guest, lost and returned, prized and fussed over.

Heinrich insisted on saying a prayer together before they ate. Katie and Maria bowed their heads to thank God for being reunited, Hansgünther, a fledgling but convinced atheist, tutted to himself and Heinz sat still in his own thoughts.

The beef, real star of the show, came out of the oven in a pool of gravy and slivers of onion. There was a dish of potatoes and peas from the gardens. The meat was cut thinly and shared out equally. Katie saw how carefully it was done; how important it was.

"It's good, Maria," said Heinrich, chewing slowly, savouring, as if no-one had been sure it would be.

"I was lucky this morning," was all Maria said.

Heinz sensed Katie's curiosity and said, with a hint of mischief in his voice, "How did you pay for this – cigarettes or jewellery?"

Katie watched her mother with growing interest. She saw a flicker of cunning in her face, an expression she recognised, loved, in fact.

"Now where would I get cigarettes?" She gave Heinz an amused glance. "They are only interested in American ones now."

"I can get hold of those," said Heinz. She noticed how Heinz raised his voice just a little when talking to Mama.

"I'm sure you can," said Heinrich, with a certain wry emphasis that made Hansgünther giggle and Heinz's mouth twitch in annoyance.

"I used a brooch, one that I got from my stepmother." They waited, there would be more. "Of course, I told him, the farmer, that I couldn't part with it. Not just for sausages, which are what I told him I wanted." She turned to Katie, explaining, "This farmer hides down a different alleyway each time he comes. And of course, you have to know who to ask to find out." She said this in the tone of a master criminal. "He had his meat laid out in a suitcase. There was a cow's head, some sausage and this beef." They looked at the now empty plate, then back at her. "I told him it was gold-plated."

"Was it?" asked Katie.

"No." Maria's eyes flashed at her daughter. "Then I told him I couldn't swear to it, but I was pretty sure the little stone was a diamond." Heinrich shook his head in mock disapproval.

"That's when I pretended to notice the beef." She smiled at them all. "He couldn't wait to do the deal."

"It took you long enough, but you seem to have got the hang of the Black Market at last." Heinz looked approvingly at his mother, who took the opportunity of the distraction to scrape half a potato from her plate onto Hansgünther's which he gobbled up before anyone could notice or object.

*

The stories are gentle at first, down-played, made funny. I listen carefully, trying to picture it all. Like the story of the sausage, saved by being rammed down Mama's knicker leg in the nick of time. Like throwing the Youth who had come to recruit Hansgünther down the stairs. ('He tripped.' 'No, she pushed him, I saw it.'). Hansgünther's encounter with the Americans and his first taste of chocolate for three years. ('What? You were recruited?' 'I nearly learned how to use a gun.')

*I'm watching your faces as you tell me these things and I
know there is so much you are not telling me, keeping me from
the truth, because I wasn't here, and I will never understand.
Even the bombings are downplayed. I know you were lucky,
didn't lose your home but your poor eardrums, Mama, were
shattered, blood on the pillow for weeks. You shrug, it's a small
thing, a small thing. And Papa, you are quiet and look at me and
nod and smile. What are you thinking? That I was saved from
it all, somehow uncontaminated? Is that how you feel? Smeared,
sullied? You cried, was it with pleasure, when I gave you the tie?
As if it was too good for you. Your left hand trembles all the time;
I didn't notice at first because you cover it with your other hand
to stop it. Those thin wrists, mended cuffs slipping down.*

*Heinz, you seem sure of what you want. You want it over.
You want to work, to rebuild, to make things better. Well of
course you do. Your eyes glint with possibilities. Forget college,
forget training. It would take too long. Becoming a doctor was
always a pipe dream. You tell me about Anna, your American
girlfriend, sent over because of her perfect German. Fraternising
is not allowed but neither of you care. You meet in secret, it's
exciting to defy the authorities. Your eyes slide over my listening
face, gauging my reaction. I want you to meet her, you say.*

*And Hansgünther, you lose yourself in your drawing. People
mainly. Mother and Father in various poses. People you've
noticed in the street. The shabby and the smartened-up. Sharp
lines denoting hope or despair. Your fingers fly over the paper,
eyes squinting, concentrating. I need colours, Katie, colours! In
two years, I can go to Art College. Papa doesn't want me to,
thinks I should become an architect, or draughtsman. Never!
You declare. The world needs Art – I shall be a good artist. I
think you will, little brother, I'm sure you will.*

*

Maria tells Katie that straight after it was over the Americans
and British delivered pictures of the extermination camps to all

households. They had to do it, Katie, absolutely had to. There was – is – so much denial. If you lived near one you were taken there to walk around it, look at it, smell the stench. *You* did this, *you* did this, the pictures seemed to say. Hansgünther couldn't eat, couldn't speak, couldn't draw. Spent hours outside roaming around the rubble, never told us what he got up to. Then the schools started again. He went back mainly to see his old art teacher, reinstated after they got rid of the Nazis, who told him there was more than one kind of 'duty'. And his was to make the world a more beautiful, thoughtful place. And more honest.

*

"Will you come with me to visit Mina?" Maria asked quietly one day. Her voice suggested she expected a refusal.

"Of course, when do you want to go?"

It was three or four days after her arrival and Katie was helping her mother with the washing downstairs. There were half a dozen other women at the stone sinks battling to clean their old clothes, bedding and towels in cold water. Not enough fuel to heat the stoves yet. The house was packed with relatives and strangers, bombed out, waiting to be rehoused. People had lived down here, Maria told her, and up in the roof, under the rafters. It's more manageable now. Everyone keeps rabbits on their balconies. They had had one but then couldn't kill it, had to get someone else to do it.

"Tomorrow, we'll go tomorrow." Maria sounded pleased. "The tram hasn't started running yet so it means walking."

*

"Your father won't come with me. I've tried to persuade him, but he says it is impossible. It's not a question of forgiveness, he said, that's not for him to do. It's about not forgetting." Maria and Katie were walking at a good pace south towards Neudorf, heading gradually towards the railway lines and the old workers' apartments where Mina and her family had always lived. It was good to walk with her mother. The streets were quiet, and they could talk, as long as Katie turned her head towards Maria and spoke clearly.

"The boys won't go either." Maria shrugged. "I won't make them. Maybe it's going to be up to the women to keep families like ours going." *There will be a lot of families like ours*, thought Katie.

She hadn't thought twice about going. She wanted to see her aunt and uncle and cousin. She remembered the warm and happy days of family gatherings and parties. And Friede had had a little boy in 1943, maybe a little too soon after she had married her soldier. They had managed to find a couple of Heinz's old toy trucks to take with them. Maria was also carrying four large potatoes and some runner beans, the last of them.

The building looked dilapidated. It had always suffered from being so close to the railway lines but was now in great need of repair. Roof tiles were missing; a crack ran down the side of the house from the broken guttering down to the ground. The gardens that surrounded it were overgrown, neglected.

"They're hoping repairs can be done before winter sets in," said Maria.

Greetings between the women were warm and genuine. The toddler, a smiling and well-built little boy, took up most of their attention. It was clear who got the lion's share of the family rations. Mina, thrilled to see them, wiping away tears of joy, was enthusiastic in her praise of Katie's looks, loud in her apologies at not having real coffee 'yet', and extravagant in her thanks for the gifts. Friede echoed and copied her mother's mannerisms and reactions as she had always done. Katie remembered the shrill laughter and now found it false, unconvincing. Yet she loved them and began to pity them. When Albrecht and Karl, who had been out, returned, the greetings were more restrained but their delight at seeing Katie was heartfelt. Karl, a grey, dull man, expressed pleasure at meeting his wife's cousin for the first time.

Conversations over a plate of sandwiches were kept light, meaningless, difficult subjects avoided. They stopped asking her about England and the British after listening to her deliberately overdone and not entirely truthful descriptions of extraordinarily generous and considerate treatment 'at all levels'. They nodded and smiled but she sensed their incomprehension, their discomfort. She watched the thin coffee being poured from a porcelain pot and looked around at the heavy kitchen cabinet, both wedding presents from her grandfather and somehow out of place in the dark, low-ceilinged room, a room that had been rendered soulless as if pictures and ornaments had been scooped up and hidden.

Only once did a note of embarrassment creep in.

"And how is the work situation, Albrecht... Karl?" Katie was surprised at her mother's tone, a sharper edge to it as if she wanted to inject a little reality into the talk. There was a silence as she looked first at one then the other.

Both men were out of work. Albrecht had had to resign at the end of the war. It had been humiliating. Karl had been injured during the last days, held for a while by the Allies then sent home.

Mina said, a little too quickly, "Well, it's taking time, you know."

Katie waited, interested. Albrecht was looking intently at his plate, fingers playing with the crumbs, lips, pressed tightly together, moving, angrily mobile.

"What do you mean?" She couldn't resist it.

"Oh – it won't be long now, I'm sure." Her uncle collected himself, tried to look jolly, slapped his hands on his thighs, wanting to change the subject.

"We have to answer questions," Karl said. He hadn't said much up to now and now he might just say too much. "How we feel about this; did we know about that; then they write it all down..."

"Ridiculous. How could we know all that stuff?" Albrecht's tone was surly, almost a whisper. Katie looked sharply at him. She had heard the stories of the half-hearted, according to her father, attempts to 'de-Nazify' the nation after the Allies took over. The man she was looking at was no longer the comfortable uncle, the memories were slipping, replaced by something nastier.

Karl decided to continue. "We go once a fortnight to see them – the English."

Albrecht shifted in his seat. Katie tried to imagine the scene, her uncle, still a big man, sitting opposite an English soldier, having his past raked over.

Mina touched his arm. "It'll be over soon. These men are needed." She sounded sure.

"Well, of course," put in Friede, "the country needs all the workers it can get now that the foreign…"

"The foreign workers have gone home," completed Maria. *And everyone else is dead*, thought Katie.

Mina looked at her sister; she still had her hand on her husband's sleeve. "Albrecht and Karl did nothing wrong, Maria." The statement was final. It was what they believed. What they had to believe. For themselves and for the toddler, grown restless and crawling around their feet. Maria waited a moment, holding her sister's hard gaze, "I know, Mina, I know." She said it slowly as if to emphasise that the words were for Mina alone. They meant something else, they meant 'I won't abandon you, don't worry'. Mina nodded, placated, and poured more coffee. Thin lips satisfied.

For a second Katie felt anger; why help this woman lie even if only to herself? But when she looked at her mother's face, she saw nothing but a sister's understanding which she couldn't share, something that stretched beyond the last terrible years which had twisted lives out of shape, back to something gentler which needed resurrecting. Katie breathed in. *That's real love*, she thought. *You are a lucky woman, Mina.*

*

"A couple of years of feeling important, that's all he got out of it." Maria had firm hold of Katie's arm as they started the long walk home. Katie let her talk.

"The 'foreign workers' were slaves. Czechs, Poles, Russians. At the end they were roaming all over the city, starving, scavenging. You'd catch a glimpse of them sometimes, newspaper tied around their feet to keep from freezing or bleeding. In the last days the Gestapo, what was left of them, went out and shot any they could find. Then they went home and some of them shot themselves." Maria stopped walking. Katie looked at her anxiously.

Maria, stricken, said, "How do we live with this? How?" And she looked at Katie as if begging for an answer. Katie put her arms round her. "I don't know, I don't know."

She held her tight, wanting to squeeze the poisonous images out of her. "You don't have to talk about it, Mama."

Maria shook her head, eyes closed, leaning away. "Sometimes, sometimes…" Katie, fearing she might fall, cupped her hands around her elbows, trying to keep her upright, keep her rigid.

"I'm all right, darling, I'm all right," she said after a moment and they walked on, away from the railway toward the forest. There was a bench on the side of the road, scratched and little paint left but still sturdy. The women sat side by side and looked at the forest over the road. It was a warm afternoon, just a slight wind moving the beech trees. Great survivors, their leaves, already russet, just beginning to drop and float down onto the ground.

"It will get better, in time." Maria patted her daughter's arm as she spoke, wanting to make her feel better. "It's what time does."

A cyclist laboured past, took off his cap, and wished them a very good evening. They replied and watched him pedal up the slight incline towards Neudorf.

"The important thing," Maria continued, once more in control, "is you young people. You have your lives to live, and life is precious." Katie thought of Friede's boy, clawing at his mother's skirt, wanting food, drink and finally indulged by Albrecht who scooped him up, tickling him, making him laugh. She wanted to dislike the man. She did dislike him. What time might do is make these meetings easier. They would all perfect ways of avoiding unmentionable subjects. As the boy grew, references to the past would be taboo, except for the odd talk of the awful lack of butter and meat.

"Maybe you shouldn't go there anymore."

Maria sighed and shrugged. "She needs me, she always has."

"But why should you try and make her feel better about herself?"

Maria thought about it. *Is that what she was doing? Was that so bad?*

"She's my sister, Katie. Going there once in a while won't harm anyone."

Probably not and Katie could see that her mind was made up.

They got up and walked on up Lothar Strasse, the huge beech trees swaying and nodding them on their way.

38

November 1946. After the war, Germany had been divided into four zones. The American, British and French in the west and the Russian in the east. The Cold War had already begun with the West wary of Soviet ambitions.

After a while she stopped asking about people she had known, for fear of what she might hear. Most of the young men were dead. Otto and Jens had both been killed in torpedo attacks on their submarines. Her old school friends had lost husbands and brothers. Her aunts had survived but Lisl's husband was missing in action in Italy. Lisl herself lived in Berlin. Her uncle, Claus, had been arrested at the end of the war and died of tuberculosis. Margarethe, heartbroken, continued to live with Johanna in the big house along with all manner of wounded and destitute.

Aunt Botha had been killed in an air raid while visiting her sister in Essen. A direct hit. No bodies had ever been found. Flesh, bone, heart and soul reduced to grey ash in the violent blaze. Anton, dazed, continued to work. There was always work for a mechanic in a world where everything needed fixing. Heinrich had gone round every evening after the memorial Mass and the men sat in silence. Just once, tears rolling down his face, Anton said, "All she wanted was a child, all she ever wanted." And Heinrich, helpless, held his hands, his great, stained mechanic's hands, in his own, until the tears stopped and he could gently let them go. Maria would wait for him to return from these visits and sit with him in their silent kitchen until his heart warmed up enough for him to face sleep.

On the radio they listened as the Nuremburg trials came to

an end. The criminals had been executed or had taken their little cyanide pills, some of the snake-tongued had got away with long prison sentences. Maria watched nervously as Heinrich listened every evening, head bowed. Sometimes she pleaded, 'Turn it off now, that's enough!' But he ignored her. 'Leave it! Leave it on!'

And as the American, the British, the French and the Russian judges and lawyers and investigators packed up their documents and, relieved, caught their planes home, Heinrich sighed and said again and again, "It's not over, not over. It's not enough."

*

One afternoon, in late November, Heinrich at work, Maria shopping, Hansgünther goodness knows where, Heinz came home, flung his jacket on the floor, himself on the settee and said to Katie, "They're sending her home. Anna has to go home." He looked around the room, lifted both his hands and let them flop at his side. "Because of me, of course, because we were…" his voice cracked. Katie hadn't seen him cry since he was fourteen.

She had met Anna, a gentle girl, very pretty and clearly in love with her brother. They had talked a little in English, then in German so that Heinz was included. She was interested in Katie's experiences in England, wanted to go there one day.

Heinz brushed the tears away. "She is an employee of the US army and any fraternisation is completely out of order."

Katie sat close to him. "It was always risky." He nodded, forlorn. She felt his misery, remembered her own. "I'm so sorry, she was lovely."

A week or so later Heinrich came home with an offer for Heinz from a friend of his in the Buildings Department of the council. 'We need good, bright young men to get things going again,' he'd said, 'God knows there's a lot to do. The scum have been cleared out.' He added this for his friend's peace of mind, knowing how he felt about it. 'Training on the job. Start after Christmas.' Heinz jumped at it, bright eyes now firmly on the future. From the ashes that were left he would rebuild, restore, transform. Concert halls, theatres and art galleries would rise again. He would devote himself to it. Make it happen.

*

The scum hadn't been cleared out of all departments, however. Far from it. The de-Nazification program was watered down and eventually shelved, blind eyes turned, documents filed away in deep cellars. Expertise was needed to make this fledgling democracy thrive and grow strong. More important to create a bulwark against the encroaching power pushing from the east than to weed out the perpetrators of little crimes. They were all just obeying orders after all. Let the administrators administrate. They are good at it.

Maria said, "Well, maybe it's better, more Christian, to forgive, to let people move on." Katie wanted to agree with her.

"No! No! No!" Heinrich looked up from his paper. "Silence is not the answer. Burying it is not the answer. Do I have to walk around with my lips stapled together?" He looked from one to the other. Katie was startled at the cruel image. He clearly had more to say but seemed to change his mind. More quietly he said, "It will all blow up in our faces one day. Truth must come out."

Maria pressed her own lips together, not wanting to say anything that might make him angrier.

*

"Why didn't you say something?"

"You were nineteen. You wouldn't have listened to me."

Katie and her father were walking in the forest. It was cold and dull, but the air was good, and the floor crunched beneath their feet.

"Anyway, it was more important to get you out, it was too good an opportunity." They had been talking about Eric. Easier to talk here, walking arm in arm, the rustle of branches and the odd bird call to fill the silences.

"What made you suspicious?" she asked.

"Too interested, too knowledgeable. But it was only a suspicion. Behind my back I had my fingers crossed."

Katie thought about it. "I wouldn't have listened, you're right.

It took years for me to accept what was right in front of my nose."
Suddenly it was easy to admit, here under the trees, a world away.

"I've still got his ring, you know." She thought of the little ring
with its three rubies buried in a drawer in Streatham.

"Well for Heaven's sake, don't tell your mother, she'll swap it for
a pound of sausages."

She laughed and squeezed his arm. They walked on.

After a while Heinrich stopped. "This is where you came off your
bike that time."

"Was it?" She stared up through the canopy, trying to remember.
To the left there was a crater, hollowed out earth, broken saplings,
scorched bark.

"Courtesy of the RAF." He shrugged and they moved on. "There
are a few of them, bombs dropped before they headed home."

"I shouldn't have left. I should have stayed here with you all."

"No. Definitely not." She looked at his profile, his wire-rimmed
spectacles bent and rebent into shape, his mouth firm and sure. He
turned to smile at her.

"Listen. You can't imagine how glad we were that you were in
England. There's a country that truly understands democracy." *Here
it comes*, she thought, *there was no limit to his admiration for all things
British.* "Ever since Magna Carta," he raised a finger for scholarly
emphasis. "Can you imagine? Seven hundred years! For seven
hundred years the English have been protected – by law – against
despotic rulers!"

She smiled to herself. She had yet to hear an Englishman or
woman wax lyrical about the Magna Carta.

"How about Eric and his pals?"

"But don't you see? That's exactly why the British Fascist Party
was doomed to failure." Heinrich sounded exultant, his theory
proven. "It's just not in their nature."

There might be something in that, she thought to herself. What
she was beginning to realise was that she would never be able to share
their, her people's, experience of the war. The six years' separation was
a black chasm she couldn't cross. She could read about it, hear about
it but never understand how it was. To live among them but not to

have gone through the worst of times with them suddenly made her feel fraudulent.

"I don't know what to do." She hadn't meant to say it out loud, but the words pushed themselves out and to her surprise they sounded desperate, her voice cracked.

Heinrich stopped and faced his daughter, putting his hands on her arms. "I can't make that decision for you." He looked at her carefully. "Sometimes having a choice is harder than having no choice at all." Up above, the wind quickened and the branches rustled gently. Heinrich turned back towards the path. "Let me tell you about work."

Katie listened. The forest seemed to free her father, from tension and trembling, enable him to speak in a way he couldn't at home. She knew this was especially for her, that she must really hear what he told her, pay attention.

"For five years no-one in the office spoke to me. Not one word. They turned away when I walked past; messages were left on my desk – 'traitor', 'Hitler will punish you' – that sort of thing. They were not all bad men, just frightened. God knows so was I, but I just couldn't wear that badge, join the Party. For some reason they didn't sack me, just ostracised me."

Katie already knew this. She nodded. "In England they call it 'sending someone to Coventry.'"

"What? The city the Luftwaffe flattened?" She nodded again. Heinrich shook his head in disbelief. "Extraordinary." Then he continued.

"It was very hard, Katie, to be invisible. To be talked about in voices just loud enough for me to hear, to be pushed aside by fourteen-year-old office boys. Day after day I sat in my corner, filing bits of paper, collating lists of figures, praying that no evil lurked within those columns. And it probably did, Katie, it probably did." He stopped for a moment, studying the path, head in the past.

"Then, the day after the surrender, while they waited for the British to arrive, walls were stripped of the portraits and flags. The little busts of Hitler that had stood so prominently on their desks disappeared and their damn badges were thrown in the gutter. It was that easy, they thought, to obliterate the past. I thought them fools."

An image of Bettina's blood-red shrine to Hitler flashed unbidden into Katie's mind. She hadn't thought of it in years but there it was, as sharp and monstrous as the day she'd seen it.

"The days went past. The Ministry was closed by the Allies, while they checked and questioned. At last, I thought, at last. I got my old position back quite quickly and a couple of good new men arrived. Now new laws would come along and the best of the old resurrected and we can move on. But after a few months, who do I see? Grühl, his cronies, and even little Franz – the weasel – all back! Working in various offices, laughing and joking, slapping each other on the back." He turned his head away from her and stared into the trees.

"Well," he answered Katie's unspoken question, "things needed speeding up. Who else knew the ins and outs of the civil service? Apparently, they, those crooks, are necessary." Again, he fell silent. Katie waited.

"And that will be happening all over the country, people lying to each other and to themselves." They had been walking very slowly and now Heinrich stopped and looked at her.

"Why should you live your life in a place like this?"

Because she loved it, she loved her parents, her brothers. "But you have to live here." She was feeling desperate, oppressed by the picture he had painted. "Heinz and Hansgünther would never leave!"

"It won't bother Heinz. He is strong and knows what he wants. Hansgünther, if he pursues this damn foolish notion of being a painter, will move in completely different circles. But what would you do, Katie? What would you do?"

*

He didn't mean to, she told herself that, but his words crushed her. She could think of nothing to say on the way back. He probably wanted to guide but instead she felt immediately defeated. Once back home her father retreated into the usual silence, the conversation never revisited; he must have decided that enough had been said. The little voice that had been growing, telling her that she could train, it really wasn't too late, as a teacher, or a nurse maybe, became a whisper, then a half-hearted whine before it fell silent. Hadn't it always been the same? Her brothers were allowed ambition, encouraged to make plans but for her it was 'What would you do Katie? What on earth would you, already twenty-six years old, do?'

She knew he loved her, understood her even. He knew how hard it would be for her to live among the self-deceivers. And among the ghosts. But the ghosts had children, innocent, playing in the rubble, faces pointed towards a future manipulated by frightened governments. 'Yes, maybe, but what would you do, Katie?'

*

The words rang in her ears as she sat on the edge of her bed that evening. Her mother joined her.

"Father thinks I should go back to England," Katie said, looking at her.

"Is that what he said?"

"It's what he thinks. He said there was nothing for me here." She changed the nuance; it's what she would tell herself and others from now on.

Maria's hand slipped into Katie's and held it gently. "Except us, of course." Katie's head slipped onto her mother's shoulder.

"I think he might be right." Tears came and rolled down her face.

"Well," said Maria, "think for a minute what there is in England for you."

"For a German, you mean?" Katie straightened herself. Fading smiles, mouths setting into straight lines, eyes steely with distrust and suspicion. She had seen it dozens of times. But there was London, where you could lose yourself, where no-one was very interested in where you came from and there were concerts, art galleries, Streatham, Lisebette, laughter. She spotted a letter from Lisebette on the bedside table which had arrived days before, her plans for Christmas, questions from friends wondering when, if, she was coming back. And that nice man they met at the party – remember? The chap from the Black Forest? He hasn't forgotten you, you know.

She did remember, thinking back, an image of his face swimming into her consciousness. Bill. Yes, he was nice.

She looked at her mother just in time to see her expression change from sadness to encouraging smile. She put her arms around her and held her, rocked her.

Maria sighed. "We are all damaged here, Katie. In one way or another. Your father…"

Katie broke away and said, "He's all right, isn't he? He will be all right?"

"Yes, he'll be all right."

She nodded. She needed to believe it because she had nearly decided. She needed to believe that the tremor would go away, that the prolonged silences were nothing to worry about and that the dark shadows would fade. She would make a final decision after Christmas, she told herself, lying on the bed and rereading Lisebette's letter, blurred memories of the party she'd gone to, unwillingly, just four months ago, coming into focus. Gentle faces, laughter, gentle jokes, recalled in whispers, pushing away the rubble and the anguish and the exhausting soul-searching and, as she slipped into sleep, she drifted forward into that world of confidence, of hope, a world filled with the smell of roses in summer heat.

*

"Remember the roses under the bay windows at Opa's house?" Heinz nodded. "Well, that's what it reminded me of." Katie knew he had better things to do but she wanted someone to hear about the party, wanted him to understand its significance, which she had only just realised herself.

"OK," he said, "you didn't really want to go but this Lisebette of yours made you go. You arrive at this nice big house. Then what?"

Katie studied her brother for a second. In many ways he had grown older than her over the past years. She decided to cut her story short, concentrate on the atmosphere of the party itself, the people she had met there, how different to anything possible in Duisburg right now.

So she wouldn't tell him about the fun they'd had buying dresses at the market, pink for Lisebette – out to impress her boyfriend's parents – and navy blue for her. Or the fury directed at her from the bathroom an hour before they were due to go.

'Don't even think about changing your mind!' Lisebette had shouted at her from behind the door. 'I recognise the signs, you know. And you've suddenly gone quiet.' She'd watched from the bed as Lisebette swept her hair into a 'victory roll'. A hugely complicated task involving several partings, hair swept up and rolled into the nape of the neck and two full rolls carefully pinned high at each side of the head.

'I'm not changing my mind, it's just that…'

'No, you're not. You're expected. You're coming. And you will enjoy yourself.'

And that had been that. Stomach churning at the thought of a roomful of strangers but bolstered by the dress and her new 'Britannia Red' lipstick, off they'd gone.

Heinz was looking up at the clock, willing her to get on with it, the same clock which had managed to tick its way through bombs and sirens and hunger. Katie pressed on, searching for the right words.

"It was the people. The people at the party. All sorts." Heinz waited, interested. Then, as if a large penny had dropped, he said, "Aha! What was he like?"

He was pleased to see he had made her blush.

"No!" she said crossly. "Well, there was someone but that's not what I want to tell you."

The two men had turned their heads when she'd walked in, then resumed their conversation with another couple. They were laughing and pouring beer into glasses. She'd noticed, then become distracted by introductions to Richard, Lisebette's lover, and his parents, whose house it was. Attention wandered back to the two men intermittently, one very blond and the other dark. Brothers, it occurred to her, something about the set of their shoulders.

"There were so many different types. Doctors, musicians. Jews, Austrians, Germans." She wanted Heinz to see what she was remembering.

"So they didn't mind inviting the enemy?"

"No. That's the whole point."

Mrs Bell, Richard's mother, had linked arms with Katie immediately and begun to walk her around the room.

'So, you're German, Katie,' she'd said. Her gaze was very direct and had it not also been very friendly her heart would have sunk. Without waiting for an answer Mrs Bell continued, 'We travelled extensively all over Germany in the twenties, such a beautiful country. Where do you come from?' Her hair was nearly white, pulled back from her face, her voice, as if she sensed Katie's nerves, seemed to be extra calm and slowed down whenever she responded to an answer. 'Duisburg? No, we never went there but we did go to Cologne, wonderful concert, I remember.'

Gradually she was introduced to some of the others in the room.

"There was a woman called Lee," she told Heinz, "an English Jew and her husband Bruno, Austrian." She remembered Lee's small, neat frame and her laugh that lit up the room. And she remembered the sadness behind Bruno's tired smile as they asked her about her life, her plans. 'Of course, of course,' they'd both said when she'd told them of her need to return to Germany to see her parents.

"Then there was the couple who owned a musical instrument shop, good friends of Richard, helped him choose his cello."

Heinz's eyes were wandering once again towards the clock.

"Look, what I think I'm saying," she was working it out as she spoke, "is that it was London in a nutshell. Different people, different backgrounds all jumbled up. Not minding. Accepting each other."

Heinz paused, more pennies dropping into place. "Not like here, you mean?"

"Not like here," she repeated, nodding slowly.

"OK. I get it, London's a wonderful place. But there is still something you haven't told me, isn't there?" Get on with it, his eyes told her, get to the heart of all this. He really was much older than her now. It must be the sexless, manless void she'd been living in since Eric. She knew so little. Become timid. She told him the rest.

"There were quite a few ex-internees there, most of them had been on the Isle of Man, like me. They all seemed to know the music shop owner."

Lisebette and Richard had appeared at her side and taken her away from Mrs.Bell, steered her towards the drinks table.

'This is Franz, owner of Winkler's Musical Emporium and his lovely wife, Helena.' Richard delivered the introduction with a flourish, the friends laughed. Names were exchanged.

It was the blond brother, Albert, tanned skin, who'd offered and lit the first cigarettes, smoke blown high amidst exclamations of surprise at the fact that five years of their lives had been spent in such close proximity. She drew on her Player's Navy Cut and sipped at her wine, aware of 'Britannia Red' on tip and rim. She needed both to cope with the male eyes now scanning her face. Richard spoke, an arm swinging over the darker brother's shoulder.

'Bill plays the clarinet in our little orchestra.' Her eyes flicked over a fine face, dark hair swept back.

'I'm a tailor. Very much an amateur musician.' His voice was gentle. She noticed the self-deprecation.

'But you're good,' Richard drained his beer. 'You should take it up professionally.'

Bill shrugged, smiling, looking all the time at Katie.

Heinz listened as Katie told him about the orchestra Bill and Richard played in, that he was from the Black Forest, from a large family, that he had a kind voice with no anger in it. An interesting description, Heinz thought and said, because he knew she wanted to hear it, and because it was true, "He sounds right for you, Katie."

Bill had stayed close to her that evening, asking questions, telling her about himself. There was something untainted about him, something safe.

"And," Heinz was getting up, "you don't need anyone's permission to go back. You know that, don't you?"

Katie looked at him gratefully. "I think that's what I want."

"So do I. Now, I have got to go." He jumped up.

She watched him, smiling. "Who is she?"

He grinned. "A redhead called Magdalene. She's very nice and cheers me up no end." He threw his jacket over his shoulder.

"You'll have to meet her before you…" He stopped short, biting his lip. His eyes stung, so did hers.

He gave her a hug, a real one, a big brother hug, before leaving her. She heard the glass-panelled apartment door click, gently, and the sound of his footsteps disappear down the stone steps.

She sat for some time, Heinz's voice and presence tuned out and the party chatter once more filling her ears, her memory. She was firmly back, in London, the smell of roses wafting in through the open bay windows on that warm summer evening. She and Bill had moved away from the group and fallen effortlessly into speaking German together. She hadn't spoken to many Black Foresters before and found his accent charming, soft and lyrical. She told him of her plan to go back to Germany, to see her family, maybe to stay. Did she imagine a look of brief disappointment? But he did say, like Lee and Bruno, 'Of course, of course.'

He had no plan to return, she tried to recall what he had said, two brothers in London, another in Germany but he hadn't wanted to talk too much about it, looked down at his hands as he spoke. Hands that looked suitable for neither clarinet nor sewing needle, she remembered thinking. She also remembered how animated he became when he talked about the orchestra, how talented the conductor was – a woman – how she and Lisebette must come to the concert planned for early in the New Year, if she was in London, of course. She remembered leaning back against the windowsill, watching him speak, their shoulders brushing.

That evening she wrote a letter to Lisebette. She would spend Christmas at home, she owed her parents that at least. And New Year's Eve. It would be cruel to abandon them before *Silvester Abend*. Too important a celebration. And they would find things to celebrate. She hesitated but not for long before writing, 'If you happen to bump into Bill, tell him I'll be back in time for that concert. Make sure to get me a ticket.'

*

Heinz was adamant. Only book the ticket for the steamer to Dover. He'd find a way. And of course, he did.

A few days after Christmas he came home, slamming the door

behind him, rattling keys ostentatiously in the air and ushering them all to the window. Down below, parked directly beneath their apartment, stood a grey Volkswagen.

"Is it yours?" asked Maria.

"Not yet."

"What do you mean?" Heinrich said. He'd stopped being surprised at what his enterprising son could procure long ago. Since the wine at Christmas. Since the camera.

"Uncle Anton!" Ah. Of course.

Heinz explained, "I went to ask him if he had something I could drive Katie to Ostend in. Just to borrow. He took me out into the yard and produced that," nodding proudly down at the dull roof of the car, "from under a tarpaulin."

"Like a magician," Katie said, smiling at her brother.

"Yes!" smiling back.

They trooped downstairs to have a better look.

"Is it safe?" Maria looked at it dubiously.

"As houses," said Heinz, tapping the bumper fondly.

"It will be if Anton's let you use it." Maria was slightly reassured by Heinrich's words.

Some minor official – there had been a lot of those – had left it with Anton in '45. A slippery clutch. Anton had fixed it and waited. And waited. If Heinz was willing to pay the repair costs – yes, he could wait until the end of the month – Anton was happy for him to take it off his hands. The deal was done in ten minutes flat.

Heinz had learned to drive during the war, delivering messages, supplies and men in either a 'Kübelwagen', a jeep designed by Porsche, or a truck. The best of days, he'd loved it. Didn't last long. The vehicles were left rotting across Russia. Along with the messages, the supplies and the corpses. Driving the Volkswagen through Belgium to Ostend would be an adventure. He couldn't wait.

*

It was a muted adventure. As familiar as they were with bombed-out cities and flattened streets, the piles of rubble, neat now, ready for rebuilding, dulled their excitement. They drove into a broken Aachen, the renowned border town, scene of ancient battles, and saw a dozen jagged spires, the bare bones of the churches, toppling mediaeval walls. Sparse, well-ordered traffic, women with children navigating streets bereft of landmarks.

A delay at the border, a special queue for German number plates. Visas and passports scrutinised, questions asked and repeated by Belgian police then British soldiers. It was to be expected and they had allowed time for it.

Then a bumpy ride through Belgium, keeping north of Brussels, over shallow waterways and past shattered villages, valiantly putting themselves back together again. Outside Bruges they found a petrol station. Heinz pulled in and found the francs he had exchanged in Aachen, enough to fill the tank to get him back to Germany. He drew breath before he got out of the car, money in hand, and braced himself. The attendant, a shabby man of about sixty, shuffled towards him, taking in the German number plates, the healthy young man standing by his 'people's car', the young woman in the passenger seat, and spat vigorously out of the side of his mouth before unscrewing the nozzle and filling the tank. He took the proffered bank notes, walked back into the garage and slammed the door behind him. Back in the car Heinz and Katie exchanged a long look that simply said, 'What can you expect?'

A lopsided road sign informed them that Ostend was twenty kilometres away. After a while he wound down the window, expecting a smell of the sea, but the icy blasts that hit their skin brought complaints from Katie. They rode to the port in silence, readying themselves for the final goodbye. Heinz felt his foot lift, just a little, from the accelerator, slowing down time, delaying the moment.

Afterwards he leaned against the car and watched her walk away, turning once or twice to smile at him, towards the embarkation point. It was cold, a wind licking off the North Sea, and he tugged his jacket across his chest, keeping his eyes on her dark coat until it merged with the others and she was gone. Then he remembered. He opened the car door and reached in to grab the camera lying on the back seat. He'd meant to take a picture of her as she was leaving. He aimed it at the ship, motionless on the quay against a slate-grey sky, lines of passengers tramping up the gangplank. He thought he spotted her. Click. As he wound the film on, he scoured the railings of the ship, tiny figures – maybe that was her. Click. And again. People were waving. He waved back in case she could see him. Years later he found the photos, tipped out from an old box and spread across his huge teak desk, and had to scratch his head. A ship, funnels, that grey sky. "Of course! Ostend. The day she left; when we lost her."

*

And what of Katie on that day at the beginning of 1947? What of her conflicted brain, her torn heart?

She'd turned once to watch her mother and father recede into the distance, Maria leaning against Heinrich, her arm raised in farewell, held quite still as if afraid to lower it. The last goodbyes were positive, full of smiles, encouragement. They wished her well, it was a good decision, for the best. She caught a glimpse of them in the side mirror, specks, then gone. Only Hansgünther, true to his soul, had remained upstairs. 'I don't want to watch you leave, I want to remember you here, at home, with us.' He allowed himself his moment of resentment before breaking into a smile and wishing her good luck. The memory of the smile broke her, and she wept. Huge, gulping sobs that soaked her handkerchief and distressed Heinz so much that he asked if he should stop, go back.

"No, no!" She waved her hand frantically, blowing her nose, trying to regain control, "Go! Go!" But the heaving gasps had to run their course and slowly, slowly it was over, and she slumped down in the seat, swollen-eyed and exhausted, watching the landscape change from grey to wintry green, patches of frost glistening where the sun couldn't reach. Aware that Heinz was casting frequent anxious looks in her direction she said, "I'm all right, it's all right."

And as her breathing settled and her heart relaxed, she began to feel relief. Relief after days of bottling up her dread, holding back. And relieved that she was still sure she had made the right decision, heading in the right direction. She felt sleepy and her lids drooped.

The last days had been busy. Getting her travel permits, saying goodbyes. Friede had come with her boy, said she would miss her, did she really have to go? She was a sweet woman, Katie realised, and she would miss her and said so. She would never blame her for her parents' mistakes. As her eyes closed, she remembered her aunts, Margarethe and Johanna, coming to visit, smiles as warm as ever but thin and worn. Pre-war clothes patched, washed and, like them, faded. They had become old ladies. Eyes displaying kindness and sadness in equal measure. She wanted to squeeze away the memory.

In Belgium, as Heinz ground the gears and negotiated the pot-holes on the roads she gradually took more notice – of the flattening landscape, the sodden deserted fields. They talked about the garage owner, his inability to look Heinz in the eye. He thought it would take a few years. Katie looked at him. That's not what her father would say. Decades more like.

They arrived at Ostend and found a place near the dock to park the car. Now they could smell the sea; a few disgruntled gulls squawked overhead.

"Don't forget to write." How often during the last few days had she heard those words? This time they were addressed to Heinz.

"Well, of course I will," he said, taking her suitcase out of the boot. She smiled at him. He wouldn't, she knew that. Too many plans, too much to do. She hugged him tight and walked away.

*

Did she recognise the convulsive sobbing that had gripped her in the car as grief for what she was losing? She wouldn't remember it until the telegram, ten years later, announcing the death of her father. Then, locked in the bathroom, gripping the sides of the wash basin, tears rolling and falling, chest heaving as if it would crack open, then she remembered.

But today, the steamer cutting through an ice-grey sea, she remembered her first crossing; the two women who had, she realised now, thought her a spy. And the frantic families packing the deck, desperate to get away. Today the mood on board, like the sea, was calm. Men and women moved about, heading for the indoor benches, searching for spaces, taking out thermos flasks to ward off the cold, steam curling from the cups.

And what was she thinking as she watched the Belgian coast, still strewn with the barbed evidence of battles and invasions, slip out of view? What were her dreams as the ship turned and she faced the other shoreline, her chosen future? How conscious was her choice? The teeming anonymity of London. Battered, a little dreary, but not desperate, not defeated, not guilty. She leaned over the barrier and spotted the odd fishing boat bobbing far away, intent on their business. On the horizon there were cargo ships slowing down, awaiting permission to dock, their plumes of smoke temporarily halted. She pulled her hat more firmly around her ears and held her collar tight under her chin. The steamer had picked up speed, and the cold was penetrating. She closed her eyes and took a deep breath, imagining the smell of England, of steady normality.

She found a place to sit, near some ropes and life buoys strapped to the side of the ship. From here she could feel the odd splash on her face from rogue waves and listen to the throb of the engines. Their relentless rhythm eased her, soothed her. Drop by drop thoughts of that home behind her were evaporating. She was leaving her ghosts behind. Her skin and flesh felt lighter, buoyant. Peace seeped into her bones.

If she dipped her head and looked up, she could see clouds thinning, a promise of blue above the wheeling gulls. She thought of a fine jawline, of intelligent brown eyes and a voice without malice and allowed herself a smile.

Bill's Tale

Albert and Rosina Ragg run a baker's shop on Pratt Street in Camden and live above it with their children Rosie, Albie, Joe and John. The First World War, which began on July 28th, 1914, rocks the world of all the thousands of German immigrants living in England. Their lives become gradually more fearful and uncertain. It was into this atmosphere that Bill was born.

1

Camden, January 1915

"Papa, please." Albert looked down briefly into the blue eyes of his daughter. Whatever she wanted, now was not the time. Too much to do. His arms worked the bread on the enormous wooden table, lifting and pushing the pile of sweet-smelling dough with the heels of his hands. It was still sticky, and he threw a handful of flour over the mixture with an expert sideways flick, then the rhythmic kneading began again.

Rosie had learnt that this time of the day was the safest to approach her father when she wanted something. When those strong hands were safely busy with their work, they were less likely to lash out in the direction of a little ear or backside. The children were all wary of his temper and relaxed when the floor-length white apron was pulled over his head and, sleeves rolled up, he started to mix flour, water and yeast, becoming calmer in the process. Leaning against Rosie, four-year-old Albie looked up with curiosity at his sister. What was she up to? Why wasn't her arm around his shoulder as it usually was? He could sense that her body was rigid, alert, ready for something. He had already learnt that approaching Papa could be a risky business.

The children's fingers, resting side by side on the edge of the table, Albie on tiptoe so he could reach, were dusted with flour. So were their noses and eyelashes. Rosie's mouth twitched in determination. She watched the dough become pliant and elastic. Still the muscular

271

forearms continued the pushing and pulling. This period of calm would end soon. She gave Albie a gentle push with her hip to give herself space and a little more courage. A big breath…"Papa, it's not fair. Mitzi down the street is going. Her little brother is going. I should be allowed to go." Too fast, she was talking too fast, but she wanted this so badly, and any minute, the spell would be broken and she'd lose courage and another chance lost. "I want to learn to speak English, and they have books, oh Papa, books with pictures, big pictures. Look, look I can already write my name." She carefully wrote on the floury table R… O… S… then stopped as the kneading stopped, and her father's arms became briefly motionless before gathering the white dough and tipping it into the huge bowl where it would grow and grow. Seconds passed.

He leant heavily on the table and glanced again at his daughter. These two were like him, pale-skinned, but her eyes were like his wife's, sharp and bright. His heart lurched with love but his arms, his body, didn't know how to show it. He had work to do. Loaves needed to be brought out of the oven and the next batch put in. Cooled bread needed to be stacked on the shelves in the little shop front, coal needed to be added to the fiercely hot fire that heated the oven. In less than half an hour, the heavy front door would be unlocked, and the shop would be open.

"Rosina – where are you!" The impatience in his voice could so quickly turn to anger. He knew it himself. He swallowed down his instinct to listen to his bright-eyed girl, he couldn't look at her. The call to his wife broke the silence.

He wasn't a tall man, but powerfully built; to the children he seemed enormous. Rosie's heart was beating not just in her chest but in her throat, in her ears. She gripped the table to give herself courage. The words came out of her mouth almost in a whisper. She wasn't sure if it was her voice or not, she couldn't hear it properly because of the thumping and rush of blood in her ears. "I want to go to school; I want to go with Mitzi and Jacob. I'll be home this afternoon; I—"

"Enough!" The side of his fist came down on the table, not so hard but hard enough to send a little shower of flour up into the air. Albie took a step back. Rosie held her ground.

"Dammit, girl." The curse shook her more than the fist. Her fingers fell away from the table; she clutched her skirt and looked at his face. How angry had she made him? His mouth, half covered by a wide and shaggy moustache, was thin and grim. But his eyes, looking straight at her, were not dark and thunderous; there was a light there, something quite unfamiliar, something dancing, trying to find words. Then it was gone.

"You are needed here. Your brothers need you. You know this perfectly well."

She felt Albie's hand creep into hers as hope and excitement left her. There was prickling behind her eyes. I won't cry. I won't cry. And she squeezed Albie's hand a little too hard in her efforts to ward off the tears.

"School would be a waste of time. You will be working in the shop next year." Papa's voice was firm. He was convincing himself that he was right.

Something else was growing inside Rosie. Not fear, not disappointment but anger fuelled by injustice. This time she didn't think about her words, didn't think about how it would come out.

"You'll let Albie go when he's bigger. I know you will. It's not fair. Not fair!"

She knew she had shouted. Her fingers flew to her mouth to press her lips shut. Papa's eyes grew hard; he moved towards the corner of the table where the children stood, both frozen, motionless, shocked by Rosie's outburst. He no longer saw them, only heard the petulant, rebellious voice. He couldn't allow it, couldn't allow his authority to be questioned. His big hands moved first across the floury table then in the air as if deciding by themselves what action to take.

"Albert!"

The door leading to the storeroom and the staircase had opened, and Rosina came in. All eyes turned towards her. Albie walked over to her and buried his face in her skirt, and she absentmindedly pushed her fingers through his hair as she took in the scene in front of her. Rosie looked carefully from Mama to Papa; he straightened up and folded his arms across his chest.

Mama kept her gaze on him as she said, "I think she should go.

Let her go." Rosie stopped breathing. The silence was absolute and seemed to last a long time, but Papa broke it.

"You know she is needed here. How will you manage when the new baby arrives…?"

Mama kept her eyes on Papa. "Rosie, go upstairs and find your coat."

Rosie hesitated for only a fraction of a second before bolting for the door. As she reached it, she hesitated and took a quick glance back at Papa, whose mouth had taken a grimmer turn and his hands had moved to his hips. "Go on, girl," said Mama and Albie went scampering after her up the stairs.

Albert glared at his wife but as his arms dropped to his side his shoulders drooped slightly and his gaze became questioning rather than angry.

"This has gone on long enough. She has been begging us for months now. Let her have a chance at some learning."

"But you know how difficult things have been getting…"

"Yes, and they will probably get worse. Mrs Brinkman told me yesterday that fewer and fewer people are using their hardware shop and our own sales are down…"

"Nonsense; people will always need bread."

"But they don't have to buy *our* bread. Women who used to be good customers turn their faces away when I see them in the street. Let Rosie go to school. Only God knows what the future will bring for us."

Albert hated it when his wife talked like this. Everything he knew, everything he wanted was here at 34 Pratt Street. It had taken him ten years to build his little business. The war would be over soon, and everything would go back to normal. He turned back to the dough that had been rising and began to form it into identical round, smooth loaves.

*

Rosie burst through the door at the top of the stairs and stood puffing and panting, legs apart, staring in unbelieving triumph at the two little faces that were turned towards her. Albie finally made it up the steep staircase – he needed knees and hands to climb it – and took up his usual position next to her. John, lying in a large drawer that served as a cot, smiled sleepily, ready for play. Joe was sucking with great determination on a piece of bread.

"I'm going to school. I'm going to school now," she announced with emphasis and then, clearing her throat, remembered her position. She pulled Albie towards the little ones and sat him down then lifted John so that he could sit up but ignored the outstretched arms. Two-year-old Joe continued sucking and chewing the bread but didn't take his eyes off her. Albie sensed the importance of the moment and that he had a privileged place in it. His chest expanded a little as he waited for Rosie to say more.

"I'm seven years old," she said this gravely, as if it would serve as an explanation for whatever might come next. John found the tone of her voice unfamiliar, and the corners of his mouth turned down. Joe stopped chewing. Albie was impressed; seven was, after all, a great age.

"I have to go to school and you all have to be very, very good while I'm away." Albie wasn't too sure about being very, very good.

"Albie will be here to play with you," she looked meaningfully at him. "I will be back later this afternoon."

Joe sensed that something in his secure little world was about to change. Instead of picking things up, tidying things away, wiping his face and hands, Rosie was washing her hands at the stone sink in the corner then running her fingers through her own hair. They watched as she put on her coat. Mrs Behan down the street had given it to Mama just before Christmas because it was now definitely too small for her Mary. It was too big for Rosie, but she loved it. She tried to turn the sleeves up a little but for some reason found that her fingers weren't working properly; they seemed to have become fat and jittery and stiff. She gave it up and walked quickly to the fireplace and bent down to pick at a small piece of tile that was loose in front of it. She poked inside the hole under it until she found what she had hidden there – a tiny piece of chalk the size of a button. She held it up between her finger and thumb to show the others.

"I'll need this at school to write with. It's what happens, Mitzi told me." Rosie had found it in the street; she had been watching a greengrocer write his prices with it on his board and throw it away because it had become too small for his bulky fingers. She'd raced to pick it up. Now she put it carefully in her coat pocket, the one without a hole, then straightened herself up. She smiled bravely at her brothers and gave one last firm look at Albie before turning to the door and closing it behind her.

At the bottom of the stairs, she found her boots, also a little too big, and battered from previous use. She pushed her feet into them and made as neat a bow as she could with shaky fingers with the string that served as laces then, with a straight back, went into the baking room.

Papa had his back to her, bent over the oven, rearranging the loaves of bread; Mama was carrying a tray of baked bread into the shop and indicated to Rosie to follow her. Rosie and her mother quickly lay the warm loaves on the counter behind the first batch, four on the bottom and three on the top.

Rosie looked anxiously at Mama's face – suppose she changed her mind? Her heart skipped a beat as the tray was propped up against the wall. Mama hadn't really looked at her as they arranged the bread. Her lips were pressed tightly together, and her eyes were shinier than usual.

Suddenly she spoke. "Don't forget to work hard." Still she didn't look at Rosie. The words had come out more harshly than she intended but she was fighting very hard to stop her voice cracking. "And it's time you were off." She wiped her hands on her apron, brushed away something on her cheek and finally, finally looked down into Rosie's anxious upturned eyes.

"Come here." Rosie, relieved, put her arms around her mother, now really quite fat with the new baby growing inside her. "Of course I'm going to work hard." She felt a little indignant; what else would she do at school? Rosina smiled.

Rosie had laid her head on the bump but took it away quickly as she felt something push gently but very definitely against her cheek. She looked with alarm at her mother, but Mama was laughing. "Looks as if this one is saying goodbye to you too!" Rosie laughed back and with her mouth close to the bump whispered, "Goodbye baby, I'll be back soon."

"Now go and say good-bye to Papa – it'll be all right." Rosie wasn't sure about that. She hesitated before going back into the baking room.

Papa was leaning on the table waiting for the final batch of bread to be ready. His eyes narrowed when Rosie came in. He looked at her oversized coat and her scruffy boots and at her shining, expectant face and fought hard at hiding his sudden feeling of tenderness towards her.

"Don't be late back, your mother needs you," was all he could say, but his voice sounded a little hoarse and there was a wateriness in his eyes that Rosie found so strange that she found the courage to go up to him and quickly hug him around the waist and whisper, "Thank you, Papa," before turning away and walking back through the shop and out into the street where she breathed in the cold, damp air and felt it lick around her bare legs.

2

In Belgium and France, the German generals were trying to get to Paris and the British and French generals were trying to stop them. Thousands and thousands of soldiers were dying on the battlefields. Neither side could get past vicious machine gun fire and barbed wire fences.

Rosina watched her daughter turning right out of the shop door, walking slowly at first then shooting across the road, dodging a horse and cart as her coat flapped around her pale legs. Mitzi was on the corner of Camden Street, opposite the church and grinning from ear to ear at the sight of Rosie skipping and racing in her too big boots towards her. The girls linked arms and disappeared, laughing, towards the school.

The shop suddenly felt very quiet. Rosina smoothed back her black hair and adjusted the tight little bun at the nape of her neck. Maybe she should have pinned Rosie's hair into a bun before she set off, but that straggly head of fair hair would not behave itself. She thought of her own mother roughly pulling a comb through her tangles before setting her off on another task. No school for her. She couldn't remember a time when she wasn't expected to help scrub the table and floors, peel some vegetables, wash dishes under a freezing tap out in the backyard. She closed her eyes; for a second, she was back there, outside the wooden house, by the tap, the snow squeezing between her toes, falling off the pines next to the house as the wind tore through the branches.

Albert walked into the shop. He had put on a clean apron, ready to serve the customers. He carried the last of the morning bake in his arms, hot and sweet-smelling. He laid them onto the window shelf and took up his place behind the counter. She watched him assume the look of a businessman, capable and in charge as he brushed a few crumbs off the counter and checked the little box under it for pennies to give as change. She was proud of him, this silent and difficult man who had worked so hard to get the bakery up and running and make it successful.

"Go up to the boys, I'll open up," he said without looking at her.

She stayed by the door, giving her back an involuntary rub and looked up the street. Each day it seemed to get quieter. There used to be such bustle and noise, people shouting greetings to each other across the road. When she had first arrived with her new husband the neighbours had come round one by one to welcome her. Trudi, who was from Switzerland, became a great friend; they could talk in German and made each other giggle because of their similar dialects. Maria, from Italy, came with Trudi one day to say hello. And Rolf, a German who had helped Albert scrub out the shop and fix the oven before they had got married. Rolf had married Edna, a young English girl. Liveliest of all were the large and noisy Irish families. The Kavanaghs and Behans seemed to live mainly on the street, there were so many of them. Always friendly but try as she might she never managed to understand a word they said to her, so she smiled and returned the waves.

Now the street had become calm and sombre. A couple of the Behan men had suddenly gone back to Ireland; there was trouble over there apparently, so Albert told her, trouble with the English. Some of the English lads had joined the British Army; the Dray brothers had gone to sign up almost as soon as war was declared. Mrs Dray had come in just before Christmas, and said she was very sorry, but her husband had told her she wasn't to come into Albert Ragg's bakery anymore from now on. Albert and Rosina were stunned into silence. She had been a good and friendly customer. For a little while they couldn't understand it.

Albert brushed past her as he went to unlock the door just in time to let in the first customer.

"Good morning, Mrs Swain, how are you today?"

Rosina was always impressed by her husband's ability to switch to English in the shop; all those little phrases he used with the customers – 'how's the family?', 'that's a pity', 'glad to hear it', 'what can I get you?', 'windy day!', 'rainy day!' In the days when there were queues of people waiting to buy the warm fresh loaves, Albert enjoyed these mini conversations, handing over the bread and rattling the pennies, sixpences and shillings in the box under the counter.

"Not too bad thanks," Mrs Swain looked at Rosina and down at the bump, "and 'ow are you luv? That baby comin' soon, is it?"

"In a few weeks, a couple of weeks, maybe," Albert answered for her while Rosina smiled and nodded. She wanted to say something to this cheerful woman but was stopped short when Mrs Swain spoke again.

"What a time to be born, right in the middle of a bloomin' war! Poor little mite! Not 'is fault, is it? Not your fault neither what your lot are up to over there." She shook her head violently and pursed her lips as if to stop herself from saying anything else. Rosina's throat felt tight, confused by the sudden anger from this nice woman.

Albert shuffled his weight awkwardly from one foot to the other. "The war is crazy, crazy. I don't understand it," he said it quietly, almost as if talking to himself. Then, a little louder, repeated his favourite phrase, "It'll be over soon."

"Yes, maybe; but my Reginald says that bloomin' Kaiser needs teaching a lesson." She pushed the large loaf roughly into her bag but when she lifted her head she looked directly into Rosina's worried eyes with a mischievous look on her face. "Maybe a good kick up the arse 'll do the trick, eh?" She gave a little kick with her booted foot, so Rosina understood straight away. She smiled back broadly, out of relief and gratitude and laughed at the disrespectful joke about the Kaiser.

"Well, ta da then, and look after yourself," said Mrs Swain to Rosina, nodding at the bump. The heavy door clattered shut behind her.

3

As stalemate in the trenches continued, hatred of the enemy in Britain was gaining strength. All Germans were considered 'enemy aliens'.

One evening last August, just after war had been declared, Rosina and Albert were in the shop tidying up. The door had been bolted. Albert was locking up the day's money in his metal box; Rosina had finished sweeping and was heading for the stairs, back up to the children when there was a sharp banging on the door. They stopped what they were doing, surprised at the force behind the knock, the unfamiliar urgency, and looked at the two men standing behind the glass doors. One was in policeman's uniform, buttons glinting in the low evening sunshine; the other wore a long coat and hat pulled down over his eyes. The one in uniform put his face close up to the glass, using his hand to shield against the glare of the sun and peered in. He knocked again just as urgently. Albert glanced at Rosina then went to pull the bolt back and to turn the key in the lock.

The men came in, without a word being said, without being invited; they seemed to fill up the space in front of the counter, looking around, sizing things up. They had never been afraid of the police before. There was a bobby who came in to have a chat and to buy bread. He always had time for the children and had once lifted Albie high into the air, making him squeal in delight and let him have a go on his whistle. This felt very different.

Upstairs Rosie had heard the insistent banging, not a sound she had heard before, then the scrape of the bolt and turning key and the clatter of the door opening. What was strangest, was the silence that followed; no greeting, no welcoming chat. Something alerted her to put her finger to her lips and ask the boys to be quiet for just a moment. They all listened; John couldn't crawl yet so he sat watching as Rosie walked to the top of the stairs and slowly went down.

"Now then, Mr Ragg, as you know, there is a war on." It was the policeman who spoke.

"Yes, yes, I know, I'm so…" Albert was about to apologise, as if saying sorry could make any difference.

The policeman ignored him and puffing out his chest ever so slightly continued to speak. "My name is PC Haldane, and this is Mr Brooke from the Home Office. We are here to make a few things very clear to you, to both of you," he added, looking at Rosina. Rosie had reached the bottom of the staircase but had come in so quietly that no-one had noticed her. She stood behind her mother, staring at the white knot of the apron tied around her waist. Did she imagine it trembling? She moved her head slightly so she could see the men.

Rosina's muscles had tightened at the words 'Home Office'. She, like Albert, knew that that was where power lay. They had successfully overcome all the hurdles that the Home Office had put in their path in the past; permission to stay and work in England, to set up the business. With a stroke of a pen, it could all be taken away from them at any time.

PC Haldane gave a small cough and a sidelong glance at Mr Brooke who, at this signal, reached into his inside coat pocket and took out a sheet of paper which he unfolded. As he was about to read from it, he caught sight of the blonde head and one blue eye peeping out from behind Rosina. He faltered for a second and cleared his throat before starting.

"Under the Aliens Registration Act all Germans over the age of eighteen are requested to register at their nearest police station. This must be done as soon as possible… if you fail to do so it will be taken as an act of… you will be detained under His Majesty's…" The man was very young and Rosina watched his lips move, as he delivered his speech and noticed the soft hair on his upper lip. Albert clutched his box under his arm, standing straight and motionless; he fought to pay attention to the formal and difficult words, but they seemed to grow dim as he struggled to make sense of what was going on, what these strangers were doing in his home.

Mr Brooke stopped talking. Rosie had crept out from behind Rosina and stared up at the man who blushed slightly as he folded the paper up again. Albert suddenly realised how uncomfortable all this made the young man; he put his box onto the counter, he felt a little calmer and looked carefully at him.

"Why do I have to register? We have lived here for years—"

The policeman cut him short. "Now don't get lippy! Mr Brooke has made it quite clear, and you should have been listening. First thing in the morning you get yourselves round to Albany Street Police Station. We can't have Germans walking around London! You could be up to anything!" Albert had learnt that there were some Englishmen that were so wary of foreigners that it was always best to remain silent with them. This policeman was enjoying his work.

Albie had made his way downstairs and now stood on Rosina's other side. Her arms slipped around the children's shoulders. Mr Brooke looked from Rosie to Albie then, with a sigh, handed the paper to Albert.

"You'll need this tomorrow. Take it with you." The policeman walked to the door, opened it, and stepped outside. Mr Brooke turned to follow him but stopped to face Albert again. "This war will change everything." He gave Rosina a nod and Rosie a half-smile before adding, "Take care of your family," and closing the door gently behind him.

*

The next day Albert and Rosina walked together down Delancy Street, over the railway bridge then past Regents Park. It was a beautiful day. The great trees rustled above their heads. This is where they had gone for walks, as a young couple, and later brought the children on Sunday outings. Rosina thought of the words Mr Brooke had used. She and her family were now aliens, a word she had to ask Albert to explain. She let her fingers bounce along the iron railings bordering the park, the way Albie and Rosie did, when they came here, and felt the barrier between herself and the world on the other side where strollers were out, enjoying the warmth. They seemed sure of their place in the world. She now felt she may be in the wrong place. Alien. She knew that Albert did not feel like this. He was indignant, angry that they should have to go through this. He said little to his wife as he strode towards Albany Street, where the police station was, determined to get this registration business over with then get back to the shop and wait for the war to end, which it would, he was certain, by Christmas. In fact, he would give the police a piece of his mind.

But of course, he didn't. At the police station they were directed to sit on a bench with other nervous German men and women, all holding a paper like theirs in their hands. They greeted each other quietly, shaking hands in the polite German way, aware of the suspicious glances from the officers when they spoke. As they waited the men slumped forward, rolling their caps around in their hands. The women whispered to each other occasionally, asking names, where they came from.

"Georgiana Street."

"Lyme Street."

"Caroline Street."

One by one the names were called until it was Albert and Rosina's turn. The paper was shown and checked against a list. They were asked about the children and told they were not allowed to travel out of London without telling the police first. The officer was polite, stamped the paper and gave it back to Albert. It was over.

4

On February 4ᵗʰ, 1915 Kaiser Wilhelm stepped up the tension by declaring the North Sea a war zone. This meant that any ships sailing into it could be attacked by German U-boats. It was done in retaliation for the naval blockade imposed by Britain which meant that food and supplies could not reach Germany.

Every afternoon when Rosie came home from school Albert said the same words: "About time!" She would whisper, "Hello Papa," sidle past him, slip off her coat and run upstairs where Albie would grin at the sight of her, Joe would smile happily with a "Rosie back, Rosie back" and run towards her, followed by John who crawled as fast as he could towards his big sister, sat down when he reached her and put out his hands demanding to be picked up, which she did immediately, planting big kisses all over his grubby, happy little face.

Later on, much later on, when things were difficult, Rosie would remember these happy homecomings; a little cup of milk on the table, especially for her, and just occasionally a big biscuit, warm and smelling of cinnamon, which she would have to share with the others. It was good to listen to her familiar language, the lilting sounds of the Black Forest dialect, easy and warm. She never thought about it like that, of course, but she was aware of coming away from a sharp and difficult place and returning to a comfortable one. Albie was usually desperate to tell her what had happened through the day, often involving something unforgivable that one of the little ones had done; Joe would want his own cuddles after John had been put back down on the floor, determined to resume his newly acquired and important crawling duties, exploring every nook and cranny of the kitchen. Rosina, usually at the stove stirring something, would listen to the chatter for a while then ask her daughter what had happened at school that day.

Rosie had learnt how to handle this daily question in a way that made her mother happy and made her feel better too. At first, she had answered with, "It's good," or "Yes, fine," or, out of desperation, "I can't remember." The early days were really not so easy. But Mitzi was with her; held her hand in the playground where the big boys charged around, told her where to line up, where the classroom was. Everything was busy and noisy and unfamiliar. To her disappointment she couldn't stay with Mitzi but was sent to a class with much younger children because she hadn't been before. She had stood in front of the headmaster and a teacher on that first morning and listened to them speak over her head of the unexpected arrival of this new girl. She answered their questions nervously, pleased that she understood everything but watching their expressions grow suspicious when they heard her speak.

"Where are your parents from, girl?" Mr Fleming, the headmaster, wearing a high tight collar which made his neck red and bulgy, stared down at her.

"Pratt Street," said Rosie innocently; there couldn't possibly be anything wrong with coming from Pratt Street, everyone she knew came from there, but she knew she had done something wrong; and it had something to do with the way she spoke. She watched Mr Fleming's neck grow darker, and a little vein just near his left ear began to throb. She dragged her eyes away from this mesmerising sight in time to hear him say,

"I asked where your parents are *from*, stupid girl. They're German, aren't they?"

Not speaking seemed safer so she nodded. Her chin dropped but she kept her eyes on the two people in front of her. She understood a little of what Mr Fleming muttered next, something about 'they should be sent back' and she heard 'no right to be here'.

Suddenly Miss Roberts spoke for the first time. Ignoring what Mr Fleming had been saying she said quietly, "There is a place free in my classroom and since this silly girl hasn't come to school before I think that is the right place for her, what do you think, Mr Fleming?"

Rosie knew she wasn't silly but there was something about the steady gaze of Miss Robert's large brown eyes and the tone of her voice that made Rosie trust her. Mr Fleming seemed slightly appeased that putting this child in a class of five-year-olds went some way to punishing her for having German parents. "Hmm. Take her then," he said and disappeared through a large dark door, slamming it shut behind him.

"Come on Rosie, follow me." For a second Miss Robert's fingers touched Rosie's shoulder; it may have been to guide her in the right direction, but it was also, Rosie felt, to reassure her, to tell her that things would be all right.

So Rosie joined a class of little children, including Mitzi's brother Jacob, who giggled when he saw her walk in and take her seat at the back of the room. Miss Roberts put a stop to that with a hard stare and took out the register where she quickly added Rosie Ragg to her list of pupils and Rosie learnt to answer with a 'present' when her name was called out. She chanted the letters of the alphabet along with the others although she already knew them. On her chalk board she practised writing letters with her tiny bit of chalk until Miss Roberts noticed and with a small smile gave her a bigger bit. She loved doing this and soon started to copy the lovely loopy letters and words that were up on the walls as examples. She glowed with pride when Miss Roberts called her up to look at her work and almost imperceptibly nodded approval. Rosie loved every moment she spent in the classroom, concentrating, with her head bent, only the sounds of scratching chalk and the odd sniff and cough from the others. She was always finished first so had time to either watch Miss Roberts, in her starched white blouse with frilled collar, which Rosie thought very pretty, or study the huge map on the wall. It took a little time to work out the letters at the top of it. It said 'The British Empire' in heavy black print. All over the map were pink shapes which stood out boldly; presumably this was the empire. She had heard her father say that the Kaiser had an empire as well and wondered where it was and what they were for.

The playground was a different matter. At first, she looked forward to seeing Mitzi and they played quietly by the fence near the road. But as the days went by, she became aware of the name-calling by some of the bigger children. She didn't understand the words at first – why did they call her a 'Hun'? Why did she hear 'Kraut'? There was finger-pointing and once someone kicked the back of her leg. Her eyes stung with tears, but she said nothing. Silence always seemed best; the cruelty ended quicker that way.

There were other German children; two brothers who didn't keep quiet. One playtime shortly after Rosie had started there was a fight at playtime. Mitzi and Rosie heard the shouting first then the shocking explosion of fists and kicking feet. When the boys were dragged apart the German boys were red in the face, furious, tears and snot running over cheeks and chin. Rosie was horrified; she had never seen a fight like that or anger like that. The brothers were hauled off to the headmaster; the others given a cuff round the ears and sent back to their classroom.

*

So, there was a lot she couldn't tell Mama about school, although she wanted to. Was the war really all her fault; or Mama's; or Papa's? It seemed it must be because she was, after all, German. Miss Roberts's kind, brown eyes didn't seem to mind. Her voice didn't change tone when she spoke to Rosie. Instead, Rosie would tell Mama about the map on the wall, the praise she got for her writing and whatever story Miss Roberts had read out that day. The story was the very best thing about the day. The whole class would sit, elbows on the table, chins resting in hands and listen to tales of pirates, princesses and giants. And Rosie, whose understanding of English was growing daily, disappeared into those stories.

As she faced one-eyed pirates brandishing glinting swords, she would forget the taunts and little cruelties of the playground. As wolves chased her through dark and fearsome forests, she could forget how tired Mama was looking, how worried she seemed whenever she left the shop. As Miss Roberts's voice told of princes chasing ogres, or crocodiles snapping at the heels of brave hunters she stopped thinking of Papa pushing his floury fingers through his hair and rubbing his mouth and chin in agitation at something he read in the paper. Once, a newspaper had been thrown through the door by a passer-by with the words, "See what you lot are doing now." It landed at Rosie's feet and she had got a glimpse of a picture, soldiers with staring eyes and bayonets, before her father had sharply scooped it up, folded the paper in half and tucked it under his arm. For just a little while the stories pushed these images, which bubbled up more and more frequently, out of her head.

One evening Rosie was attempting to tell one of the stories to the boys. As usual Papa had sat down by the fireplace and asked Albie to fetch his pipe and tin of tobacco. It used to be Rosie's job but now Albie was considered old enough for this important task and he sat up straight and expectantly, pleased with this new responsibility, waiting for his father to glance at him and nod over at the pipe hanging on a hook next to the mantelpiece and say, "Bring me my pipe, lad." Albie jumped up. He fetched the tin first so Papa could get the lid off and pick out some tobacco. He was just tall enough to unhook the pipe from the wall; it was large, brown and shiny with a curved stem and handled by Albie with great reverence. He gave it to Papa with both hands, then everyone watched and waited while he slowly stuffed the tobacco in the bowl of the pipe with his thumb, light a taper and held it over the bowl, sucking in deeply three or four times. The children always watched this procedure with fascination; especially the way the sucking dragged the flame from the taper downwards into the bowl, making the tobacco glow. Then there was the puff, puff of smoke out of the side of Papa's mouth.

Rosie wanted to choose a story that wasn't too frightening and had decided on Tom Thumb, the heroic tiny boy who is cleverer than everyone around him, although there was the bit where he gets swallowed by a wolf. But she quickly decided that Albie, in particular, would enjoy that so she started the story. Albie and Joe were snuggled up, but John was more interested in examining Papa's socks. Papa was sitting with his legs crossed, one foot swinging. It was this foot, with its woolly, frayed sock that John was trying to grab hold of. He had lit his pipe and had a newspaper spread on his knee. The smell of the tobacco added an air of calm in the little kitchen; as Papa smoked, blowing clouds around his head, he relaxed and so did everyone else. He stopped his foot moving to allow John to get a grip of the sock then bobbled it about gently, making him wobble about and giggle in delight.

Albert, needing distraction from the horror unfolding in the newspaper spread across his lap, watched as Rosie told, in German, the familiar fairy tale and watched Albie's face as it reflected with a grin Tom Thumb's success at hoodwinking the thieves and then with wide eyes the fear of being swallowed up. It was a moment of rare calm. John in the foreground clutching at his sock, the children melting into one another and into the tale, Rosie trying her hardest to make her voice, just like Miss Roberts's, rise and fall and change to add to the excitement and, in the background, there was Rosina, clearing away the plates, turning occasionally to look at her clever girl and who, quite suddenly, turned her back to them, grabbed hold of the sink and froze.

When in the long years to come he lay in his narrow, hard bunk at night, his family so far away, exhausted and trying to sleep, listening to the snores of the other men, he would try and bring back this picture, struggle to remember details, John's laughter and dribbly, toothy smile; Rosie's earnest face struggling to get the story right; Joe enjoying the shared warmth of the words, fighting sleepily to stay awake. As those months in the camp crawled by, this was the image that he tried hard to keep in his heart although it became more blurred, more distant and unreal as the days and endless nights went by.

Albert became aware of his wife's rigid back and her white knuckles gripping the sink. And as she relaxed her grip and breathed out noisily, he slowly and dimly remembered what this might mean. When she turned round, he was left in no doubt; after all, four babies had already been born under this roof and he recognised that look of gritty resolution. Amid the rising panic he told himself that he knew what to do, but even so he dropped his pipe and scattered the newspaper across the floor and stumbled as he stepped over John to get to Rosina. Rosie, who was just reuniting Tom Thumb with his parents after his adventures, stopped mid-sentence, taken aback at this unexpected movement.

Rosina, as usual, took charge of the situation. Her voice sounded calm, but Rosie knew something special was going on and she prepared herself. "Take the boys to bed now, Rosie. Albert, put the kettle on and then go and ask if Mrs Kavanagh across the road can come over."

Albert, grateful to be given firm instructions, was already putting his boots on and, after slamming the kettle on the kitchen range, pulled on his cap and left the room. The children were frozen into silence. They never saw their father panic or hurry. Rosina looked at Albie. "Albie, everything is all right." His face was beginning to crumple, and tears were squeezing out of his eyes. "The new baby is coming and when it arrives you can come and say hallo. Go with Rosie now and get into bed. Papa won't be long."

5

February 23rd. In 1915 having a baby was still a dangerous thing. Women preferred to have their babies at home since more babies and women seemed to die in hospitals. This was because doctors still didn't realise how easily infections could be passed from doctors and nurses to women having their babies.

Albert crossed a deserted Pratt Street. It was a cold and drizzly winter's evening. People were inside by their fires, eating their meals and reading the newspaper accounts of the war, as Albert had been doing, worrying about the young men they knew who were in Belgium and France. It took a while before one of the Kavanagh children opened the door. Albert poked his head around the living room door where he was met with the smells of cooked food, stale tobacco smoke and washing drying on the pulley that hung above the fireplace. Trying to keep the urgency out of his voice he said, "The baby is on the way, can you come and help us?"

Mrs Kavanagh looked at him. She was sitting at the table peeling potatoes into a huge pot of water; a toddler was sitting on the table dipping his fingers into the pot and splashing the water gently. She put the knife down, gathered the boy in her arms and deposited him on the floor.

"Sure, I'll come, it's going to be number five, isn't it?" Albert nodded.

"It'll be in a hurry then," she added and as she made for the door, she looked sharply at him and said, "You know I charge two shillings?" Albert nodded again. *Just please hurry up*, he was thinking.

"Watch the kids, Eileen," she spoke to a thin girl who was concentrating on threading a needle, ready to tackle some mending.

"Sure, Mam." Eileen was used to anxious-looking men coming to the door at all hours, day or night. She managed a thin smile for Albert before licking the thread again and poking it carefully into the eye of the needle.

Meanwhile, Rosie was trying to settle Joe off to sleep. John, as usual, went to sleep as soon as he lay down in his makeshift cot. Albie lay down and closed his eyes, but the excitement made sleep difficult, and he listened to Rosie as she tried to calm Joe, who had woken up properly, wanted Mama and couldn't understand why she wouldn't come. Rosie had already left him once to see if Mama was all right. She was sitting on the side of the bed and didn't seem to want to talk. Rosie watched her mother's face for a second or two then quietly sat next to her and held her hand. Rosina gripped hard for a minute then relaxed and breathed deeply. She looked down at Rosie's face frowning up at her.

"It's not easy having a baby, Rosie, but it will soon be over. I want you to stay with the boys. Papa will be back any minute." Joe's yelling was getting more insistent. She looked directly into Rosie's eyes and smiled. "Off you go, I'll be fine."

There was a clattering on the stairs. Rosie peered round the door and saw Mrs Kavanagh roll up her sleeves and shout to Papa to bring hot water and soap to the bedroom. She shooed Rosie out of the way and bustled into the room and her bulky body hid Mama from view. She was shooed out of the way again as Papa came past carrying a large bowl of steaming water, which he put on the floor near the bed. Then he was shooed out of the room, the door firmly closed on them both and suddenly the house felt calm once again. Even Joe had stopped yelling, but Rosie went to the bedroom to sit with the boys, and soon became aware of the smell of tobacco. Papa must have relit his pipe; that had to be a good sign. She concentrated hard on the voices of the women next door but could hear very little. Gradually her heart stopped beating quite so fast, her eye lids became droopy, and she lay down next to Albie and Joe's warm bodies and fell asleep.

6

William Ragg was born on Monday February 15th, 1915. Soldiers were battling in the mud and cold of Europe and countries across the globe were becoming involved. Feelings against the Germans were becoming more bitter, more extreme.

Joe was the first to wake up in the morning. He wriggled out from under the blankets and made his way down to the end of the bed where he turned round onto his tummy and stretched down to the ground. He walked towards the door and was surprised by Papa, carrying John.

"Where's Mama?" She was always there when he woke up, not Papa, never Papa. He was somewhere else, downstairs.

"Come and see," said Papa. He took his little boy by the hand and led him into the other bedroom. It smelled of soap and sleep. Mama was sitting up in bed holding something close to her breast and had her eyes closed. She opened them when Joe tried to climb on the bed and smiled at him.

"Good morning, little man. This is William, your new brother." Papa's arm gently pulled him back from climbing so he had to peer up at the bundle his Mama was showing him. Joe wasn't quite sure what to make of this little red object with tightly closed eyes. Then things got a little more interesting as the tiny lips pushed and puckered and the whole bundle seemed to squirm before a very audible burp came out of that mouth. Joe smiled delightedly in recognition of this proper little person. William's head turned and stretched towards his mother looking for something which Mama clearly decided he was not going to get. She settled him higher up on her arm. Albie had

294

joined Joe by now and, rubbing sleep out of his eye with one hand, reached the other up to William's cheek and stroked the brand-new, petal-soft skin. Mama stroked Albie's cheek with her free hand and gently pushed his hair out of his face.

Rosie was watching, leaning against the doorway. She watched Papa. Winter sunshine was creeping its way through the window into the small bedroom casting a little light on his face. His mouth and eyes were relaxed and for a while he looked tender and younger, absentmindedly nuzzling into John's dark hair. William continued to cast a spell over them all in the early morning silence until John, with a wriggle and a protesting shout, decided that enough was enough and it was time for breakfast.

"Take the boys downstairs, Albert. Mrs Kavanagh has got things ready for you." Mama sounded tired, but she looked at Rosie and motioned her over. "Rosie hasn't said hello yet."

Mrs Kavanagh had indeed got things ready. The kettle was boiling on the stove and there was bread and butter and milk ready on the table. She was buttoning up her coat as Albert and the boys came in.

"Now remember, she needs a day in bed. You could bring her a cup of tea – she'll be thirsty. I'll pop over later on to check she's all right. That's a fine healthy baby boy you've got there, Mr Ragg – no worries at all. Now if you just settle up with me, I'll get back home." She had been up all night but was still all bustle and practicality. Albert, dumbly grateful, slipped the two shillings off the mantelpiece where he had left it during the night and put it into her hand. He walked with her to the door. "Thank you, thank you very much," and watched her turn to go.

Mrs Kavanagh paused before crossing the deserted street. "Look after those kiddies, Albert. Things are not going to get any easier." It was a still, chilly morning. She spoke to him as if she would never speak to him again.

"Oh, I will, I always will." He meant it; with all his heart he meant it. As he walked back to the boys, he felt the dull fear of the last months return.

In the bedroom Rosie had settled down on the bed next to

her mother. After studying her face for a second and deciding that whatever happens when you have a baby, she did seem all right, she had a good look at William. She didn't mean to say it with such a regretful sigh but, "I really wanted a sister," were the words that came out; she had been quite sure that the baby would be a girl, a friend for her to look after and play with, an ally against all the boys in the house. She looked quickly at Mama, hoping she hadn't said the wrong thing, but Mama was smiling and said, "Would you like to hold him?"

Rosie took William into her arms and looked into that slightly wrinkled face with skin that seemed to have been sprinkled with the finest dusting of flour. One tiny fist was poking out of the blanket next to his face and the frail bluey-white fingers with transparent fingernails were unclenching, exploring the air around him. Suddenly and unexpectedly, she felt hot tears stabbing at her eyes and fall down her cheeks. She couldn't understand why she was feeling so, well, angry. It was as if all the bad things that were happening, at school, in the street, in the world, bad things that just wouldn't go away, might hurt this tiny boy who was so vulnerable, so innocent. It was the first time she had ever felt such fierce love for anyone and as she gulped away the tears and sobs her grip around William grew tighter.

"Rosie, Rosie, what's the matter?" Rosina leant towards her.

"Oh Mama, nothing must ever happen to him, ever!"

Rosina stroked her arms. "Nothing will happen to him. We'll make sure of that. Papa and I will make sure that nothing will happen to any of you."

Rosie slowly calmed down and handed William back to Mama, who said, "Come right up here next to me." Rosie leant against her mother.

"Papa will need your help for the next week or two. The shop won't open today or tomorrow but then it's back to normal. You know what that means?"

"No school."

"That's right."

"That's all right. There is a lot to do here." Rosie suddenly knew where it was important to be.

"Good girl. Now go downstairs and ask Papa to bring me a cup of tea, nice and sweet."

Rosie nodded and smiled back at Rosina, reassured by this request. She slid off the bed but not before giving William the softest of kisses.

7

In Europe neither side could advance. The German army was developing the Zeppelin airships and both sides were thinking of using poison gas, in order to break the stalemate that existed in the trenches.

William, almost immediately renamed Billy by everyone, wasn't very interesting in the opinion of his brothers. Considering the fuss he caused, he was no fun at all. He slept, cried a bit and took up all of Mama's time. Worst of all they were being told to be quiet all the time by their father. So Albie, Joe and John played their games quietly and kept out of the way of Papa, who stomped about keeping the stove alight, self-consciously making tea and boiling potatoes. At least he didn't bother combing their hair, which was always painful, or telling them to put on some socks or tuck in their vests. He only just remembered to tell them to wash hands and faces before bedtime.

Rosina slept for most of the day and night, waking when Billy woke, to feed him. The following day she got up and came downstairs, sitting in Papa's chair. Billy took up residence near the stove in a small wooden crate which Rosie had lined with an old clean woollen blanket. John climbed onto Rosina's lap. She rubbed at his messy hair and pulled off his jumper to turn it the right way round before he wriggled free of her. She looked with tired amusement at her husband. He might make the best bread in Camden but in this little kitchen he really couldn't or wouldn't do a thing.

"Albert, I think I'll make a soup today. Go and get some vegetables and a little meat."

Soup was the children's very favourite meal; four heads turned to watch their father go quickly to get his coat and cap, surprisingly quickly as if relieved to be going out, to have something else to do. He grabbed the tin on the mantelpiece where money was kept and took a couple of shillings. Rosina nodded. "That will be plenty. Hardcastle's on the High Street has good meat with bones." Albert was already at the side door that led into Queen Street. There was a brief chill as the door opened. "I won't be long," he said and closed the door again firmly. Rosie, sitting on the floor next to Billy, watched him leave with a sense of unease. He rarely left the house these days. She glanced up at her mother's face and caught a similar flicker of concern, but it was gone in a flash and her attention shifted to Billy, who began wriggling restlessly.

"Pick him up, Rosie, he needs to get used to you; walk about with him for a bit." Rosie didn't need telling twice. She lifted him gently from the crate and popped him on her shoulder the way she had seen her mother do it. His head wobbled about until he nestled into her neck. She walked up and down swaying from side to side, feeling his little body relax and enjoy the motion. She looked at her mother from time to time for confirmation that she was doing things properly and felt a definite sense of achievement when Billy fell asleep again.

Joe, seeing an opportunity, crawled onto his mother's lap and put his arms around her neck. Gentle Joe, not as tough as his brothers, had always needed a little more attention. She held him close and nuzzled his ear. But her eyes were fixed on the door, waiting for Albert's return. The clock on the mantelpiece ticked away the minutes; a half-hour was all it should take. It was an hour, before they heard the door open and slam shut again. Albert put the food on the table, took off his coat and sat down.

Rosina looked at him. He was always on edge when he left the house, they both were. People they knew weren't exactly unfriendly, but they would hurry past with the quickest of greeting. Some turned their heads away. But this felt different. She waited for him to speak.

"I saw Frank Harker outside Hardcastle's."

He sat heavily in his chair; his chin sunk onto his chest. He raised his eyes to look at her. "His boy, remember George?" Rosina nodded slowly. "He was killed, they found out a few days ago." She had never seen him look so sad. "I couldn't face him. I should've spoken to the poor man but I couldn't even walk past him. I went to Bayham Street instead."

One man gains a child, another man loses a child under the most appalling circumstances; Albert looked as if he had had the joy sucked out of him. It was as close as he could get to admitting that things were never going to be the same. She got up, stood behind him and put her hands on his shoulders. He was a difficult man to comfort but they stayed like this for a few moments. She bent down and spoke into his ear, "I'll make good soup, and dumplings. You must have got so cold."

8

On March 21ˢᵗ news came through of a Zeppelin airship raid
on Paris. The Zeppelin had already been used to drop bombs on
Liege, in Belgium and in the south of England. The Daily Mail
showed pictures of destroyed houses.

At around the time Billy started smiling, a shy smile as if embarrassed at getting so much attention from so many people, the boys began to ask questions about the Zeppelin airship. The raids from these giants had begun in January and struck fear into the hearts of Londoners. They had seen a picture, pasted up on a shop window, of this monster machine with searchlights beaming down on London. It was a poster encouraging more young men to join the army.

Rosie, who had learned about the Zeppelin airships at school, decided to share her expertise with the others. She took the role of Miss Roberts, who had stood by the blackboard and spoken in a very sombre voice of the importance of remembering exactly what she was about to tell them. Rosie cleared her throat.

"If the Zeppelins come there are three things you must remember."

The four of them were under the table. Rosie had decided that this would add to the mood. She had managed to stop the boys' giggles and fidgeting with her best 'Miss Roberts' glares. "To keep safe, you have to KEEP INDOORS; PUT OUT THE LIGHTS; and KEEP QUIET. Now I want you to repeat those three things back to me."

Albie and Joe looked confused. John had spotted a bit of food on the floor and was making a grab for it.

"Look, it's really important. If a Zeppelin comes over our house, doing this will keep us safe. We'll learn it slowly. Say KEEP INDOORS." She gave them an encouraging look.

"KEEP INDOORS," said Albie and Joe. John was examining his find.

"Now say PUT OUT THE LIGHTS."

"PUT OUT THE LIGHTS." They were getting good at it now and enjoying saying the words in loud, bossy voices.

"And now KEEP QUIET."

Albie and Joe, in unison and as loudly as they could, "AND NOW KEEP QUIET." They fell against each other laughing.

Rosie glared at them and said, "Zeppelins always come at night time."

"So we can't see them," said Albie, paying attention again. Joe was still rocking from side to side laughing to himself.

"That's right, so they can't be shot down. They are like a giant dragon, flying silently high, high above in the black sky." Rosie was enjoying herself now.

"Always watching, always listening for sounds below so it can attack. Because it is so silent it can hear everything, especially boys laughing." Rosie narrowed her eyes at Joe who had in fact stopped and was listening again.

"And it looks for any signs of life, candles, lamps, things moving about. If it sees or hears something the searchlights shine down and the men in the machine get ready to drop the bombs." She wasn't quite sure that she wanted to think about what would happen next, so she decided to go back to the dragon. "Just like a dragon with his fiery breath."

There was silence for a few seconds as various images skipped across their imaginations. Albie was dissatisfied; he did want to get to what would happen next.

"Bombs fall down, and everything blows up and…" and he started to make explosion noises which Joe and even John copied with great enthusiasm; all three got out from under the table and twirled and lurched around the kitchen and fell down in a heap, Albie announcing, "We're all dead."

Rosie, still under the table, legs crossed, knew that this would never happen in Miss Roberts's classroom. She sighed, crawled out and stood above them with her hands on her hips. "Well, you will be if you make that much noise when it comes."

Albie sat up and looked at Rosie. "I want to see one; I really want to see one. If it does come, I won't stay inside, I'll run outside and watch it fly over."

"Oh, Albie!" Rosie gave up. She decided to go over to Billy. His arms were visible, waving about above the edge of the crate. He was looking around and smiled as he caught sight of her; she gave him her finger which he gripped firmly.

"Hey, Rosie – look at John!" She turned quickly to see John take his first steps; podgy legs making their way unsteadily towards her. He fell back down onto his bottom before making it but got up again straight away to complete the journey.

"You clever boy!" said Rosie. "Albie, go and get Mama. Tell her John's walking."

That evening belonged to John. He was sent walking from Mama to Papa; from Rosie to Albie; from Albie to Joe and each time was clapped and cheered. John beamed with pride and sometimes lost his balance as he watched the delighted faces of his audience. Rosie, with Billy lying on her lap, listened to the laughter and watched Mama and Papa's faces, relaxed and happy, and wanted this moment to go on for ever.

9

April 1915.

Rosie looked at the dust bursting into the air as Mama beat the rug hanging over the washing line in the backyard. Thwack, thwack, thwack went the beater, Rosina attacking it a few times before giving it a final shake by hand and laying it down in a sunny corner. Warmth was creeping through the streets of Camden at last, encouraging the women to clean away the winter dirt. Windows were opened, bedding hung over the sills. Doors were left ajar as floors were scrubbed. Rosina lowered the line a little and hung out a couple of mats. She handed the beater to Rosie.

"Get all the muck out of them and try to keep your face away from the dust." Rosie was delighted to have a go and, lips pushed together, began beating with glee and determination. She hadn't been to school for weeks now. She missed Miss Roberts; but she was needed at home. Mama gave her lots of jobs to do. She gripped the beater in two hands to beat harder and watched the dust float up into the sky.

Rosina went back into the shop. Billy was there in his crate; she glanced at him briefly, pleased that he was fast asleep. Albert stood by the window looking down the street. There were no customers. They both knew that things could not go on like this. Hardly any bread was being sold. It was hardly worth while lighting the oven. Money was getting scarce, and their savings were running low. They kept to the routine of opening the shop but swept and tidied up a little earlier each day.

Sometimes friends would come to the shop in the afternoon, caps pulled down over their faces. They came through the door quickly as if relieved to be off the street. The men would lean on the counter, heads together, quiet voices, trying to convince themselves that the war would end soon, even though all the newspaper reports talked of stalemate, with neither side able or prepared to move; or that, somehow, they and their families would be able to sit it out, stay put, even though everyone was making it quite clear that they were now not just unwanted but despised. But their talk soon changed to worries about their families, about what would happen if they were arrested. There was a lot of shaking of heads and rubbing of chins, big, square hands gesturing hopelessness. Rosina made weak coffee – there was very little left – the smell of it, the normality of it calmed them. Sometimes Joe or John was picked up and perched on the counter, tickled or joked with, before being told to play somewhere else. At the door hands were shaken warmly, promises of mutual support given should the worst happen, then a slight hesitation, checking the street, before they left.

10

May 1ˢᵗ. The liner, the Lusitania, set sail from New York to Liverpool. It was the fastest liner afloat, and the Admiralty had helped build it so that it could be used in times of war.

On the first day of May Albert was sent by Rosina to the chemist to buy something to settle Billy's tummy. She had been up all night with him draped over her shoulder, his little body tense with pain and all the tapping and rubbing on his back didn't help. "Go to Cohen's on the High Street; they will serve you there and it's too far to send Rosie."

Rosie was watching; she was fed up with staying in all the time. "Can I go too?" Silence from both Mama and Papa. "Please, I haven't gone to the High Street in ages."

Rosina was about to say no, she was safer indoors, when Billy started wailing again. Distracted, she turned away to gather him into her arms and said instead, "OK. Go on then…" Rosie raced to put on her boots.

Papa put on his cap and jacket; Rosie was at the side door, hand on the handle, itching to get out before anyone could change their mind. Papa took his time, tying his laces, checking he had some money in his pocket, mumbling something about watching the shop in case a customer dropped in. Before joining her at the door he turned up his collar. Finally, they were outside, and when she lifted her face, she felt the warmth of the sun like a welcome stroke. She automatically searched for Papa's hand to hold, and when he firmly held hers, she realised how unusual it felt. Before when they had all gone out together for walks on a Sunday she had always walked with Mama, held her hand when it was free. Papa often walked in front, guiding the way, carrying Joe when he got tired, telling Albie to hurry up.

Today she had him all to herself. She looked up at him; below his huge moustache, his lips formed a tight, straight line. He glanced quickly up and down the road before setting off towards Bayham Street. It was busy and took a while to cross. There were horse-drawn buses, and carts and the odd motor car. Papa dragged her this way and that to avoid bumping into wheels and hooves and people. There was noise, and dust was being kicked up, getting into Rosie's eyes and nose. Drivers and pedestrians shouted at each other to "watch out", or "get out the way" and Papa usually did the same but today he kept his lips firmly together, tightened his grip on Rosie's hand and finally got them across. Once on the other side they walked straight on towards Camden High Street.

It was quieter now and Rosie was feeling a tingle of excitement. The best shops were in the High Street; shops selling clothes, cups and saucers, brooms, toys, food. There was always something going on; she had seen a monkey dancing on an organ once and Mama had told her about the German bands that had played before they were forbidden. The sun was warm on her head and, as she breathed in the spring air, she felt light and brave and her legs started to skip, once, twice, three times, her boots scraping on the pavement.

"Calm, calm child," Papa cautioned but he was smiling down at her. When she looked up and caught the smile she grinned back. It was the biggest smile she had ever shared with him and they both knew it was a precious moment. For a little while grumpy Papa forgot that the world had become so unsure and was free to enjoy his daughter. He lifted her arm to the rhythm of her skips, helping her get higher and higher. She giggled, already out of breath and he felt the unexpected tightening in throat and chest as laughter bubbled up. She heard it and the surprise of it was squashed only by the sudden din coming from the High Street as they got to the corner. More carts, some pulled by boys, some by horses, more people. Down the centre of the street ran the glinting snakes of tram lines and every so often, the clattering carriages would cause a brief pause in the endless crossing and manoeuvring before the bustle began again.

They turned left and bumped into a large pig being coaxed by a couple of boys with sticks to go down an alley next to a butcher's shop. The boy at the front was pulling the pig, grunting and squealing in protest, by the ear, the one behind poked and kicked it. They were spattered with dried mud and neither boy was wearing shoes. The shop front had blue and white tiles and behind the window on the display shelf were a few sausages and some fatty pieces of meat. Rosie and Albert passed a tobacconist shop, a small newspaper kiosk, and then a hardware shop with its goods arranged carefully on the pavement. Metal buckets, small, medium and large; brooms and brushes; coils of rope. Behind the window Rosie spotted a small section where some toys were piled untidily. Albert allowed himself to be led towards them. There were a couple of balls, some skittles, a large hoop and, wound round polished wooden handles, a skipping rope.

She knew better than to ask for anything but couldn't help whispering, "Oh, Papa, look." Albert did look; he rubbed his hand over his moustache and said, "Come on, let's get that medicine for your brother." They walked on towards Cohen's.

On the other side of the street Rosie suddenly saw, in the middle of the little shops with their canvas shutters pulled down against the sun, a large entranceway, with a curved metal and glass awning decorated with wrought iron. Lights twinkled behind the doors. Rosie slowed down and looked up where the roof towered above the other buildings. It was the most beautiful building Rosie could remember seeing with its carved arches and pillars. Albert stopped and crouched down beside her.

"It's the Theatre of Varieties; it's where you can see people singing and dancing." There was a sign announcing twice-daily shows which could be seen for threepence, sixpence, ninepence or one shilling. He didn't tell Rosie that he had wanted to take Mama there when they were first married and had been told in no uncertain terms that she would never, ever set foot inside such an ungodly place where women in skimpy clothes danced about on a stage. They walked on.

*

Albert was surprised to find the door of the shop closed; it was usually propped open, especially on a fine day like today. He peered in through the window. Mr Cohen was behind the counter as usual and looked up sharply when he heard the door being pushed open. The worried frown gave way immediately to a smile of greeting.

"Ah, Albert, good morning, good to see you, it's been a while." He shook Albert by the hand and then took Rosie's hand in both of his, smiling and saying how she had grown. Then he asked after Rosina and the boys and Albert told him about the arrival of Billy and that it was for him that they had come today.

The Cohens had come from the same part of southern Germany as Albert, Baden, and had decided to come to London twenty-five years ago. His chemist shop had done well but Albert could tell that he was having the same difficulties as he was. The two men looked at each other with unspoken understanding. Mr Cohen, palms up, lifted his shoulders in a heavy shrug before reaching over and putting his hand in a large glass jar that stood on the counter and was filled with bright, shining yellow and orange boiled sweets. He handed one to Rosie with a smile. The shop was empty, so they spoke in German; Rosie listened to the men start their conversation as she first felt the enormous sweet, hard and sticky, and then popped it into her mouth. Sharp sweetness slowly melted onto her tongue. Bliss.

"Things are looking bad, old friend. I never know who is going to come through the door nowadays. I've had a picture of the King on the wall since the coronation and God knows I have no time for that crazy Prussian Kaiser, but I am German and that makes me, to some people, an enemy. Last week two fellows came in, drunk, swearing, threatening to smash the shop." Rosie, sucking on the orange-flavoured sweet which made her cheek bulge out, watched as Mr Cohen told his story. He used his hands to show where the men were, clenched his fists to emphasise their vicious words.

"Thank God there are good people in the world. Some others came in off the street, calmed them down and dragged them out." He shook his head slowly. "I'm worried, Albert, worried for Ilse and the children. What will happen if…"

He suddenly remembered Rosie. She had stopped sucking her sweet, waiting for Mr Cohen to finish what he was saying.

"What am I thinking of; I haven't got you that medicine for little Billy," he smiled at her, "I dare say he's yelling the house down." He found a small bottle of white liquid on the shelf behind him and put it in a brown paper bag. "That'll be threepence ha'penny and let's hope it sorts him out." Albert dug into his pocket for the money and handed the package to Rosie.

Mr Cohen leant over the counter and grabbed a handful of the sweets. "Take these home for your brothers, Rosie, and give my best wishes to your mother."

Rosie said she would do that and stuffed the sweets into her pocket. She thanked him again and walked towards the door, expecting Papa to be right behind her. But he was listening to Mr Cohen who was talking quietly, urgently. Papa nodded, replied and finally the two men shook hands, more warmly than before, Rosie noticed, each of them pressing their free hand on the other's arm. At last Papa turned, joined her and together they went back out into the street.

The sun shone into their eyes as they walked past the shops, awnings pulled low, busier now, past the Theatre where a woman was scrubbing the front steps, past the hardware shop where, unexpectedly, Papa slowed and then stopped. After the briefest hesitation he marched straight into the shop, Rosie close behind. They walked to the corner of the window. "Go and get it," he said it very quietly, in English. He nodded down at the skipping rope with the shiny handles. For a minute Rosie couldn't believe it. "Go on!" he said with a more determined nod. First, she handed Papa Billy's medicine, which he slipped into his pocket, and then reached in and took it. The handles were smooth and the rope white. Papa waited a second and reached back in for a ball, green and made from rubber. As if speaking to himself he said, "For the boys." Both precious items were put on the counter and paid for without another word being said.

Outside the crowds seemed to have got thicker, busier, enjoying the spring brightness. Rosie couldn't stay quiet for a second longer.

She felt she was going to burst with happiness. The sunshine, holding Papa's hand, seeing the Theatre, Mr Cohen's sweets and now, best of all, the skipping rope. Until the other man spoke nothing could spoil the day. She hugged Papa and, beaming a smile up at him, said how she couldn't wait to show Mama. Until the other man spoke, she continued babbling about how the boys, especially Albie, would love the ball. Albert listened to her, pleased he had made her happy, laughing, saying it was high time to get back home, forgetting that they were speaking in German – until the man spoke. He was a little taller than Papa. Rosie didn't realise he had come so close. Suddenly his face was in Albert's. "Krauts! We'd be better off if you and your brats were all locked up!" Rosie froze. Albert looked confused, any feeling of anger giving way quickly to the need to get away. Someone nearby said, "Leave 'em alone." Someone else, "Nah, they should be locked up."

There was more shouting, and someone spat, a glob of spittle landing on Albert's shoulder. Arm around Rosie, he forced his way past broad, blocking shoulders, avoided grabbing hands. Rosie's face was pushed against rough wool coats, her hair caught on a button; she could see hands balling into fists, white-knuckled, she could see brown and black boots shuffling around her. And then they were free of the crowd and turning right into Pratt Street, away from the noise. Albert dragged Rosie closer to Bayham Street, looking over his shoulder to check if they were being followed. They weren't. He stopped and crouched down in front of Rosie; he took the package which she had tight hold of and put it onto the ground between them. Then he put his hands gently but firmly on her arms. Her body was trembling. Her pale face had become paler and greenish shadows had appeared under her eyes. Albert waited till her eyes met his.

"Rosie, these people are angry, angry because of what is happening. Too many people are dying." He looked at her frightened face, searched for the right words. In the end he told the lie, "They are not really angry with you or me, just with the war." And he added, "You must understand that."

No, she didn't understand that. They were angry with her and they wanted to hurt Papa. Why would they want to hurt Papa or

Mama when they hadn't done anything? She stared at him but somehow didn't see him, her head was too full of coats and boots and smells of anger. Her mouth wouldn't form words, nothing came out. It was only when Albert put his arms around her and held her close, that her face crumpled, and tears poured down her face. She sobbed on his shoulder for a long while and he waited until she was calmer. As he held her Albert's own thoughts began to clear. He wasn't angry, only certain that things were about to change.

*

Rosie's sobbing grew calmer; she tried to wipe her face dry, and Albert helped, with his big fingers, the unaccustomed gentleness bringing a fresh bout of sniffing and yet more tears, which she tried to swipe away with the heels of her hands. Finally, he felt she was listening to him again.

"This isn't going to happen to you again, I'll make sure of that." She looked at his face. It had changed. He didn't look worried, but he did look very serious. She took comfort from this. She believed him. Papa knew what to do.

"Now we must get home, Mama will be worrying about us." Rosie nodded and grabbed the package.

"… and Billy's tummy medicine…" one last sniff and she stood up.

"Goodness yes, Billy's medicine," Albert also stood and patted his pocket where he had put the little bottle. "Better if we don't talk about this to the boys, no need to frighten them. I'll tell Mama." He paused a moment to make sure she had understood. Her hands felt the hard round shape of the ball.

"Can I give them the ball?"

"That's a very good idea, Rosie. And I want to see you skip!"

They walked back home slowly. Hand in hand.

11

Mama took one look at Rosie's face and knew something had happened. Rosie silently put her arms around her waist and, relaxing into Mama's soft body, felt tears force their way back into her eyes and throat. Rosina looked at Albert, who put his finger to his lips.

"We've got the medicine. Mr Cohen sends his greetings." Papa's voice sounded falsely jovial. "How about giving the boys their present, Rosie?"

Rosie reluctantly broke away from Mama; she still had hold of the package with the ball and the rope in it. It had become wrinkled, squashed and smeared on the journey home. She opened the bag and showed Mama the contents.

"The skipping rope is for me," Rosie managed a thin smile.

Mama bent down and stroked her cheek. Another glance at Albert. "It's beautiful. And the boys will love their ball – they are in the back yard, go and give it to them." Rosie nodded and walked off to find them.

Joe and Albie were running around the yard with John following them and getting in the way. Rosie sat on the step and put the paper package on her lap.

"You have to guess what is in here." Rosie looked at her brothers in turn, first at Albie, then at Joe, who returned her gaze very seriously and then at John who, as ever, just wanted to laugh with her; he leant against her knee. All three turned their attention to the bag which Rosie kept tight hold of. "Papa has bought us presents."

Albie looked at her questioningly; this was certainly unusual but very exciting. None of them could come up with a guess. "OK." She pretended to open the bag; three heads bent lower. Then she closed it again. "One of the things is long and one of the things is round." Blank looks. "You can throw and catch and kick the round one," and with a flourish she put her hand in the bag and produced the ball. Albie grinned and grabbed it. Seconds later he was kicking it around the yard chased by Joe.

"The ball is for all of you," Rosie shouted. But Albie was concentrating on his feet, watching the ball ricochet off the wall, stopping it going anywhere near Joe.

"Have a look at this, Joe." John had reached into the bag and with two podgy hands and with Rosie's help taken her present out. She looked at the gleaming white rope for a moment then handed it to Joe, who unravelled it and she watched as it slowly fell onto the dusty ground.

In the kitchen Rosina was watching Albert as he told her what had happened. It was unlike him to describe something so clearly. It was ugly and frightening. He wanted to be sure that she understood that, but his face showed no anger; it remained sad and serious.

Finally, he said, "Tonight we talk about what we are going to do. We can't live this way." They were sitting, she with her hands in her lap, Albert leaning towards her, forearms resting on the table. His voice was steady and certain, and she could think of nothing to say. She was dimly aware of the children out in the yard, the thump of the ball against the wall and of Billy sleeping in the box near the fireplace, exhausted from crying. She knew he was right, had known it for longer than he had, but now the heavy weight of decision-making hung over them. One of her hands reached over to him across the table. He covered it with his own. In the silence they suddenly both became aware of a *slap... slap... slap* coming from the yard. Albert had a good idea what the noise might be. They got up and walked to the back-yard door.

Outside Rosie was skipping. Up and round, up and round went the rope, kicking up a little dust each time it slapped upon the ground. The boys watched hypnotised as they listened to the rhythm of Rosie's booted feet jumping without missing a beat. Then she speeded up, skinny knees going higher, wrists twisting the rope over her head faster and faster. She looked up and saw the rope slice into the puffy clouds again and again until, laughing and breathless, she stopped. For a moment she enjoyed the feeling of exhilaration as her heart thumped in her chest and the boys clapped and Mama and Papa said, "Well done." They were standing together in the doorway, Mama smiling and Papa proud. She didn't want to look at him for too long, didn't want to remember that morning. Mama turned away; she had heard Billy's crying and Papa followed her, leaving a black and empty space. The boys were chasing the ball again and Rosie sat on the warm step rewinding the rope around the handles.

12

The Lusitania sped on towards Liverpool. On board were 1,924 passengers, men, women and children. There were also hidden gun mounts, ammunition and goods supplied by the Americans to help Britain's war effort.

The next morning Mama put clean clothes on Billy, wrapped him in a thin woollen blanket and set off to see Mrs Swain. The medicine had done the trick and he was smiling again. Rosie stood at the shop door watching Mama walk down the street, Billy's round face bobbing happily on her shoulder.

"Come and help me carry these loaves, Rosie." Papa had baked a small batch that morning and they needed arranging in the shop window. She didn't ask where Mama was going; there had been no talk of it before Mama left. It felt like some sort of plan.

Mrs Swain lived at Number 14, very close to the engineering works. The works were enclosed behind tall heavy wooden doors but clanking and drilling noises could be heard. Rosina knocked on the door and waited. After a while the door opened wide; Mrs Swain looked at Rosina, managed to hide her surprise – just a slight raising of her eyebrows – and said, "Good to see you, come on in." Rosina followed her into the back room, small with fresh-smelling washing piled onto the table which Mrs Swain had been folding. She pushed it all to one side to make room for them to sit.

"Looks like you've got a fine boy there, can I have a hold of him?" Mrs Swain had spotted the nervousness on Rosina's face as she handed Billy over and devoted her attention to Billy's good looks and gummy smile to give Rosina time to speak.

Rosina finally found the words. Her English wasn't as good as Albert's, but she managed well. Mrs Swain listened as Rosina told her of Rosie's experience the day before; how Albert was prepared to put up with it but now they were too worried for the children; how the business was shrinking and money running out; how the only answer was for them to leave.

They were sitting in the little kitchen; Billy, wide awake and looking at the unfamiliar surroundings, was being rocked about gently on Mrs Swain's knees but her attention was fully on what Rosina was saying. Albert wouldn't be allowed to leave but now it seemed impossible for her and the children to stay. She would have to take them back to Germany. Somehow. Rosina paused and leant forward to take back Billy and plant an unconscious kiss on his head.

She had decided to go to Mrs Swain for advice because she trusted her and hoped she would be able to direct her to where to find help. She and Albert had thought about going to the Catholic Church, where they had taken each child to be baptised but the memory of Billy's baptism put them off. They had put on their best clothes and walked for forty minutes to the imposing building with its gothic windows and arches. They sat at the back of the church waiting for the priest. It was cool and still with a lingering smell of flowers and incense. The priest stood near the wooden side doors talking to two very young servicemen and their families, wishing them good luck, warmly congratulating them on being able to go and fight for their country. Having given his blessing to these young men he turned his attention hesitantly and self-consciously to the German family waiting quietly to have their new baby welcomed into the church.

The priest had cleared his throat before asking them to follow him to the stone font. Albert held John while Rosina adjusted Billy's clothing. Rosie, Albie and Joe watched as the priest took a little silver jug and poured drops of water over Billy's forehead. The priest performed the ceremony quickly. Albert and Rosina were very aware how little warmth there was in his voice, how difficult he found it to meet their eyes.

"Albert thinks it's only a matter of time before he's taken away." Rosina said this quietly as if to herself, her fingers playing with the corner of Billy's blanket. She wasn't used to saying things like 'taken away' or 'back to Germany' out loud. She realised she was as bad as Albert at pretending things could go on as they were.

Mrs Swain tried hard to put herself in Rosina's position. Five small children and a husband about to be put in a camp. She would have nothing. The government had been talking for months about rounding up all enemy aliens; they'd tried it once but released them again because there too many of them. But it was hard to feel sorry for them; she was more worried about her own boys, still too young to be called up. But if the war went on for a long time... she couldn't bear to think about it.

Rosina straightened up. "I'm not taking them into the workhouse. We've been told it's where they might take us once the men have gone." Her voice was more rushed; there was a hint of panic. Mrs Swain was taken aback by this.

"That won't happen, not the workhouse." She sounded genuinely shocked at the thought.

Rosina nodded, "It's what we've been told." Her voice was calmer. She didn't want to sound desperate; it was hard enough asking for help.

"Let me think..." Mrs Swain's fingers were drumming gently on the table, catching Billy's sleepy attention. Rosina watched the expression on her face change from attentive listener to indignant problem solver. Her mouth was working silently, summoning up some hidden information lurking at the back of her mind, and her eyes scanned the room seeking inspiration.

The suggestion of the workhouse had triggered a deep-seated fear and reaction in Mrs Swain that even Rosina wouldn't understand. The workhouse was a place for the lowest of unfortunates, not for the respectable people in Pratt Street, no matter where they came from. Good heavens, not even if they were German! And everyone knew, that once in one of those places it was very unlikely they would ever come out.

"Let's hope this lot can get you out of your pickle." Mrs Swain was bending down over the table, slowly copying an address from a newspaper onto a scrap of paper. Rosina didn't understand the word 'pickle' but accepted the paper. "It says here," Mrs Swain was looking at the newspaper, "that they 'offer help to all those in need', so with a bit of luck that includes you."

Outside, Billy propped over her shoulder once again, Rosina looked briefly at the address before putting it in her pocket, then walked quickly back home to talk to Albert.

*

He was in the shop by himself; a few customers had been in and he was thinking of making another batch of bread for the afternoon. Rosina came in the shop entrance.

"Look at this while I put Billy in his cot," and she passed him the address. She was back in a few seconds.

Albert was looking doubtful. "I'm not sure. The Red Cross helps soldiers and people caught up in the fighting. I don't think they'll help us." He rubbed his chin and looked at Rosina; his pale eyes had lost some of the steeliness and determination. She looked back at him firmly. She needed him to be strong.

"They are good people. It's worth going there; maybe they can tell us who will be able to help."

"Yes, yes, they are good people," he nodded slowly, "maybe tomorrow…"

"No, today; I'll go today." Rosina sounded very sure.

13

The German Embassy in the USA had published a warning that vessels flying the flag of Great Britain were liable to destruction by U-boats. Fifteen U-boats patrolled the seas around Ireland. The British and Americans ignored the warning; the Lusitania could outrun any U-boat.

It was a small office near St. Pancras Station. Rosina stopped a short distance away from it. Billy slept in her arms, which were beginning to ache; she swapped him over to the other arm and stretched her back while she watched. There was a large Red Cross flag pinned up in the window and another draped above the door, which was propped wide while some men and women carried in some bags and boxes. Further up the street, parked nearer the station, were a couple of army trucks. Soldiers in puttees and hobnailed boots jumped down heavily and grouped together, lighting cigarettes, laughing loudly. The khaki uniforms looked new and uncomfortable; the little brass buttons blinked in the sun. Rosina looked back to the Red Cross entrance, where a woman was closing the door behind the last of the delivery. She walked up to the office and peered into the window. There were women on one side of the room emptying the bags and sorting out clothing. Others were carrying smaller boxes into a back room. A loud shout distracted her, and she turned, to see the soldiers being organised by their sergeant and marched off towards the trains; the trucks pulled away onto Euston Road. Taking a breath, she turned back and opened the office door.

Betty, the manageress, was aware of someone coming in. "If you've brought clothing put it over there on the table and if you want to make a donation pop it in the box near the window," she said without looking up. The tone was matter of fact. She was concentrating on filling in columns in a ledger, the ink pen scratching as she wrote.

"No, no. I'm sorry, I... I've come for help." The woman spoke quietly, nervously. There was an accent.

Betty paused and looked up. Worried brown eyes met hers. She put her pen down and blew on the wet ink. In the ledger were lists of destinations in Belgium and France where Red Cross supplies were to be sent and lists of what was most urgently needed. Places where makeshift hospitals had been set up for wounded soldiers and names of wrecked villages where men, women and children had lost everything. She rubbed her eyes, which had dark shadows underneath them.

"Are you German or Austrian?"

"German."

Betty sighed; she really didn't have time for this. A voice from behind the German woman called to her.

"There's a consignment of sheets and blankets over here, Betty. I've parcelled them up. I need the labels." The woman who had spoken gave Rosina a brief and apologetic smile as she approached the desk.

Betty said, "Yes, they're going to the hospital barge in France, the new casualty clearing station. I've got the address labels here." She reached towards a small stack of large labels, checked the address and handed two of them over. Each had a red cross printed on the corner. "Put it with those packages over there, Vi, it's all due to go to Le Havre this afternoon." Vi took the labels and with another small smile directed at Rosina returned to the packages.

She turned her attention once more to the German woman. For the first time she noticed that the woman was holding a baby. She got up and pulled a chair across and motioned to her to sit down. "What sort of help do you need?" Betty's head ached, ached with tiredness, with worry. Reports had come in of a poison gas attack by the Germans. Thousands dead. It was unbearable but she had to bear it, so she packed up parcels, wrote her lists, glued on the address labels.

Rosina, arms relieved of Billy's weight, waited. These women didn't talk like the women in Pratt Street. Their voices sounded clipped, unfamiliar; Mrs Swain would have called them 'proper posh'. Betty sat very straight in her chair and listened to Rosina as she started to talk. Her English wasn't good but she made herself clear. She spoke of her five children; that it was probably only a question of time before her husband would be taken away, that she didn't feel safe anymore. She needed help to go home. Then she stopped talking.

Rosina had in fact confused herself using the word 'home'. Where exactly was 'home'? It should be here in London where her children were born, a place she had grown to love. Her eyes scanned the room without seeing as she struggled to find the words, the English words, to make it clear that she was beginning to feel desperate.

Finally, and quietly she said, "I'm frightened."

Betty's face remained impassive. She fought to remove the images of blinded, terrified men stumbling over dead bodies; she struggled to make sense of Rosina's "I'm frightened" and failed; what could this woman know of fear when young men were enduring such extreme suffering. She looked down at the baby. Billy chose that moment to wake up and as usual, so used to having a friendly face ready to greet him, smiled before he opened his eyes. Betty took a breath. She was looking at two human beings caught up in something they didn't understand and had no control over; but like everyone else, they knew that a predictable world was suddenly turned upside down. Of course she was frightened; Betty relaxed her shoulders, focussed and began to speak.

Rosina left a little later, armed with information and a little hope. More trucks were arriving at the station, more young men jumping down and marching off towards the trains.

14

May 5th. The Lusitania ploughed its way through the Atlantic towards Ireland. On board, passengers, Europeans and Americans enjoyed the luxuries it had to offer.

At home Albie was watching his big sister's face. She hadn't looked quite the same as usual for a few days. It was harder to make her smile and she didn't listen properly. They were sitting at the table and he was drawing a picture for her. Rosie had noticed that he was good at it and asked him to draw Mama and Papa. He used pencil stubs that Papa had given them. They were the ones that lodged behind Papa's ear, when he was in the shop, till they were too short for his thick fingers to use anymore. But she wasn't watching him.

It had been a few days since Mama had gone out; she had been out all day and come back tired, sinking into Papa's chair and feeding Billy. She didn't talk about where she had been but Rosie knew she would tell Papa later. Whispered conversations that broke off whenever she was in earshot. She could sense the disagreements; sense the urgency, sense when a decision had been made. And in between life felt almost normal; Mama washed, maybe more than usual, put meals on the table. Papa baked a little bread. But there was something hiding in the air, something waiting, something coming to an end.

*

Rosina was frustrated with Albert. When she had told him that Betty didn't think there was any immediate danger, he had agreed too

readily as if they could ride this storm and it would soon resolve itself
and people would return to normality. He had to be forced to hear
that old people, women and children were already being helped to get
across the channel. That internment camps were being built across
the country for prisoners of war. The determination he had had, and
which had given her the strength to go to Mrs Swain and then to
the Red Cross, was replaced by a stubborn, half-listening expression
which infuriated her.

As she told him of the Society of Friends, the Quakers, who
would help them Albert was muttering,

"You wait and see, we won't need them, just wait and see." Had
he forgotten so quickly? Forgotten Rosie's shocked face; imagine it
couldn't happen again?

"Albert, we must be prepared." She tried to keep her voice calm,
not let her frustration show.

"How? How can we prepare when we don't know from one day
to the next what is going to happen?"

But Rosina was preparing. Some of the preparing couldn't be seen,
because it was going on inside her head. If they had to leave, there was
only one place they could go. Back to Germany, to the Black Forest, to
Neustadt. Tiny, quiet, hidden Neustadt which she had left when she
was eighteen. Up until now she thought she would never see it again,
never see her mother or her sisters. Now she dragged up images of
people she had known, places she remembered. She traced in her
mind the path from her grandmother's house to the road that took
her to the village. She tried to remember the shops, the blacksmith,
the pub. But there was too much she didn't want to remember; her
grandmother's coldness, her mother's determination that life would
be better for her if she left the village. Go, go somewhere else where
there was work. Work suitable for a girl like her. 'Like her' meant
for a girl without a father. England or America – that's where there
was work and opportunity; go girl go! So somehow the fare for the
passage had been found and she joined a group of other hopefuls and
left everything she knew. Horse and cart took them to Freiburg then
an endless train journey to the sea which she had never seen before.

She thought of these things at night while stroking Rosie's head to lull her to sleep. At night-time, the boys already in bed, Rosie would talk about the 'bad men' who wanted to hurt Papa. The tears would come, and she would sit with her and whisper, "You're safe with us. Here at home, you are safe. Don't worry, don't worry. Shh. Shh." And she gently moved Rosie's sticky-wet hair off her forehead and stroked her cheek, her hand, until she fell asleep.

In the corner of the children's bedroom was a large, black bag. Rosina hadn't used it since coming here with Albert years ago. In it she had put a set of clothes for each of the children and some for herself. In a skirt of hers she had sewn some money, shillings that she had taken out of the tin downstairs – Albert would never notice. Betty had told her she wouldn't be allowed to take money if they were forced to go. Among the clothes she hid the small crucifix that stood in the bedroom and the brooch she had worn on her wedding day and on special days, the only piece of jewellery she owned apart from her wedding ring. Now Rosina avoided looking at the black bag; when she did, fear bubbled up into her throat. Once it had signalled a beginning; now it seemed to be a reminder, a warning of something dark to come.

15

On May 7th, passengers had dined, babies had been put to bed in the ship's nurseries and at 2.10 a German submarine, the U-20, fired a torpedo into the side of the Lusitania. A second explosion ripped the ship apart. Within eighteen minutes the 'Greyhound of the Seas' had sunk.

Albie was the first to hear the rap on the door. He was clambering up the stairs to join the others in the kitchen. The rapid knocking made him climb more quickly, made him a little breathless.

"Mama, someone's banging on the door."

Rosina and Albert had heard it too by now. They glanced briefly at each other, caught unawares. Rosina stopped putting the plates on the table. Albert froze while drying his hands at the sink. Rosie, newly alert to changes in the atmosphere at home, held tightly onto Billy who was playing with her hair, noticing how long those few seconds lasted. Rosina had a sudden image of the huge pine trees outside her grandmother's house, swaying and creaking in the bitter winter winds. She looked again at Albert who nodded and headed towards the stairs. She leant against the table, listening to his heavy steps, the side door being opened and an urgent woman's voice before more footsteps clattered back up the staircase.

It was Mrs Swain. Thank God it was Mrs Swain. Rosina, who had briefly forgotten to breathe, gulped in some air, and moved towards her. Her friend's face was pinched, concerned, she had something to say. More than that; as she looked from Rosina to Albert, she seemed expectant, as if they would know why she had come. Confused, they waited for her to gain breath, to explain.

"You 'aven't heard, 'ave you? My Reginald says that's the end, the bloomin' end for you lot. I thought of you and Billy, thought I'd come over quick and warn you."

Albert and Rosina continued to wait, still perplexed, no idea what could have brought her here this evening. Mrs Swain sat down suddenly, heavily.

"Look, there's going to be trouble." She was distracted for a moment by Joe who had his head cupped in his hands, elbows on the table, his brown eyes looking at her with a serious steadiness.

"It's the *Lusitania*." No response. "One of your lot's submarines, U-boats, or whatever they're called, sunk her. Giant explosions. Over a thousand dead. Civilians. Americans." Mrs Swain's voice pitched higher and higher at each outrage. "Terrible, terrible; they didn't stand a chance."

Rosina was racking her brains. What did this mean, what did it have to do with them? Why did Mrs Swain want to warn them? But Albert did understand. He had read about the *Lusitania*, the pride of the British and American navies. But it was a civilian liner. Civilians, dead; innocent people dead.

"Even little babies…" Mrs Swain looked at Billy, wriggling a little now in Rosie's arms. "The papers are full of it. People are angry." She looked Rosina in the eye. "There's talk in the pub. Reg says there always is when the men have had a skinful, no end of things those drunk so and so's would like to do to a Kraut if they could catch one. But this time it's different."

Rosina was still trying to make sense of it. What would they do? Would they hurt them?

"They're going to smash things up. They'll look for shops with German names, places where they know Germans live." Albert looked stunned. "You never know, you may be lucky, your name isn't as German as some round here, but I wouldn't count on it."

Albert and Rosina remained speechless.

"That's what I wanted to say. Reg'll go mad when he hears I've been round, but I had to tell you. Be careful, tonight, tomorrow. Just watch yourselves. Right, I'm off." She levered herself up and onto her feet then added, "It's when the pubs close; that's when there might be trouble." The children's eyes followed her as she made for the door, Rosina, after a confused hesitation, got up and went after her. The women went down the stairs and stood at the side door. She held Mrs Swain's hand. Felt the sturdy warmth of it, the strength in it. She didn't want to let go. Finally, she said, "Thank you, thank you for coming over to tell us. You have been a great friend." Mrs Swain looked slightly surprised then smiled gently. "Goodbye Mrs Ragg, and good luck." Rosina watched her broad back as she walked quickly down Pratt Street then locked and bolted the door.

*

Upstairs the children sat watching Albert put food clumsily onto their plates. They didn't dare speak; Papa looked so grim. Albie glanced across at Rosie to see fat tears roll down her cheeks and fall onto her potatoes. This silence, this misery, was too much and his face puckered up, his mouth quivered, and he let out a howl. Rosina came back into the room in time to see Albert slam the saucepan down onto the table. The howl stopped.

"Albert! Sit down; I'll do that." He was leaning on the table, head down, fighting the impulse to shout. Rosina took his arm and pushed him towards his seat then picked up the saucepan. She saw that Billy was propped up in his cot; even he knew better than to make a noise at this particular moment. She filled Albert's plate, put some on her own, replaced the saucepan on the cooker and sat down. No-one had spoken, no-one had moved except John who was feeding himself with his fingers.

"Eat your dinner. When we've eaten, you will go to bed," Albert said it with a tone of finality and picked up his fork with his paw of a hand and began to eat. He couldn't look any of them in the eye.

"But Mama…?" Rosie's eyes pleaded; she wanted an explanation, some reassurance, anything.

Rosina's answer came swiftly, "Later, Rosie, later." Her look was sharp. Rosie picked up her fork and forced herself to eat.

*

Rosina could only taste the metal of the spoon. The sourness in the air was also in her mouth. Albert chomped on his food while his eyes flicked across the table restlessly. He was lost; Rosina knew he was lost. She struggled to remember exactly what Mrs Swain had said. There would be trouble. What sort of trouble? What could these men do? The throb in her throat worsened as she wondered what to do next, what to tell Rosie, how to bring Albert back.

First John, then Joe was put to bed. Finally, finally Albie, argumentative and tearful, gave up his fight against sleep and cajoled by Rosie's voice, closed his eyes.

In the kitchen Rosina waited while Albert lit his pipe and had taken a few deep lungfuls of the sweet tobacco. Rosie had come down and was sitting next to Billy. In reply to Albert's, "Send the girl to bed," Rosina had said, "No, she can stay with us for a bit, she won't sleep." He sat down in his chair and gave them both a heavy look; Rosina saw that the anger had gone, and she breathed a little more easily. He had checked the doors downstairs; pulled the blinds down securely. It was dark now, but he'd not lit the gas lamps. There was a single candle flickering on the table and wobbly shadows played on the walls. They were sitting close together, their world reduced to the circle of light cast by the candle. For a while he told them about the *Lusitania,* famous for its beauty, its speed. What a mistake, what a crazy mistake. Then silence while Albert shook his head and blew out great puffs of smoke. Rosie crept nearer to Mama and the three of them waited, the only sound the odd snuffle from Billy's cot. Rosina dragged it closer to her side.

There were often sounds, outside, on the street, at night-time. The odd bellow or shriek, sometimes a shout of laughter; but always followed by silence, the city swallowing up whatever joy or terror the sound signified. Tonight, the silence felt deep and black. The flickering candle stirred memories.

"At home, you know, in Germany, it was always quiet like this." Mama's words surprised Rosie; she hardly ever talked about Germany. "I didn't dare look outside because it was so dark." She remembered how the trees seemed to suck away the light as the sun disappeared.

"But there must have been lights, lights on the streets?"

Rosina smiled to herself and said quietly, "No streets where I lived, no lights." Rosie could imagine it well, just like pictures she had seen in books at school, houses like the one Little Red Riding Hood had lived in.

Again, they sat in silence; Rosie's eyes grew heavy as she leant against Mama. It was a slight tensing in Mama's body that made her listen. There were voices, shouting then quiet again.

"That's the Tavern closing up." Albert was listening. "Sam 'll be telling the last of them to get off home." Sam was the landlord of the Tavern, just down the street on the other side. His wife used to buy their bread from him. Years ago, Albert had gone occasionally for a pint of beer and chatted to Sam, about business, the price of things. Comfortable times, days full of hard work and hope.

They listened again; shouting in the distance, it went on for a long time. Was that the sound of smashing glass? It was too far away to be sure of anything except that it wasn't normal. The shouts rose and died away, then rose again.

Albert was leaning forward, very alert. He got up and walked over to the window, parted the curtains by a fraction so he could see the street. Rosie held Mama's hand tightly.

"It's coming from the High Street," he said.

Getting louder, Rosina was sure of it. The shouting, made up of individual voices blurring together into a distant but distinct roar. Rosie remembered the angry men and imagined a multi-legged, brown-booted monster. Her limbs felt as if they had been turned to stone, nothing would move, her breathing was quick and shallow. Nearer still and nearer. At one point the roars crescendoed like an exultant hurrah before breaking and scattering back into steady murmur.

"I can't see anyone." Now there were single cries followed by agreeing and disagreeing yells, running footsteps disappearing, others coming closer. A definite sound of boots on streets, very close. Rosie watched Papa move a step back from the window. Now it was Mama's grip that tightened.

It looked to Albert as if the three men were running away from something. Out of breath they paused opposite the shop. They were Albert's age, paunchy, not used to running. One pointed at the shop sign saying, A RAGG, BAKER, and said something to his companions. One shook his head, the other shrugged his shoulders. The first man seemed angry, excited. "It is! It's a Kraut. A bloody Hun! What are we waiting for?" Then, distracted, the three men turned their heads in unison in the direction of the High Street where there were more sounds of clattering boots. They paused for a brief second then ran and disappeared down Queen Street.

"Policemen," said Albert. A silence followed, less menacing and Rosina and Rosie, eyes glued to the back of Albert's head, felt their breathing turn slowly back to normal. After a while he carried Rosie upstairs to bed and Rosina and Billy followed. Rosie's arms, tight round his neck, had softened and relaxed into sleep before he laid her down next to Albie and she quickly nuzzled into her brother as she did every night. Then, knowing that sleep wouldn't come, he went back down.

*

In the still, dead hours that followed, Albert sat in his chair. The candle had long since flickered its last. His world felt shrunken and silent. He felt sure this was only the beginning. Violence could be contagious, there would be more. More people would feel angry and aggrieved, and they would want them gone. As the grey hours passed, he realised for the first time with perfect clarity that the unthinkable would happen. It was now inevitable, there could be no going back. His home and business would be taken away from him. His family would have to leave. The enormity of it had been beyond his imagination until now; he had fought and fought against it becoming a concrete possibility. He could still feel Rosie's arms tight around his neck and, for the first time since he was a child, he felt the prick of tears behind his eyes. He rubbed them, embarrassed at the unfamiliar emotion.

His own father would sneer if he cried. He remembered looking up at that tobacco-yellow moustache and thin lips; "Don't you cry, boy. Don't you dare. I'll give you something to cry about." And he felt the sting of his father's hand as it slapped hard against his ear. The old man had died before Albert left for England. He hadn't loved him, and he was glad to get away. He was twenty when he arrived in London and the noise, the dirt, the sheer effort of survival had pushed away the memory of his mother's face. He'd left her alone. He wanted more than a life sweating on someone else's land, being worked to death like an old horse. He'd ignored her tears and walked away.

As the first pale light crept around the room, he thought for the first time of what she had lost, wondered how she might have coped alone, relying on the kindness of family and neighbours.

He pulled himself out of his chair and walked over to the window. The street looked unchanged; he could hear the sound of a cart being dragged over the cobbles. It would be Mr Heaney off to collect the daily supply of fruit and veg for his shop. Somewhere else there was a whisper of a shutter being pulled up. How he missed the beautiful normality of routine. He walked over to the sink. He would light the stove and put water on to boil for breakfast. Rosina would be down soon.

As he bent to light the wood with the tapers, he heard steps outside; no voices but the steps faltered, close, then stopped. The crash of smashed glass caught him shockingly unawares. He ran down the stairs, unbolted the middle door and saw the bright jagged shards spread impossibly across the shop. He stepped forward and heard the crunch beneath his feet. Big pieces of glass lay on the shelf below the window, smaller pieces scattered as far as the counter. Rosina, barefoot, had appeared behind him; her hand flew to her mouth when she saw the damage.

"Go upstairs, I'll see to this." She didn't move. He turned towards her and gripped her shoulders. "Go up! Make coffee; cut the bread. I'll clear this then I'll be up." She looked up at his tired face and nodded.

So, they'd come back. Chased away by the police they had waited till everything was quiet then returned. Or maybe it was someone in the street, someone they knew. She stared at the gaping hole left in the window frame and the little flecks of dust coming in from outside, dancing in the early morning sunshine. How easily their world could be shattered, how flimsy the line between safety and danger. Bolts and shutters couldn't keep it away; all it took was one stone.

16

There had already been mob attacks on German shopkeepers in Manchester and Liverpool. In London the attacks were more serious, especially around the docks area where there were so many German bakers and butchers. The Guardian *newspaper reported that angry mobs tore through houses, threw Germans through windows and looted everything in their homes.*

The black bag was dragged out of the corner of the bedroom. Rosie watched Mama putting small items in it then take them out again. Blankets for Billy, the small lace-edged runner that lay on the cupboard, one of Rosie's warm skirts. Rosina moved about distracted, folding and unfolding, walking from bedroom to bedroom. Billy lay on the bed watching and gurgling.

There had been a lot of noise coming from downstairs, from the shop which, this morning, the children were forbidden to go near. Some boys had stopped to look at the broken window and shouted and laughed until their mothers had pulled them away. There was the sound of sweeping and glass dropping and shattering into an old box; Albert cursing as he cut himself. Some men bawled from across the road, "Go home. Get out." And more, that Rosie didn't understand, and that made Rosina cover her ears, so she couldn't hear it. Finally, there were calmer voices, followed by hammering. Albert told them when he at last came back upstairs that a policeman and Mr Roos from down the street had brought a large sheet of wrought iron to wedge in the window, some protection at least. He'd brought the policeman up with him.

Rosina, carrying Billy, and Rosie went down to the kitchen when they heard the men's voices. Albert washed his hands at the sink, not seeing the little drops of blood turn pink and swirl away. He carried the coffee pot, still warm on the stove, over to the table and sat down. The policeman stayed standing. He was a familiar face, one of the bobbies that sometimes came into the shop.

"There's been a lot of trouble, Albert. Much worse than this. Is there anywhere your family can go? It's too risky here." He was aware of Rosina's gaze; he didn't want to say too much. But Rosina was thinking quickly. It was now; the time had come. Not for plans, not for waiting for things to get worse.

"I know where to go." The men looked at her. Her voice was steady. "I know where to take the children."

The policeman nodded and went on, "A couple of us have volunteered to visit all the German families," he looked at Albert, "to tell you what's likely to happen. Albert, you'd best get yourself to the police station before they come here and arrest you." Albert's heart was thudding in his chest. Like Rosina, he realised it was now, no time for thinking. As the policeman turned to leave, he remembered to say, "Thank you, thank you for your help." Always a grateful foreigner, whatever was thrown at him.

17

After the riots and in response to public opinion, the Government became increasingly harsh towards 'enemy aliens'. They refused help to those made homeless. Requests for repatriation increased. Both the Red Cross and the Society of Friends, the Quakers, offered help.

It was late afternoon and Miss Sarah Bassett had been at the Meeting House since six o'clock that morning. By midday the two back rooms as well as the meeting room had been organised; neatly folded sets of blankets and pillows were stacked by the walls and rugs and carpets put down on the floors; supplies of food would come tomorrow, they weren't sure how many people might arrive. The Red Cross had sent word that there would be an increase in families needing help; so far they were managing but accommodation was in such short supply the Quakers would certainly be needed to help out – there would be no help from the government, which didn't want to be seen helping enemy aliens.

Sarah lifted her arms and stretched out her back. The others had gone home for the day and now she sat alone at her desk in the front office. In a minute she would get up and make a cup of tea, but first of all there was just one more set of papers to see to. Requests for help from two Belgian families; two widows who had arrived in London with their children, needing somewhere to stay. On her desk was a newspaper with yet more details of the riots across London as well as the latest reports of the fighting in France. She glanced at it once again. Why would intelligent people invent something as horrible as poison gas? Thousands had died within minutes. It was incomprehensible. Her father would say when there was a war each side would do anything and everything to move their side forwards, to win. When she asked him if Britain would ever use such a weapon, he had said that now that it was there everyone involved would use it. He was a gentle man, made thoughtful after fighting in the Boer wars where he saw what men were capable of. He couldn't shake off his belief that the British Empire could be a force for good, but he taught his daughters to question everything, with the result that Sarah did, with a vehemence reserved for the young, and joined the Women's Patriotic League until it became too involved in the war effort. She then decided to join the Quakers, where she found like-minded friends and could devote her energy to helping the victims of war.

There was a sheet of paper on the corner of her desk. She pulled it over in front of her and moved her finger down a short list of addresses. "Ah. This would do," she said out loud. A house in Holloway, not far from here. A woman, Mrs Emily Winters, had offered to put up a family of refugees. She had two rooms spare. She glanced back at the names of the Belgian families; Mrs de Ruyt had one child, Mrs Martens two boys. "I wonder if she would be prepared to take both families." Sarah thought she might just have time to go round to see Mrs Winter before packing up for the day. That cup of tea would have to wait.

She got up to collect her hat and jacket from the coat stand in the corner of the little office. As she fixed her hat, she became aware of a faint knock, a pause and then another. She looked round over her shoulder and saw through the small panes of glass in the upper part of the sturdy wooden door the shape of a small woman peering in. Her face turned away for a moment and there were voices, children's voices, then her face reappeared. She walked over to the door and opened it. The woman had a small child draped, limp, over her shoulder. She looked exhausted, dark circles under her eyes which seemed uncertain, ready for rejection, as she explained that she had nowhere to go, needed a little help. Next to her stood two little boys, one blonde and one dark and just behind them a girl carrying a baby. Sarah opened the door wide and let them in. The woman bent awkwardly to pick up a large black bag and she took it from her and dragged it in.

Beyond the office was the larger meeting room where the Friends would gather for worship. She opened the door to this room so that they would all have somewhere to sit. It was cool and light, large windows along one wall, and it smelled of polish. Sarah looked at the children's faces as she pulled over a bench for the children to sit. They looked dazed, close to tears but too weary to cry. Their mother spoke to them quietly in German and addressed the girl directly, taking the baby from her after the sleeping child had been lain down next to his brothers. It was the girl's face that particularly caught Sarah's attention; nothing had been said so far, only that first plea for a little help. The boys had looked at her with a degree of interest, but the girl wouldn't meet her eye. When she wasn't looking intently at the baby in her arms, she stared vacantly around, not focussing on anything. She asked gently if anyone would like a drink of milk, and as she left them, to go to the scullery, which was through another small linking room, she heard one of the boys whisper something to his mother. She understood a little German but couldn't catch what he said. She filled the kettle and put it onto boil, then found enough cups, some milk and the biscuits that had been bought for the next meeting and put them on a tray. As the kettle heated up, she thought of the Belgian children she had met. The word she had learned to describe their numb, unsmiling misery was 'trauma', something some doctors were beginning to understand. They had seen things no children should ever see and retreated into shocked silence.

Rosina allowed her eyes to close for a few seconds and felt a brief moment of peace in this perfectly silent room. Albert's anguished face swam in front of her eyes, Rosie's hysterical screams as he pulled her arms off him and shouted at her to "Go with Mama, now! It's not safe here anymore!" She opened her eyes quickly to get rid of the thoughts and looked down at Billy. He was looking up at her and smiled his slightly wonky, gummy smile as their eyes met. She couldn't smile back.

Albie was leaning against Rosie, swinging his legs under the bench. Joe, who hadn't moved a muscle since sitting down, turned his head slowly towards his brother and whispered, "When are we going home, Albie?" He knew he couldn't ask Rosie because she had stopped talking and Mama was too sad or too busy with Billy, but soon they would have to go back because this wasn't home and that was where they had left Papa.

"We can't go home, Joe. Too many people shouting. And throwing stones. You heard them." Albie had been thinking about this. It was the stones that were the worst. Banging and banging against the new metal window. He had hidden under the bed to get away from the shouting outside but no matter how hard he squeezed his hands against his ears he could still hear the clanging of the stones and bricks.

"But Papa is still there." Rosina looked at Joe's worried face and reached across to hold his hand. She summoned up the right words. "Papa wants us to stay away. He will be all right because the policemen will look after him." She was aware of a glance from Rosie as she said it and tried to keep her voice controlled. "He will be all right."

There was a tinkling sound and the family turned to see Sarah put a large tray on the table. At the sight of the biscuits Joe nudged John, who was just beginning to wake up, and Albie stopped swinging his legs. The boys looked at Mama then took a biscuit and began nibbling at them, concentrating on the crunch and sugary sweetness.

"You must be hungry," Sarah brought a cup of milk over to Rosie. She shook her head. Sarah put the plate of biscuits and milk down and knelt down next to her. For the first time Rosie looked at her. Sarah said gently, "I'm sure you could try a little drink of milk, it'll do you good." Her serious, kind face reminded Rosie of Miss Roberts, who would probably want her to have a drink of milk. She was very thirsty. It had been hard work carrying Billy. But she still couldn't make her voice work. And the memory of Miss Roberts had brought a lump to her throat.

"I'll leave it all here for you. Take some when you want. I want to give your mother some tea now." Sarah kept her voice quiet and steady. She had seen a small light in the girl's eye, a look of recognition, of recovery.

Rosina was feeding Billy by now. "You'll need this." She put the sweet tea into Rosina's free hand and sat down close to her.

"I need to ask you your names." She addressed this to Rosina, but it was Albie, recovering fast, who answered. "My name is Albie, this is Joe." This was something Albie could say well in English, Mama had taught him. "And that's John." He gestured to John who was sitting on the floor now making a mess with his biscuit. Sarah looked at the little boys, who had rings of milk around their lips, and glanced at Rosina who gave the slightest of smiles. Sarah kept her eyes away from Rosie, who she sensed needed just a little more time. She waited for Rosina to speak.

"My name is Rosina Ragg. We've come from Camden." Sarah nodded and waited, bending down to help John with his drink. She knew Rosina was struggling. To say the important things, to get the English right, above all not to cry. She took the cup from Rosina and held it for her. "A policeman went with us to the Red Cross. My husband said go, go, take the children and go. People were shouting at us, but my husband can't come with us. He has to stay, he can't come…" The words were rushed, Rosina swallowed back her tears. "At the Red Cross they gave us this address."

"We got a bus," Albie said brightly. "It was good, wasn't it, Joe?" Joe nodded. The boys remembered the wooden seats, watching the streets speed past through the windows as it rattled along.

"My husband… he's by himself…" Rosina suddenly felt the loss of Albert as keenly as her worry for him.

"Rosina, listen to me." Sarah could feel the rise of panic in Rosina's voice and sensed its echo in Rosie. "Your husband, what's his name?"

"Albert." Rosina fixed her eyes on Sarah's gaze.

"You must believe me that Albert will be safe. He'll be taken with other German men somewhere safe and looked after. The government has a plan for them."

"But Papa doesn't want to be a soldier so why can't he come with us now?" Anger released tears which streamed down Rosie's face as the words, choked, strangled their way out.

"Oh, my dear," Sarah fought back her own tears at the sight of this distressed child, "there is such a terrible war going on. Bad things are happening to everybody. Isn't it good to know that your Papa is going to be safe?"

At that moment there was a banging on the door. Sarah turned her head towards the sound and with a glance at Rosina got up to answer it.

"Rosie, come over here," she said. Sarah's words were sinking in slowly; it was time for her to take over again. "The lady is right. Papa will be safe. People will look after him." Rosie buried her face into Mama's arm, reluctant to agree and wiping her wet face at the same time. "Now, drink that milk and eat a biscuit before the boys eat the lot." Albie and Joe rammed the last morsels of their second biscuit into their mouths in case someone took them away.

18

Sarah had to send word out to other Friends to come and help that evening. They hadn't expected people to arrive so quickly. An elderly couple took up a space near Rosina and the children; they had come to London to be with their son and family but now they wanted to go back to Frankfurt. Next, two younger women, who took themselves off to the far side of the room. Then a woman with two little girls. More and more came through the doors of the Quaker house in Upper Holloway. A giant tea urn was set up in the room where they had talked to Miss Bassett; bread was produced from somewhere with apologies that it was too late to provide a hot meal. As warm sweet tea was drunk the room slowly filled with the murmur of quiet conversation and sharing of stories.

"Mama, look." Rosie had noticed that the woman with the two girls hadn't moved from where she had sat down. Rosina watched them for a minute then handed Billy over to Rosie. She got a cup of tea from the urn, stirred two spoons of sugar into it and took it over to the woman. The girls were sitting either side of her, just as silent.

"Come on now, drink this and you'll feel better." Only the woman's thin, pale hands were moving, fingers interlocking and unlocking and rubbing together. Rosina noticed scratches on her wrists and a dark bruise on the side of her head. She put the tea down and gently took her hands into her own. Slowly, the woman's head lifted, and she looked at Rosina.

"They threw me on the floor." She spoke in a whisper, wisps of hair falling over her eyes. Rosina waited and continued to hold her hands which were quieter now. She looked at the girls and smiled into their grey frightened eyes.

"My husband, my husband… they hurt him, kicked him. I don't

know where he is…" Now the tears started to roll down her face and the two girls joined in simultaneously.

Rosina knew this wasn't helping; tears had never been her way of coping. Whatever horror had happened she had to get on with the next thing and the next thing was going to be drinking this tea, wiping her face and talking to her little girls. Rosina didn't know where this hardness was coming from, but she knew it was the only way. She rubbed and patted the woman's hands to somehow bring her back, into the room, next to her children.

"Your husband, like my husband, is going to be OK. The police will look after them and put them somewhere safe." Rosina had to believe this was true and her voice had all the certainty of conviction. For the first time the women's eyes met. "What's your name?" Rosina's tone was kinder now as she saw the woman begin to take notice.

"Gertrude."

"Gertrude, we are with good people here. Tomorrow we will get some idea of what is going to happen." She offered the tea once again and it was accepted. "There are some jam sandwiches over there; I'm sure your girls would like some."

Gertrude sipped at the tea and nodded automatically. She smiled weakly at Rosina. "Are your children here with you?" Rosina nodded in the direction of her family. They were biting into large jam sandwiches, John getting very messy and Albie and Joe looking as if life couldn't get any better. Rosie had Billy on her knee as he craned his head around looking for his mama.

After a pause Gertrude said, "How will we cope without our men?"

"I don't know. But we are going to have to, aren't we?"

19

J oe stopped when he reached the bottom of the greasy gangplank. He'd watched people shuffle slowly up it, dragging bags and boxes and children. It sagged and creaked and when he looked up towards the ship it moved gently against the skyline. It was clearly a bad idea to get onto things that were moving and the whole thing was on water, for goodness' sake. He decided to stay where he was. He was unsure about what lay in front of him; too many people he didn't know, none of them were smiling, babies crying, sailors shouting and throwing things about. He didn't need to turn round to know that behind him were things he understood. Certain, solid things. Like Papa.

"Come on Joe!" Ahead of him was Rosie carrying John. Albert was close behind, slipping on the wood, grabbing the handrail. No, he would stay here. It felt better.

Suddenly he was lifted by two great arms. A silent gasp as his feet left the solid ground, his world tilted and spun round as he was flung over a broad navy-blue shoulder. There was Mama with Billy bundled and buttoned into her coat. And behind her an endless throng of women and children and old people, unable to move fast, pushing and being pushed. The air was full of the sound of seagulls squawking, clogs and hobnailed boots scraping.

"You nearly caused a pile-up, lad," said the giant. Joe closed his eyes and only opened them as he was lowered down onto the wet deck and claimed by Rosie.

"Joe, come here and hold my hand. Albie, you have to look after John, I can't carry him anymore."

Then Mama was with them. She looked around at the people, no-one really knowing what to do, heading in different directions, clutching their bags and scant possessions. Over the loudspeaker someone was shouting instructions, hard to decipher but people were moving towards a narrow staircase and climbing to the next deck.

"Come on, let's go up there, find somewhere to sit. Joe, stay with Rosie. Stay together." Joe didn't need telling. He was squeezing Rosie's hand so tightly it hurt. Albie had a firm grip on John's arm and was dragging him towards the staircase, following Mama. She had a cloth bag over one shoulder and carried the stuffed black bag ahead of her; Billy's eyes were open and he kept them fixed on his mother. Finally, they were all up and pushing towards a space on the deck not far from the railings. Rosina threw the bag down and then her weary body to claim the territory and gather the children round her.

*

They had stayed at the Quaker house for two nights. A steady stream of people arrived and on the second night the floor was full of makeshift beds; a second tea urn was brought from somewhere and a vat of soup was prepared in the little kitchen. Miss Bassett was no longer available. She was busy talking on the telephone to the Aliens Advisory Committee, the body responsible for the repatriation of the families. It was also responsible for the detention and imprisonment of able-bodied German men. Instead of a steady trickle of people wishing to go home there was now a flood and the Committee was thrown into a period of mad activity organising travel visas, trains and steamers to get the families over the channel. About the able-bodied German men – the women were clamouring for information – Miss Bassett could find out very little, only that they were being 'held'. She added the word 'safely'.

On the third morning of Rosina's stay, she was told that her visas had arrived and they would be leaving straight away. This was the moment she had been expecting and dreading. They were leaving Albert behind, there was no going back. Rosie watched her mother's face change from surprise to shock and then into a mask of calm practicality.

"Help put our things into the bag, Rosie. Leave the little blue blanket, I'll wrap Billy in that one. Then I want you to watch John. Albie, come here. When we leave, you're to hold Joe's hand and always stay next to me. Do you understand?" Albie didn't but nodded anyway.

Rosie, still not speaking, took her cues entirely from her mother's face which she watched and studied almost constantly. She had registered the relief because they were getting help and knew that the shock of being told they were to go was to do with Papa not being with them, not knowing where he was. She stared hard at her mother. She couldn't, wouldn't, think of Papa. Of the way he had wrenched her arms from around his neck and told her to "Go with Mama! Now!" He sounded angry; his face was grey.

Keep looking at Mama. She was calm; she was certain, wrapping Billy, taking the bread and butter from the lady and putting them in the cloth bag, along with some clean nappies. And now, on the deck of the steamer, gulls screeching overhead, Rosie watched again as Mama unravelled Billy and made a nest for him out of her coat, told the boys to sit down, lean against the black bag and not move away, as long skirts, booted feet and battered luggage dragged and shuffled past.

Rosina forced her fingers not to shake as she sorted out Billy. She had noticed how little milk she had that morning, it seemed to have disappeared overnight. He was hungry and it was only the incessant moving and noise that was preventing him from crying. It would start soon though. Her eyes flicked from child to child, all tired, the boys watching the gulls and the ship's funnel spewing smoke. She realised she didn't know where they were going; no information had been given out, but she thought she had heard Dutch being spoken by the sailors and someone had said it was unlikely they would be going to Belgium or France – too dangerous, nothing but troop ships. And then what…?

Rosie had crawled over to lie down next to Billy. Rosina watched her reach out and take hold of his hand, drawing comfort, then close her eyes. The shadows had got deeper, darker, skin whiter than ever.

Around them families grouped themselves, grandparents grimacing as they lowered themselves down, exhausted women checking on their children. Suddenly, the ship's horn hooted, half-heartedly, and the steamer slowly edged away from the dock and Rosina stared at the coastline as the expanse of water widened. Something stretched inside her, as if it would snap. Grey sky over a flat landscape. Home, Albert. She had never been away from him. The lump in her throat stopped her breath and tears came and fell.

Only Joe noticed. Crestfallen, he got up and, wobbling on the unfamiliar rocking deck, came and put his arms around her. "Never mind, Mama. Never mind." He said it very quietly into her ear. And for a few seconds, face buried in his soft little neck, she allowed herself to mind, to mind very much indeed, before finding herself again, gently pulling away and drawing him in to her side.

Albie was looking at the coastline intently. "Are we coming back?"

It was the question everyone was suddenly thinking. Rosie, sitting up again, unexpectedly supplied the answer, "Of course. We have to come and get Papa."

Rosina watched as England faded away. Nothing snapped, it felt more like a dissolving, as if it had never been real. Camden, London, England had just been on loan. Something else was penetrating, a kind of peace. The voices and quiet conversations around her, all German, different dialects but all recognisable. Here, on this boat she was no longer a foreigner.

*

"Can we go and explore?" Albie felt revived after his sandwich and ready for action. The water was calm and the boat was rolling gently. Its motion pulled his legs in unexpected directions; there seemed to be a magic force coming from deep below. He stood in front of his mother, swaying and smiling, then addressed Rosie.

"Come with me, Rosie." Rosie looked at Mama; Mama looked at the deck with its little groups of people huddled down and then at the railings with just the odd splash of water rising up. It should be safe.

"Go on, Rosie. How about you, Joe?" Joe was up, encouraged by Albie's smile. So was John. Not quite two years old and never happy to be left behind.

"No, you're too small." This from Albie, John would get in the way. John scowled then his face threatened to crumple.

"I'll watch him, Mama." Rosie got up and took his hand.

Rosina watched the four of them set off. Just then the steamer gave a short hoot and picked up just enough speed to increase the ship's rocking. Albie took the lead, he and Joe spreading their arms in an exaggerated need to keep balanced, shrieking with delight. And Rosie, laughing, thank goodness, laughing with John who was bravely wobbling and lurching from side to side, legs dumpy and determined, keeping up. Quite an adventure. She watched as they skirted around bags and people, sometimes losing their footing and being helped on their way by a nearby adult. Her attention turned to Billy.

*

The children found the toilets which were visited very quickly on account of their smell and heat. They could feel the throb of the engines beneath their feet. They held their noses and shouted at each other to hurry up. Then onward towards the stern where a woman was being sick and only had the energy to look at them mournfully. They moved a little away from her and the four of them stood next to each other and, holding the rusting metal railings, they stared at the ship's frothy wake which led all the way back to England. John stretched his arms through the bars as if reaching out for it. Rosie had firm hold of the back of his coat and leant her body hard against the barrier as she used her free hand to push her wispy hair out of her face and behind her ears. She strained to see the hazy blur on the horizon where Papa still was. The briny wind smelt clean and fresh, cool on her face. She breathed it in. He was going to be safe. Mama was sure of that. Safe from spitting, kicking men. She watched the little waves at the edge of the water trail, each with a fleck of white foam, each receding and disappearing into this great grey sea. Occasionally a splash reached their faces and made them laugh.

Joe said, "Let's go back to Mama." They turned for the return trip to be met with the giant sailor who had carried Joe up the gangway.

"Found your sea legs, have you?" He grinned down at them. They, in turn, looked down at their legs, wondering if they had changed somehow, gone green? Turned watery? They looked up, perplexed. He laughed and said, "You'll be proper little sailors by the time we reach Holland, especially this one." He crouched down in front of John, big thighs splayed. John smiled and babbled. "Probably time to get back to your mother now," he said, rising up again, "it's going to get a little rougher soon. Where is she?" Rosie and Albie pointed. "Come on, then. I'll take the little 'un." John was hoisted up onto the powerful arm of the sailor and they made their way back along the crowded deck. *To be a sailor would be a fine thing*, thought Joe, as he watched the big man stride off after Rosie. But as he thought it the swell got more pronounced, and he got a funny feeling in his throat.

*

Rosina was trying to feed Billy, but she knew she had nothing for him. He wriggled and squirmed, trying to suck and giving up in frustration. They looked at each other in mutual hopelessness. She sat him up and buttoned up her blouse. Billy was summoning up the energy to yell. She became aware of someone standing next to her.

"Tea, dear?" She looked up to see a woman wearing a Red Cross armband carrying, with difficulty, a tray. "Milk and sugar's in."

"Oh, yes please. Thank you." She shifted Billy a little to free up a hand and carefully took the tea.

"Baby looks a bit cross," observed the woman. Rosina nodded and shrugged. Give it another minute and the whole boat would know just how cross he was. The woman moved off. Rosina dipped her finger in the warm tea and let Billy suck. He liked it so she blew on the liquid and held it carefully to his lips. A little made it into his mouth, a lot dribbled down his chin.

"Mama, we're back." Rosie flopped down next to her, face pink, eyes brighter. John was lowered from above and deposited next to Rosie. Rosina looked up, past knees, leather belt with a sailor's jersey tucked in, up to broad shoulders and a grinning face complete with ginger bristles.

"Proper little sailors you got here. That one's gone a little green though," he nodded in Joe's direction. He spoke in German, rough and clipped. A Dutchman.

"Best if he lies down, that should help." Joe had indeed gone a pale shade of green, his mouth was turned down and he looked at his mother with bleary eyes. He lay down on the blanket and closed his eyes.

"You've got your hands full," said the kindly giant.

Rosina nodded. "Thank you for helping them." He nodded down at them all before heading off. It occurred to her that she was in a place she didn't want to be, going somewhere she didn't want to go, and yet, she seemed to spend the whole time thanking people.

"He's our friend," said Albie proudly. "And we've got sea legs." He stood solidly on the tipping deck. "See?"

Rosina looked at her smiling son and felt profoundly ungrateful.

*

"How much longer, Mama?" Rosie wasn't feeling too good. The ship was swaying erratically, the odd wave visible above the railings.

"A little while yet." Rosie groaned and slumped against Mama's shoulder. Billy was on her lap now and was trying to respond to Rosie's voice, but hunger was definitely getting the better of him.

Rosina remembered the long journey to England when she was eighteen years old. That had also been seven long hours from Holland. The same black bag half-empty, excitement all mixed up with fear. She had had a lot of attention from the sailors, she remembered, until she found a couple, from Mainz, to sit with. He was a butcher, joining his brother in Bradford. A wonderful place, lots of opportunity. She still had no idea where it was. What were they doing now?

Billy's protests were unusually subdued, the rocking and noise around him keeping his eyes and ears busy and the frequent visits by the Red Cross women with tea made him think he was being fed. Rosina had managed to ask for a teaspoon and had successfully got a little sweet liquid down him. Joe, after an hour's sleep, tried to get up but promptly felt ill again and resumed his position. John crawled about or tried to walk, heading towards groups of people who engaged in conversations with him, glad of the distraction. He fell on his bottom more than once and was helped up, pointed in the right direction by thoughtful hands.

"Why don't boats sink?" Every so often Albie had a question that he only half expected an answer to. This one felt quite important. Rosie shrugged. "They just don't. I think they do if there is a hole in the side." She paused for a second, remembering something, "Like the Titanic." They scanned the horizon for icebergs.

Albie thought about it. "It would have to be a big hole; small ones wouldn't matter."

"No."

"Bombs would do the trick. Ships have torpedoes. I've seen pictures. They race through the water. You can't see them." Again, this time more urgently, they searched the waves for signs of danger. Far away were shapes that could have been ships but the waves, the foam, made it hard to be sure.

Rosina, looking at Billy, felt inside her coat; her breasts were still empty. How could it happen so suddenly, so completely? Maybe the milk would come back but what was she going to do for the rest of the journey? She felt Rosie grab her arm.

"Mama! I think he's going to be sick!" Just in time Rosina grabbed Billy and held him away from the children. Up came the brownish tea, up came any remains of the morning feed. It splashed in a little sour-smelling puddle, just missing Albie's feet. He grimaced and proceeded to scrape the mess away with his boot.

Billy looked shocked at this minor explosion then resorted to heartfelt wailing. John chose that moment to return to the fold and, not getting one second of attention, decided to join in with the crying, pulling at Rosina's coat as she tried to clean Billy up and placate him somehow. Rosie had, of course, heard plenty of family noise before but this seemed worse. The rocking of the boat, the unfamiliar nausea and not knowing where they were headed was all getting too much. Against her will she felt her bottom lip tremble and tears prickle behind her eyes.

Joe, woken by the racket, sat up. Through bleary eyes he watched as, ahead, a large form blocked out the grey sky, the tilting deck. He was quite unsurprised to see his giant suddenly materialise next to Mama. Of course, he was there. He would make everything all right. And he closed his eyes once more.

The sailor stood with his hands on his hips. "Well, well, what a hullaballoo." And for the first time he looked at the woman carefully. Her sharp brown eyes were flitting from child to child, quick glances at the two older ones, a hand darting out to the toddler lying down then the same hand removing the other one from her coat sleeve, one arm cradling the baby, still yelling. Her gestures were automatic but half-hearted, her face frozen in an expression of forced calm which threatened to break down at any moment. She glanced up at him and away again quickly to avoid his gaze. This woman was never going to ask for help. He crouched down to be nearer them all. John immediately and trustingly moved over to him and was grabbed and placed on his knee. His sheer bulk demanded that he had their attention.

"What I think is needed here is something warm to eat." He spoke in German. "*Etwas warmes zu essen.*" Albie had been practicing the word 'hullaballoo' under his breath and was only half listening. Rosie wiped her nose on the back of her sleeve and watched the man.

"What do you think, Mother?" Rosina was forced to meet his eye and nodded. Something warm would be good for them. It still left Billy hungry though.

"I know just the job. My wife swears by it." He carefully placed John back on the ground, stood up and walked purposefully towards the entrance that only the Red Cross workers seemed to have access to.

The family, even Billy, watched the entrance for some minutes, before giving up and only stopped their grizzling when Rosina bad-temperedly told them to stop. Albie said, with confidence, "He will come back." And Rosie was sure he was right.

Quite a long time passed and just as Albie was beginning to doubt his certainty, their sailor re-emerged from the small, metal door carrying two dishes, one in each hand, with spoons propped against the edge of each. He was carrying them carefully; a little steam was wafting above each dish.

The bowls were placed on the deck; six heads, in a circle, bowed over them.

"Porridge!" Their sailor sounded pleased with himself. "It took a little time to persuade the woman in charge, but I convinced her in the end!"

A thick layer of sugar covered each one and to Rosie's eye they sparkled.

"I'm going back for another one." Their giant disappeared.

"Albie, share that one with John, make sure he gets enough. Rosie, start on this one. Save some for Joe." A minute later the sailor placed another bowl in Rosina's hands. "Make sure you eat this," he said. He waited while she laid Billy down and took the bowl. Porridge was Albert's favourite. Back in Germany it was often made with barley. This tasted good. She crunched the sugar with her teeth and watched it melt in the dish. Almost absent-mindedly she offered Billy the spoon. He licked and looked up at her. She popped him on her lap and offered him a tiny spoonful. His tongue pushed out a grain, but his legs kicked in anticipation of more.

"Well, what do you know?" The sailor grinned.

"He likes it, Mama." Rosie watched him rolling the food round in his mouth and swallowing. Rosina gave a silent prayer of thanks and blew on the next spoonful.

20

"I don't think we can go in," Rosie said, squinting through the gap in the folds of the tent, sounding unsure. Albie pushed her so that he could get a glimpse of what was happening inside.

Rosie's fingers slid down the thick black canvas and she realised it was an opening. She widened it carefully and Albie squeezed in front of her and stepped through into a rectangular space. They could smell food but there was no sign of any. Some benches, chairs and a table stood in disarray along one side as if a lot of people had suddenly got up and left in a hurry. While Rosie searched in vain for something to eat Albie's curiosity was roused by the sight of a large white sheet of canvas hanging at an awkward angle at the far side. Nearer to them a man was unscrewing a brass-coloured tube from a large polished wooden box. Next to him a woman in a white, mud-stained apron was talking, hands on hips. Rosie grabbed hold of Albie's shoulder to stop him exploring any further. The man was concentrating on his task, bending over it. They hadn't been noticed.

"Just stay one more evening." She wasn't pleading. The tone was more an exasperated demand, as if she had run out of ways to convince him. The man's shoulders locked stubbornly, and he wrapped the brass tube, which had glass in it, in a piece of soft cloth.

Rosie whispered, "Come on, let's go and see what else there is." And they slipped out backwards, through the gap in the tent, uncomfortable intruders.

*

After they got off the boat they were taken in trucks to a camp, set up not far from a small village. They jostled about in the truck for an hour. Then the jostling got much worse as the truck drove over the dried-up ruts in the field and they finally came to an abrupt stop which sent John flying forwards into the bony knees of an old man with a bundle on his lap.

They were to stay the night in a specially erected wooden shed. There were lots of them and each one could accommodate about twenty people. There were bunks and a couple of chairs. When Rosina walked in the room smelled stale, the floor was dusty; one of the chairs was upturned. A woman followed her in, side-stepping the children. She started to throw blankets on the beds.

"The Belgians all left yesterday. Suddenly this camp was to be made available for you Germans." She looked flustered, put upon. Her hair was falling out of its pins. "It's all a lot of work, you know." And she glared at them all before turning and leaving. In Dutch, of course, but Rosina caught the drift.

She was weary, bone weary and longed for sleep, longed to lie down on one of the bunks and think of nothing. She said to Rosie, "Go with Albie. See what there is. See if there is a place where we can get something to eat."

*

"Just one more night. They leave tomorrow." She wasn't going to give up just yet. He stopped dismantling a small wooden frame that slid out of the front of the box and looked at her. He squeezed his eyes up as if to emphasise what he was about to say one last time. "I'm not doing the show for a bunch of Germans. That's not what I signed up for." He laid the frame on the cloth and squared up to the woman who was still standing with her hands on her hips. She sighed and gave up. She had really thought she would be able to persuade him.

"Women and children and old men, Hendrik, they're tired, confused…"

"And their men have slaughtered Belgian children! I'll have nothing to do with any of them."

"Their men live in England, as innocent as you or me." She'd already said this.

He shrugged. "Give them half a chance and they'd do the same. There is something wrong with Germans, it's obvious." He had more to say but paused. Behind the woman was a movement and two pale blond heads came into his line of vision. He nodded at them to indicate their presence. Gerda turned round.

Rosie and Albie had come back in. There was nothing else to find outside, some latrines and people wandering about. It was getting dark. The man and woman were talking Dutch; they'd understood nothing, although it sounded as if they were both cross. Hunger gave her courage and she decided to try in English.

"Excuse me, is there somewhere where we can get something to eat?"

Gerda turned and saw two children, the same dark circles under the eyes, the same hopeful request. The girl looked resigned to hear a negative answer; the boy was looking curiously at the wooden box. He had caught sight of another box on the table containing pieces of coloured glass.

"What's that?" Albie had to ask. He craned his head forward and looked up at Hendrik.

Gerda, with a glance at Hendrik said in Dutch, "They look murderous, don't they?" then addressed Rosie in English.

"The food is late. You can tell your mother that it's being brought over from the village."

Rosie nodded slowly. Gerda felt she only half believed her. "Where have you come from?"

"London. On a boat," and she couldn't help adding, "our Papa is still there." It felt necessary to say it, not leave him out, on the other side of the sea. She was about to turn and leave.

"What are those?" Albie really needed to know. He'd been working it out.

Hendrik coughed and tried to avoid looking at the boy, hoping he would go away.

Albie badly wanted to talk to the man about the glass pieces and that wooden thing. He could only do it in German. "Those," he pointed at the glass slides, "will fit in there, won't they?" and he pointed at the frames.

Gerda could sense that Hendrik was weakening. His fingers were reaching for a slide. They were his pride and joy. He selected one and held it up. A clown with a ball. The colours were beautiful, reds, pinks and yellows. Both children were enchanted, thin faces for a moment forgetting everything and transformed. Gerda knew Hendrik would find the reaction irresistible. He never tired of demonstrating the magic lantern's power to captivate children.

The look he gave Gerda told her that he knew he had been hasty; she was probably right, children were children, even German children. She smiled at him. *A good man,* she thought.

"Later on, I will show you. After you've eaten."

Albie grinned at Rosie. "Let's go and tell Mama." He grabbed her hand and they ran off.

21

The train carriage was packed. Bags and cases were piled onto the rack above the seats, more squeezed in around people's feet. Opposite Rosina sat two sisters, Eveline and Mathilde. In the corner, sitting either side of the door leading to the corridor, were a nervous-looking woman and her two children, older boys, slumped down in their seats, maybe thirteen or fourteen years old. There was a false start, whistles blown, the great wheels grinding to a halt. Frederika, the nervous woman, became agitated, telling her boys to sit still and not speak, although they hadn't uttered a sound so far. Then the train dragged itself out of the station and set off on its journey through southern Holland.

Albie's head was still full of last night's lantern show. Rosina had been desperate for sleep but revived a little after a meal of boiled potatoes, sausages and cabbage. There was caraway in the cabbage which she found very comforting. Albie ate quickly, one eye permanently searching for Hendrik, who appeared as dishes were being cleared and began to assemble his box. The screen had been righted and was hanging, momentarily ignored, at the edge of the tent. He'd raced for a seat next to Hendrik and beamed at him, ready to be welcomed. Hendrik nodded at him, told him firmly in English to watch carefully and to get ready to be amazed.

Rosie was remembering as well. As the train pushed and steamed its way towards Germany, she smiled at the memory of the little man up on the screen with the hat. Hendrik had asked them to blow hard after the count of three and the hat had simply blown off. Up on the screen they watched the man touch his hat to greet the lady and the next second the hat was gone, caught in the branches of the tree. Then there was a horse eating hay, head bobbing up and down. Best of all was a snoring man; he had a big black beard and opened his mouth very wide when he snored. Hendrik asked everyone to make snoring noises which the children – and adults – did with great enthusiasm. Suddenly a little mouse ran up the bed straight into the man's open mouth! A woman in the audience shrieked. It wasn't Mama, though, she was laughing. It was good to hear her laugh.

Albie had been torn between watching the screen and watching Hendrik manoeuvre the slides.

"I know how it all worked," said Albie, to no-one in particular, but some did listen. "For each little story there were two pieces of glass, the man called them slides, and he moved one on top of the other." Albie was proud of his knowledge and thought he could draw pictures on glass too. Rosie leant against Mama's shoulder. Summer sun was shining through the train's dirty window and through half-closed eyes she saw flat land, cut through with slow-moving, shining water. Then, in the sleepy warmth there were clowns and cottages with barking dogs and a dancer with yellow hair and pointing toes. Soon she was dreaming and dancing with her.

Rosina closed her eyes as well. Billy was on Eveline's lap, the boys silent and caught up in the train's rhythm. Everyone was tired from yesterday's voyage and the early rise this morning. Bread rolls and thin coffee for breakfast at six o'clock then collected in trucks and taken to the railway station. The Dutch wanted to get rid of the unwanted Germans as quickly as possible, it seemed. The Red Cross gave her milk for Billy, extra to take with her. He managed the bottle with difficulty. She still hoped her own milk would come back. Now, Rosie's warm head on her shoulder and lulled by the motion, she had time to think.

Going home now, going home now. The train tried to convince her. As the sun warmed her face, she tried to remember summer in the Black Forest, those few months when the air smelled of pine and she could walk barefoot, stepping around the tiny white flowers that grew through the needles, collecting the cones to burn in winter. There was a sunny patch at the side of her mother's house where she grew peas. She remembered the peas, shelling them, making soup, preserving them for winter, her grandmother telling her she hadn't done it right.

Maybe the old woman was dead now. She had never learned to love her granddaughter; not having a father made it too shameful. Her body remembered the pain she had carried around with her until she left, left it buried in the forest, never thought about in the din and roar that was London. Welcome or not there was nowhere else she could think of going. Her village, Neustadt, her mother, she needed them both. No going back, the train said, no going back.

The carriage was silent, dust danced in the summer sun. All were busy with their own thoughts. Billy had fallen asleep on Eveline's breast and she was holding his hand, looking out past Rosina at the land flashing hypnotically by. She and her sister had come to London with their husbands only two years ago, musicians, so many plans.

The travellers were roused from their daydreams, their worries, by a guard walking down the corridor announcing imminent arrival at the border. The train slowed down and after it had crawled endlessly along for mile after mile finally came to rest at a small station. Frederika was the first up. She gave each of her boys a bag to carry and told them to remember everything she had told them. "Ernst, take this one, Sepp, this one and walk between us." Rosina smiled at the shortened form 'Sepp' for Joseph and was wondering if Joe would become a 'Sepp'. Albert had insisted on English names. Then, as she looked at Frederika's sons, she guessed the reason for her nervousness and her eagerness to get onto German soil. The boys looked awkward in their short trousers, muscular legs, developing bodies. She must have fought to take them with her. A couple more years and they could probably be soldiers.

There was a shout to get off the train. Bags grabbed, Billy returned, four children clustered around her legs; somehow, they got off and stood waiting on the platform. It was hot, not yet midday, and apart from the hundred or so people there was no-one else. No-one knew what to do. No-one felt like talking. It was eerily quiet. Some stragglers were still clambering down from the carriages; an old man tripped, and he was helped up. When everyone was on the platform the train gave a heave and their heads turned to watch as the train shunted backwards, receding, getting smaller then noisily stopping with a final blast of steam, a snorting mother abandoning her young. Were they in Germany now? Or was this still Holland? It was certainly the end of the railway line. On the other side of the platform stood a hut with a sign on it saying Winterswijk.

"We're still in Holland," said Mathilde. In the distance the rumbling of a truck, no, a few trucks, broke the silence. "Looks like transport has arrived." German trucks, German flags – black, white and red, fluttering from the windows, Red Cross signs along the side of each, trundled along the rough roads and ground to a halt some distance from the little platform. The great steam train seemed to watch for a while, waiting for the group to move on.

"Come on," said Eveline. She smiled down at Albie and offered her free hand. "Let's go and find some good seats for your mama." Albie thought for a moment, then took hold of the hand. Rosina buttoned Billy back into her coat, although it was far too hot, in order to free up her hands. Rosie turned her head once and the steam train was gone.

The trucks loaded them up quickly and took them across the border. A short delay as papers were examined, then one bit of dusty road gave way to an identical bit of dusty road and they were in Germany.

They went first to Munster where the travellers split up. Some went to the great ports in the north, some east towards Berlin. Some, like Rosina, began the long journey south, down the centre of the country, avoiding the belching factories of the Ruhr. Past rolling hills to Kassel. The children moved through tiredness, fractiousness, bad temper to a sort of stupor relieved only by food and drink that was brought at odd times and sometimes not at all. They spent the night in railway sidings outside Wurzburg. There was water to share and nothing else. Rosina had to throw some of Billy's dirty things away and ripped up a skirt to turn into makeshift nappies. Still no milk but the Red Cross did check on the state of the children occasionally and bottles were given to women with babies.

Eveline and Mathilde went with them as far as Stuttgart. They were heading home to their parents' home in Munich. They came from a large Jewish family and both knew they would be overjoyed to have their girls back. During conversations on the train Rosina learned that a lot of the men in London had been taken to Alexandra Palace but that another place would have to be found, as there were too many of them. God only knew where that would be. Rosina listened and it all seemed so far away. London was suddenly another world. As she hurtled towards something that was familiar and yet fearful, she had difficulty even picturing the street, the kitchen, the shop.

The sisters said farewell, rummaging in their suitcase to find things to help Rosina, gifts of handkerchiefs, a scarf and, to a whoop of delight from Mathilde, a long-forgotten little bar of soap. "Take it, take it. We'll soon be home." They kissed the children's grubby faces as if they had known them all their lives and told them to look after their mother. She watched them disappear towards another platform, another train. They had linked arms, looked at home in the busy city, sure of what they were doing. She felt forlorn, looked about her for some clue as to what to do next; the children sat in a heap around the black bag. They were beginning to look like vagrants, the sort you would cross the street to avoid.

A station guard approached and asked her what she was doing. Papers were again produced, and she said she needed to get to Freiburg. He looked at her for some time then took her to the platform, then to the train, then to the carriage, where he spoke to the guard. They shook their heads and tutted, sidelong glances at the bedraggled little group, shrugged their shoulders and found her a place to sit.

*

And now they were in Freiburg, alone on the platform, not a soul to be seen and Rosina, who had lost all track of time, could think of no alternative but to start to walk. Towards the village, like a homing pigeon, the only place she knew. She didn't know how far it was, only that it was south from here, south and uphill, where the trees were blackest, the paths narrowest. She looked down at the children who seemed to be past crying, past asking for something to eat and then up at the darkening sky. She closed her eyes. Suddenly, defeated, she sank down to the ground.

"Mama!" Rosie, worried, pulled at Rosina's hand which had gone limp. "Mama, please!"

"Just a minute, Rosie, just a minute." She lifted her head. A place to sleep tonight, that was what they needed. A wall to lean against, to give a little shelter. She looked up and down the street. Behind them the station was now in total darkness and ahead there was the rough path that led to the town. One dim gas light marked the entrance to the path. That might be a better place to spend the night, a little comfort for the children. Maybe a little warmth. Even in summer Black Forest nights could get cold. They stumbled over and settled underneath the light, which by degrees grew dimmer. The boys fell asleep straight away and Rosie lay close to her mother. Billy grunted gently next to her breast. The darkness was complete, thick and heavy as she remembered it could be. She dozed and dreamed. So tired. Tomorrow she must find, beg for something to eat, for milk then they would start the walk. She felt swaddled by the dark... so tired... Suddenly, right in front of her, clear and solid, was Albert. "What on earth are you doing here, out in the open, on the street, are you mad, woman?" His face was white, young, and his bright grey eyes fixed on her. His voice unnerved her, roused her. He was angry with her.

"What are you doing?"

Through closed lids she was aware of a yellow light, swaying and rocking to and fro in front of her. Then the voice again, clearer, calmer. "What are doing here, goodness me!" She struggled to open her eyes; it couldn't be... she forced her eyes open.

"Good heavens, four children, oh my goodness." A face came slowly into focus, a moustache like Albert's and the voice, the dialect so familiar. The station master, on his last round of the night, peered at the little group.

"Have you nowhere to go? You can't stay here, you know." Rosina sat up, leaning on an elbow and Billy's sleeping face came into view.

"For heaven's sake, a baby as well." He steadied the lantern he was carrying and put it down.

Rosina saw herself as he saw her, ragged and dirty. She tried to sound dignified. "We have to go to Waldau," her voice sounded hoarse, dry and small. She coughed and continued, "My mother lives there. We must go there." She knew she could say no more.

"Well, well. Waldau, eh?" The man had crouched down to look at them all properly. "Waldau," he repeated it before standing up and holding the lantern above their heads, "Let's think about that tomorrow. You can't sleep out here. Come on, we'll make room for you, come on."

*

The children, when they woke the following morning, couldn't remember how they had got here. As their eyes opened, they could hear voices from nearby. Rosie, awake first, saw a little table with a small milk bottle on it, empty. Near her was Mama, fast asleep, Billy at her side. They were covered with a knitted blanket. Albie was sitting up next to her, Joe and John stirring, waking, and staring at the room, bright with morning sun, through squinting eyes. All were very hungry, bellies empty.

The voices came from a room nearby, a man's low voice and a woman's, rising occasionally, discordant.

"Where are we, Rosie?"

Albert's question was met with silence. The four of them were enjoying the stillness, lack of motion, warm muggy air and the sunshine playing with dust through the window. They breathed sleepily, looking occasionally at the half-closed door where a smell of warming bread made their tummies ache. It must be for them.

Then Rosina woke with a start and got up off the floor, straightening her skirt, pushing her hair back. The spell was broken as she hustled them to get up, fold the blankets, get ready.

"We must go, leave these good people, must go." Rosie folded and tidied in response to Mama's distracted commands, stopping only when the man opened the door carefully and came in.

"Good morning, good morning!" he smiled at them all. "I hope you all slept well." He looked at dishevelled hair, grubby faces. "There is some warm water in the kitchen for you to use," he moved his weight from foot to foot, looking at Rosina then sideways at the kitchen door, where there was the sound of a table being noisily laid. "But maybe something to eat first...?"

The children's faces all turned to Mama. Rosina's instinct was to leave straight away but what was she thinking? "Thank you, thank you very much. This is very kind of you."

The man's wife had put bread and milk on the table. The man brought out some bilberry jam which Rosina refused until he insisted. He spread it thinly on Rosie's bread, transforming it into a shining blue-purple delight.

"Have you never eaten bilberries before?" he asked. His wife had not joined them at the table. She had remained quiet, brought them milk, busied herself behind them. "They grow in the forest."

Albie swallowed his piece and declared it very good. The man smiled and with a look at his wife's back said, "My wife makes very good bilberry jam." Her aproned back seemed to relax just a little.

After breakfast and when all the children had individually said their thanks, a bowl of warm water was carried into the back yard and Rosina was able to clean and tidy them all up a bit. Billy had a bad rash which was making him grizzle but there was nothing she could do about that. She wet and smoothed her hair and pinned it properly, which made her feel better. From the kitchen came raised voices. She heard the woman say, "No more!" and thought she heard the word 'English'. Of course, the enemy had changed.

Rosina wanted to go. They went back inside and there were copious thanks given to the once more silent, disapproving wife; the children were told to shake hands and say, "Thank you very much," one by one, even John.

She was grateful but unhappy at the need for charity and she hadn't prepared herself for it, hadn't expected to feel so ashamed by it. Outside she was surprised to find the station master following her.

"I've been thinking," he said. "You need to take the train to Neustadt. It's a long way still from there to Waldau." She knew it. The names of the villages were coming back to her, Kirchzarten, Hinterzarten, Titisee. Miles and miles of walking ahead of her.

"I have no money. I must walk."

The station master put his hands on his hips and looked at

the children. "It's at least fifty kilometres. They can't manage it." He paused, watching her face. "Neither can you."

Her bag suddenly felt very heavy. The children looked pale and small.

"The first train to Neustadt leaves in half an hour. I will give you a ticket."

Rosina nodded. They were standing by the lamp, under which he had found them. The station was coming to life. Freiburg was a big town, a university town. People were gathering around the station, busy, things to do. Rosina nodded again, recognising her own foolishness, thanked him with her eyes and took the children to wait on the platform.

He watched them set off and shook his head, pleased he'd helped. At breakfast the boy had said, "We are English, you know," which had caused a clattering at the sink and his wife's back to rigidly straighten. *Good luck, little family,* he thought. *It won't be easy.*

22

The station at Neustadt had opened in 1887. The number was set in stone above the entrance. In the distance was the goods yard where engines were repaired, freight loaded and unloaded. Rosina noticed none of it. She headed into the town. In her pocket were two marks which the station master had given her. She would buy something to eat at a baker's shop, some milk. Then head off north to Waldau where her mother lived. She looked neither to left nor to the right, aware that her clothes and her pale children were attracting attention. The locals, with their headscarves, and sunburned skin recognised difference when they saw it. She told the children to wait in the street while she went into the baker's.

A plump girl in an embroidered dress came and stood in front of Rosie. She stood for a while, staring and saying nothing. Rosie stared back.

"Where are you from?" said the girl. She was staring in particular at Rosie's blonde hair sticking out in wisps around her head.

"England." It didn't occur to her to say anything else. She was thinking that the girl had a vacant, stupid face and indeed there was no reaction. Maybe she had never heard of the place.

Rosina had been asked the same question in the shop and answered with the explanation that she had had to leave. The two or three women in the shop muttered among themselves but were not unfriendly. She told them she was off to Waldau.

"Who have you got there?" said someone.

"My mother." Rosina looked at the woman and added, "Berta." Eyes narrowed; the air became flinty.

"Ah, I know her. The woman with the red hair?" And the household of brats, Rosina knew it was what they were thinking.

"You're the daughter who left, I remember." This comment from the oldest woman in the group. They were all dressed in black, skirts down to their ankles.

"Yes." Rosina was surprised. But of course, these people had long memories. In London you didn't know who lived in the same street. She felt the old ways of the village seep back into her soul. The village was their universe.

"She hardly comes down anymore. Looks as if you've got quite a surprise in store for her." All eyes were directed towards the doorway where four faces had suddenly appeared.

The woman who knew Berta directed them to the path to Waldau. "Up there and you'll come to the track."

The little group of women watched them go.

"Well, fancy that," said one.

"She's got her hands full," said another.

A third shrugged. "Well, what can we do?"

*

The path started to climb steeply straightaway. None of them was used to it. It took a while before they reached the cart track, which was flatter, a mixture of white pebbles and hardened mud. There was the odd copse but they could see the town, the valley with its fields.

"We'll walk a little more then I'll show you what I bought in the shop."

With an early evening sun behind them they walked for fifteen minutes and came to an opening leading to a huge farmhouse, ramshackle, untidy. Chickens were running about and there was a cart with children playing on it. Behind them was the immense sloping roof, almost reaching to the ground. The children on the cart stopped and gawped at the travellers. They in turn stopped in their tracks and stared back.

"It stinks." Rosie wrinkled her nose. A heap of dung steamed gently near the cart, flies buzzing around it. Piles of broken timber were strewn about. Further back three cows were being brought in for milking, Rosina guessed, each with a bell around its neck. They clanged, deep irregular notes, as a farmer tapped the animals with his stick. He waved and they, a little uncertainly, waved back.

"Going to Waldau?" he shouted.

"Yes."

He paused, nodded and said in a slow drawl, "Long way," then he continued to tap the cows towards the side of the house and disappeared into the milking shed, all part of the same building.

They watched until the last cow was gone. "Come on, let's go." And on they went. Rosie had John on her back, Joe trailed behind. They came to some logs lying at the side of the road.

"We'll sit here for a bit." The children threw themselves on the ground with relief. Albie was intent on finding out what was in the paper bag Mama had brought out of the shop. A roll, each with crystals of salt on top to lick off.

Rosina put Billy to her breast and watched the children discover the pine cones, strewn around the logs. She closed her eyes. Still so far to go. Soon the track would start to rise. There were short cuts through the forest, but she was unsure of them and Joe would find it too difficult. Poor Rosie was going to have to carry either Billy or John a lot of the time. She looked up at the white scudding clouds. That could mean rain later. She sighed; her knees were aching already.

An hour later they were on the move again. Rosie was beginning to ask questions, about Waldau, about their grandmother. "Will she be glad to see us?" The only thing she knew about grandparents was what she had learnt in stories. At school there had been English children who had them, lived with them. The ones in stories were usually kind. "Does she know about us?" It occurred to her that she might not. "Is there room for us?" Each question drove home to Rosina how much she was hoping for the impossible. She had sent a letter home telling her mother about getting married to Albert. So long ago. There had been no reply. The silence had stopped hurting after a few years.

There was a faint sound behind them, a quiet thudding that became the clip clop of a horse's hooves, the scrape and rattle of wheels on the track. Albie turned round and saw the head of a horse nodding and bobbing towards them. Bigger and bigger, brown and solid. They stepped off the track and waited and watched as it stomped past them then came to a halt. The driver, high up on his seat, turned around and spoke.

"Good day to you all. Off to Waldau, eh?" Of course, the farmer down below would have told him. He jumped down and stood square in front of them all. The children gathered around the horse whose powerful shoulders glistened with sweat. Flies danced around its withers.

"Mind his feet," he said, "he could stamp on you." Rosie squealed and they all jumped back.

They stared up at the beast for some seconds. "Do you think we can touch it?" Joe asked Albie quietly.

Albie thought about it. "Maybe not," he said, and the horse shook his head in agreement, sending insects and dust flying.

The man watched Rosina, arms hanging slackly by his side, waiting for her to speak.

"My mother lives there." She explained. He cocked his head to one side, broad-shouldered, dark brown eyes studying her.

"Berta." She said it defiantly with sharp eyes.

He nodded, unfazed. Everyone seemed to know her. She suddenly felt her heart contract, breath leave her. What was she doing here? Returning to the woman she had been so pleased to get away from?

"I can take you. There's room." His voice was steady. She saw the load of freshly cut timber on the back. It lay in neat piles across the width of the cart.

"I'm delivering this to a furniture maker up there."

Something stirred in her memory. "Old Peter?"

"No, he died in '11. Young Peter took over."

She looked again at the wagon. "I have no money. I'm sorry. I can't pay you." She tipped her chin up as she said it. She would not allow herself to look ashamed.

He shook his head, "No need for that." And he started to rearrange the wood, pushing some forward, some back until he had created a space. As he picked up first Joe, then John, wedging them safely into it, he said, "I can take you to the fork in the path, the one that leads to Red Berta's house."

Rosina remembered and nodded. "You two, climb up." While Rosie and Albert scrambled up the side of the wagon, he told Rosina to get onto the front seat. She produced Billy from inside her coat and he held him as she hauled herself up. The children sat very still, feeling both nervous and excited and jumped a little as the wheels of the wagon jerked into motion.

"It'll take a couple of hours," he said, as he picked up the reins loosely and the horse, which clearly needed no instruction, walked slowly on, tail flicking lazily, flies dispersing.

Soon the children demanded to be allowed to sit at the front and they took it in turns to sit between the man and Mama. Joe got there first. Billy was propped on her knee and seemed mesmerised by the swaying back of the horse and the sound of his hooves.

"You all have names, I suppose?" He said it over his shoulder and was met with shouted replies.

"I'm Joe," said Joe, "and he's Billy."

"And I am Gustav. Pleased to meet you." The children laughed. Rosina smiled but said nothing. Seconds passed.

Gustav bent down towards Joe, "And your mama, does she have a name?" Joe looked across at him. "Well, of course, she is called Mama!"

Rosie laughed, "Her name's Rosina, silly!"

"Frau Rosina Ragg," Rosina said it firmly. Her formal married title seemed important: all she had left.

"All the way from England?" Gustav was genuinely amazed at this. He thought for a moment and said to her, over Joe's head, "The English, what are they like?"

The English… other people, not her, not Albert, not even her children with their English birth certificates…

"Well, they don't like us very much at the moment, that's for sure," and she breathed the sweet air in deeply and looked down at Joe. He was grinning happily. Gustav had given him the reins to hold, and he felt like a king. His cheeks had a pink glow to them. That was why she was here, why she would have to face her mother.

Gustav shrugged and shook his head. "Never thought we would be fighting the English. The French, well of course, always fought the French. But the English?"

They carried on along the gently inclining path. Rosina told him about the shop in London, about her husband. He listened to her and shook his head from side to side. He had no pictures in his head of a life in London. but he could imagine the devastation of such a loss.

He held Joe's hands to guide the wagon to the side. "Let's give Ulli a rest, shall we?"

They clambered down and Gustav led the horse over to a fast-running brook. They watched carefully as Ulli drank greedily, and then, to their delight urinated with a great gush.

"You can all get a drink too but go a little further up away from the road. It's safe enough but don't fall in." They trooped off, Joe following Albie, John stumbling along with Rosie.

Gustav looked away as Rosina put Billy to her breast; that morning she had felt as if there was something to give him. He sucked with vigour. She watched the children work out how to get a drink; they were nervous of the fast-running little stream. After a few seconds they lay on their stomachs and scooped water into their mouths with their hands, exclaiming how cold it was. The hills in the distance looked black against the sky. A few more weeks and the weather would turn, cold winds would blow up from the Alps and winter would settle around the hamlets. No gentle autumn to forestall the shock. But today it was warm, the gentlest breeze just moving the air. And quiet, so quiet. To right and left of the track the land was flat enough to plough. Barley, and some rye, were ripening and there was the odd glimpse of green shoots, potatoes probably.

When the children returned, he produced a sausage and gave them each a slice which they watched him cut with the knife he had on his belt. Then back on the wagon, Rosie in the front holding the reins, John wedged between Albie and Joe. Rosina's gaze returned again and again to the dark hills, tinged with cloud. She tried to picture her mother's face, haggard and disappointed, and feared for the welcome she might get.

*

Red Berta had quite a reputation. Gustav sensed there was little love lost between mother and daughter so shared what he knew with her, choosing his words as carefully as he knew how. These days she only left her home to go to church in Langenordnach, a hamlet just up the valley towards St.Märgen. Before, she had gone down to Neustadt fairly regularly, especially in summer, to sell a few vegetables. She'd take a few of the girls with her. The epithet 'Red' was because of her hair, which had been quite a talking point in her younger days but had become an expression of her infamous record as a mother of seven illegitimate daughters. Eyes were raised to heaven and signs of the cross made hastily by both priest and villagers when they had dealings with her. But God help any prospective buyer if they tried to bargain with her over the price of a kilo of peas. And pity the poor shopkeeper who expected to get a fair price for a bag of flour. Her voice would rise at the injustice of such a price. How could a poor woman, permanently down on her luck, be expected to pay that!

Rosina listened without commenting. He was trying to inject a note of admiration into his words, the woman has pluck, has nerve. We have to give her that at least. With a sideways look at her he implied respect. She kept her face impassive.

She recognised the instinct for survival. Berta had had a tough life. Farmed out by her own mother to local farmers to wash and clean she had returned home time and again with a big belly and given birth weeks later. Rosina had been the first, then Petra. But she was sent out again to earn a pittance and told to keep herself to herself. No mention made of the fathers.

"One sister is married now, I think. Some... of the others... have left." He coughed slightly as he said it, to cover any embarrassment. Both his and hers.

Maybe it was Petra who was married, she had been fourteen years old the last time she had seen her.

"The old woman?" She meant her grandmother.

"Died in the winter of 1912 – a bad one." Rosina nodded and the silence lasted a few minutes.

"You may have your work cut out with Berta." Rosina shrugged her shoulders but felt Gustav's last remark had to be answered.

"She's always been difficult," she said. "I'm sure she'll want to help her grandchildren." She was sure of no such thing but saying it gave her a little courage. She put her arm around Albie whose turn it now was to twiddle the reins. He was speaking encouragingly to the horse who pretended to listen. As the familiar valley of Waldau came into view, thicker forest, giant, older trees casting darker contours over the land as the sun began to dip, her heart sank a little.

"I'm staying at Young Peter's tonight. Tomorrow I'm collecting a load of timber to take to the paper mill in Neustadt." She listened to him and wondered why he was telling her. He had taken the reins from Albie and was pulling at them. The wagon slowed and stopped.

Gustav pointed. "There's the path to Berta's place." Already in shadow it veered off obliquely through tall conifers. Rosina remembered the day she had left, carrying the same bag, emerging from this path and walking down the track alone and anxious. Now, Billy tucked back in, and in spite of four children standing around her, she felt seventeen again.

"Good luck," said Gustav as he climbed back up.

They stood in silence for a minute watching Gustav and Ulli head off. He turned and raised his arm once to them all and they waved back.

"I love Ulli," said Joe quietly and sadly, somehow voicing what they all felt, a happy interlude now over.

Rosina looked down at them, sighed and said, "Come on, let's see your grandmother."

*

Albie and Rosie looked at the wagon disappear on the still bright track then looked at the path Rosina was walking towards. Joe was following closely behind Mama and John had hold of Rosie's hand, wondering why she wasn't moving.

"Come on you two!" Mama had stopped in half-shade, "we are nearly there."

One more look and they followed her into the gloom. The temperature dropped immediately, and Rosie remembered the breadcrumbs Hansel and Gretel dropped to find their way back home. She took Albie's hand as well and slowly they all clambered up the rough footpath until they reach an overgrown clearing and a house. They watched their mother approach the door. Joe dropped back. The house had the traditional sloping roof, but it was broken-looking, tiny windows giving nothing away. Rosie bent down and picked John up.

The house was much as Rosina remembered it. The water pump was there and there was an untidy wood pile pushed under the shelter of the low roof. A sack of pine cones leant against the wall near the front door and some abandoned vegetable peelings mouldered in a dish. The door, unpainted, much mended, swung on its hinges. She went to the door and pushed it open. There was a dull glow coming from the stove and a sudden movement as Berta emerged from a dark corner and faced her daughter. For a moment they studied each other.

Outside John started to cry. Rosie shushed him as she watched, a little fearfully as Mama pushed the door and disappeared through it.

*

"Well, fancy! I never thought I'd see you again." Berta was older but her face had the same hard stubbornness.

"I had to come home. The war…"

Berta cut her short. "I know all about the war."

She straightened up and put her hands on her hips, glancing over at the door. "What have you brought with you, apart from that one?" She nodded at Billy who was struggling to be free.

The children, anxious not to lose sight of Mama, crept in, first Albie, then Rosie with John and finally Joe. Berta looked them over with glittering eyes and they, frightened, stared back.

"Say hello to your Oma." They whispered their hellos.

The little light that came in through the windows showed a wooden table and chairs, a mat on the floor and curtains. There were oil lamps and candles on the windowsill. Around the stove were large pans and a flour sack. On the table stood a forlorn little bunch of wildflowers in a cracked jug.

"Is Petra here?"

"She's out at the vegetable patch. With her two."

"The others?"

"Only Leni left here. The others are working in Freiburg. War work."

Rosina nodded and shifted her weight about. Finally, she put down her bag and released Billy from his bondage.

"I'll take him," said Berta and she placed him on her hip while he examined this stranger with frank baby eyes.

"How long have you been travelling?"

Rosina had to think about it. "Four days," she said. Berta's face remained impassive. Billy's hands were aiming at tendrils of auburn hair, streaked with grey, which had escaped the tight bun pinned at the back of her head.

"You will be tired and hungry." It was a statement of fact rather than a sympathetic observation. "Petra will be back soon."

The children were drawn to the stove which glowed faintly. Bertha gave Billy back to Rosina, told them all to sit down and filled a saucepan with water which she set to boil. She pushed another log into the stove and poked at it with a stick until the embers were coaxed back into life.

Rosina realised she was being treated like a visitor. She looked around, remembered the tiny rooms upstairs, and now six more mouths to feed...

Berta, busy at the stove, spoke with her back to them. "Her husband's a soldier." She was talking about Petra. "He signed up as soon as the war started. Money comes in regular as clockwork every month." Rosina sighed. Seemed like the war was good for something.

When Petra walked in, two grubby boys following behind, she dropped the cabbage and beans she was carrying.

"Rosina!"

Still a girl but a very tired one. The sisters hugged and looked at each other's children in awe. The children looked at each other in silence.

As the soup bubbled on the stove and Rosina talked of London and Albert, Berta softened a little, played with Billy, told Albie not to venture outside in the dark because the little forest men would catch him.

"No, no Albie, there are no such things," said Rosina quickly.

"Oh yes, there are. I've seen them," Franz, Petra's eldest said with great conviction. Albie and Rosie exchanged a worried glance. Rosina laughed but it was too late. The seed was sown.

The soup was eaten, with relish by the children and with guilt by Rosina, who knew that every mouthful was one less for tomorrow. As the minutes passed and the food disappeared, she swallowed down the growing certainty of the inevitable rejection by her mother which would surely come. And once the children were put to bed, head to toe in the old beds upstairs, it did.

"You know you can't stay here." It was said without preamble, without sorrow.

"What will I do?" was all Rosina could think of saying.

Petra looked down at her thin soil-stained fingers. "Maybe we..."

Berta was quick to smother any soft dissent. "It's not possible. You can see that for yourself. Go to Neustadt. The town council will think of something." Berta knew the ropes, all right. Rosina couldn't bear the thought of it.

And before either she or Petra could say anything else she added, "Tomorrow. Get back down there tomorrow." She had thought about it, she had decided; it was what would happen.

*

What had she expected? A warm welcome? She was too tired to feel anger – it hadn't been a comfortable night and they were up at five o'clock – too bowed by humiliation to stay a moment longer than necessary. Her mother didn't want her, had blotted her out of her life the day she'd left. The children, bewildered by the coldness, wanting something more from this new phenomenon of a grandmother, whispered their goodbyes as they had whispered their hellos and set off down the path, walking in single file, not looking back, following Rosina with baby and black bag.

And Bertha moved to the door and opened it a crack to watch

them go, watched the little dark one with his sturdy but reluctant legs, his sister holding his hand. Watched the blond boy kick at the late summer grasses and the quiet one hurry to catch up with his mother. She felt a stab of something in her heart, at the back of her throat, but swallowed it away. Too long a time, too hard a life. She had nothing to give. She wiped the back of her hand across her mouth and closed the door.

They were back on the track. The morning was still, low sunshine peaking over the hills. Their shoes crunched gently on the pebbles. The air felt cool against their skin and smelled of grass and sun-kissed cones. There was the whisper of a wind chasing them and rustling the pines, towering and ancient above their heads. Rosie and Albie peered between the trees, both eager and fearful at catching a glance of the little men who inhabited the darkness. Joe heard something else above the hypnotic swishing, a more definite crunch, a firmer tread. He stopped and looked back and waited. The sound was now unmistakable. The rhythm of heavy hooves, the grind of wheels. They all stopped.

"Ulli!" exclaimed Joe. His grin grew wider as Gustav pulled up and stopped alongside them.

Part Two

1

November 1915. Knockaloe was a camp built in 1915 on the west coast of the Isle of Man in order to intern enemy aliens. A few thousand were originally expected but, by 1916, Knockaloe would house 20,000 men from Germany, Austria, Turkey and other countries.

Albert was standing in line outside the canteen block. He was listening carefully to a conversation going on behind him.

"Come on, Arthur. If you've got any sense, you'll come with me."

"What's the bloody point? We'll be out in a couple of weeks."

They had broad cockney accents. Albert turned round briefly and nodded a greeting. They were young, clearly brothers.

"Maybe, maybe not, but this'd give us a chance to earn a bit of money."

Albert, interested, said, "Paid work?" There were men among them who had money or families who sent them money. They all had to live in the same huts but the fortunate soon made themselves more comfortable.

"Yeh, layin' the roads. Tons of railway sleepers come from Peel and they want to get the roads laid before winter sets in." The railway had been extended from the nearby village of St. Patrick to the entrance to the camp and brought in the internees and vast amounts of supplies. Albert stored the information away.

They shuffled up a little towards the canteen. The winter was already setting in, cold, damp winds blowing off the Irish Sea, that grey-green expanse that held them captive. Collars were turned up and hands dug into pockets.

He turned back once again and asked, "Where are you from?" It was always the second question the men asked of each other.

The older one spoke. "Whitechapel. Dad was German, died five years back. We was born in London." He must have told his story hundreds of times. Albert shook his head in sympathy. Everyone had a tale to tell. Most were beginning to accept their lot. They reached the canteen, and their tins were filled with a thin stew and some potatoes. Albert hurried back to his hut to eat before it got cold.

The huts were built in rows close together. Albert climbed the wooden steps up into his, found a place next to Rudi at their table and lifted his legs over the bench. The room smelled of tobacco, stale food and damp clothing. The men ate in silence and scraped out their tins noisily. Then pipes and cigarettes were lit. The need for tobacco seemed to be universally understood and was always available.

Later he walked to the works office at the perimeter of the compound, dodging the odd football and ignoring the watchtowers which were dotted about, more being built a good mile away where the new camps were going up. No-one talked of escape. They were surrounded by water and where on earth could they go? Most realised they were safe here. Some of the younger ones were ready to fight in the trenches, had friends who were already there, some already dead. All were unclear what the war was about. All were convinced it would be over soon. Albert had been there for six months.

He was given a slip of paper and told he could start tomorrow morning, eight o'clock sharp. The sleepers needed offloading from the trains and taking to the areas of the camp still in need of roadways – narrow, sleeper-width paths. The land was flat, already worn smooth by hundreds of boots. The winter rains, sleet and snow would soon turn it into a mud bath. Pocketing his work slip, he pulled his cap closer over his ears and did what he did every afternoon and walked the perimeter of the whole camp, between five and six kilometres, he reckoned. He stayed close to the barbed wire so his eyes could stretch across the fields where the land rolled with gentle hills, brushed with scudding clouds and he got the occasional smell of the sea. On the other side of the wire, he saw the odd sentry, dressed in a blue uniform. Some ignored him but there was one who always raised his hand and said, "All right?" to which Albert would reply with a nod and a wave. Sometimes he saw locals who would walk near the wire to catch a glimpse of the 'Huns'. If he saw children, he made a semi-circular detour away from them. They tended to throw stones.

Today there was a threat of rain, blustery winds, and there was no-one about. He dug his hands deeper into his pockets and, head down, watched his boots, scuffed and stained, as they strode over little tussocks of dying grass. He had heard nothing from Rosina but had been assured by the others that families were being helped home. He tried to imagine what she would do when she got to Neustadt. Would she find anywhere to live? What help would she get? As he trudged round the camp, he imagined the faces of each of his children; already it was getting difficult, Albie's round face, John's black eyes. Already he couldn't quite remember their voices. He missed his wife, her hands on his shoulders, her warm shape next to him in bed. When the war was over, he would bring them back, even if it meant starting from scratch. He had done it before, he would do it again. His pace speeded up as he thought about it, daydreamed it into a sort of reality. Wouldn't be long now, he thought, ignoring the construction of wooden buildings and laying of roads that was going on all round him. Wouldn't be long.

*

In a matter of weeks roads were down, and dozens more buildings were up. Internees were concentrated into huts all built to War Office specifications. Each hut measured thirty feet by fifteen and held thirty men. Six of these huts were placed together with only a thin wall as partition. Five such arrangements comprised a compound of a thousand prisoners and they had a bath house, latrines and recreation room. A kitchen was added where they could sometimes do their own cooking. Within the hut, there were three wooden tables and chairs. Bunk beds were stacked in threes. Each man had a mattress and three blankets.

Christmas 1915 came and went.

The Red Cross were beginning to bring post, which brought immense relief and joy to the men. They were also able to send post. There had been nothing for Albert at Christmas and he had to watch others open their parcels and display their images of family. Then, at the beginning of April, came the photo.

The envelope had been opened, of course. There was a team of censors kept busy on this task, checking incoming and outgoing mail and parcels. The photo was folded within a larger sheet on which Rosina had written:

> Dear Albert,
>
> I hope that all is well with you. Some good people in the town helped me to find out where you are, and I wanted you to have this photo of us all. As you can see, we are as well as can be expected. We have found somewhere to live, and I get a little help from the town council so please don't worry about us. Rosie and Albie are both at school. (There followed a line which was blacked out). I have seen my mother and am trying to find out if your mother is still alive and living in Baden. Please take care of yourself. We are all looking forward to seeing you when (following words blacked out).
>
> Love and greetings, your Rosina.

Albert stared at the photo. There was a photographer's stamp on the back. They were all in clothes he had never seen before. Well-made little trousers and shirts, Rosie in a pretty dress. Rosina looked composed. All were well-scrubbed, hair neat and slicked. They were his and yet they were unfamiliar, staring and smiling at an unseen photographer, expectant and ready for the flash. Billy he hardly recognised, cheeks filled out, a direct gaze aimed straight at his heart.

Rudi looked over his shoulder. "A fine family, Albert."

The lump in his throat prevented Albert from answering and he turned his head away. A little later he pinned the photo next to his pillow, the letter he slipped under it. At the beginning he touched each face before he went to sleep. Or tried to sleep, because it was never quiet in the huts. Men stumbled about in the middle of the night, crashing into the furniture, others swore at them, others groaned with their nightmares, shouting in their sleep. The partitions were so thin between the huts that laughter, arguments, snoring could all be heard.

Later he would stare at it and try to add years to those faces, saying their names, sometimes getting confused. Later still a stubborn anger seemed to take hold and he refused to remember, turning a cold shoulder to the photo, preferring to harbour a resentment that was strangling his soul. But that was later.

One day he learned that a bakery was being built; men were needed to bake the 15,000 loaves needed every day. He presented himself as the master baker he was and was taken to the industrially sized room with its machines for mixing, stacks of warm shelving for proving, a dozen ovens with chimneys stretching up into the wooden roof. He inspected the quality of the flour, although no-one asked him to and didn't think much of it. The risen dough still had to be weighed and put into the tins by hand, an activity he would supervise carefully. He hated the scale of the place, the uniformity of the sub-standard loaves. No chance of a good crust in these conditions. Blank looks greeted his requests for rye flour, caraway seeds.

But, for those first couple of years, it gave him purpose. Other men made furniture, baskets, toys. Some formed an orchestra, a couple even set up as portrait painters. The governor and warders could do little about the barbed wire, the enclosed spaces, the noise and lack of privacy, but they could do something about the boredom, possibly the most dangerous threat of all. So activities of all kinds were encouraged. Albert shunned them. Each morning, before the sun rose, he went to the bakery, taking his turn at the machines, at the ovens and at the sinks. He was the first man in and the last out. And then, regardless of the weather, walking the perimeter, letting the Irish winds tug at his clothes, the damp air settle into his skin. From time to time, he would unfold Rosina's letter, and let his eyes travel over the words, look at the shape of her round careful handwriting, but her face and voice turned misty, became indistinct.

"You should write to her, Albert," said Rudi, "tell her you're OK, you know?" Albert's shrug suggested a 'maybe', but he never wrote to Rosina, preferring to imagine the resumption of normality in Camden and, when that dream crashed, to becoming an unsmiling automaton, resentfully bowing to the will of circumstances he felt were beyond his control.

2

Neustadt, November 1918. The Armistice, pronouncing, at long last, the end of the war, was signed. The nation, previously certain of victory, was now grappling with the death of the myth of Prussian military invincibility. The Kaiser had fled, and Germany was now a republic.

Billy crawled over to the window and pulled himself up onto the wooden bench where his mama sometimes sat looking out. At three years old there was no surface he hadn't scaled and no corner he hadn't explored. He watched Rosie and Albie walk hand in hand down the track to school. Joe and John were playing outside, making patterns with pebbles and fir cones, and then seeing how far they could kick them. The cones had been collected during the summer and there were piles of them in the kitchen and under the shelter at the side of the house. Rosina came up behind him and fondled his hair.

"Don't you want to play out with your brothers?" He nodded half-heartedly.

She kissed the top of his head. It was the same every morning. He hated Rosie and Albie leaving for school. Albie had started in September and it had taken a month for Billy to stop crying for a good hour every morning. If she shouted at him to stop it just got worse. Now he watched miserably until they disappeared around the bend in the track.

"Back in a few hours," he said sadly, repeating the mantra she had said every morning.

She watched him climb down and walk as slowly as he could,

dragging his feet, unwilling to let go of the sadness, towards the door, pull it open and slip outside. Within minutes he was joining in, laughing at something John did, kicking hard in the boots that were a size too big. She studied the sky. Not long before the first snow. The clouds had begun to take on the dense, particular shade of grey that heralded the first falls. She would make use of the hour she had to go and pull the last of the carrots and the cabbage and tidy the patch up a bit. The baby would sleep for a while longer.

As she walked past the boys John, readying himself for a lifetime's best kick, paused and called out, "Is Uncle coming today?"

"Tonight, maybe." John nodded and kicked his cone towards the nearest tree, cheering his own effort.

"Joe, if Hilda wakes up, go in to her. I won't be long."

"Do I have to?"

"Yes, you do." Her voice was as firm as it should be although she knew that his disgruntled tone was half-hearted. He tried to copy his brother's more robust rebellion when it came to chores but found it difficult.

"OK, Mama."

Billy thought briefly of following her into the garden but decided to stay put and practise kicking instead.

*

Gustav had rapidly become 'Uncle'. At the beginning he had given them shelter in a barn that he rented not far from Waldau. He used it to store wood which he cleared out. It had the benefit of a wooden floor so when he brought the stove and an old bed it began to look habitable. Water had to be collected from the stream and the wind blew through the gaps in the walls. Rosina buried her humiliation deep and did what was necessary. She took the children to the town council and managed to secure a small amount of money that could be collected each week. She also went to the church, and the priest told her that many people needed help during this time of war. There were widows whose husbands had died for the Fatherland, but in view of the fact that she had five children two marks could be collected after Mass every other Sunday. Whenever Gustav visited, another pot or blanket was added to their meagre belongings. She accepted everything and didn't ask where it came from.

The first winter was shockingly hard. Snow banked up the sides of the barn and leaked in through every crevice. Gustav brought wood and food but sometimes days passed without him appearing. Rosina spent the days fighting the cold, nursing the children who all became ill and praying for spring. Petra came down once in a while to bring whatever they could spare but often the paths were too bad to walk along. The snow stayed till May; slowly the earth warmed.

Gustav's visits were welcomed, not only for what he might bring with him but because he spent time with the children and of course always brought Ulli. They were now great friends with the animal though warned each time to watch out for his hooves with their occasional unpredictability. Ulli allowed them to pet him and smooth down his strong flanks and muddy legs with the stiff brush that was kept under Gustav's seat on the wagon. And they liked the way he made Mama laugh.

Late in spring Gustav came and told Rosina about a house that had become vacant nearer to Neustadt. An old man had died and now the farmer was looking for a tenant.

"How will I afford it?"

"You will," he told her, ending the conversation, and their belongings were loaded onto the wagon and they moved into the house on the outskirts of town. The house was in a bad way. Damp patches on the walls, a chimney that pushed smoke the wrong way. Gustav mended and fixed and the children helped make up the beds, stack the pots. Rosina examined the patch of garden and made plans for it. Now it was possible for Rosie and Albie to go to school, only a thirty-minute walk away.

The following winter was as severe as the first. Sometimes the snow was so deep that Gustav had to stay the night, Ulli bedded down at the back of the house. The children were glad to see them both in the morning.

*

And now, as she bent down pulling the carrots and wondering if the cabbage was good enough to preserve, she tried to work out if she could buy Rosie some new boots for school. Summers were so much easier; the children didn't need shoes.

"Only the poorest, scruffiest children go to school in bare feet, Mama!" Ten years old now, her daughter could summon outrage. She'd squeezed her feet into the old ones for long enough.

Well, they were poor. And scruffy. Impossible to keep them clean when soap cost so much and half the time there was none to be had. The nit comb would come out every week. Shame was a thing of the past, no time for it. If Rosina caught a glimpse of herself in a window, she would avert her eyes quickly, and lift her chin, a habit so well-honed that others thought her haughty.

Shoving the carrots into her apron pocket, she made a decision. She would buy some boots out of next week's stipend and cut down on food. Maybe Gustav would have an idea. There were places to go for second-hand clothes. She would never take money from him, though. He'd stopped offering long ago.

She stood up to stretch out her back and examined the bare soil. It wouldn't grow much but she had learnt to make the best of it. The surface was growing cold, hardening because of the morning frosts, but if she poked down, it was still crumbly, a memory of the brief summer. She spotted a turnip, the greens dead now but it would still be edible. Farmers grew them further down the valley for animal feed, but she had discovered it tasted good in soup. Her thoughts drifted towards this evening when Gustav said he could come by. He would bring her news of the war, the peace. Thank God, the peace.

Why were people so shocked? There was no food in the shops, no fuel coming from the east. Wounded soldiers were already drifting back into the villages, some minus an arm or a leg. Yet they believed the newspapers with their insistence on imminent breakthroughs and ultimate victory.

When Gustav had brought her the news of the armistice, of Germany's defeat, she felt the conflict of relief which had to be kept secret and the sudden looming certainty that everything would change. The silence that day was thick with all the things they couldn't talk about, had never dared talk about.

"Mama!" John's urgent voice broke into her thoughts. "Joe says Hilda is crying."

"Yes, yes, I'm coming." John ran off and Rosina tuned into the distant howling. Hilda. Eight months old, healthy and beautiful.

*

That evening Rosie watched her mother and Gustav fuss over Hilda. She knew how babies were made; after all she was ten years old now and had talked in unsavoury detail with her friends at school about the process. She knew that somehow Hilda was wrong. And that might mean that Mama was wrong too, but that was hard to think about. But she was such a pretty baby and so loved by Mama and the boys, and Gustav, that she became right. Gustav had brought over a small bag of flour and Rosina had made some little griddle cakes which they were munching on now, their warmth and softness stopping all chatter. Later, when it was quite dark, Hilda asleep on her lap, Rosie saw Gustav and Mama talking quietly near the door. He was shaking his head, but she couldn't make out what was being said. She glanced at Mama and saw her wipe at her eyes. Not long after he walked slowly to the door, lifted the latch and left.

3

Neustadt, June 1919.

"There's a man in our house." Billy and John had walked up the track to meet the others on their way home from school. The sky was blue, cloudless, and the sun had warmed the ground beneath their bare feet. It was Billy who made the announcement. John had gone quiet.

"You mean Uncle?" said Joe after a pause. He was tired and hungry. It was a long walk home from school and he had eaten nothing since breakfast.

"No. Someone else," said Billy, slipping his hand into Rosie's. The stranger had walked in about an hour ago and he hadn't liked the way Mama had had to sit down, as if there was something suddenly wrong with her legs. John had stared and run out of the kitchen and he'd followed, frightened at the reaction.

Rosie knew who it must be, but couldn't speak, couldn't form it into a coherent thought. No visual memories or pictures came to her, just a sense of the man, a presence, the shape of him.

They walked slowly towards the house, which had taken on an air of foreboding despite the blue sky and green, sloping fields to either side. The forest started further back and had lost its winter black. The landscape had become part of them by now, the gradations of wind, the smells of summer, the silence of the night, the animals they were learning to name. Even the little men who lived in the forest; they could all swear they had seen one, hiding, darting about among the trees, causing them to shriek, call to each other and run home fast.

They paused at the door, where they saw an abandoned bag. It sagged, half-empty, against the wall. The door was ajar, and the apparent silence gave Albie the courage to push it open. Mama was standing stiffly at the stove, her back expressive in its unwillingness to show them her face. Hilda was standing by her, holding tight to the hem of her apron. She was pouring milk into a saucepan as she did every day when they came home from school. The farmer brought her a jugful every morning, a kindness Rosina could never repay. A man sat hunched over the table. He had his back to them and seemed to be deciding whether to turn his head towards them. After some seconds he did turn and looked at them over his shoulder. Just then Hilda ran towards Joe, as she always did. Joe had time for her, looked after her. That's how it was. Joe and Hilda. Billy and Rosie. Albert and John.

The man took it in and turned more fully towards them. They didn't notice that he was thin. Everyone was thin, everyone was hungry. Food was so scarce even on the farms. Meat had to be sent to the towns, as did the milk. They didn't notice how his jacket, an old English tweed, was worn out, seams coming apart, or how his trousers bagged around his ankles.

Rosina had noticed. When Albert came through the door and she had had to hang onto the table, she had seen how grey his skin looked, how he had shrunk, and how his left hand trembled even when he stood still. And she had noticed how, when Hilda had stood in front of him, between them, bright brown eyes, black hair down to her shoulders, expecting smiles, he had known who she was, what she was, and with one look at Rosina had sat down at the table.

"Well, don't you recognise your Papa?" His voice was rough, as if he hadn't used it much. Rosie and her brothers took small steps towards him. He did look like the man she talked about with Mama sometimes. Yes, it was Papa.

Albie, remembering he was the big boy who ought to be aware of protocol, took a breath, straightened himself up, walked up to him and offered his hand to shake. He lost his nerve and could only stutter the unfamiliar, "Father…" Albert grunted at him. It felt like a rebuttal and, although he forgot the incident, he remembered the beginnings of rejection. Never forgave him for it.

Rosina carried the saucepan of milk to the table and was about to fill the six little cups when Albert suddenly plunged his thick, travel-stained finger into the warm creamy liquid and pulled out the skin that had formed on the surface. It dangled, dripping, on the end of his finger. He looked at it for a moment then licked his finger clean. The children watched, dumbstruck and looked nervously at Mama. If any one of them had ever dared do such a thing… she paused briefly, said nothing and continued to pour. Her own chipped cup she filled to the brim and pushed over to Albert.

*

That night Albert made a bed for himself on the floor near the table. It was the closest he could get to the bunk he had been sleeping in for the past four years. He felt he might drown in the silence and woke regularly, peering into the blackness, missing the snores and shouts and indecipherable murmurings coming from behind the thin partitions. Even at the end, especially at the end – men losing their minds – the place was always full of noise.

Now his head was too full of the journey back to Germany, of resentment at being sent back to a country he didn't want to be in, to think of the people he had seen climb the narrow staircase to share the beds upstairs, under the eaves of the house, this house that had nothing to do with him.

He had tried hard to be allowed to stay in England, go back to Camden and start his business over, but he'd been refused at every turn. The internees who wanted to go back to Germany had been released in the weeks after the treaty had been signed. But he and a hundred or so others had hung on, pleading with the Home Office to resume their former lives. Only a handful had been successful. The months of waiting took their toll. Everyone was sick of them, feeding them, guarding them. They wanted to get back to normality. The camp bakery had shut down. Apart from a couple of blocks to house these remnants the place was being dismantled – the materials could be put to good use elsewhere.

I have a right to live in England, he declared, to whoever might listen but it turned out he had no rights whatsoever. To imagine he had rights was laughable. He watched as his companions became distracted, mumbling, insular. Patience eventually came to an end and he was deported. Sorry, mate, get off back to where you came from. He packed his clothes, mended, threadbare though they were. And the photo.

Upstairs Billy, sharing a bed with Mama and Hilda, whispered, "Is he staying? That man downstairs, is he staying here?"

"He's your father, Billy." A short pause. "Yes he's staying, here, with us." She lay very still, listening and finally, much later, falling asleep to the sound of the mice chasing each other in the rafters.

4

The bad times. The hard times. This is how people would describe the years after the war for decades to come. In the towns there were street battles between factions on the left and factions on the right. In the villages, thoughts were concentrated on finding food for the table. For Rosina the battle was to manage the vagaries of Albert's mood and temper, to protect the children from them. It was a battle she would lose time and time again, each strategy coming up against a bulwark of fierce silence, repressed resentment that would occasionally spill over into violence.

There was no work for him, but he made sure the authorities knew of his presence. When, after a week or so, he walked for the first time into Neustadt he grimly ignored the returning soldiers shuffling around on crutches, the thin faces of the women and children. At the Town Hall he encountered much muttering and shaking of heads; after all, the money would be better spent on the returning soldiers who had risked all for their country. Luckily for him the new republic had resulted in universal suffrage and there were now four women on the town council and a liberal mayor called Karl Pfister. They had made it their mission to protect the men and women of Neustadt regardless of background – even a British one – during this grim time. The family's stipend was duly increased.

The children avoided him; moved around him, responded as best they could on the rare occasions he spoke. Rosie began to recall moments she had buried away, lighter moments. Albert's presence, in spite of its sullen heaviness, made her remember the kitchen in Pratt Street, walks in Camden High Street, Sundays in Regents Park. She felt cheated that this shadow of her father had been returned to her.

What hurt her most, and she could not have found the words for this, was his attitude towards Hilda.

Hilda, approaching two years old, unaware of family tensions, was sure she could win over the affections of this stranger, as she could with everyone else. Smiling and laughing had always brought success before and to Rosina's amazement it worked with Albert. He petted the child in front of the others, dandled her on his knee, fed her at meal times. Rosie watched, unable to fathom the unfairness of it, to understand the need for Albert to claim the child as his, to take the child that had been Rosina's own.

Rosina watched and accepted it. Only once did she speak of Gustav to Albert.

"We would not have managed without him." Albert had sneered at this, but it was never mentioned again. And Albert never spoke of his time as an internee. Rosina tried once or twice but was met with shrugs and exhalations of air that seemed to say she would never understand. She kept to herself the odd ungenerous thought that at least he had come home. At least he still had all his limbs. At least he hadn't had to live with rats for four years.

*

Billy became Willi when he went to school, the diminutive of Wilhelm, John was now Johann, and Joe, as Rosina had predicted, had his name, shortened from Joseph to Sepp. Rosie and Albie were fortunate that their names were comprehensible to teachers and friends and could remain unchanged. It wasn't a problem. At home, all the names were used in different circumstances, depending on whether a little English was called for. Albert joined in with the English episodes, enjoyed demonstrating his superior knowledge. But they were all happiest with the Black Forest dialect, a comfortable and musical language which fitted well with the slow and rhythmic way of life and contrasted with the hardships all were enduring.

School was also an endurance. Teachers, mostly men, were of the opinion that children should be beaten as an example to others for the slightest misdemeanour. Albie, and later John, especially John, learnt this the hard way. Smart boys, they couldn't resist making their pals laugh and paid the price again and again. Joe, ever watchful, a thinker, avoided the beatings, did what was required of him and looked forward to home-time.

Billy, round-faced, popular, lived for playtime. There was a football they could use and there was no greater joy than getting his feet, bare or booted, behind it, running and kicking as far as he could get before it was taken off him. In time he learned control and strategy. He was quite a player.

They moved to a house in Neustadt. Here Rosina could make a little money from taking in washing. Albert worked occasionally for local wood merchants, farmers, but the jobs never lasted for long. Now the journey to school was shorter and come what may on Sunday mornings Rosina would lick them all into shape and take them to Mass at the Church of Christ the King and listen to the priest read the latest proclamation from the Pope railing against the evils of communism.

Winters, in spite of the freezing temperatures, the lack of warm clothing, boots too small or too large, would be remembered as magical. Sliding down the steep sloping roof of the house and falling into metres of soft snow, strapping wooden planks to their boots with blue fingers and skiing to school and, when they were old enough, going to the lake and borrowing makeshift blades, learning to skate on the frozen water. And Christmas would bring, to their delight during these hardest of years, some biscuits, some nuts and once, from somewhere, somehow a single orange, startling in its colour and vibrant taste, to share.

5

The German revolution had brought a very uneasy democracy to a divided land. The Weimar Republic was doomed from the start with parties on the left refusing to co-operate and the right using this weakness to try and regain power.

At thirteen years of age, they could leave school. They had all learned to read and write, manage simple arithmetic, they could navigate a map of the world. They knew that Germany had been decimated and defrauded by the war. Now it was time to join the world of the grown-ups, a world where there was little work for the likes of them, where even a village the size of Neustadt had its warring factions. It was 1925 and Rosie had had enough.

The previous year Anna had been born. After years of not going anywhere near Rosina Albert had finally decided to reclaim his marital rights and the result was the new baby. The pregnancy and birth had exhausted Rosina, left her ill, incapable of feeling anything for the baby who was handed, mewling, from sibling to sibling, Rosie bearing the brunt of it, of course. Hilda, discovering that a real baby was no doll, lost interest fairly quickly.

Rosie didn't like the way her life was panning out. For three years she had been rented out to local farmer's families, cleaning, cooking and avoiding the attentions of fathers and their sons, which she did with a viciousness her mother approved of, but which lost her job after job.

At night, in the bedroom she still shared with her brothers, Albie and Joe, she talked about going to England. "Why not?" she would say when they doubted the wisdom of the move.

"Mama went when she was eighteen."

"You can't leave her," said Joe, "I know I couldn't. Ever."

"What would you do?" asked Albie, interested.

"What I do now, I suppose, but for rich people." She turned her back on them and stared at the wall, conjuring up a life where she would have her own room, time to herself, time to be grown up.

It took her a little time to work up the courage to talk to her mother about it. And she had to pick her moment, when Papa wasn't around, when Rosina could listen.

Rosina did listen and didn't say what she wanted to say – *don't go! I can't manage without you* – although Rosie knew it was what she was thinking.

"You left your Mama." It was a low blow.

"Yes, but she wanted me to go."

"There's hardly any room for me here anymore, Mama." The room she really craved wasn't physical space, it was distance from servitude, distance from small-minded finger-pointing.

"Then go," Rosina said it sadly. How could she stop her? She was right. To lead any sort of life it was the thing to do.

When Albert heard about it his reaction surprised her.

"England?" His pale eyes wandered around the room as if recalling, remembering something. He squinted up at her from his usual position at the table.

"Yes, there'll be work. I can speak the language." She wasn't sure what was coming.

After a thoughtful pause he said, "You'll need money."

"Yes, I know." Was that all he would say?

She realised she wanted him to put up some sort of opposition so that she could pretend to herself that he felt something for her. None came. Later that evening he put some money into her hands.

"For the crossing." She looked at the money then at him. She had so rarely looked at him properly, into his eyes. There it was. A glimmer of the father she had known, a suggestion of the man who used to know how to love her.

"Thank you, Papa."

He grunted; the surly persona was back. "Be careful, when you get there, be careful." It was 1926.

*

When Joe left school to go and work on the farm, Billy found himself in charge of Hilda, seeing her safely to school and back again. It was an unbelievable nuisance. No more kicking a makeshift ball about on the cobbled streets with his brothers or his pals. No more hanging around the baker shop in the hope of a broken cake or biscuit. Frau Hemels was a kind soul.

No, orders were to bring her straight home. But today he was distracted, he couldn't resist it. The town band was practising outside in a little square near the church and he had to go and listen. Hilda was happy to go along. She was happy to go anywhere with Billy, to whom she had transferred her affections. Joe had to stay the whole week at the farm, returning at weekends with the money he had earned and handing it straight over to Rosina. He had become monosyllabic, morose and it worried Rosina. He refused to speak about it, answered no questions.

Billy stood near the tuba player. He didn't know it was a tuba at that point, but he was wondering why the man was sad. And bored. The conductor tapped the music stand with his baton and called for attention. It was an early March afternoon, bright enough but still cold. The musicians were wrapped up in dark blue overcoats and blue trousers, double-breasted with brass buttons going up to the collar. On close inspection they were shabby, ill-fitting and the buttons had lost their sheen, but to Billy they looked marvellous. They started to play but were immediately stopped.

"Well, that won't win us the competition, will it, gentlemen? Two weeks to go; if we're going to take the crown from Freiburg we need to start in unison, as you all well know." His tone was firm but not hectoring. Everyone, including Billy, listened to him. The conductor lifted his baton, looked over the musicians and paused.

"Again. And by the sixth bar I want the crescendo to reach the top of the church tower behind me." Billy and Hilda both automatically turned their heads and craned their necks back and up to look at the distinctive steeple, bells silent, white against the blue sky.

A perfect start this time and the music grew louder and quieter by turns. There were little pauses, different instruments changed the mood and it all made glorious, perfect sense to Billy, who grabbed Hilda and moved to stand next to the glockenspiel. Like the tuba player, this man had a long wait for his moment of glory but when it came the sound shimmered through the notes, cascaded over the children's heads. Billy peered at the sheet music they had their eyes locked onto, as well as somehow watching the baton point and direct. He'd seen the dancing, incomprehensible black notes before, at school, laid out on the piano. Fraulein Waldvogel came in every Friday morning to play and smiled at the children as they filed past.

When the music ended the perfect unity of the band gently collapsed as the session ended. Instruments were put over shoulders or tucked under arms and one by one the musicians left.

"Can we go home now?" Hilda tugged at his arm.

"Yes, yes. We can go now." His ears were ringing with the music. This is what he had to do. Be part of that. But how?

*

Old Jakob lived not far from them and spent the spring and summer outside, making things out of wood to sell, baskets mainly but he also knew how to make whistles. Billy had watched him and asked to be shown how to do it. Jakob looked at him from under very bushy eyebrows, deciding whether it was worth his while to stop. The boy had a round and eager face, eyes fixed on his hands that were expertly cutting into the wood at an angle with his ancient and sharp knife. He liked the look of him.

"First thing you have to do is recognise an elder tree. Do you know what one looks like?" Billy shrugged his shoulders, mesmerised by the expert fine chiselling with the knife, so narrowly missing the old man's fingers.

Jakob rested his hands on his knees. He nodded towards a copse of trees dancing in the sunshine. In the background, as always, the black of the pine, but here on the perimeter of the town, it was open, and the only movement was the breeze causing a gentle rustle.

"There's apple and cherry growing there. The elder is the low bushy one with the white flowers." Billy spotted several. He knew the fruit trees well enough. He'd filled his empty belly with those cherries many times.

"You'll need a straight branch a fraction bigger than this finger," and he held up a forefinger, thick and gnarled, the nail yellow from tobacco. Billy nodded and turned to go.

"Wait. What are you going to cut it with? Tearing at branches damages the tree, can't do that." And he got up, winced and rubbed his back, and headed to the side of the house and into a small lean-to hut.

Billy followed. It smelled of fresh wood and there were curls of pine all over the floor, ready to be swept and burned. Two big brooms were propped up behind the door. Racks of tools on the walls, carefully hung in order of size. Chisels, knives, saws – dozens of them. On a work bench were rulers and planes. Billy felt he had come into a wonderland. *I'm having a room like this one day*, he thought to himself, *where I can do stuff*.

"Here, use this. Shouldn't do too much damage with that one." Jakob handed him a small saw which Billy handled with reverence.

"To the tree, I mean. Your fingers are your responsibility." Billy looked up at him and saw the twinkle; he grinned back. "I'll be careful." And he was off.

Standing within the bush he tried hard to remember just how thick that bent old finger was. He found something that he thought would do and started to saw, expecting resistance but it was easy to get through. He raced back with it.

Jakob was still in the hut when he got back. He frowned. "Well, fine mess you've made of that." He'd torn the end of it.

"Let's tidy it up." He picked up an even finer saw and deftly cut off the broken end, laying it on the table. "Now you do the same to the other end, easy now, always gently." Billy managed it. It wasn't much longer than Jakob's finger.

Jakob picked up the stick and looked at the end carefully. "It's a good piece, look at it." Billy looked. "You've got a good quantity of soft pith in there. It's just what you need. Once you've scraped off the bark, we'll hollow it out." Billy took the knife offered and began to scrape away at the bark. Jakob was patient, showing him once or twice how to angle the blade so that only the bark was removed. Apart from a few gouges it wasn't badly done. Now the soft pith was pushed out and the hollow smoothed out with a small stiff stick. "That's why we use the elder, the soft pith." Jakob gave Billy time to finish the smoothing, holding it up to peer through it, the beginnings of a thing that could make music.

"Now for the tricky bit, to make the mouthpiece. Today I'll show you. Then you have to practise."

He made a cut about an inch from one end, then another at an angle to meet it. He took his time for the boy to take it in. He laid the embryo whistle down, picked up the discarded wedge of elder and carved a small shape to fit into the mouthpiece, all-important to produce sound. He flattened one edge with a rough sanding tool and slipped it into the mouthpiece where it fitted snugly. He handed it to Billy, who put it to his lips and played it by blocking the end with his finger.

"Find a different elder bush, boy. You'll need a big one and that one's mine." Jakob chuckled as Billy walked off with his prize. A dozen attempts later Billy managed to make something that worked. Later he changed the design so that it was a bit more like a recorder, more notes to produce. Rosina watched, impressed, and listened to his plans to join the band. Albert harrumphed at the mere idea.

*

Billy began to bother the band leader, Herr Thoma. Practice nights were on a Thursday and Billy hung around, watching the players, keeping out of the way until Herr Thoma finally said,

"What the devil makes you think you could play?"

"I want to do it; I like the music."

Herr Thoma saw the enthusiastic face. "What you just heard was Strauss. Have you heard of him?" Billy shook his head. "How about Beethoven? Or Schubert?"

"Yes, I've heard of Beethoven." Fraulein Waldvogel had brought a phonograph into school one Friday afternoon and played the class a record. "This is Beethoven's 'Pastoral Symphony,'" she had said with reverence. She'd explained what the word 'pastoral' meant. They had had to lay their heads on their arms on the desks and listen. Some went to sleep. Billy listened to every note, could hear the mountains, the streams and the birds.

By now he had learned the names of all the instruments. "I'd like to play the flute," he told Herr Thoma.

"Mm…" Herr Thoma looked at Billy's fingers, square and short but strong. "How about having a go at the clarinet."

An instrument was produced and Peter, the clarinettist, showed him how to pull his lips over his teeth to make a good fit for the mouthpiece. He explained that the reed gave the clarinet its particular sound. First attempt, second attempt, no sound. Then, manoeuvring his tongue slightly and licking his lips there was a squeak. Fourth attempt and there was a full high sound, like the laugh of a girl. The beautiful black rod with its intricate silver keys felt right in his hands and Herr Thoma and Peter nodded approvingly. He watched as Peter took it apart and laid the five pieces into a lined box.

"You'll have to learn to read music. But it's an easy language – and the most beautiful. Come next Wednesday, after school."

He ran, hopped and skipped home to tell his mother. Albert snorted as if no good would come of it, but it was a beginning, and he would never look back.

6

1928. While Germany struggled, along with the rest of the world, with the great depression, Neustadt was in the fortunate position of having a mayor who tried to insulate the town from the worst ravages of the recession. The mayor, Karl Pfister, managed to borrow money to keep small businesses afloat.

Billy looked at the pile of soft steaming shit and considered his options. The cows in his charge – he had eight of them but Schummi had begun to calve in the middle of the night so there were seven – were pushing their noses into the snow and finding the odd bit of nourishment, their bells chiming sadly, muffled, in the damp, wintry air. His job was to watch them, and to bring them back down to the farmhouse, in a couple of hours' time. "Just before the sun hits the Old Man," Herr Eiche had said, pointing with his head to the low hill in the distance. The sky was filling, grey and heavy with snow and the cattle would probably be kept in tomorrow. These huge Hinterlands were strong but there was no point in their being out in the deep snow. Tomorrow he'd be busy in the barns. Mitzi, his favourite, was close by him and he scratched at her huge, rough tan and white back, the way she liked. It was Mitzi's deposit he was staring at.

He was freezing. So cold that he could hardly feel his fingers and his feet hurt with it. He had a pair of old boots on his feet. Frau Eiche had found them for him, but they were ancient and leaked. His bare feet – he'd never had a pair of socks in his life – squelched in them, icy crystals creeping in as he stood. He thought about it; he'd seen farmers do it but never thought he would. Then the promise of heat, the delicious comfort it would bring, and the way Mitzi seemed to look at him, as if to say, "I did it just for you," made him decide. He shook off the boots and plunged his feet firmly into the heap. He was in it up to his ankles. It was heavenly. Warmth crept up from his toes, he sighed with pleasure. He stood there for a while, contemplating the darkening sky and wondering if he would get home on Sunday. If there was little work to do the family would take him into Neustadt for the day when they went to Mass. Sometimes the snow was too deep for the trip.

He had been here in Langenordnach since he'd left school the previous summer. Joe's miserable experience, which he still didn't like to talk about, hadn't stopped his father finding a place for Billy. It was something he could do before starting some sort of apprenticeship when he was fourteen. Encouraging his boys into work was something Albert took seriously. During the summer Billy had travelled over to the farm, where he spent his days and most nights with the cows in the field. Herr and Frau Eiche were kindly. After Joe's experience Rosina questioned Billy intensely about them. Billy, happy to talk, reassured her that he was given enough to eat, that the nights outside were no problem. In fact the nights were a little frightening, at first. As long as there was a light somewhere in the valley to focus on, he was OK and he was usually so tired that he went straight to sleep under his blanket, head on a pillow of ripped-up grass.

But sometimes the murmur of the trees, never completely silent, the movement of the cows, sent his imagination spinning. The little men of the forest, the creatures of folklore were there, spying on him, waiting to wreak impish havoc. He'd sit up and stare into the darkness and see – there, and there – something move, something jump. Then Lola or Mitzi would low, bells muffled by darkness, giving the gentlest of sounds. Nothing there, nothing to worry about. Slowly his eyes would close, and he would drift off to sleep.

The hardest thing was missing his clarinet lessons. As he wandered in the fields he imagined his fingers covering the keys, pictured the notes on the page, the scales he had been learning.

"Never mind." Herr Thoma could see how upset he was. "You'll be back soon. You are good at this, you know, you'll soon pick it up again."

Now Billy looked first at the hill in the distance then down at his feet. He wiped the shit as carefully as he could on the snow-covered grass and slipped the boots back on. He reached into his pocket and took out one of his whistles and blew to catch the attention of the cows. They turned their heads towards him, muted bellows showing gratitude, breath sweet and milky, forming clouds in the cold, grey air. Boy and beasts started their slow walk back to the farm, to the warm barns with their meagre heaps of soft straw and, hopefully, a new arrival.

*

Albert had infrequent need to wander around Neustadt. The busy little town with its well-established social and family links, its deeply held religious prejudices, its traditions honed over centuries, hemmed in by the mountains and proximity of the French and Swiss borders, made it all alien to him, the man from Baden who had broken free and had found success in London. Twice an outsider.

Occasionally he would stride through the town, maybe to the council, maybe to the hardware shop, but rarely would he greet or be greeted. He would walk past the old soldiers' meeting places where they sat talking about the injustices suffered by Germany after all their sacrifices. Recently there had been a couple of new faces, louder voices berating the lies told by the new republic, its weakness, the need for revenge. The taverns were pleased to see them. More beer was being drunk. Once or twice, he had stopped for a beer, and listened to them.

The old soldiers had plenty to complain about with their diet of potatoes and their thin beer. The Steel Helmets, who had raised money all over Germany for the brave comrades injured in the war, now strutted about in uniforms, encouraging anyone who would listen that something had to be done about the communists and their Jewish collaborators. The war wasn't over for them, Albert thought, they were still fighting it.

Today Albert was on a mission. Rosina had seen the signs. The intense frowns, the prolonged silences. His sons were growing up,

Albie now seventeen and keen to leave home and make his way in Freiburg. He had done well at school, not as clever as John but nonetheless had his school certificate. For all of them their English birth certificates were a hindrance. He was sure of it. He had himself been insulted in the street as 'that English traitor'. It had for a time confused him. He listened, scowling, when Rosina told him she had had the same thrown at her by some of the women in town, women, she tried to remind herself, who had lost husbands and sons for seemingly nothing. She kept to herself the time she had been called 'an English whore', soon after Hilda's birth. It was months before she could face the market again.

Albert pondered on it and decided that he would force officialdom to come to the aid of his family instead of waiting for the state to cause trouble, as English officialdom had done before. His English-born sons needed to become German citizens.

So, he climbed the steps of the Town Hall and found a bureaucrat who could tell him what to do. Birth certificates would have to be produced, his and Rosina's. Their parents' as well. It would take time but soon those fine boys would be welcomed into the Deutches Reich and be able to take their part in building the nation to its former and even greater glory. At least that was how Albert interpreted the gleam in the bureaucrat's eye and he didn't argue with him.

For Albert, the piece of paper he eventually received, stamped, signed, dated and ennobled with the Baden crest printed at the top, ensured his sons' safety. Just a few years later he would be climbing more steps, this time with Albie at his side, to procure documentation to prove his family's Catholic heritage, to prove that not a drop of Jewish blood flowed in their veins. Ridiculous, of course, but people were doing it, just as a precaution, to cast aside any doubt.

7

1930. The Weimar Government was faltering. In the major cities there was endless street fighting between right and left.

Billy's young life had moved on. Albert suddenly announced that he had found him an apprenticeship at Mayer's, the tailor. Albert scoffed at his musical ambitions and told him he should bring some money into the house, like Joe, who, after a few false starts had finally done the right thing and found work with a plumber. Dirty work, scrabbling under floors and behind walls, but money appeared on the table every Friday. Billy, startled at the unexpected turn of events, started his apprenticeship when he was fourteen, spending long hours squatting cross-legged on the enormous table, training his young bones, learning how to thread a needle and use a thimble. As light relief he had to run errands, sweep the floor, scrub the irons, put the marking chalks back in the boxes and pick off the fluff and grime that attached itself to the sewing machines. This year he had moved on to felling linings, which involved a complicated stitch and pressing. His day started at seven-thirty and he finished at five.

At the end of his first year, he had been hung upside down by his braces on a hook on the wall, grabbed by the stronger arms of the three other apprentices. It had happened quite suddenly without warning, although he remembered being curious about the silences and suppressed chuckles from the others that morning. After an age of struggle and pleading they turned him the right way up and then deserted him, amid hoots and loud laughter. They returned with a camera. He didn't smile when Herr Mayer took the shot. In fact, it took days before he could laugh about it, heartened only by the fact that at some point he would be able to inflict the same humiliation on the next unsuspecting victim. The photo was his to keep.

He was busy. By the time he had put in a ten-hour day at Mayer's he had to find time for band practice or race to the football 'pitch' for training and matches at the weekend. Saturday mornings consisted of being shouted at by his sisters because he was always out and why should they do all the jobs, cajoling his mother, avoiding his father and getting out of the door as quickly as possible.

The Neustadt team practised and played on a flattish piece of land by the side of the road leading to Donaueschingen to the east, where the great Danube rose. Bigger teams, when they came, sneered at the lumps and bumps on the pitch but they had no idea how much effort they put into keeping it as flat as it was. A great cement roller was pushed across it regularly but every spring, once the snows had finally gone, the tears in the soil reappeared as if there were icy, angry fingers under the surface, affronted at the very idea of flatness. Grass grew in hard little tussocks and caused many a trip, useful when you wanted to take the ball from under the legs of an opponent.

Today he was walking home through the town with John. They played in the same team, in cobbled-together kit and the boots they wore every day. Billy a centre forward, strong, never flagging, John an excitable striker, prone to histrionics but deadly accurate with his left foot. They had beaten Löffingen 4-2 and were talking happily about the good moments and generously about a Löffingen player called Feigelman, small and nippy and very much what their own team needed. John had an arm slung round Billy's neck, longer-legged and thinner than his brother, black hair brushed back off his forehead, dark clever eyes scanning the town as he walked. They parted at the old mill in the centre of town because Billy wanted to pay a visit to old Jakob, who was spending less time outside his house these days.

John walked up the slope of a road and turned right towards the tavern. He walked more slowly as he approached it because a group of men and women, not just the old soldiers, had their faces turned towards a man who was speaking loudly enough to attract attention; he moved his hands as he spoke, using gestures that seemed to draw in the crowd. John leant against a building and listened. Soon he found himself moving closer and paying heed. The man was persuasive. What he said was worth thinking about.

*

Meanwhile Joe had spent the afternoon with his friend Marco. Joe had stopped playing football, preferring to hang around the market square where there were girls to look at. Marco was the brave one, he could make them laugh, but Joe had his followers. His shyness and warmth seemed to hold an attraction for a particular type of girl. Susannah had let him hold her hand and promised to look out for him tomorrow at Mass. Now the two young men, eighteen years old, were on their way home and the conversation had taken a serious turn. It was why he loved Marco. He could switch from girls to socialism in a heartbeat. And their hearts did beat loud and strong to the sentiments of Marx and Engels, the speeches they read by Friedrich Ebert, founder of the republic. It still excited Joe, young enough to be convinced that a struggle would inevitably turn out in their favour. An election was coming up. Too young to vote but happy to deliver leaflets, help put up the posters.

"We've got to steal their thunder, Joe." Marco was talking about the Communists. It was a running theme with him.

"How can forming a splinter group help anyone?" Joe was rarely angry but his frustration with his friend was showing.

"People will follow us, once it becomes clear that the old way isn't working."

"There are enough choices for people to turn to without yet another one."

"Nonsense. We shouldn't be tempted to dilute the message in order to gain—"

"What? Votes?" Joe shouted, incredulous. "Power is what we want, isn't it? No change without that!"

They glared at each other for a split second then broke into grins. They knew that in Neustadt it was a largely academic question. Here people voted for the Catholic parties and nothing would change their minds. The extremes were dismissed with hasty signs of the cross and shakes of the head.

They sat down on a felled tree trunk that lay parallel to the path. Their caps were pushed back, and they leaned forward, with their elbows resting on their knees. They were on the edge of town and could see swathes of rough farmland and beyond the forest stretching away, dark even in the afternoon light.

"Are you serious about leaving the Party?" Joe looked at his friend. Marco grimaced, breathed out and turned his head slightly away. "Not sure." He shrugged and made to stand up. Joe touched his arm to stop him.

"Don't. We need to stick together. This Socialist Workers Party of yours hasn't got the answers, especially for people like ours," Joe gestured towards the town, to the fields and farmhouses.

The men shook hands and parted. Joe kicked at the ground as he made his way home. Marco would leave, he felt sure. And not just their Party but Neustadt itself. Albie, now in Freiburg, came home with stories of street fighting, unheard of in Neustadt, Nazis making trouble at every opportunity. They didn't behave as if they kept losing elections. Marco wanted to challenge that and not just with posters.

Despondent, troubled, he made his way home.

*

Billy heard the voices of his brothers before opening the front door and was then pushed aside by his father, storming out, scowling. "Your brothers are arguing, and I can't be bothered with them." He headed off towards town.

Joe, unusually red-faced, was staring at John, hands flat on the table as if to steady himself. "How can you believe this rubbish?"

"I'm not saying I believe anything, just that what he said made sense – and it was making sense to the people listening." John was sitting back, away from Joe's anger, which he had never seen before and which excited him. He leant forward. "When was the last time any politician actually thought of the little farmers around here, the ones that work their fingers to the bone for the landowners?"

'This was new for Joe. He was used to discussing the many facets of socialism, communism, collectivism with his comrades and, most recently, the thing that was dearest to his heart, pacifism. His brother, two years his junior, quick-witted and articulate, had picked up the biggest weakness in the socialist narrative and he didn't know how to counter it.

"They lie, John. All the time, the Nazis lie."

"Tell people what they want to hear, and they'll vote for them." Sixteen-year-old John looked steadily at his brother, knowing he had scored a point.

Billy listened to his brothers, looked over at Rosina sitting squarely at the other end of the table, waiting for her to stop it. He remembered the paper, the *Echo*, lying on Jakob's work bench yesterday evening with a photo of that respectable, besuited politician, Herr Hitler, and Jakob's finger jabbing at it. "That man wants war, that's all he's after." Billy was shocked at the angry tone and the sad shake of the head. He knew that Jakob had lost two sons in the war. "It mustn't happen again, Billy." He said it very quietly, almost as if Billy wasn't there. Then, to Billy's relief the conversation had returned to music and clarinet practice.

"Enough, boys." Rosina stood up. "I want to put food on the table." Anna and Hilda carried plates and spoons and a pot of barley soup was brought over from the stove. They ate in uneasy silence. John and Joe, aware of unformed ideas, decisions yet to be made, glanced at one another occasionally, unwilling to allow differences to escalate.

As Billy ate, his mind wandered. He wished Albie were here; he would want to talk about the World Cup, taking place in Uruguay – without a team from Germany, too far away, couldn't afford it. And Albie, man of the world over there in Freiburg, listening to the radio, would know what was going on. He wished they could have a radio… but all that, as his family sat momentarily unhappy with itself, lost its significance. He looked guiltily over at Mama.

And Rosina regarded them all. Too much bound them together, for a rift to widen between these people she loved. She had learned not to show it, her face had set itself into impassivity, scrutinised as she knew it was by Albert for any sign of sentiment, or weakness.

Once, when she had been comforting Joe, just thirteen, after a bad week on the farm, agreeing that he needn't go back, he had threatened to throw them both down the stairs, face white with anger, hands gripped on Joe's slim shoulders. "We need the money. The boy has to toughen up." She remembered how fear had constricted her throat, how for the first time she felt deep and pure hatred. The next day, alone in the house with Albert, she told him that Joe would stop work at the farm at the end of the month. Albert looked at the cold steel in her eyes and said nothing.

She sometimes wondered where this fierce love of hers came from. Where did she learn it? Not from Berta, who, she had convinced herself, was incapable of it. For Berta, the girl with the beautiful red hair, every violation became a lesson in survival, every injustice hardened her, had to harden her, against pain.

But when Rosina looked at her children's bright faces, her own eyes discerning everything, she burned with love, folding it into a tiny corner of her heart which was just for them.

She read the papers, she heard the talk in the town, listened to Albie's fears when he came home to visit, knew how the world was shifting. And they were all finding their feet, edging away from her, noses always pointed at the door. She prayed every Sunday at Mass that Albie wouldn't leave, like Rosie. Her golden boy, her clever boy. But he was the one that devoured his sister's letters full of news of London, of work. He ached to go. Rosie had found a position in a house off Russell Square; her descriptions of her employers dripped with venom, the family incapable of doing anything without servants, they would starve without the Belgian cook and the German maids and the gardener whose English she couldn't understand a word of, she had to point and wave her arms around to make herself understood. Albert complained that she never sent any money home. Rosina was glad she didn't.

8

London. September 1935.

Albie, standing in the narrow hallway, stared at his sister through the open door. They smiled uncertainly at each other.

"Well, come on in." She stood awkwardly in the middle of the room, not sure what to do with her arms. It had been eight years since she had left, since the day they, crestfallen, had watched her disappear out of the door.

"Someone downstairs told me where to go." She drank him in. Blond and handsome, smart woollen jacket, grey trousers, a raincoat over one arm. He was well-prepared for London although with that tan he would stick out like a sore thumb.

"That'll be Mavis, I told her to keep an eye out for you."

"May-vis." He smiled at the unfamiliar name. Rosie had changed, little lines at the side of her mouth, between her eyes. She was wearing a flower print dress and a red cardigan with bright red lipstick to match. Her fine hair was permed in a halo around her head, accentuating her broad forehead, summer freckles beginning to fade.

"It's not her real name. It's Helmine, she's Swiss, but Lady Boynton can't pronounce it so she's Mavis. I think she always calls her downstairs maid Mavis."

Albie pulled an 'I see' face, turning the corners of his mouth down and stepped in, putting his suitcase, small and new, on the floor. The lino was dark brown, shiny and cracked. No carpet, a bed by the window and a chest of drawers with some female clutter on top of it.

"The family are away so you're OK to stay here. They wouldn't notice anyway, and the cook won't say a word. There used to be a butler but now there's only Mavis. You can sleep on that." She spoke quickly, pointing to an old sofa pushed up against the wall; a couple of blankets were laid there, ready. Why was she so nervous, shy of him? There was so much to ask, it had been so long. She felt tears prickle her eyes.

"Oh, Albie, it's so good to see you. How is everyone? How's Mama?"

"Rosie! What I'd love is a cup of coffee. Or a beer! Then I'll tell you everything."

She laughed, feeling easier. "Too early for the pubs – we'll go later. Come downstairs and I'll get you something to eat. The cook is German, Bettina, she'll like you!" She gave him a self-conscious hug, surprised how much taller he was, how muscular he'd become. "Come on."

Bettina, round, and every inch a cook, made him a plate of sandwiches, ham and chicken, and a pot of coffee. She folded her arms under her bosom and smiled down on him as he wolfed it down. It had been a long time since he'd eaten and he didn't look up till he'd finished, wiping his mouth with the back of his hand. Then Rosie placed something else in front of him.

"What is it?"

"A scone. It's an English delicacy. Lady Boynton has one every afternoon."

"Oh." He looked at it with reverence.

*

They took the 49 to Earls Court, where Rosie's favourite pub was, on Old Brompton Road. They sat upstairs and smoked. It turned out that Rosie had changed employers several times, something she didn't mention in her letters home. She had left the family in

Russell Square for reasons she wouldn't go into and gone to work for a banker, not far from St. Paul's Cathedral. Then to Chelsea to work for a woman, a socialist writer, who treated her poorly, like a skivvy, she said. On to someone called Sir Ralph who had fallen on hard times and had had to let the staff go. Now, here she was in Belgravia where Bettina was training her to be a cook. She was staying put this time although it went without saying that Lady Boynton was a fool.

Once in the pub Rosie began to ask her questions. They sat in a corner of The Drayton Arms, half-hidden in the convivial fug where they could talk in German without turning heads, pints of brown ale in front of them, Albie sipping his with interest, gradually getting to like it. Albie told her about John's plans to travel to South America, Joe's devotion to socialism even though it was now banned. Mama was fairly well. 'You know Mama,' he said with a confident smile, 'strong as an ox.' Father was, as always, quiet, silent even, unless crossed. Rosie nodded at the memory. She didn't ask but listened to him tell her about Hilda, everyone's favourite, it seemed. And Anna. Nervy, difficult, not doing well at school, a worry for Mama. Rosie shook her head gently, remembering, and waited a while.

"And Billy, tell me about Billy. What's he up to?" Albie looked at Rosie's face light up, the little brother she loved. They both remembered the tears he had had to swallow back when Rosie left. Their father had glared at him – thirteen was too old to cry.

"Ah, well now, Billy." There was plenty to tell her about Billy.

9

Neustadt. August 1935. The Nazi Party was increasing its hold on the nation. The first race laws came into effect. Marriage between Jew and non-Jew was forbidden. Complex laws around employment rights came into existence regarding those who were half or quarter Jew.

"You can put those straight back on, sunshine, if you know what's good for you!" Sergeant Schrenk paused only briefly in front of Billy and his tone was not friendly.

They were sitting on the side of a lake, taking a brief break and he had taken off his boots and peeled off the socks to examine the blisters and the bloody mess which was what had become of his heels and toes. Years of only intermittent shoe wearing had left his feet unprepared for the rigours of army training.

"Here, wrap these around before you put the socks back on." Helmut handed Billy two strips of torn material, old shirt by the looks of them. "Got to get yourself kitted up, my friend, no-one's going to do it for you." Billy nodded and wrapped up his toes before carefully levering the socks back on and, wincing, first one slightly too big boot then the other.

The call-up to do his duty for the Fatherland had arrived a couple of months before. He could have got out of it, made excuses, like Joe who was helping build houses outside Hufingen with his plumber, but he thought he'd get it over with, just as he was beginning to earn some money at Mayer's as a fully qualified tailor, just as he was given a clarinet solo to play in the upcoming concert in Freiburg. It hadn't been a total surprise. Albie had been called the year before, pulled

419

out of the business course he was taking. He had to listen to him plotting to run away to England, tried to persuade him against it. Albie did his stint, kept the authorities sweet, then, the minute it was over, spent his money on new clothes, a suitcase and was gone.

Mama hadn't left the house for a week; she seemed to shrink, close down. For once their father's sneers and rough jibes had no effect. Instead, he faced their broadening, shielding backs and it registered that a turning point had come.

Only weeks before he left, they'd been swimming in the Titisee, practising handstands; Albie could walk on his better than anyone, girlfriends in their swimsuits cheering them on, bodies brown and glowing. So much to laugh about while the sun shone.

Now life consisted of tramping across the hills, camping out, rifle cleaning, boot polishing. He, Helmut and others kept out of the way of the Nazis, who ran faster, polished more thoroughly, dismantled and cleaned rifles more efficiently and shouted louder when required. They, the Nazis, were a small group, in this Catholic backwater of a place, but favoured by the officers, applauded by the Gauleiter, who had replaced the benign, kindly mayor in '33 and who visited their camp on the odd occasion. Billy watched them from a distance and tried to figure out what made him most uneasy. It was their certainty, their blind belief that unsettled him. He thought of Joe, also a believer – lately in internationalism, so many 'isms' in Joe's world – borders were unnatural, he had read somewhere, we are all the same, nations need to unite, not fight. John had laughed. He said I think you'll find Herr Hitler will be no respecter of frontiers, just wait and watch! Joe glowered at him. John was no Nazi, but anyone could see the way the tide was turning.

Billy had time for none of it. Hardly listened to it. Music was what transported him, nothing had that power, except perhaps Irmgard's blue eyes, watching him hungrily on the shores of the Titisee, and very little could compare with scoring a goal for his team, the only time he was capable of real aggression, muscles pumped. No. He had time for none of the speeches, the hysteria. Till now. Now he began to take more careful notice.

Billy, for whom life was about making a room light up, bringing a whole orchestra to the point of dangerous laughter by playing the wrong note, so perfectly pitched and timed for there to be no doubt it was a joke, at home lifting Anna's morose mood and reducing Hilda to helpless giggles, this same Billy was beginning to make connections. It was like a fast-moving picture show; his bloody toes, the sneer in the voice of the sergeant, the barking of orders throughout the day, the change in the way the villagers interacted with each other. The images tumbled over each other. The world he had held at bay for too long was crashing into his universe. Not because he was blind, or unthinking, but because it was his nature to dismiss the uncontrollable and make things better in any way he could. He feared those men in his platoon, men he knew he could run into the ground if he chose to; he feared their devotion to an individual whose rhetoric seemed to stem from some soulless place, a humourless place that was alien to him. It was a painful awakening, tearing up the blueprint he thought his life would follow, forcing him to imagine alternatives, different futures because the future is all there is when you are twenty and impatient for life.

*

It was Albie who had brought the radio home, back in '33, all the way from Freiburg. The price of radios had dropped but Albie wanted a better model which could pick up foreign stations. Rosina looked at it dubiously.

"Must've cost a lot of money."

"You'll never get it to work here," said Albert and by way of explanation, "The mountains..."

Ignoring his father Albie said, "Worth every penny, Mama." He was working for a musical instrument supplier with plans of owning his own business one day. "Soon we'll be able to listen to London," he said, as he plugged it in to the one socket in the kitchen.

"London?" said Albert from his corner, pipe in mouth, twitching with interest. He watched his sons gather round as Albie turned the tuning knob. Only crackles and hisses emerged. Albert grunted an 'I told you so.' John and Joe started giving advice.

Billy sat on the edge of the table watching and thinking. At last, he would be able to hear one of the matches that were broadcast on Saturday afternoons. *Today is Friday*, he thought, *tomorrow Hertha Berlin were playing Leipzig – it would be a bloody affair*. They had taken over from the mighty Nurnberg and were winning everything. And he, Billy, knew why. He had listened to scraps of games on Jakob's set – the old man was one of the first in Neustadt to get a radio – and he became more and more fascinated by the analysis which made him think how his team's play could be improved. He and John would discuss at length whether the new ideas borrowed from England, from a club called Woolwich Arsenal, were really responsible for Hertha's transformation. Or was it just the fitness of the players? Both, they agreed. The defensive system paid off but only if the men were fast enough to scoop up the lost balls and sometimes there wasn't enough for the midfielders to do...

The sound of identifiable human voices taking the place of the hissing broke into his thoughts and he moved over to the set, Mama too. Albie beamed at them all. It seemed that everything mattered in order to get a reception. The position of the radio, the position of other objects, even where they stood seemed to have an effect.

"There you are, Mama. It's an episode of *The Dortmeyers*, a drama about a Stuttgart family. They're hooked on this in Freiburg." Rosina looked doubtfully at the contraption.

"Don't they have better things to do than listen to the radio?"

Albie laughed. "It lasts for fifteen minutes, Mama. My boss's wife is a great fan. She listens with her afternoon coffee." Rosina tried to imagine such decadence and then, in response to Albert's mutterings of disapproval, decided she might give it a try. They listened for a few minutes to doleful chatter about a forthcoming visit from an aunt who lived in Munich. For some reason they weren't looking forward to it. Rosina was immediately interested but Albert broke in,

"Where's London, then?"

John was at the controls. "Let me find it." The red stripe passed over Europe in a flash and lingered over the BBC. A little fine tuning brought indistinct but raucous music hall into their home, followed by laughter, silence and a time check. They looked at each other and smiled. An English voice, English noises, even an English silence. For a minute Albert and Rosina sank into unfamiliar and separate worlds of memory. The others marvelled at the possibilities, doors opening, minds expanding.

*

The local newspaper had by 1935 become unreadable. *Der Hochwächter* had been a weekly luxury for Albert and Rosina for years, with its summaries of national events and local news. In '33 it was taken over by the Party and its stain was imprinted on every article, its virus contaminating each page. When the full-page adverts appeared describing Jews as a national scourge who needed flushing out of the sewers, Communists as a national enemy, red in tooth and claw, Albert had had enough. Rosina agreed but missed it; there was a good women's page she enjoyed, and Billy missed the Sport section. For years he had waited for his parents to finish with it so he could turn to the football news, follow the fortunes of his footballing heroes, Dresden's Richard Hofman, Schalke's Fritz Szepan and many others.

And his interest in the English game was fanned by articles he read, especially about what was happening at Arsenal. Every so often there would be an article about the revolutionary manager Herbert Chapman, who from 1930 onwards had produced title after title for the team. Billy learned to say the names of the English clubs, Huddersfield, Aston Villa, Sheffield Wednesday, Everton and found out where the towns were; starry-eyed he devoured information about the star players like Ted Drake, Les Compton and Cliff Bastin, goal-scoring legends. In January 1934, snow in Neustadt two metres deep, came the news of Chapman's death from pneumonia. Billy feared for the season, but they still won the first division. Now, Albie gone, he would listen to the radio. On Saturdays he heard news of Arsenal's successes, his father even translating when he didn't understand.

Lying in bed at night, a bed still shared with a brother, he dreamed and planned. He would save his money, somehow, go to England and watch them play then come back and tell John all about it and make Neustadt the best club in Baden Württemberg.

Of course, other news came into their kitchen, sliding unbidden from the speakers, filling the spaces between stove and table, table and chair until Albert switched it off. Vengeful voices enraged at the injustices the Fatherland had suffered, expansion threatened in the east, enemies within. Billy, home for a weekend's leave, trying to get a chance to play his clarinet – still not his own but he was trusted sufficiently by Herr Thoma to take it home – or joining a training session at the football ground, heard it all, filed it away. Not for him, none of that was for him.

It was Herr Thoma who watered the seed of an idea already firmly planted. "What are you going to do, lad?" Billy looked at him over the music stand, where Bach's intricate notes danced, and held the clarinet loosely on his lap. "Those hands of yours aren't meant for rifles."

And my feet aren't meant for army boots, thought Billy, but kept the thought to himself.

10

January 1936.

They sat together at the top of the ski slope, looking down at the half-dozen skiers who had already set off. They preferred to wait a while and stare out over the snowy hills, down towards the treeline. The air was cold and dry, the sky a perfect blue, they wouldn't be able to sit for long before it crept through their clothing and froze their bones. But they were strong, used to the temperatures, and never tired of the beauty spread out before them. Every year they clambered up the Feldberg, to the top of its 1,277 metres and then hurtled down on their home-made skis, whooping and shouting as they went. This time Billy, John and Joe had used the ski lift and could see, eyes smarting and squinting against the bright, icy glare, as far as the Swiss Alps, every angle, peak and outline familiar to them, always spell-binding. More people were coming in every year as skiing as a sport became more popular. Hotels in Titisee did good business.

"You'll miss this," Joe said, nudging his brother.

"I'm coming back, a couple of months that's all. See Albie and Rosie." Billy had it planned.

"Mama doesn't think you'll come back."

Billy looked at Joe. "Is that what she said?" Joe nodded.

"Of course I'm coming back."

"You might not get the chance." John was unwrapping sausage sandwiches and took a huge bite out of one of them.

There was a lot of talk of war. The old men talked of little else, said it was inevitable. The young brushed it aside, better things to concentrate on, things were looking up, after all, at last they had some money in their pockets. The sun dipped a little lower in the sky, casting longer shadows over the bottom of the valley.

"I'll never leave," said Joe, shaking his head.

"Well, 'comrade', you might just have to."

John had told Joe on many occasions to ditch his Socialist nonsense; it was going to get him into trouble. There was a concentration camp being built outside Freiburg, more in the pipeline. Communists were being rounded up all over the country.

Joe shrugged and looked at John, putting his hand out for a sandwich. "I won't leave her." They knew he meant Rosina.

John nodded and there was a few seconds' silence. "Well, I'm certainly not going anywhere. Whatever happens this is my country and I'm staying put." John took a deep breath of crisp, German air while his brothers wondered what was actually going on inside his head. He caught their expressions, raised his brows and set his mouth into a thin, stubborn line before slapping his hands on his knees and saying, "For God's sake, why are looking at me like that? This is my country! Whatever happens in it I will not leave." He stared furiously first at them then towards the mountains in the distance. He'd done a bit of travelling recently, once up to Karlsruhe and once to Stuttgart, taking odd jobs as he went. It had changed him. He was planning a trip to Munich although their mother was against it. He knew his ambitions to see the world could be curtailed.

"Whatever happens?" Joe asked deliberately. They had talked about the Jews, agreed it was wrong. So many laws. Cruel laws. It had been a step in Billy's awakening when Jews were no longer allowed to play in the League teams. Now they were banned in the smaller teams as well. The stupidity baffled him.

"You can't defend what's happening, John."

"I don't defend it," John looked less comfortable, "but I want to be here, be part of…" His voice trailed off. He couldn't help being excited by what was happening. The bad stuff would stop soon, he was sure, when the country was back on its feet, when other countries took it seriously again. His brothers didn't understand.

"You'll have to join the army, you both will," Billy said. Joe shook his head.

"You'll have no choice, you idiot!"

For Joe there were always choices, between good and bad, right and wrong, right and left. He couldn't imagine a situation where he would be unable to choose, ever hopeful, although the signs were bleak. The Nazis hadn't gone away as he and his friends had predicted in 1933; they were not a temporary aberration.

They looked up at the sky, recognised an imperceptible change in the quality of the blue, darkening down in the valley, a slight quickening in the coldness of the still air around them. This place was part of their souls; their understanding of the landscape, the seasons, went beyond words, more a matter of smell and touch. The names of the valleys below them were ingrained, the pathways that linked them had been walked a thousand times. They stood in a line and set off together in perfect formation, knees swaying gently one way and then the other, sticks stroking the snow, eyes assessing the swells and dips ahead. Always together until, swerving left, they came to rest near the road that would take them home.

*

Here he comes, smart, ready to go. My boy, my little boy, I mustn't show you how my heart is breaking. Don't go. Look at you. Smooth-skinned, such a boy. Come here and tell me you have changed your mind. But I can see you haven't. The gleam of excitement in your eye, shoulders stiff with apprehension. You've got your suitcase, same as Albie, had your hair cut short and fashionable. New jacket you made yourself, a beautiful thing. You don't know that I can still feel you, damp and warm, tucked up in my coat as we arrived here. How did I do that? How did any of us do that? I mustn't spoil it for you; you want it so badly. I know, I know. But how will I bear it, you are my bright star. John makes us laugh but you make us smile, inside and out. No crying, I promise, I've already done that. You'll remember me with red eyes and red hands from doing too much washing. Will you come back? I don't think you will.

Billy hesitated at the door. Rosina was sitting on the little wall waiting for him. He turned, taking his time to shut the door firmly while he gathered himself together to face her. Don't cry, Mama, please don't cry. As he approached her, he could see she was calm, mouth forcing a smile that didn't reach her eyes. He put his suitcase down and sat next to her, took her hand.

"Mama…" A mixture of sadness and embarrassment. They had all learned not to show emotion, safer that way for all sorts of reasons. Rosina covered his hand with hers and squeezed it gently. "Give my love to Rosie and Albie," she was smiling properly now, "oh, and give this to Rosie." She searched in her apron pocket and brought out a little shiny, gold and red bow with silver bells attached. He recognised it and nodded, feeling more miserable by the second.

"It was her favourite, she always wanted to put it on the Christmas tree, remember?" He couldn't but nodded anyway. "I always wanted her to have it."

He could think of nothing to say so she continued, filling the silence, "Be careful when you get to London. It's so big…" She stopped, catching her breath at the thought of her boy alone at the station, facing that traffic, that noise.

"Mama, I'm coming back soon," he had to say it, this was unbearable. "Just a few months, see everything, then I'll be back." She stood up, wanting it over, not wanting it over. She brushed down her apron.

He put his arms around her; she felt so small, her forehead leaning on his shoulder. She was surprised at the strength in his arms, felt comforted by it. They said their brave goodbyes and she watched him head off down the road towards the station, fields, forests, hills spread out either side of him. She'd watch until he disappeared around the bend in the road, and he knew it. Relieved to turn the corner, relieved to be gone, every step feeling lighter, head brimful of the adventure ahead, chest puffed with excitement. If he had turned back, he might have seen Albert, shoulders taut, at the window, rubbing his thumb and forefinger across his eyes.

11

Neustadt. Spring 1938. Germany marched unopposed into Austria. In September the Sudetenland, part of Czechoslovakia, was annexed. In November, synagogues the length and breadth of Germany were destroyed.

"How long have those two been hanging around?" Albert had noticed the boys walking past the house, stopping a little further up the road and walking back slowly, peering over, cockily, making no pretence of their interest. Rosina joined him at the window.

"Who? Ah, Hans and Walter." She looked carefully at the boys who had been at school with Hilda. Loyal Party members, who, after two boisterous years in the Hitler Youth, were now toadies for the Gauleiter who recognised certain talents and loyalty.

"Are they interested in the girls?" Albert moved away from the window and resumed his seat in the corner.

"Well, I'm certainly not interested in them!" said Hilda firmly. Boys from school were very much beneath her. Anna looked up from mending her stockings, terrified at the mere idea.

"It's Joe they're interested in, isn't it?" Albert tapped his foot angrily in the air, reaching for his pipe. "Where is he, anyway?"

"Walking. He wanted to go across to the Schluchsee, set off at six this morning," Hilda told him. Walking was Joe's passion, a time to think things through, come to conclusions. He used to go with Billy when he was still here, when he had time. Now he went by himself.

Rosina watched Hans and Walter shuffle off, hunched up against the wind, abandoning their watch in the face of the cold and at the prospect of food back home. Frau Beckman was sure to feed her brood of rowdy boys with meat twice a day. Frau Beckman wore her Party badge with pride, pushing it into the faces of the few women who wouldn't follow her example.

'Maybe, maybe,' they would say when she pressed them.

'Let's see how things pan out,' they'd add, trying to avoid confrontation.

'You should show your loyalty to the Führer. Look what he's doing for the country.' The women smiled and wandered away, to church, where the priest was in no doubt about the infamy of the man in charge but spoke in code, about the equality of all men, the sanctity of human life, the authority of the Pope.

Rosina said, "It's not just Joe, you know. It's all of us. They are suspicious because we lived in England."

Frau Beckman had had little difficulty sowing seeds of doubt about Rosina. The family were no better than foreigners, making use of our country when it suited them. She had been whispered about since she arrived. Daughter of Red Berta? What do you expect? It had got better as the children grew up, popular and friendly, but now as three of them had drifted back to England, it had started again, certain backs turned, silences as she walked past.

"No, it's Joe," said Albert, staring at the ground, sinking into thoughtful silence punctuated by sharp shakes of the head and puffing more noisily than usual on his pipe.

It was after eight o'clock before Joe got back, ruddy-cheeked and exhilarated after walking all day. He'd walked through icy valleys, still untouched by the low spring sun and the lake had glistened, mirror-like in the still air. He would never tire of it, the rhythm of motion keeping his brain and muscles in tune. He would add the word soul to that if he believed in such a thing anymore.

Albert waited until he had eaten and the girls, Hilda protesting, had gone up to bed.

"You are going to have to go too." No preamble from Albert, blunt as ever. For a moment Joe looked confused, unsure what he meant. He had finished his meal and was about to carry his plate over to his mother at the sink before heading up to bed himself. He sat still, waiting for more from his father. Rosina had turned to face them and was leaning back against the low stone sink, her face drained of colour, looking at Albert.

"Join your brothers before it's too late." His eyes were darting about the room, brain busy. "It's only a question of time before they come for you. Unless you join them, of course," and he looked keenly at his son, narrowing his eyes, challenging him.

Joe snorted. "Never, you know I won't."

"Not like your brother?" John had joined the Wehrmacht, started his basic training.

"John hasn't joined the Party, he never would," said Joe.

Albert shrugged. "He's going to be fighting for them, same thing." He kept his hard gaze on his son.

Joe glanced at his mother. "I can't do that. I talked about it with him. I can't do that."

"Then go. Before you're arrested." Albert leaned forward. "You can still get out but only if you go now."

Rosina and Joe looked at each other. In spite of their pounding hearts and Joe's numerous promises that he would always stay to look after them, they knew Albert was right. They wanted to fight it but could think of nothing to counter the simple truth of what he was saying. Joe would have to choose. Either go against everything he believed in and fight for this monstrous regime or leave. Or be locked up, and he knew enough about the concentration camps to know that he might never come out. Rosina watched her conflicted son and, hands balled into tight fists to keep herself under control, said, "He's right, son." She fought to keep her voice steady. "The police will come for you, the Beckmans will make sure of that. Go to England. Then I can rest in peace." Joe slumped over the table, heartbroken. Within the week he was gone.

12

London, 1936. April 25th.

It was Cup Final day. The roads to Wembley were blocked with 93,000 fans heading to the ground. Sheffield United fans, excited after their train journeys, heading to one end, Arsenal fans to the other. Some had banners, all wore caps and coats.

Inside the stadium there was a roar as the teams came onto the pitch, people stood yelling, swaying and cheering. Sheffield captain, Harry Hooper, kicked off and Arsenal narrowly avoided going 1-0 down in the first few minutes after a fumble from the goalkeeper saw United players charge in and an Arsenal defender clear the ball just in time. Gasps and cheers from the supporters. There followed a furious ding-dong of a first half, no players succeeding in breaking through. That continued in the second half, the crowd falling almost silent in disgust at the lacklustre play. Then, in the twenty-ninth minute, Arsenal's Chris Bastin sent a clever cross to Ted Drake, who scored. Minutes later Sheffield counter-attacked with a header from Jock Dodds. Premature cheers turned to groans as the ball rebounded off the crossbar. Arsenal lifted the cup and later paraded it outside Islington Town Hall to the delight of the whole of North London.

Billy, glued to the radio in Rosie's room, listening to every move, heart in mouth, seeing it clearly in his mind's eye, whooped with joy at the result. Already forgetting that he was meant to be going home again soon, he vowed that next year he would see it all for himself, every home match, if he possibly could.

1937

It came as a shock to Billy that there were Nazis in London. He watched news footage of October's Battle of Cable Street, waiting for the main film to start. It took a while for him to realise that the police were fighting the anti-fascists. Mosley's Blackshirts had sneaked off out of harm's way.

He had come with Rosie to watch *The Charge of the Light Brigade*. She was a great fan of Errol Flynn and Billy used the films to improve his English, and if he was lucky there would be some reports on the previous weekend's football matches. Tonight, however, there was no mention of football. After the brief film showing the police dispersing the anti-fascists in the East End, Pathé News had a long and slightly disapproving report of the King's holiday with Wallis Simpson. "That woman is after his millions," Rosie hissed in his ear, eyes glued to the screen. *For someone who was so scathing about her aristocratic employers,* thought Billy, *she is certainly fascinated by the Royal Family.* The King had declared his decision to abdicate before Christmas. Now no-one could talk of anything else.

Billy was learning a lot about the British. Their innate snobbery, their keen sense of class and rank, their ability to laugh at anything and everything, which he found confusing sometimes. There was a lot to learn.

Riding home on the bus from Leicester Square Odeon he looked out at London's West End twinkling back at him. He loved it, starstruck at the vastness, the noise, the pace. He had explored these streets by bus and on foot. He'd got the hang of the Underground and disobeyed Rosie's command not to venture east of Liverpool Street – he would fall prey to thieves, crooks and, interestingly, foreigners. He walked around Whitechapel and looked at the Jewish shops standing side by side, going about their businesses, pavements teeming with black-hatted men talking, gesticulating and… yes, safe, thought Billy. Down the alleys and side streets he saw half-naked children playing, fighting, laughing. Other streets were being demolished; better housing promised.

Rosie got off the bus at Knightsbridge while Billy continued to Earls Court. Albie would be home. He'd been working in a music shop near the British Museum for a year now and was seeing a girl he had met there. Billy had had a variety of short-term jobs. Washing up, window cleaning put money on the table, but it wasn't what he wanted. Finding a tailoring position had proved more difficult than he had imagined.

Finally, he said to one disdainful prospective employer, "Who do you think made this jacket?" The man hadn't noticed it, keen to dismiss the youngster. He looked expertly at the perfectly fitting shoulders, the pressed lapels, the hand-sewn buttonholes.

"You made this?" Eyebrows arched.

"Every stitch," said Billy.

"Come on Monday morning, we'll give you a try," said Mr Ravanelli, looking him up and down with increased interest. Ravenelli's was a good enough establishment but it was off Savile Row, near Conduit Street. As far as Billy was concerned this was but a step on the ladder. He had had to wait until 1938 before being taken on by 'Ravenelli's Gentleman's Tailoring (High-Class)'. Before that he continued with odd jobs, saved a few shillings when he could towards the cost of a clarinet, borrowed Albie's bike to explore possibilities and followed the misfortunes of Arsenal, for whom, in spite of George Allison's proud boasts on the steps of Islington Town Hall, further success would be elusive for some time yet.

*

1939. The Munich Agreement had been signed the previous September. Few believed that war could be avoided.

So now they were four. Joe found work easily enough, there was always work in London. Billy took him under his wing when he arrived, sensing his unhappiness, his unwillingness to talk. Walked with him to Camden to have a look at Pratt Street, the old shop, the park Rosina had taken them to. Joe could remember nothing. For days they criss-crossed the famous streets looking at all the sights their parents had told them about. They visited Rosie often, looking at her cut-out pictures of the coronation of George VI which covered the wall above her bed, and sat in the kitchen being fed by a delighted Bettina who, over plates of English cake, enjoyed their chatter in familiar dialect.

Slowly Joe opened up – telling them about John, now set to fight in the German army, about increasing fear in the village, his own fear of arrest. And about his guilt at not staying, in effect, running away. Nonsense, said Albie. He had more need to get away than the rest of them. What would be the point in dying in a concentration camp.

Joe listened to what they said and took some comfort from it but decided that his future lay out of London. He took himself off to Oxfordshire. He'd heard it was a gentler place with rolling green hills. And it was. But for Billy and Albie the sights and sounds and stink of this great city had seeped into their bones and they became part of the place, part of its heaving underbelly of hard-working, contradictory masses, accented in a thousand different ways and grateful for a haven while reading the papers, watching the news reels. Austria, Czechoslovakia, the Munich Agreement. And now Poland.

*

After the fall of France and Holland in May 1940 and the rescue of the British expeditionary force at Dunkirk there was a real fear of invasion by Germany and a worry that the German community in Britain harboured spies. Churchill directed the immediate arrest of all enemy aliens.

After war was declared by Germany in September 1939 the siblings were at first frightened, wary. Then, seeing life go on almost as before, relaxed into a normal though much quieter rhythm. Albie was kept on by the Austrian owner of the music shop. Billy, well settled in at Ravenelli's, was told quietly, "Tell anyone who asks you're Swiss, OK?" Rosie seemed safe at Lady Boynton's.

It was late in the evening of May 20th when Albie and Billy were caught unawares. They were chuckling among themselves at the film they had just seen, laughter lubricated by the pints they had swallowed on the way home. Rosie had had to miss out on *Alexander's Ragtime Band* because Lady Boynton was throwing a dinner party, in spite of the new blackout regulations, and the imminent threat of bombers which never seemed to come. The room the brothers were sharing, was in a house off the Cromwell Road. The gas lamps were very low as they approached it, and they didn't notice the two men leaning against the wall near their front door. The men straightened, pushed themselves off the wall and came towards them as Albie forced the key into the lock. They caught the look in their eyes as they approached, not particularly unfriendly but one of confident, grim authority, permission granted from a higher source.

"All right, gentlemen," were the first words spoken, "are you Mr Albert Ragg and Mr William Ragg of Leopold Terrace?" The two men stood square in front of them. One of them fished out a piece of paper from his inside coat pocket and started to read from it. The brothers waited for what was to come. They'd heard of Germans who had been arrested but no-one would be interested in them, surely? They'd convinced themselves of that over the last few months. The man with the piece of paper in his hand started to speak in a formal, flat tone and Billy, suddenly fearful, couldn't take in what he was saying. The voice droned on.

"... reason to believe you to be of hostile origin... sympathies with a government with which His Majesty is at war..."

"No, that's wrong, we came to get away..." someone said in a small voice.

"So under the Emergency Powers Act we are arresting you..." This couldn't be happening.

"You have fifteen minutes to collect anything you would like to take with you. Detective Barker will accompany you while you do so."

Albie began to say something but thought better of it. Only minutes before they had been talking about their mother, how she would have loved *Alexander's Ragtime Band*, suddenly excited at the thought of somehow bringing her over here. Now they trudged up the stairs in silence. Detective Barker, a portly man, sat down on one of the chairs by the small table and peered around.

Albie cleared his throat. "Look, I really think there has been some sort of mistake. We are not hostile…" Detective Barker looked surprised to hear him talk.

"I wouldn't waste my breath, mate. Get your stuff together. By my reckoning you've only got ten minutes left now." The brothers looked first at his podgy disinterested face then at each other. Billy shrugged. They each put anything that came to hand into their little suitcases. As they clicked them shut Barker stood up. Billy suddenly remembered something.

"Birth certificates. We mustn't forget them." The papers were in the little drawer attached under the table.

"Excuse me, please." He waited for Barker to step away and he opened and removed all the papers in the drawer. "OK. We're ready now." Billy grinned at his brother. "Let's go."

Albie smiled to himself at his younger brother's gentle assertion of authority. Barker didn't notice.

13

There were 75,000 Germans and Austrians living in Britain in 1940. Some were second generation, and many were Jews. All were rounded up.

He and Albert, Albie would now always be called Albert, childish things being put well and truly behind him, shared a cell, fully expecting to be released in the morning once they had a chance to talk to someone – someone who would understand their position. When the lights went out, he lay with his hands behind his head, staring into the darkness. There were the odd scrapes and rattles, and a drunk was brought in amidst shouts and obscenities which lasted a while. Then silence. He shared a few words with Albert but both men felt the need to process what was happening in their own way. Neither slept much.

*

Superintendent Fairfax looked at the two piles of paper on his desk and sighed. There were outstanding murder and burglary cases he'd rather be concentrating on. Now he'd be tied up with dealing with these foreigners. Why was it his job? The army should nab the lot and lock 'em up. Or send 'em to Australia. He took his jacket off, hung it over the back of his chair and rolled his shirt sleeves up. Better get on with it. He picked up a sheet from the right-hand pile.

"All right, constable, send the next one in, will you. And get me a cup of tea. And open the window." The constable, young and pink, dithered for a moment with these conflicting instructions, headed to the window and opened it an inch or two.

"Open it, I said!" Fairfax glared at him, watched him push it wide open and shook his head as the lad, growing pinker, walked back across the room and out the door.

A minute later a dark-haired young man was standing in front of Fairfax. He looked at him briefly then looked at the sheet of paper on the desk.

"William Ragg. Formerly of Baden…" Fairfax squinted at the word 'Wurttemberg' in front of him and gave up. "Do you speak English?" The young man nodded.

"Says here you've been living in London since 1936." He looked up at Bill. "So what have you been doing with yourself?"

"Working. I'm a tailor. Me and my brothers came…"

Fairfax narrowed his eyes.

"Brothers, eh? A little gang of you is there?" Fairfax leaned back in his chair and scratched his forearm.

"No, we just…"

"Save it, lad. You're off to Brixton. You can save your tales for them." He slammed the piece of paper on top of the left-hand 'done' pile. "Off you go, the constable will take you out."

*

So when did Billy, little brother Billy, finally become Bill? Was it when the plain clothes policeman approached outside his home? Was it when the man sat uninvited in their room and watched as they stuffed underclothes and old shirts into their suitcases, the same suitcases they had taken such trouble buying in Brunwald's Leather Goods shop in Neustadt? Or perhaps standing in front of Fairfax, a new sensation of humiliation flooding his chest as he realised the man was not interested in him at all, would never believe a word he said. Or was it right now, as he, separated from Albert, was driven past what seemed to be miles of brick, through enormous wooden doors and into the dank courtyard of Brixton Prison. More brick walls, small barred windows. If he had looked up, he would have seen the tall Victorian chimneys on the grey slate roof. But he didn't. He concentrated on staring straight ahead, seeing little, hearing less, stomach cramped, breath coming in short, shallow bursts.

"*Sei ruhig, junge Mann, sei ruhig,*" a man sitting next to him put an arm on his, "*Es wird ganz bestimmt nicht so schlimm sein.*"

The man's blue, kindly eyes looked straight into his and held his gaze. It wouldn't be so bad, the man had said. He fought to bring his breathing under control. It was the first time he had experienced panic. Was it because he was without his brother? No. It was the lack of control over what was happening to him. Everything that happened to him now lay in the hands of people who regarded him as an enemy. He struggled to recognise himself, who he was. What was he doing, being dragged out of the lorry, pushed up clanking stairways and down long corridors to cells that contained a bucket, a plank for a bed and a blanket?

Another man was put in the cell with him. He didn't look at him, just sat on the edge of the bed looking down at his feet. It wouldn't be so bad, the blue-eyed man had said. It would definitely not be so bad. Gradually he became calmer. He lay on his back and stared at the ceiling, where over a century's grime and cobwebs and memories had collected, and closed his eyes. He thought first about his brothers, were they here somewhere? Would Rosie be arrested as well? She may well be left alone in that big house of hers. He decided that when his turn came in front of the judge or the magistrate, or whoever would be deciding his fate, he would say nothing about Rosie, or Joe, if he was lucky enough to still be in Oxfordshire. Would he be able to write home? From prison? What would his mother think of all this? Far better if she didn't know. He drifted off into sleep, waking to shouts and hollers that came at him from different directions. Back to sleep and woken again this time by a bell, piercing and metallic. He got up straight away, for a second unsure where he was, and was confronted by his cell mate. He looked about eighteen, tousled hair, frightened eyes. Just a kid. They looked at each other for a minute, appraising.

"Bill," said Bill, and stretched out a hand.

"Hans," said Hans, taking the offered hand and shaking it with the gentlest pressure while his lips formed a question.

"They'll let me out, won't they? My mother is all alone." What could he say? He looked at the young face, pale fluff on his cheeks and chin, eyes bleary from tears and lack of sleep.

"I'm sure they will. We'll all get a chance to talk to a judge. You can tell him about your mother." He was making this up but his voice sounded sure, and it seemed to quieten the boy.

"Right now, though, I need to use that," and he pointed to the bucket in the corner. The boy nodded and turned his head discreetly to one side.

*

At meal times men talked quietly, sharing information which they had picked up. A lot of it contradictory. We'll have to stay here, thought some. No, no, there was a camp being built outside Liverpool, we'll all be going there. What sort of a camp, said a worried voice. No, not *that* sort of camp and there was another being built on an island somewhere. For god's sake, an exasperated, impatient voice interrupted; that's all rubbish, most of us will be released soon. Nonsense, said a voice from the other end of the long table, they don't care, we're here for as long as the war lasts.

Jews sat together, not comprehending, suddenly fearful once again. British fascists and Nazis found each other and talked with heads close together, enjoying the fear.

And suddenly there was Albert. Standing right in front of him. The brothers grinned, shook hands and clasped each other, delighted that each was safe and that they were reunited. Bill introduced Hans, his cell mate who was now a permanent fixture at his side. "He'll be going back to his mama soon."

"*Hoffentlich,*" said Hans quietly with a nervous smile.

"Definitely, I would say, Hans, no 'hopefully' about it," Bill told Albert. "He and his mother came over from Mannheim last year after his father was arrested for being a Communist. They haven't heard from him since."

Albert looked at Hans, that baby face, and shook his head in sympathy. It occurred to him that he and Bill had no such story to tell. He had come here to work, like his father before him. 'Not liking' the regime back in Germany sounded like a poor excuse.

A few weeks passed before the interviews began. Meanwhile the word got round that Oswald Mosley had been arrested and was being held somewhere in the jail. This excited the fascists to such an extent that, whether to impress their leader, or whether to express their fury at his arrest, they got together to do what they were good at – beating up a few Jews. Word came out that the Jews didn't take it lying down, just the opposite. They put up a good fight, cuts and bruises sustained on both sides, before the sorry little episode was brought to an end by the guards. If ever there was evidence that the Jews should have been released straight away, there it was, but government saw otherwise, and they stayed under lock and key.

*

Each man would be questioned; a variety of judges and magistrates were employed to head the hearings, make decisions. Once the tribunals started Bill began to think carefully about what he was going to say. The truth, of course, but he had his birth certificate, the precious document proving that despite his childhood, his accent, he had been born in the heart of England's capital city. As he waited for his turn, he read and reread the piece of paper grown limp with folding and unfolding with its pinkish background and typed affirmation of his preferred nationality. There it was – Birth in the Sub-District of East St. Pancras in the County of London. In spite of his father's determination to safeguard his sons by ensuring their German nationality, Rosina had kept the birth certificates, hidden from view, maybe as a memento, maybe as some sort of insurance. It was the last thing she gave each of them as they left.

And now it lay on the desk, in front of a Mr Forsythe. Still folded. So far ignored. Bill stood in front of the desk, a warden behind him, guarding the closed door. In case of what, he thought – sudden crazed attempts at escape? Next to Mr Forsythe sat a secretary, a woman of about fifty who scowled first at him then at the piles of paper which were clearly her responsibility, as was note-taking throughout the proceedings.

"Now then, Mr Ragg," Forsythe had some information in front of him which he was peering at, "you came over here in 1936. In your own words can you tell me why?" And he leaned forward slightly, cupped his chin onto criss-crossed fingers and stared at Bill as if into his very soul in order to discern the truth.

Bill was discomfited but began, "I wanted to see London. My brother was already here. He told me there was work. I'm a tailor and thought there would be more opportunities here for me." He had rehearsed this; his English was good, but he wanted to get it right.

"Did you intend to stay here?"

Bill tried to remember how he had felt when he first came. So much had changed. "Not at first. My mother was expecting me to go back home after a few months."

"Indeed." Forsythe withdrew his intent gaze and looked again at the paper in front of him. "What changed your mind, I wonder?" Was he meant to reply to that? There was something in the tone, that very English sarcasm that had caught him unawares before and that made him hesitate.

"What are your feelings towards the current regime in Germany?"

He'd been expecting that. "Hitler is a disgrace to Germany. His policies towards the Jews are disgusting." Those grey eyes were again fixed on his face. Again, he looked down.

"Mmm." Forsythe fiddled with the paper. "It says here you volunteered to join the German Army in 1934?"

"I was nineteen, sir. I wanted to get it over with."

"Old enough to know better, I'd say. You volunteered." This time he put emphasis on the last word. Bill became unsure where this was heading. The man obviously didn't understand that 'volunteering' in Nazi Germany was an entirely different concept to any that he might be familiar with. Forsythe was still speaking.

"Not the action of someone who finds the regime 'disgusting', is it?" He looked around as if remembering something and in an angry tone said, "Have you any idea what some of those men you trained with are doing in Poland, in Czechoslovakia?"

Bill felt the bile at the back of his throat. He had heard and decided not to believe it. Such murderous crimes; it couldn't possibly be true. But...

There was a silence in the room that had the smack of guilt about it and Bill wanted to get rid of it. He needed this man, that woman to know he wasn't like that, no Nazi.

"I was born in London, sir." It sounded lame. The secretary leaned a fraction towards the table and tapped the folded birth certificate with the tip of her pen. Forsythe opened it out and read it then folded it up again.

"So you were born in this great city, and your father made good use of it, it seems. You go back to Germany, volunteer to train in the army and swear allegiance to Hitler and when it suits you, you come back for reasons that are flimsy to say the least. This certificate counts against you! You're no better than Mosley and his crew."

Bill was reeling. What had just happened? A version of himself had been invented by this man who knew nothing, and it was now to become some sort of truth. The secretary was scribbling down something and Forsythe was announcing his fate.

"Put Mr Ragg down as a Category 18b, will you, Miss Bancroft. I believe there is a special camp being prepared on the Isle of Man. You'll be sent there as soon as transport has been arranged."

*

"Well, did you?" Hans was listening to his retelling of the hearing.

"Did I what?" Hans's blue eyes were quizzical, curious.

"Did you swear allegiance to Hitler?"

"We had to." And he realised that he was now in a place, not just physical, but a moral and political place, where that was not just a perfunctory act, laughed at afterwards with his comrades and promptly forgotten because the words were meaningless to them at the time. It had branded him. And he felt branded, standing in front of a man whose father would die for not conforming. His own soul had been stamped and tampered with.

Hans waited for him to continue. He had left the hearing speechless, stunned.

After a pause Bill said, "They made me feel like... well, like a criminal, like someone I'm not."

Hans turned his head away, towards the cell door, the long corridors that stretched beyond. "Well, there's a lot of them about."

He turned back to Bill, looking immensely sad and momentarily feeling older than him. "Come on now. The people who count know exactly who you are, what you are." He smiled at his friend, and Bill felt warmed by it.

"What is Category 18b, anyway?" wondered Hans. "I've heard of A, B and C but not 18b."

14

The Isle of Man had several internment camps in Douglas, the capital, and in Ramsey in the north of the island. Mooragh camp was a row of large boarding houses facing the sea in Ramsey. From May 1940 to August 1945, it housed Germans, Italians and Finns.

The British birth certificates probably hadn't done Bill much good after all. Not only was he a German threat but there was also a touch of the British traitor about him too. It was only after several months and conversations with others, all of whose stories were different, and most of which were as innocent as his own, that he was able to laugh at the absurdity of it.

When he was alone, which wasn't often in the confines of the camp, but when he was – digging up potatoes on the farm or breaking his back planting broad beans – he found less to laugh at. Not because he was being deprived of his freedom, or that an injustice was being done. More a nagging feeling that he deserved it, deserved it all. He'd had his head in the clouds, didn't take life seriously enough, should have made a stand. *You did*, his reasonable self told him; *you left*. Not enough. Not enough. And the reasons were faulty, selfish. *You knew that life was more than inane slogans and flag waving. You did the only thing you could.* His reasonable self was having trouble. Would continue to have trouble.

Hans was not on the boat bound for the Isle of Man. His tribunal was held by a man thankfully more easily swayed and he was deemed a Category 'C' and packed off home to his mother. Bill and Albert were delighted for him, pummelled his shoulders and shook his hand, and called him a lucky devil. Hans, who couldn't stop beaming, wrote his address on a piece of paper and told them to write to him. He would try and help, maybe send a food parcel or something. Bill thought about him as the boat churned its way through choppy waters, drizzle and poor light, towards the island. Hans would have had his head over the side like a couple of the others, that's for sure. He was sitting on the deck, propped up against some boxes. He was being hit by spray, but it was worth it to be outside, breathe the salty air, think about his father who had experienced the same journey. For the first time he felt a connection with the man. How difficult that journey must have been. A shout broke into his thoughts.

"Look over there!" Heads turned, necks craned.

"I don't believe it." "Man, we must be a dangerous bunch."

Keeping alongside the little steamer that puffed daily between Liverpool and the Isle of Man was a sleek grey battleship, nose dipping under the waves.

"Is that a U-boat?" asked Bill. Others laughed but village boy turned city lad had no idea what he was looking at. He'd make it his business to find out now.

"A battleship; packed with armed men ready to slaughter us if we revolt." Wry laughter from the men in their overcoats, caps and empty pockets. One man had brought a fishing rod, the optimism of it cheering everyone up. Another had brought a typewriter, no objection made.

The battleship veered away as land was spotted, ploughing into the grey waters that lapped against both English and Irish shores. Some of the men took off their caps, cheered and waved goodbye. Ahead was the town of Ramsey, in the north of the island, where the Queen's Pier was to be their disembarkation point. Over eight hundred men, all German or Austrian, were ordered off in batches and marched along the pier, lined by the Royal Welch Fusiliers who had arrived the day before to take up their roles as guards.

The men were assembled along the South Promenade then directed over the swing bridge. Ramsey, usually a holiday destination, had been turned upside down to accommodate the hostile aliens now shambling untidily towards the barbed wire, behind which were the houses that would be home for the next four years. Landladies and hotel owners had been given only a day or two to vacate their homes, pack their stuff and make way for these unwanted strangers. They were ordered to leave behind all furniture, cutlery, crockery, bedding and bed linen. No wonder there was some hissing and booing as they shuffled along in pairs towards the opening in the wire fence, although, on the whole, they were stared at in silence. Bill, Albert and the other Germans in their group were allocated rooms in the furthermost building.

The beginning, thankfully forgotten over the following months, was a dreary affair of sitting, four to a room, getting to know each other. Stories exchanged were similar but why there were so many Jews among them was a mystery. A few Nazi sympathisers peeled themselves off and kept to themselves, outnumbered. Hardened Nazis, the Category 'A's, were in a different camp. And the mystery of the 18bs had been solved. They, and there were many, had all done military service after 1933 and as such were suspect.

Among these bakers, tailors, toy makers, musicians and teachers Bill found much in common. Most had come after 1933. Some had lived their whole lives in England.

At first food was delivered to them in large bins. Then the kitchens were organised, as were household duties, supplies came in and meals were cooked in the houses. The authorities on the island as well as the government back on the mainland were sure that the best way to treat the internees and minimise unrest was to leave things up to them. They were quick to form interest groups; musicians and painters found each other and procured materials and instruments. Academics and teachers set up classes and one could be found on almost any subject.

And there was sport: hockey teams, cricket teams and, most popular, football teams.

Men adapted, formed their own routines, chose their friends, wrote their letters, and waited.

*

There were better clarinettists than Bill in the camps. Much better. Some of the interned musicians, Jewish or otherwise, had studied at the best music colleges in Berlin and Vienna. He listened to the pianist Marjan Rawicz and to the violinist Peter Schidlof and while listening realised how much he had to learn. At Hutchinson camp in Douglas instruments were procured and an orchestra set up. No such luck where he was up in Ramsey. He cursed his misfortune but eventually did manage to borrow an instrument and practised whenever he got the chance. But he had little music, and he knew that he needed tuition to improve. In February '42 a package arrived. It wasn't sent from heaven, although it felt like it. It was from Hans.

"I came across this in a music shop. Did I ever tell you my mother plays the piano? I wanted to buy her some score that she wanted. I thought of you straight away and how you told me that you wished you had found the time to get some tuition. This might help. If you can get hold of an instrument that is." It was written in German in a fine sloping script. The second paragraph was entirely blacked out.

The brown leather-bound book slid into his hands and very soon after into his heart. *Treatise on the Clarinet (Boehm System)* was written by Rudolph Dunbar. There was a photo of him at the front of the book. It must have been taken a few years before. He was dressed in formal musician's attire, pinstripe high-waisted trousers, short waistcoat, black jacket with peak lapels. All beautifully cut. Around his neck was a floppy silk bow. He was looking down at the instrument, dwarfed where it lay in his long-fingered hands, with a half-smile on his face. A beautiful photo, the photographer had caught the sheen on his fine black skin, the ripple on his slicked-back hair.

"I remember you saying you liked the music of Duke Ellington. I think this book mentions jazz," wrote Hans. Yes, it was true. He loved the Black American jazz bands. The musicians took liberties with their instruments that Herr Thoma would certainly disapprove of. Banned in Germany, Bill had discovered the excitement of jazz in the London cinemas. Unfortunately, Rudolph Dunbar, born in British Guyana, educated at the New York Institute of Musical Art, was a stickler for 'thoroughness' and 'upon the importance of studying assiduously the major and minor chords and their scales.' Herr Thoma would certainly approve of that. This composer and founder of a music school for clarinettists believed in 'slow practice – no hurrying over exercises or groups of passages.' *Ah well*, thought Bill, as he opened the book and paged through the very carefully graduated lessons.

There was a history of the instrument and a meticulous explanation of how the jaw, cheek muscles and lips had to be coordinated, in order to produce the perfect sound. Thankfully, it seemed that Herr Thoma had taught him well, and he derived huge satisfaction when he learned that his own physiognomy made it easy for him. As Rudolph said, it is all to do 'with the planes of the jaw or the facial angle and the muscles of mastication'. It seemed that this meant that when the instrument was in his mouth, he was automatically ready to produce a good sound. Rudolph Dunbar, who as a boy of fourteen had joined a militia band, just like him, spoke to him across the waves, across cultures, and kept his musical mind and fingers nimble.

*

Tiredness seemed endemic across the camps. Men falling asleep propped against sunny walls. Disappearing to rooms, and emerging puffy-eyed. Afternoons, no matter the season, were silent and sluggish. It seemed to be what enforced incarceration did to you. There were hours of activity in the morning, classes to attend, animated conversations to enjoy then, as the clocks chimed two or three o'clock, the mood changed, a collective and exhausted sigh. What are we doing here? What's happening at home?

And at night there were the dreams, extraordinary and complex, disturbing and incomprehensible. Bill would wake from some tangled mess in his head and stare at the ceiling, asking the questions he avoided thinking about. How was his mother, his father? Was Rosie OK? And then the darker thoughts. How could he lie here – safe in

450

a warm bed – when there was hell going on in all four corners of the world? Could he have made different decisions?

One such night, arms locked behind his head, Bill lay thinking about his father. He'd heard stories from one of the guards, an older man who remembered the first time Germans were brought to the island. No weather-proof boarding houses for them. Albert would have been housed in draughty wooden huts, not much to do. Bill was trying to imagine a man who shunned others as much as Albert did crammed into a small space with thirty others. When, if, he got home again he would try to get him to talk about it. He drifted off to sleep and images of his father's angry face loomed up at him, shouting at him but he couldn't understand what he said – some other language – but his face so close he could see the spots of saliva at the corners of his mouth, that nicotine-stained moustache. Suddenly a crash outside followed by yells and loud voices broke into his dream and he got up, pulling on a pair of trousers as he stumbled over to the window.

The Finnish sailors had arrived that year, transferred from a camp in Douglas, which had closed, and were now lodged in the buildings next to Bill's. They had been warned about the Finns. Word had passed throughout the various camps that they were loyal Nazis, ill-educated, happiest and most violent when drunk, and knowledgeable as to how to increase the potency of the weak beer rations by adding boot polish or white spirit. They kept themselves to themselves usually, glowering at the Italians, housed further along and disappointed that the Germans gave them the cold shoulder.

On this particular night they were more disappointed than usual with those they had mistakenly taken to be their allies. It was April 20th, a date all recognised but most in the camp were relieved to relegate to the status of unimportant and to be ignored. It had been a public holiday in Germany since 1933, Hitler's birthday. The Finns were, Bill learned later, hell bent on celebrating, ransacked the stores for beer and spent the day drinking.

By the time Bill and a few others had got themselves into the street outside they were in time to witness the aftermath of a murder.

Staring through the dim gas light they saw a huddle of men gathered around a lifeless shape on the ground and then turn with a howl and set upon a swaying figure standing alone a little way off.

Two rows of barbed wire separated the Finns from the Germans and Bill was left watching helplessly. Seconds later a police van drove up, five or six guards got out and with some difficulty broke up the fight. They watched as things calmed down and the bloodied loner and the rest of them were taken away. The corpse was left on the ground. Bill, his fingers hanging on the wire, looked on as the man left to watch over him found a discarded jacket and carefully laid it over his head. He was touched by the gesture and didn't follow the others back inside.

"Come on back in," Albert said, "nothing much we can do."

Bill looked at his brother. "In a bit." Albert nodded and left him.

He sat on the step, keeping vigil, and looking over at the body, already becoming part of the cold, sober earth. So shocking on this little island. Moments before, this man was alive, shouting the praises of a monster he knew nothing about. Bill buried his head in his hands and thought of the bodies littering Europe, thought of John, who would have seen many bodies by now, and wanted more than anything to know if he was alive.

The wind, out of respect, had died down and in the dark and silence he could hear the guard shuffle on his feet, give the occasional cough and, once or twice, the two men caught each other's eye through the wire, and all the time the shapeless heap that was once a man grew cold and stiff and somewhere a mother would, in the weeks to come, read about her son and the manner of his death.

Dawn broke gently and an orange glow spread itself across the sea's horizon, tipping the bobbing waves with gold. In the growing light he noticed the pattern on the jacket covering the man's head. A black and red dogtooth. Then a distant rattle of tyres on tarmac and an ambulance arrived, breaking into the morning silence. As the men arranged his body on the stretcher, he saw first the blackish-purple stains of blood on the pavement then the boots, hanging and flopping as they carried him away. They were polished. He had polished his boots in Hitler's honour. Bill stood up, limbs stiffened in the morning chill, and the guard, as he climbed into the van, turned his head and gave Bill a discreet nod. Later in the day the darkening stains had been washed away by the afternoon drizzle.

15

(Location blacked out), September 1942

Dear Albert and Bill,

I've been told that I shouldn't write to you about the war, but you said you get a newspaper so I'm hoping you are up to speed. I have heard from Mother. She worries about all of us, of course, but most about John. Her letters are heavily censored. There is still food to be bought but things are hard there. They are luckier than people living in the cities.

I've been travelling around quite a bit. I joined the Non-Combatants Corps (NCC) as soon as the war got serious, and they send me wherever there is a need. Once people get used to my accent things usually go very smoothly. Apart from the 'conchies' like me, some older fellows who remember the first war, there are lots of chaps who for one reason or another aren't able to enlist. By the way I met a girl in (blacked out). She's really nice. I hope you meet her soon!

Your loving brother, Joe

P.S. Hope the pound comes in handy. Can you get hold of the odd beer?

May 29th 1943

Dear Albert and Bill,

Hope you are both keeping well. The cake is a fruit cake made with margarine, can't get hold of butter, and it should stand the journey. And I hope the ten-bob note comes in useful. You told me there are places for you to shop.

Things are OK here. Things are fairly quiet. I've met a soldier. He takes me dancing when he's in London. He's asked me to marry him and I think I will. His name is Cecil.

I heard from Mother. She is fine and says that Hilda has married the soldier she was seeing. She has heard from John. He was (blacked out). Father is also well. Joe visits when he is in London. He has (long sentence blacked out).

That's my news. Take care of yourselves, Rosie.

(location blacked out) November 1943

Dear Albert, Dear Bill,

Thought you might like to know I've got married. Me and Nellie tied the knot last week. We got fed up waiting for the damn war to end and really didn't fancy waiting any longer. I've written to our mother to tell her and sent a photo. I hope it arrives. Can't wait for you to meet her and for us to be together. It was a very small wedding. Rosie couldn't make it.

All the best from Joe and Nellie

*

Precious letters were rare, but the *Daily Mail* came regularly and for some reason it was delivered only to Mooragh and to no other camp on the island. So Hitler's movements were followed and hands thrown in the air when the invasion of Russia became doomed.

"That's it!" said one.

"What an idiot!" said another.

"We'll be out in months," shouted a young optimist from Bremen.

That was in 1943. There was a long way to go. News of lost convoys in the Atlantic brought groans, all pretence at German patriotism gone apart from the few who called it all English propaganda, then relief as the anti-submarine weaponry got the upper hand. Quiet admiration for Rommel's soldiering gave way to cheers for Montgomery. General Patton got a toehold into Italy. Greece seemed to be liberating herself. Good news, good news. And all the time anxious eyes looked for places their brothers, cousins, friends might be, fighting for the wrong side, killing and being killed. As the bombs rained down on Essen and Cologne many wept, wrung their hands.

John, John! Where are you in all this? Bill tried to imagine his loud, football-loving brother holding a gun, aiming it, firing it.

And all the time rumours of horror and atrocity hardened into ugly and poisonous truth. Massacres in Warsaw, Krakow, Katyn exposed, raw and unbearable.

"Can this be true?"

"You know it can."

Then came the Normandy invasions. Not long now. Not long.

*

Most of the men on Mooragh camp volunteered to work on the nearby farms. Bill was one of the first. He thought he would be put to work with the cattle or in the milking sheds but that was the women's domain now that the men had enlisted. He was needed on the land, on the tractors, planting and harvesting. He enjoyed the labour, the space and sense of freedom, the exhaustion at the end of the day. His skin grew brown and tough, his muscles hardened. And while he ploughed and picked, weeded and watered and the sweat trickled between his shoulder blades he blotted out images of slaughter that plagued his thoughts at night-time. Did it make him cowardly that he was so grateful not to be part of it? If he had been asked, would he have fought for the British, been willing to point a gun, maybe at John or some other terrified German kid? He even avoided thinking about the future, because he couldn't imagine where it lay, what it could offer. He thought of his music, what he needed to concentrate on next. He was keeping up the practice, fingers staying nimble, but he missed playing with others, longed to stand alongside the oboe or bassoon, behind the flutes, looking ahead to the conductor's baton.

Twice a week there was football practice. Inter-camp matches were ferocious affairs. Teams made up of Italians, Austrians or Germans (Nazis discouraged) were supported by unashamedly partisan crowds who swore and shouted their way through each match. There were frequent fights, off and on the pitch, but somehow football prevailed, and Bill loved every minute. Unprotected shins were kicked and slashed in each glorious battle, vengeance vowed before each match. He had swapped half of one of Rosie's cakes and five Senior Service for a pair of boots. Then found himself in the tailor's workshop altering worn-out and threadbare trousers into shorts. Not a difficult job. Mooragh Deutschland had a fierce rivalry with Mooragh Italia. Bill would have loved to organise a combined team, they had some nifty players, but it proved impossible. At the very end, in a fit of temporary optimism he bartered the boots, ten cigarettes and a brick red ten shilling note for a small camera, assured it would last a life time, which it did.

*

1944

Now, through the pages of the *Daily Mail*, these not so German Germans could follow the tortuous creep and crawl from the beaches of Normandy through France towards Paris, the deadly struggle on the eastern front and the inexhaustible Soviet forces ploughing their way towards Berlin, smashing everything that stood in their way. Belgium retaken by American and Canadian troops. Greece in uproar and starving. Aerial shots of destroyed German cities, news of the collapse of law and order, children with guns. They looked and read and waited. The months went by and again they waited as the Allies completed the Battle of the Bulge and fought on to the Rhine, waited as street after street in Berlin was turned to rubble, waited as Eisenhower's demand for total surrender fell on Hitler's deaf ears. Then the pictures that were impossible to talk about. Buchenwald, Bergen-Belsen and Dachau. Men became silent, withdrew into themselves and saved tears for night-time. For a while, the atmosphere became muted, stilted, then thoughts of release took over, were anticipated. Each man put on hold his grief, his relief and, above all, a complexity of guilt that would haunt for decades to come.

16

Belgravia, London, July 1945. Clement Atlee won a decisive victory for the Labour Party. Winston Churchill was defeated.

I can't believe it. A Labour government! Bloody marvellous! Lady Boynton drew the curtains of her bedroom and stayed there all day telephoning her friends. Mavis said, in a whisper, "She's furious, Rosie." Ranted on for hours, apparently. 'What a way to thank Churchill who is such a hero. He saved this country, saved it!' And the inevitable, 'the country will go to the dogs now', repeated endlessly as she stomped up and down the room.

Well, the real heroes are the boys that fought and died. That's what I say. I'm glad we've sent the toffs packing. Good riddance. Me and Bettina had a grand time in the kitchen when the news was in, had a little sip of her best brandy to celebrate – she won't notice.

Of course, Joe is delighted. At last, he came to see me. I had to wait long enough, I must say, but I knew he would find time for his sister eventually. He brought Nellie with him. I suppose he had to really. She's a pretty girl but didn't have much to say. Apparently, they have been busy, but he didn't go into it. They are going to live in Bromley, close to her mum. She didn't eat anything either, after I went to all that trouble and made a sponge. Eggs and sugar aren't easy to come by. I didn't tell Joe about Cecil. Never heard another thing from him! They're all the same. After one thing then – goodbye!

No word from John, Joe reckons he is probably a prisoner of war somewhere. Our mother must be so worried about him. But we would have heard if he had been killed. She knows he'll come home eventually.

They stayed an hour or so, that's all. Then Joe said Nellie was getting tired and they would have to get back. The Underground wasn't reliable yet and the journey would take a couple of hours. I was a bit disappointed; he could have stayed a bit longer. I watched them walk off arm in arm towards Knightsbridge Tube station, she put her head on his shoulder.

*

It says in the paper they are trying to hurry up the process of releasing the internees. Herbert Morrison our Home Secretary says we need the skilled workmen locked up in the camps. Of course, there are still MPs who think every German is bound to be a dangerous Nazi, but Herbert Morrison and Ernest Bevin are finding out exactly what the men can offer the country. Good news for Bill, I reckon, everyone needs clothes after all. Not sure about Albert. Not much call for musical instrument salesmen. Anyway, they'll both be coming straight here when they're released. Having a sister in London is of some use after all!

They need an address to head for before they are allowed out. Let's hope they're allocated a ration card when they come. I don't think I'll be able to feed them without one. All there was at the butcher today was pig's liver. Her Ladyship had a dickey fit. 'You see! A Labour government and all there is to eat is pig's liver.' Bettina says she feels like overcooking it out of spite. I really don't know how much longer I can bear to work for that woman. When things ease up a little I shall look for a position as a cook somewhere else. Bettina thinks I'm ready. 'Rosie', she said, 'if you can make something edible with dried eggs and margarine, not to mention trotters and tripe you can do anything!'

*

August 1945

Just as I thought, it was Bill who came to me first. He's been given the address of a factory making demob suits and has to report there next Monday. It's over Lambeth way, near the Elephant and Castle. I was surprised. I didn't think there was anything much left that end of London after the doodlebugs. I heard them over here, terrifying it was. So, there he was, my little brother with his suitcase, looking thinner and smiling at me. I'll have to feed him up, get rid of those shadows under his eyes. And a lot older. We had a bit of an awkward hug, he seemed stiff, as if he was somewhere else, not really here, hard to explain. Not got a lot to say for himself. Didn't really want to answer my questions. Bettina says to give him time. He did say that he was very well treated and that the Isle of Man is a pretty place. I don't think he liked it when I said it must have been paradise compared with London, dodging the bombs and everything. He looked at me with a very serious face and sort of nodded. 'I'm glad you are OK, Rosie. You are, aren't you?' Well! What could I say? All he wanted to know from me was if I'd heard from John. No-one has and no news is good news I told him, even these days. He wants to go and see Joe. Soon. Honestly, I thought he would spend a few days with me at least. He says he needs to buy a clarinet – hasn't earned a penny yet and already making plans. He's changed no doubt about it. Restless, can't sit still, fidgets all the time. It'll be good when he starts work.

17

Spring 1946

Bill sat on a bit of wall somewhere near Moorgate and stared at the broken buildings, up at the rooms laid bare for all to see with discarded furniture still teetering on edges, wallpaper peeling, fading and flapping in the breeze.

It was Saturday, his day off and as usual he spent it walking around London reacquainting himself with the streets he had got to know so well before the war. Then he'd meet up with Albert at the music shop. Today he had walked through the City, from the Tower, pockmarked and damaged, to the devastation surrounding St. Pauls and north to where he was now. Although he knew that more civilians died in Hamburg and Dresden in two nights of Allied bombing than in London during the course of the whole war, the loss of these buildings, the loss of these homes and these lives hurt him more. London meant much more to him than any of the large German cities. This was the city he had chosen and got to know.

He looked at the flowers that covered the ground, creeping out of the cracks, white and pink and yellow. All the bombsites were full of them, the rich London soil exposed, courtesy of the Luftwaffe, and seeds, some ancient, had burst into life. The carpet of colour reminded him of spring in the Black Forest where tiny flowers would suddenly spread wherever the sun managed to melt the ice and warm the ground. For a minute he was lost, back in the hills and forests of home.

"Hey, Mister! Got a fag?" A young voice. A boy of maybe twelve or thirteen, short trousers, patched, and a jumper a size too small. Bill was smoking and reached into his pocket for the pack with his left hand.

"You're too young to smoke." The boy shrugged and Bill smiled as he got one out and reached over to hand it to him. The boy put it into his pocket and sat on his haunches looking at Bill.

"Where're you from?" Just a few words and his secret was out. Friendliness in abundance from Londoners until he opened his mouth. Bill met the boy's quizzical eye, an eye that was both knowing and ignorant at the same time. What the hell.

"The other end." He jerked his head vaguely to indicate a direction. Where they were sitting that could mean east or west London.

"Nah." The boy shook his head. "You're foreign."

"I'm German."

The boy's eyes grew wide. "No kidding? Never met a Kraut before. You a Nazi?"

"No, I'm not," Bill kept his voice matter of fact, "I didn't fight in the war."

"My dad did. He says they're all murdering bastards."

Bill was resting his arms on his knees. He straightened a little to draw on his cigarette and said quietly, "Maybe not all," and he held the boy's gaze. The boy stared at him for some seconds, unsure whether he could believe this contradiction of his dad's wisdom. Then he stood up. After a little self-conscious cough, he said,

"Well, I've got to go. Ta da."

"Goodbye, young man." The boy shuffled from one foot to the other before turning and shooting off over the wall and away.

The image of the boy's face stayed with him. Round and guileless, like his own at that age. He looked around again at this glorious playground that the children of London were enjoying. Acres of boltholes, climbing walls, hiding places, dens, tunnels, dead people's secrets exposed. Bulldozers would come soon, flattening and clearing and ripping out the flowers.

He stood up and walked west down Holborn and on to Oxford Street where shops were coming to a bleary sort of life. The noise and bustle cheered him but right now he needed his brother, needed the familiarity of the shop with its smell of wood and brass and the comfort of talk in a mixture of languages.

By huge good fortune, the music shop Albert had worked in before the war still existed. It had been kept going by Herr Winkler's English wife, Helena, until '42 when her husband was released from internment. They had met in Vienna in the late twenties. Apart from the shop's change of name from 'Winkler's' to 'Bradshaw's' – Helena's maiden name, a decision considered expedient given the circumstances – everything had remained unchanged. Albert had been welcomed like a long-lost son and taken back on.

Bill turned into Tottenham Court Road and took a right to where the shop was. A bell tinkled as he opened the door.

"*Da bist du*," Franz Winkler beamed at him.

"There you are," Helena echoed, "come over here, I want you to meet someone."

Albert had been in the back storeroom and walked in to nod a greeting to his brother. He also raised his eyebrows and looked at Helena as if to warn him that something interesting was coming up.

"Richard, this is Bill, the clarinettist I was telling you about. Bill, this is Doctor Richard Bell. He plays cello for an amateur orchestra at the Middlesex Hospital, they need a clarinettist." She smiled broadly at the two of them.

Bill shook the hand that was offered. "Oh, well, not sure I'm up to standard yet."

"Nonsense," said Franz, still beaming, "I've heard him. And I know he works at it."

Bill now owned the clarinet that had waited for him at the back of the storeroom for five years. Or at least he nearly owned it. Allowed to take it home after paying a deposit and weekly amounts agreed on. Every Saturday, when Bill handed over a pound note, Franz would look embarrassed as if he didn't really want to continue with this transaction. Only £5 to go now.

"Would you come along to one of our rehearsals? You can see

what we're like and I'll get our lead violinist and Rita, that's our conductor, to give you a workout. They're fussy, I warn you." Richard said it with a grin.

"Well, of course. I'd love that," said Bill, hardly daring believe what had been offered, and smiled his thanks to Helena and Franz.

"Marvellous." The couple said it in unison. Musical unions and introductions were their speciality, and nothing gave them more pleasure.

"I'll get the cognac," said Franz.

"And I'll make coffee."

Already light-headed from the unexpected turn of events, the coffee and cognac made the journey home one to remember. Heads turned on the top deck of the 57 to Streatham as the men laughed and joked and forgot entirely to keep their voices down.

18

It took a while for the knock on the door to register. Since moving in they had had no visitors. Rosie had been once on a rare day off. Albert exchanged a quick glance with Bill, who was washing up at the tiny sink, and went to open it. It was Saturday, midday, and they had just had some bread and cheese. On the landing stood Joe.

"I've heard from John," he said, smiling and grasping Albert's hand. Then he walked over to Bill, who dried his hands before shaking Joe's firmly, the good news sinking in slowly. Joe's smile could only mean John was alive, somewhere.

The brothers sat down. Joe took out a letter from his inside pocket and laid it carefully on the table. Hot water was added to the lukewarm tea in the pot, chipped and cracked and found in the back of the cupboard when they moved in a few months ago. They didn't need to ask him how he'd got there. He walked. A three-hour walk was nothing to Joe. He would work out his destination and set off, walking as the crow flies. For Bill and Albert South London was plotted out with Underground train stations and bus routes and timetables; for Joe it was street names and parks and squares that could be cut across, junctions that were best avoided and tiny passes and alley ways that could save miles.

"He's OK. Somewhere in France and OK." Joe's fingers stroked the letter gently as he spoke, pulling the folded sheets out of the envelope. "Unlikely to get home any time soon, though."

Bill looked at the letter, written carefully in pencil, John's long sloping handwriting very recognisable. Joe said, "The Red Cross got it to our parents and Mother sent it on to me." The paper was grubby, stained, creases carefully pressed out again and again by John, then his mother, then Joe. The envelope had been stamped by the French Croix-Rouge, then by the German Rote Kreuz and over-stamped diligently by the German Postal Service with some evidence of the American occupying forces in the form of small stars and stripes in the corners. It had taken six months to reach them. Bill glanced up at Albert who said, "Go on, you read it." He picked it up, prepared himself by reading the first line or two and then started to read it out loud.

When he'd finished, he laid the sheets back on the table, where Albert picked them up to look and verify that familiar hand, to savour the absolute certainty that those words had been John's, that he was, without doubt alive and well. Gradually their emotions settled, their mood calmed, and they talked of their mother. She had included a note telling them of Hilda's boy – fine and sturdy – Hilda's hope of a war pension, Anna's latest boyfriend, their father, getting frail. Very little about herself. The letter, of course, had been addressed to her.

*

May 1946

Dearest Mother,

I know it is a long time since you heard from me, but I want to assure you that I am well and hope with all my heart that you too are well.

I am in France near a town called Troyes although I am not allowed to go there. I have been put to work on a farm here. The family are good to me and I have at last been given permission to write a letter home.

The work I do would be very familiar to you. I have to dig the land, pull a plough. I'm doing the work of the horse! The animals died of starvation in '44 or were eaten, of course. I've planted seeds – vegetables and salad crops. It's warm here, tomatoes are already growing. Imagine that! We had to clear the ground first. There was a lot of damage during the war because of tanks criss-crossing. There are a lot of spent shells and other evidence of the fighting that went on.

I think I'm finally being trusted by the family. Madame brought me a little rabbit stew just now. The traps I laid down seem to be effective. Best thing I've tasted in a long while. The old man has stopped supervising me as much as well. Still grunts at me as if I was a dog, though. Suppose that's what we are in his eyes.

I'm here with another lad called Werner. He's from Stuttgart and not used to farm work. But he's learning fast. I can speak French now, picked it up as I've gone along which makes things easier with the family.

Werner had to learn the hard way. The work was beneath him, he said, his father owned acres of land in Hesse. He was no peasant. Göring himself had been a family friend. Some of the local lads wanted to beat him up. So did I. I told them he was an idiot but to leave him to me. Grabbed him by the throat and said that all his father's land and connections were worse than useless to him now and that if he didn't want to either die in a local ditch or be sent on mine clearance duties where lads like him were dying in their hundreds, he had better learn to get his hands dirty.

It was quite hard when we were captured by the Americans. We were taken by truck and train to a camp near Dietersheim and spent about four months there before being brought back to France. I think the Americans had had enough of us by then and the French wanted to put us to work. Conditions were tough in Dietersheim.

Very tough.

*

May 1945, Dietersheim camp.

Grey. Grey as far as the eye could see. It wasn't the earth, or the clouds above, breaking up now and again to expose slivers of blue. The grey was the men. Thousands of them. Defeated and exhausted. Lying down, sleeping, shuffling to find a better spot under the sky. As far as the eye could see. And eerily quiet. The odd whispered movement, the odd moan, even the birds had surrendered to the inevitable.

John lay on the hard ground with Sebastian's head in his lap. Sebbi was dying but John refused to accept it. He stroked his sweat-drenched hair and talked to him about home, about the paths leading to the mountains, the fresh streams they could drink from. Sebbi, eyes closed, smiled and with difficulty reached up to hold onto John's hand, breath rasping a little.

John continued his gentle talk. They'd go to his mother's. He would like her. Best not to expect too much from his father, though. And his sisters – Anna and Hilda. He struggled for a moment to remember what they looked like. The pressure from Sebbi's hand weakened but he carried on. His village, Neustadt, had some fine pubs. They would go there and drink their fill. All the while John's eyes scanned the fence, seven foot high, and then the gates for movement. Very little. The narrow path beyond the fence was just wide enough for the odd jeep. Soldiers patrolled and leant against the wooden struts to enjoy a cigarette, but no sign of the medical help he'd asked for, no sign of food. It was midday.

On higher ground to their right sat a couple more Americans, guns ready, watching. As if any of them had the strength or desire to escape. John carried on talking, gently, bending his head towards Sebbi's. In winter there would be skiing – ski all the way to Switzerland under a clear blue sky if they felt like it. Down below a corpse was being carried to the gates, his friends were struggling with it, bending with the effort, forming an arc over the thin, dead man. John didn't want to think where they were taking him. He laid his hand on Sebbi's chest. His heart was still beating. His eyes were moving under thin, veined lids.

It hadn't been such a difficult decision to give up on the whole damn business, to ignore Hitler's obsessive command to fight on, die rather than surrender. No. Enough. They had watched their friends die, and there were thousands more dying across France in the hopeless struggle against the hordes of Allied soldiers pouring over the Channel. He and Sebbi had slipped away one night down to the river, where they slithered and stumbled through slimy mud for hours, stopping when it was light to hide. Now they were two of Himmler's malingerers and deserters that were to be shot on sight. They would take their chances.

Days of rain had been replaced by fog. Mist loitered over the stinking river. Dead bodies floated past them and caught their attention at first, then they lost interest. Too hungry, too cold. Sound was muffled and distorted, sudden squawks and splashes surprising them, coming from unexpected directions. Voices – German – coming from somewhere. They flattened themselves into the earth and waited. It was American voices they were waiting for.

They came quite suddenly. One minute the silence, the next a shout through the morning gloom. It was a young voice, unsure and accompanied with the cocking of a rifle.

John had helped Sebbi up the bank a few kilometres back. The damp and cold wasn't doing Sebbi any good, his feet were dragging, and he was shivering. He was sure they were well into Allied territory. Now on flat ground the view was obscured by the lingering fog but there was movement ahead, something approaching, he was sure. Then the shout.

The American soldier was really very young. "Hände hoch," he said, it sounded like 'hock'. Sebbi was leaning against him, crumpling; John raised his hands slowly. They had no rifles, had abandoned them to the river a couple of days ago.

"Sarge," the nervous soldier called over his shoulder, "two more here."

John looked beyond the soldier. Men were walking towards him out of the mist. As it cleared, he saw more men ahead, jeeps, tents. And beyond those there were trucks, dozens of them and men, Germans, hands clasped behind their heads, being herded into the trucks. And beyond the trucks, behind hastily constructed barbed wire enclosures, more Germans, standing in groups, watching and waiting. John lowered an arm slowly to put it around Sebbi, to keep him upright. Keeping an eye on the young Ami and his trigger finger he spoke to Sebbi.

"We've found them, Sebbi. Should be all right now."

They were searched, Sebbi toppling as the Ami pushed and poked at him.

"He needs water, food. He's ill," said John. The young soldier met his eye, surprised at the English.

"Sure. Roast beef and champagne at the end of the ride. Get over there." John missed the sarcasm but heard the disdain, the disinterest.

The truck ride took hours. One man died; a jacket was thrown over his head. The guard shouted that the body would be dealt with when they arrived. John tried to catch a glimpse of the landscape through the flaps at the back of the truck. Sebbi's burning head bounced on his shoulder. Someone had a drop of water which John poured carefully in his hand and wet Sebbi's lips with.

"We must be well into Germany now," someone said. They got the occasional glimpse of broken houses through the dust thrown up by the truck. There was little conversation. Some apprehension but overall relief that the war, the fighting, the fear was over. Months before many of these men would have sworn to fight to the death for the Führer. Now he'd been abandoned; they had chosen life.

*

That was days ago. John had lost count. Days and nights dissolved into one another. He'd left Sebbi asleep in a dug-out to find medical help but it turned out there wasn't any available. Food and drink arrived twice a day, sometimes only once. Some bread and a thin brown liquid which they sometimes called soup and sometimes coffee. There was no shelter. If it rained, they got wet, then dried in the June sunshine. John tried to protect Sebbi as best he could. The sun burnt their skin, left them parched. The men stank. The toilet area was in a field. They did their best to dig holes, cover their mess.

The Red Cross will come soon, was the hope and the talk but

they never came. When one of their senior officers asked about it, he was told they were not Prisoners of War but Disarmed Enemy Forces and as such had no rights whatsoever. Orders from Eisenhower so that was that.

John cradled Sebbi's dead body for hours before someone said, "Time to take him away," a gentle voice, and John was grateful but shook his head. Let me hold him for a little longer, he thought, just a few more moments. Through thick and thin they'd had each other's backs. Shared food, jokes in even the grimmest moments. Don't be dead! Stay with me! We promised each other. There was the world to see.

The gentle voice was back. "Come on, my friend." Sebbi was very cold now, his face, his beautiful face, turned grey. He nodded and got up. Offers of help were rejected.

"I'll do it myself." The others watched as John picked Sebbi up. He didn't weigh much but it was still a struggle as he made his way to the gates.

They saw him lean back under the weight of the body as he shouted for a guard. The gates opened and Sebbi was taken from him, put down on the ground. John made as if to follow but he was pushed back, the gates locked. A plank of wood appeared and Sebbi laid on it. John raised his arms, as if asking for something, but he was ignored and the Amis carried another dead German down the dusty path. They watched John sink to his knees, and watch, and keep watching long after the trio had disappeared.

*

There were nineteen camps like Dietersheim set up in Germany in American-held territory. They housed three million captured German soldiers and, unsurprisingly, the Americans were having trouble feeding them. By September it was decided that better use could be made of this manpower. France needed men to rebuild, to clear mines and to work on the farms. Germany also made a claim for men to reconstruct the ruined cities. The men in Dietersheim, weak and hungry but glad to be alive, were taken by truck to various locations in France.

They had learned not to meet the eyes of their captors. The steely hatred coming from those young faces never wavered. Boys and men who had seen the carnage as they fought their way over the Rhine, who had seen the horror pictures coming from Belsen and Auschwitz, some had been there, seen it with their own eyes. Better not to look at those boyish faces, old before their time. Better to stay inside their own heads, do whatever was asked of them, think of a time when they could go home.

And John, grief-stricken, locked himself away, imagined Sebbi two paces behind or in front, as they had always been, ate and drank what was put in front of him until, in the middle of September the Americans, with a sigh of relief, put him and some others into a truck and packed him off to Troyes in the very heart of France.

And slowly, when the stone-throwing, the name-calling and the odd kicking subsided, his broken heart fixed itself just enough to carry on beating. Though scarred with a hundred welts his spirit revived just enough to survive, to make himself endurable to Madame, to make the teenage farmhands laugh, and to water down Werner's many resentments.

*

So, Mother, please don't worry about me. Goodness knows when you will receive this letter and I really don't know when they will release us. There is talk that they want us for at least another year. But it's not so bad. Very quiet, especially at night. Just like home. I am given wine every evening with my meal! I think of the girls and you and Father. I think of Bill, Rosie, of Albert and Joe over in England. How different our lives have been. As soon as I can, I will be with you, even if I have to walk!
John

19

August 1946. Streatham

Bill sighed quietly and glanced at Albert, who stood next to him, holding a bunch of dark pink carnations, ramrod stiff against his chest. For the last time, just to make absolutely sure, he checked the address he had scribbled down before screwing the slip of paper up into a ball and pushing it into his pocket.

"Well, this is it," he said. They both stared at the large double-fronted house opposite with its gravel driveway and billowing rose bushes nestling up against the bay windows. It was the grandest house they had ever been invited to in London; if you discounted scrabbling down the back steps of the tradesman's entrance of Rosie's current mansion in Knightsbridge.

They couldn't refuse the invitation, no matter how uncomfortable the thought of facing strangers, making conversation, making mistakes. Richard had been so enthusiastic, and he wanted them to meet his girlfriend, fiancée, Lisebette. An Austrian! They could speak German together. She had been on the Isle of Man. So much in common. Bill had smiled at his new friend. He had been to two rehearsals with the Middlesex Hospital Orchestra, and they had gone well, very well. Of course, we would love to come, he'd said. And Richard, delighted, had explained that the party would be at his parents' house in Streatham, no need to bring anything. His mother was a great music lover and would love to meet them both.

Their feelings of unease increased as the date approached. Suits and shirts were pressed, ties selected. They thought carefully about the flowers. In Germany it was the polite thing to do if you were invited to someone's house. These carnations were chosen for Richard's mother, Mrs Bell, elderly, undoubtedly refined. Chosen for their colour, their scent. They had been pleased with their choice.

And now, pressed against the shadows, sweating inside their suits in the August evening sunshine, they made an incongruous pair, felt out of their depth, sure that they were about to be confronted by the English middle class whose vagaries were still a mystery to them. Polite words from the lips, often meaning the opposite of what was said. Disdain in the eyes. Offer of a handshake ignored.

Bill looked again at his brother and decided to make a show of confidence. "Come on, big brother," he took a step forward, "we know Richard, we know the Winklers. There is nothing to fear!"

Albert gave a resigned smile from behind the carnations and followed Bill to the kerbside. They waited for a car and a couple of bicycles to pass, crossed the road and crunched their way up the driveway.

Close up, the house showed signs of wartime neglect and damage. Flaking paint, cracked windows. There was a bell handle which Bill pulled. Somewhere inside there was a distant chime and seconds later Richard opened the door wide and ushered them in.

"Was wondering where you two had got to. Great to see you." The smile was broad and welcoming; behind him stood a couple, both white-haired, upright.

Richard introduced them. "Albert, Bill – my parents."

She, Mrs Bell, stepped forward. "We've heard all about you." She held out her hand to shake theirs, first Bill, then Albert, who juggled the flowers awkwardly before saying,

"I hope you like carnations." She took them.

"My absolute favourites. They're beautiful. Thank you very much." She had very blue eyes, sharp and perceptive.

"And which of you is the clarinettist?"

"This one," said Richard, putting his arm on Bill's shoulder. Mrs

Bell opened her lips to say something. "But right now, Ma, these men need a beer. You can quiz them later."

And Richard, after planting a kiss on his mother's forehead, steered them firmly into a large room and towards a table covered in bottles of wine, sherry and spirits. Richard handed them each a bottle of beer and a glass.

"I put a few bottles in the fridge for you – I know you don't understand warm beer. You'll need it when my mother gets hold of you – and believe me she will – she'll want to know every last thing about you, so be warned and drink up!"

Bill and Albert grinned, raised their glasses and drank appreciatively. The ale tasted very good. They felt their shoulders soften, breathing relax.

Bill recognised the first violinist, deep in conversation with a woman in the corner. And there was the bassoonist who gave him a wink. OK so far. Maybe this wouldn't be so bad.

"Lisebette shouldn't be long, might be bringing a friend, she said." Richard drained his glass and looked around the room. A small dark woman and a large man in glasses were talking to Helena and Franz who waved when they saw them.

"That's Bruno and Lee. She works in the hospital with Lisebette. Bruno's Austrian, she's a Londoner." Richard seemed to be leaving something unsaid. Bill looked at the couple, Jewish, he was sure. He wondered what their story might be. Tension crept back into his shoulders; the air hardened a little in his lungs. Franz beckoned them over.

Handshakes, introductions, fixed smiles. "Albert works with me," said Franz, "my right-hand man as they say. And this is Bill, his brother. The orchestra's new clarinettist and very pleased they are with him too, so I've heard." He clapped Bill on the back and Helena beamed. Now the conversation turned to music. Yes, a concert was coming up, maybe at the end of September, Schumann and Dvorak. Bruno was a great fan of Schumann.

"We've something bigger planned for the New Year," said Richard. "Not sure about the programme, though." He paused, looking over Bill's shoulder. "Whoops, here she comes, prepare yourselves." Mrs Bell was walking serenely towards them and heard these last words.

"Now, now Richard. You know I'm always interested in your friends." She linked one arm through Bill's and one through Albert's. Pinioned, they had very little choice in the matter and after some backward glances, grins and resigned shrugging, they were led gently into the middle of the room.

"I hear you are from the Black Forest. Such a lovely place. My husband and I travelled there in the twenties. We travelled all over Germany, until it got too… difficult." Albert and Bill exchanged a quick look over her head.

The quizzing was gentle but relentless. After a few moments she had gleaned a fairly comprehensive family history, nodding and shaking her head appropriately.

"So many widows," she said sadly when told that Hilda's young husband had been killed before the birth of their son. The news had filtered its way to London, to Rosie, taking months. The boy would be two years old by now. Albert chatted amiably with the old lady, their voices and laughter drifting past Bill who, for a few minutes, was back home with his mother, the smell of grass from the nearby field filling his nostrils, summer winds rustling the pines. Somewhere in the distance a bell chimed. His mother would be working in the garden, maybe the little boy, Hilda's boy, helping her. He fought the faint throb at the back of his throat.

The bell chimed again, more insistent, bringing him back to the party chatter, Albert talking of starting his own business someday, and Bill was aware of Richard peeling off from his crowd and making for the hallway, walking quickly, and the sound of the heavy door opening, then Mrs Bell excusing herself and following him out. Bill and Albert walked back to the table to get another beer. Seconds later a girl in pink, pretty, smiling, came into the room with Richard and followed by his father. Bill was aware of another figure coming in a step or two behind them, hesitating at the door. But all eyes were on Lisebette, blushing, happy with the attention, looking up at Richard, then around the room, then glancing back at the woman behind. Bill followed the glance. Dark blonde hair was falling against her cheek and she pushed it back to reveal a heart-shaped face, full lips. Bill noticed the smile she gave her friend, noticed the quick, shy look around the room. They were slowly moving in his direction but then Mrs Bell approached the woman, linked arms with her and steered her towards the window. Bill was sure she had noticed her discomfort and had stepped in quickly to try and help quell her nerves. It seemed to work; the woman was soon talking and smiling, her head lifted as she listened and replied. Mrs Bell was a perceptive lady.

The group gathered around the drinks table, Richard introducing Lisebette to his friends, cigarettes were lit, and wine and beer poured. Out of the corner of his eye Bill tracked Mrs Bell's movements around the room and her approach.

"This is Katie, everyone." Albert, liking what he saw, flipped open his pack of Players and offered her one. As he lit it her eyes flicked between the brothers, lingering a fraction longer on his face, Bill was sure. And, however embarrassed, fraudulent almost, he felt at being introduced as a clarinettist, he did notice she became interested, curious.

He was next to her. Mrs Bell started to talk to Albert, edging a little away so that there was a hazy space between Bill, Katie and the rest, or so it felt, a space that needed filling. With talk. He took a breath. "Whereabouts in Germany do you come from?" And so it began, in German, quite naturally, allowed now that no-one else was listening. She was from Duisburg up in the industrial belt. She had very green eyes. She had come over in '39, didn't say why. They moved over to the open window and he told her a little about his family. She listened carefully, seriously. No, he wasn't thinking of going back to the Black Forest. She didn't quiz him. London was his home now.

The room was filling with more guests. Albert, looking over at Bill and giving him a slightly envious grin, was being ushered over to a couple in the corner. Lisebette and Richard, looking radiantly happy, were with the Winklers.

"She's a nice lady," said Katie as they watched Mrs Bell work the room. She had plenty to do.

"Mm," said Bill. In fact, everyone here was much nicer than he had imagined.

"I'm glad I thought to buy her some flowers. You know, like we do at home." Katie pointed to some ox-eye daisies in a vase.

"And there's ours." Bill nodded at the carnations, in another vase on the same hefty, polished sideboard. "Luckily carnations are her absolute favourites," he added and began to smile.

"Well, that's strange. That's what she said about my daisies." They laughed, looking fondly at the back of Mrs Bell's head.

"Very English!" said Bill.

"And very nice," said Katie. And he couldn't disagree.

20

London. January 20th, 1947

B ill was standing outside Tottenham Court Underground station. He pulled his collar up. After a mild start to the year, it had turned much colder. Above, heavy clouds were gathering, casting a low light over an already gloomy London. He could smell the snow in the air. The wet English kind that chilled the bones. From where he was standing, he could see where both Great Russell Street and Oxford Street joined Tottenham Court Road. He reckoned Katie would walk that way from the British Museum where she was spending a couple of hours before meeting him. He'd been at work. To the right he could just make out the windows of Lyons Corner House on Charing Cross Road where he was taking her. In summer, the awnings would be down, waving in the breeze, welcoming the visitors. Today they were tightly rolled up. Men and women, heads down against the northerly wind, walked past the sombre buildings, grubby from years of neglect, over the cracked paving, intent on being somewhere else. Dim electric light struggled from the odd shop window. He checked his watch for the fifth time in ten minutes. It was nearly 3.30.

After the concert at the beginning of January – a great success, Brahms followed by Sibelius – they had been invited, along with Richard and Lisebette, for a meal at Bruno and Lee's little place in Clapham. Lee was pregnant, very happy and had made the tiny flat bright and comfortable. They ate chicken soup with dumplings and homemade bread. As the soup pot was brought to the table there was a power cut, so Bruno found candles. He also found a bottle of schnapps, the source of which he wouldn't divulge, which kept the cold at bay. He and Katie had been shy with each other, each pleased to see the other but unsure how to proceed. Everyone had been aware of it, of course, and there were meaningful glances exchanged between the women and Bill's opinion sought on every topic that came up, which he found exhausting. Until the third schnapps, when he discovered he had opinions he didn't know about and a talent for making everyone laugh. He found the courage to ask Katie to see him again soon.

They had met in a pub and she had told him of her visit home, her parents, her brothers. Cried a little, and he'd covered her hand with his own. He had thought about her often while she'd been away, and as the weeks and months went by had given up hope. When he heard she was coming back and wanted to come to the concert he felt not just pleasure but relief. It must mean, surely, that she felt the same as him; they were right together.

Her long absence had forced him to think about his own reluctance to return. He told himself it was because there would be no work. His mother was well, as far as he knew; two daughters to look after her, what could he do? And eventually John would be back with her. That promise he'd made to Rosina, to go back, seemed like centuries ago, but it bothered him. Joe, surprisingly, had no problem with it. "She'll understand. We can't go back to a country still full of Nazis." And Katie had mentioned the distrust she felt while in Germany, the shame that hung like a dirty mantle over everything.

Yes, he felt that but for him it was something else. He wanted to be English. He had been born here, birth certificate to prove it. Joe laughed at him. "Prove what you like, we will never sound English, accents like ours will never be forgiven." He, Joe, was resigned to being neither English nor German, enjoying the few brief years of hope that international socialism was just around the corner. His life was full, with his Nellie and a baby expected soon. Albert was increasingly disillusioned, not at all sure that England was the place for his business ambitions. Rosie seemed settled, but resentful about the cards life had dealt her. Bill often felt they were fracturing; never to the point of falling apart but beginning to invent different futures for themselves.

He would become English. There would be a way. His Englishness would evolve as he adapted to English ways and customs. Unexpressed, half-baked and naïve thoughts. Wishful.

He looked once more at his watch, once more towards Great Russell Street, at the sea of downturned faces walking towards him, none of them the one he wanted to see. He stamped his feet and shoved his hands deeper into his pockets. He wanted to tell her about his plans, about the workshop he'd found round the back of the Palladium Theatre in a grubby, narrow little street full of tailors' shops, milliners and a steaming, noisy laundry. At night it changed character when a couple of seedy bars and nightclubs opened for business. Skinny, powdered prostitutes slipping out of alleys and doorways.

21, Carnaby Street was a tall thin Victorian building jammed between the others. There were four floors, and his workshop was at the very top. No water; he would have to carry it up in buckets every morning from the little toilet room on the floor below, up the narrow, steep staircase, ancient, worn, encrusted with dust, untouched for decades. But there was electricity, so he could use his irons for pressing, when he'd located some. He'd already found a good treadle machine. Somehow, with help, he'd get it up there. He was getting a good reputation as a waistcoat maker, a couple of Savile Row tailors offering him work. Best of all was the narrow balcony that ran around the workshop. If you climbed out through the window you could walk around two sides of the building and see the whole of London spread out before you. Katie would like that, he was sure. He could taste the pride he would feel when he showed her.

And suddenly, emerging from the crowd, was one upturned head, a smiling face and she was there, just a few feet from him, lips forming words, something about I'm sorry I'm late, eyes shining. And while London bobbed and meandered past them like a grey, despondent stream, they formed their own little island, licked and jostled by the ebb and flow, but safe together. They stood for a moment talking nonsense, till Bill took her arm and guided her across the road.

Acknowledgements

For historical accuracy I have relied on Richard Evans' trilogy about the Third Reich; a wonderfully detailed, brutally honest yet compassionate account.

For insight into the day-to-day lives of Jews and others I found Victor Klemperer's diaries (*I Shall Bear Witness*) hugely valuable – dispassionate, unsentimental yet heart-breaking.

Thanks to the Manx Museum on the Isle of Man and their generous help when researching First and Second World War internment.

I want to thank my sister, Margaret, for unlocking memories of our parents' lives and my cousin Susan for supplying invaluable information. Thanks also to my cousins, Ursel in Essen and Monika in Neustadt, for details of life in pre- and post-war Germany.

Special thanks to Emma who gave me great encouragement and to the Leeds Writer's Circle who put me right on many dubious sentences.

Thank you, Soren, for your research into the fortunes of Arsenal football club.

Finally, thanks to my lovely children – John, Kate and Michael – for putting up with a mother who has spent the last four years buried in the last century.

Rita Morrison was born in 1949 to German immigrants living in London. In 1970 she moved to the North East and worked as a primary teacher. In 2000 she went to Nepal to train teachers and on her return moved to Leeds and taught English to refugees and asylum seekers. Since retiring she studied German language and history as part of her Open University degree and has travelled in Germany, visiting most of the locations in this story. She lives in Chapel Allerton near two of her children and grandchildren. She visits her eldest son and granddaughter who live in Paris as often as possible.

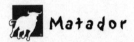 **Matador**